BEAUTIFUL & TERRIBLE THINGS

A NOVEL BY

S.M. STEVENS

Black Rose Writing | Texas

This is a work of fiction. Names, characters, businesses, places, events, and incidents are either the products of the author's imagination or used in a fictitious manner. Any resemblance to actual persons, living or dead, or actual events is purely coincidental.

ISBN: 978-1-68513-447-1
LIBRARY OF CONGRESS CONTROL NUMBER: 2024934262
PUBLISHED BY BLACK ROSE WRITING
www.blackrosewriting.com

Printed in the United States of America
Suggested Retail Price (SRP) $24.95

Beautiful and Terrible Things is printed in Minion Pro

*As a planet-friendly publisher, Black Rose Writing does its best to eliminate unnecessary waste to reduce paper usage and energy costs, while never compromising the reading experience. As a result, the final word count vs. page count may not meet common expectations.

Excerpts from *Wishful Thinking: A Theological ABC* by Frederick Buechner, Copyright © 1973; and *Telling Secrets* by Frederick Buechner, Copyright © 1991; reprinted by permission of Frederick Buechner Literary Assets, LLC.

To Natalie, who answers the call to shine a light on injustice,
even in her darkest days.

PRAISE FOR
BEAUTIFUL AND TERRIBLE THINGS

"As six very different friends navigate their lives separately and together, helping each other and the world in general, they find healing for themselves in this thoughtful novel."
–Bonnar Spring, award-winning author of *Toward the Light* and *Disappeared*

"Six friends. Five ethnic backgrounds. Four romantic attractions. Three genders. Two mental illnesses. One turtle. Disparate millennials grapple with social justice issues while navigating their personal and professional lives. *Beautiful and Terrible Things* challenges readers to move away from ingrained patterns of thinking, breathing life into modern social structures in an authentic and refreshing manner. This novel is far from tokenistic in its sensitive handling of issues surrounding the continually evolving space of gender politics and race relations."
–Annabel Harz, author of *Journey into the Dark and the Light* and *Journey into the Shadow and the Sunshine*

"A poignant, whirlwind read that grabs you. A story so relevant it vibrates."
–Tina O'Hailey, author of *Dark Drink*

"A moving, character driven story that includes frank explorations of contemporary debates on migration, and the implications of immigration law and enforcement on both migrants and those whose lives they touch. Thoughtfully conceived–an engaging read!"
–Robert Irwin, Director of Humanizing Deportation Project, University of California, Davis

"A deep dive into interpersonal dynamics among a group of young adult friends who live on the cutting edge of intersectionality and identity politics. For readers not familiar with pansexuals and the children of lesbian parents, Stevens's story will introduce them to their full humanity. Others will see themselves in these characters. And what a pleasure to find realistic and sympathetic depictions of Guatemalan and Colombian immigrants, which could have been drawn from my practice as an immigration attorney! Fear and hope, pain and compassion tie these friends to each other. Ultimately, they have much to teach us about the beauty and love that defines real friendship. It was hard to leave these characters behind at the end."
–Susan Mills, author of *On the Wings of a Hummingbird* and retired immigration attorney

"Mental illness remains feared and misunderstood. We distance ourselves and avoid understanding why and how an afflicted individual is affected by the painful activity in their psyche. *Beautiful and Terrible Things* neither avoids nor fears, gazing directly into the pain and struggle of its characters. This is a book about people living in a complex and challenging world. Stevens's readable and heartfelt prose makes this a winner."
–Richard Schwindt, MSW, RSW, author of *Emotional Recovery from Situational Anxiety*

"From the first to last page, thought-provoking characters inhabit the essence of how humane we can be despite secret prejudices and ingrained fears. S.M. Stevens doesn't settle for cautious taletelling. She dives into bigotry and heals with the truth."
–M.T. Maliha, author of the *Waverly Estate* series

"A beautifully crafted story of friendship and self-discovery set amidst the harsh realities of today's world. Superb!"
–Eileen O'Finlan, author of *Erin's Children*

"The representation of depression and related PTSD is poignant and accurate in this novel. Such a stigma exists around this disorder that a large number of people go untreated and, as a result, become isolated. The examination of Bipolar 1 underscores the well-meaning minimization of this condition. Fortunately, the protagonist here discovers a group of caring friends who help her, and, as a result, each other."
–Lucinda Nightingale, LMFT

"Stunning…The portrayal of six young adults finding their way in the world reminded me of layers of an artichoke, from thorn to bracts to choke to heart, as Stevens peels back their passions, fears, secrets, and, in some cases, anger at their situation. The emotional rollercoaster was filled with unexpected turns that kept me intrigued. Highly recommended."
–Rox Burkey, author of *The Enigma Series*

"So well-drawn that each character seems nuanced and real, the millennials in this story span a wide range of ethnicities and sexual proclivities. They grapple with issues of love and attraction, mental illness, immigration, personal loyalty vs. social responsibility, and more. Their stories form a richly interwoven tapestry that causes us to laugh, cry, and reflect. The underlying message: Like this appealing and sympathetic band of young people, life itself is not always black or white. And sometimes, beautiful intentions can yield terrible consequences. Stevens has delivered an ambitious and absorbing novel."
–Ruth F. Stevens, author of *Stage Seven*

OTHER WORKS FROM S.M. STEVENS

NOVELS

The Wallace House of Pain (Novelette)

Horseshoes and Hand Grenades

Shannon's Odyssey (Middle Grade)

Bit Players series (Young Adult)

Bit Players, Has-Been Actors and Other Posers

Bit Players, Bullies and Righteous Rebels

Bit Players, Bird Girls and Fake Break-Ups

SHORT STORIES

Inside and Out
Monadnock Underground, 2022

Two Kinds of People
Smoky Quartz, 2021

AUTHOR'S NOTE

First, I have benefited from the input of many qualified sensitivity readers and experts for this novel, in areas including mental health, race, immigration, gender identity, sexual orientation, and even a Filipino artist. None of that changes my own identity. Some will no doubt question if I am qualified to tell these characters' stories. Discussion on the important topic of cultural appropriation is warranted. I can't predict where my novel will fall or how it will be treated in that discussion. I can only say that I have tried to draw my diverse characters with respect and love, and I hope their portrayals ring true to readers.

Second, this story is set in a fictional city in hopes that you will envision it unfolding in the city you know best. The conversations and incidents in the story are happening around the U.S. and much of the world. You may not see or hear them firsthand, but they are happening, and I believe they represent our society today, for better and for worse. Thank you for humoring my generic approach.

Third, a trigger warning: This novel includes scenes depicting self-harm.

Subscribe to the author's blog at AuthorSMStevens.com to access Bonus Materials and deleted scenes.

BEAUTIFUL
&
TERRIBLE
THINGS

"Here is the world. Beautiful and terrible things will happen. Don't be afraid."

–Frederick Buechner

PART 1:
PERCHANCE THE UNIVERSE

CHAPTER 1: HARBINGERS

Early Summer 2018

Charley jerked her head away too late. The scramble of bloody fur on the asphalt imprinted itself on her brain as a shudder coursed through her body. She stopped jogging at the edge of the two-lane thoroughfare slicing through the heart of Founders Park, resisting the urge to flee past the carcass. Instead, she inched closer, feeling an obligation to acknowledge the damage and her potential role in it.

The squirrel lay on its back, mouth agape in a silent scream. A spot of red blossomed across the white canvas of its belly. She jumped as a passing breeze fluttered the wispy tail. Shuddering again, she embraced her torso, the internal heat from her morning run entirely dissipated.

"I'm so sorry, squirrel. I hope you don't have babies at home who need you."

At a loss for anything else to say or do, she moved on, crossing the street and continuing down the park trail. She broke into a fast jog, not to outrun the generous raindrops that had begun plunking on the trail, but to hasten her trip home so she could bury the roadkill image behind her rigid morning regimen.

Back in her bare apartment above City Books, she stopped in the bathroom to turn on the shower—number one—then hung her sweaty jogging shorts and tank top off the sides of the laundry basket in her bedroom—number two. Number three, while the water warmed, she pulled out black jeans and a short-sleeved top. By the time she scrubbed herself in the shower, dressed, pulled her long wet hair into a high messy bun, and scarfed down a bowl of cereal—numbers four through seven—the notion that she somehow bore responsibility for the squirrel had been temporarily tucked away in a protective recess of her mind.

Number eight, she brushed her teeth while the cat balanced on the side of the tub and watched. Number nine, she affixed her name tag to her shirt and ran her thumb back and forth over the word *Charley* before—number ten—collecting her keys and cell phone and heading downstairs to prepare the bookstore for opening.

*****

Charley raised an eyebrow as she turned the dented doorknob of the store's back entrance. Already open. Since Georgina promoted Charley to store manager of City Books last year, the owner rarely arrived first. Some days, it seemed Charley was the one in charge, which suited her fine since the shop was her home away from home or, to be exact, her home under her home.

"Happy birthday!" Georgina rasped from their small, shared office, holding out a chocolate muffin on a thin paper plate, a single lit candle precariously askew on top. Her ash-brown dyed curls bobbed as she nodded and grinned, exposing crooked, coffee-stained teeth.

Charley accepted the muffin and attempted to smile graciously. How, she reasoned, was Georgina to know that Charley's twenty-ninth birthday was not one to be celebrated? Why would Georgina know that this year, Charley would exist in constant fear of the anvil hanging inches above her head, biding its time before plunging to flatten her for the fourth time? Georgina certainly couldn't be expected to know that the universe presented Charley with a freshly slaughtered squirrel in the park that morning, a clear harbinger of another tragedy to come.

Charley blew out the candle and mumbled thanks.

"What are you doing to celebrate?" Georgina asked, smoker's wrinkles pointing to her mouth from all directions.

Charley picked at the muffin's wrapper, physically incapable of looking someone in the eye while lying. "Going out with friends, I think."

"Good for you." Georgina placed her leopard-print reading glasses on her nose and returned to her paperwork.

Charley took a pen from the desk and stuck it in her damp bun. She grabbed a notebook in one hand, balanced the muffin on its flimsy plate in the other, and headed for the front of the store.

An hour later, perched on a stool behind the sleeping cash register, Charley stared blankly at an order form for upcoming hardcover and paperback releases, a neglected cup of mint tea off to the side. She flinched when a hand nudged her shoulder.

"So sorry, I didn't mean to alarm you," the customer said. "I did utter 'excuse me' a few times, but you didn't hear me."

Charley blinked and forced herself to focus on the casually dressed man. He was about her age, tall and wiry, with a mess of dirty blonde hair almost reaching his shoulders, blue eyes, a thin, slightly hooked nose, and a short beard glistening with a few apparently unfelt raindrops.

"No, I'm sorry," she said, her shoulder buzzing as if he'd left behind an electric residue. "What can I help you with?"

He pointed to her name tag. "First, I must inquire—did you lose your own name tag?"

Her hand flew past the name tag and landed near her mouth, covering the small mole under her lip, which resembled a stray crumb from whatever she'd last been eating.

"No, this is mine," she said with a defensive edge.

"No offense intended. I only implied it might be the property of another because I've been known to pilfer a name tag or two in my time, usually because I misplaced my own. I've masqueraded as Melvin and Harry as a result." He spoke in a laid-back style bordering on a drawl, in complete contrast to his stilted, formal words. "But of course, you're Charley. It fits."

While he talked, she stared at the countertop between them. She didn't pay much attention to customers, so she couldn't be sure if he'd been in before. To Charley, a customer was merely a set of hands dropping books next to the register and handing her a credit or debit card, or an inquiry at the tiny customer service desk leading to an enthusiastic treasure hunt to find the book in question. This guy, however, to her surprise and discomfort, had physically touched her and insisted she notice him in less than two minutes.

"It was presumptuous of me to project my foibles onto you," he continued, "I do apologize." He bowed slightly with his hand to his heart. Charley half expected him to tack on "my fair maiden" at the end of this short speech. "I'm Xander, by the way. Not Harry, or Melvin."

He grinned and extended a hand. She turned away as if suddenly distracted by an essential task behind her. "Can I help you find something? Or are you ready to pay?" she said over her shoulder, knowing the second question was inane because he was empty-handed. Turning back to face him, it appeared he hadn't heard her. She repeated her first question.

He leaned in and smiled. "I seek a book on dog training."

Charley nodded, walked around the corner of the counter, and headed toward the Pets section. Xander took the cue and followed her through the store.

"*Wandering patrons. Enlightened between covers. A sight to behold.*"

Charley's head angled toward her shoulder. "Sorry, what?"

"Nothing. Just freestyling a little poetry."

She furrowed her brow but said nothing.

"My dog Fred is practically the perfect canine companion," Xander said from surprisingly close behind, making her jump although, since she was walking, the jump manifested itself as an odd twitch. "He approaches life with passion and flair, if I may say so without sounding overly proud." He stretched his words as if savoring each one as it trickled off his tongue. "But he's acquired a barking habit that may get him evicted if he's not careful. My challenge is to prevent that, hence the need for the book."

Charley nodded and moored him to the half-shelf of dog training books before moving back down the aisle toward the front of the store. At the row's end, she snuck a peek. He was bouncing on his toes while flipping through one of the books, his enthusiasm prompting a rare smile to dawn on Charley's face.

By the time he came to the cash register to pay, more customers had entered, and Charley was busy ringing up purchases.

"Found what you needed?" she asked when his turn came.

"Absolutely. I believe this one will be salubrious."

She nodded and processed his sale. "Have a nice day," she said. He smiled, his blue eyes crinkling as if she'd said something humorous. Her eyes flicked to the next customer.

"And you as well."

As he left, she scribbled *salubrious* in her notebook as a reminder to look up the definition on her phone later.

***

Charley's jumpy movements weren't lost on Xander, calling to mind a wounded bird pondering its next move.

He crumpled a sheet of paper into a ball, leaned back in his chair, paused to line up his target—the standard-issue wastebasket ten feet away in a room stuffed with six desks—and launched the projectile. It bounced off the rim of the wastebasket to join a party of other makeshift balls dotting the linoleum floor.

Ignoring the throat-clearing and mildly annoyed look from his Wilderness Protection Society colleague two desks away, Xander crumpled another piece of paper while musing upon Charley. She was quite adorable, with brown bangs teasing her eyes and an upturned nose accented by a silver nose ring. Her alabaster skin was accented by a beauty mark that hovered under her full lips, and her emerald eyes— they would be stunning if they weren't coated with self-doubt.

He half-heartedly tossed another ball at the trash can.

Why, he wondered, did someone so socially awkward work in a retail establishment? More importantly, how did she get that way, and what could he do to help?

Xander sighed and glanced at the door leading to the City Edge Nature Preserve's grounds. Where the hell was Terrance? The call could come any minute.

The Wilderness Protection Society had been trying for years to buy or obtain lease rights to the land on the west side of Long Lake to expand its City Edge preserve. Then, Wrighton's largest developer, All-American Development & Construction, finagled a deal to purchase and build on the land. Somehow, the CEO Liam Flammer convinced government officials that the replacement of a half-acre of cracked pavement, broken glass, and litter near the lake made his twenty-three-acre, mixed-use Stone Circle project acceptable. The company had broken ground on the project almost two years ago.

Then—Xander broke into a triumphant grin at the memory—a six-year-old girl walking with her father unknowingly crossed the property line between the nature preserve and Flammer's Stone Circle site and found a bog turtle. Once the species and threatened status of the turtle were confirmed, Wilderness Protection launched an all-out assault to kill the real estate project and preserve the open land.

Even though Flammer's environmental consultant had convinced government officials the land wasn't wetlands, Xander knew that was bull. And wetlands represent to nature what the kidneys represent to the human body. They extract toxins and waste, and they balance and clean the water. So Xander organized a grassroots outreach campaign using the theme "Save The Turtles, Save Our Water."

On Terrance's first day at Wilderness Protection, Xander learned the new communications director wasn't enamored with the campaign, making Xander less than enamored with the new guy.

After giving him a tour of the grounds, Xander had stopped at the concrete barrier demarcating the border between the preserve and Flammer's land. "I know you hail from out-of-state and haven't worked at a land conservation organization before," Xander had drawled, "but if you've got an alternative idea to put forth based on your vast experience, I am all proverbial ears."

Terrance scratched his close-cropped, dyed-blonde hair, which contrasted dramatically with his dark brown skin and all-black clothing. "You know I've been doing PR for clean air causes for three years, and I did policy work before changing to communications, so I think I have some idea what's going on."

Xander slouched against the barrier and drummed his fingers on his dungaree pant leg.

One of Terrance's diamond stud earrings winked in the sunlight filtering through the leaves as he turned toward Xander. "I've learned you have to evoke emotion to get people on board. Get to their hearts as well as their minds. Comparing wetlands to the city's kidneys is, well, a bit clinical, don't you think? And from what I've heard, politicians and the public are losing interest."

Xander couldn't deny that last part. "So? What might you suggest?"

Terrance leaned on the barrier next to Xander. "Everyone knows clean drinking water is important, but they only get passionate about it when there's a problem. There's no problem here. When you've been doing your outreach, what parts of the story get to people?"

Xander stroked his short beard. "The turtle." He nodded. "The bog turtle is an exceptionally cute little guy, one must admit. He's not much bigger than the pet turtles many people have as kids." He frowned in disapproval of that ghastly trend.

"Does his size make people want to protect him?"

"Sure, if they're looking at him. Otherwise, the turtle is merely a concept."

Terrance removed his heavy, black-rimmed glasses, pulled a microfiber cloth from his pocket, and wiped the lenses. "So, let's make him more real." He replaced his glasses and looked to the heavens. "Let's say the turtle is a victim here. Who's the bad guy?"

"Flammer, of course."

"Flammer and his building. What if we juxtapose the tiny turtle and the big building somehow?"

Xander's eyes brightened as he turned to Terrance. "We depict a bog turtle cowering in the shadow of a skyscraper!"

"Yeah! Maybe not a skyscraper since Stone Circle is only what—five stories? And if we used a skyscraper, the turtle would be a dot in comparison. But I like where you're going with this. We put the turtle in a tall building's shadow. That could work. We could call the campaign 'Looking Out for the Little Guy'."

Xander laughed.

"What?"

"My mother declared that very sentiment every time I saved a bug or stuck up for a friend as a kid—'That's my Xander, looking out for the little guy.'"

Months later, after that first day's fledgling rapport grew into real friendship, Xander asked Terrance if he'd had that campaign idea all along. Terrance had laughed and admitted he discovered long ago that letting other people take credit for good ideas was an effective way to achieve your goals.

Xander grabbed another sheet of paper from the bin next to him, mashed it up into a ball, and lobbed it at the wastebasket.

A moist wave of steaming air announced Terrance's arrival through the building's side door, making Xander wonder anew why his friend insisted on wearing only black in the city's pulsating summer heat. Terrance eyed the array of crumpled paper balls on the floor. "How many sheets of paper have you wasted doing that?"

"Seriously?" Xander walked to the wastebasket and grabbed a paper ball from the floor. He uncrumpled it and showed both sides to Terrance. "Scrap paper. Printed both sides. Need I say more?" He scooped up more paper balls and started winging them at Terrance. The third one hit Terrance's glasses.

"Hey, watch it, moron."

"Why don't you actually try to catch them, moron?" Xander threw another one.

Terrance dropped his satchel to the floor, grabbed the next two balls out of the air, and flung one back at Xander. As Xander reached for a high lob, Terrance whipped the other one, hitting Xander in the chest.

"So, no word yet, I presume," Terrance said.

"None. The wait is excruciating." Xander bounced on his toes and swung his arms in the air a few times. The combined actions morphed into a series of jumping jacks.

Terrance rolled his eyes in the direction of their colleague, who was trying to ignore them. "Who gave him too much sugar this time?"

Terrance braced his hands on Xander's shoulders until the jumping subsided. "Easy, Xan; we don't even know if they'll decide today."

Xander's shoulder muscle twitched in Terrance's grasp. "My contact at Fish and Wildlife said it would likely be today," Xander said between gulps of air. "It's got to—"

"Terrance. Xander." Sarah, the Wilderness Protection Society's regional director, beckoned to her communications director and campaign manager from her office doorway. "Get in here now! Connelly's on the phone."

The two men scurried after her, landing beside her desk as she hit the speaker button on her phone to resume the call. "We're all here now. What's the word?" She tucked a strand of brunette hair behind her ear, staring at the phone as if she could see her U.S. Fish & Wildlife Service counterpart on the other end.

"It's going into tomorrow's Federal Register. The Stone Circle site is being designated a Critical Habitat for the threatened bog turtle."

Sarah pumped her fist in the air and high-fived Terrance while Xander threw both arms up and jumped victoriously, his faded yellow T-shirt rising to show a band of tanned skin. "That's great news, Connelly. Tell us exactly what this means for the land."

"Well, CH designation doesn't prohibit development, but the project would have to be cognizant of the bog turtle's habitat. Between you and me, and I'll deny ever telling you this—" Xander smirked at Sarah; it wasn't like Connelly was divulging a nuclear launch code—"I don't think he'll be able to make the project economics work now."

Sarah hung up.

The three colleagues all whooped at once. Sarah and Xander let loose with a quick happy dance. Terrance took a few steps and wiggled his shoulders. Xander ran shouting into the adjacent room where his colleague sat. "We won! We beat Flammer! Go, bog turtle!"

Terrance shook his head. "Do you think just once he could observe protocol and let you make the announcement?"

Sarah shrugged. "This was his baby all along." She moved to the doorway and yelled, "Celebratory drinks after work!"

***

At half past eight, Charley locked up and slipped out of the sanctuary of the shop for the steady security of her apartment upstairs. The rain that had stuttered all day revved up into a proper summer storm, with erratic winds heaving water mercilessly against the old brick building. She wrestled the cranky wooden windows in her living room shut.

Moving through her evening regimen, she fed the cat first and checked her personal email second. The latter took no time at all because she'd generally and willfully lost touch with her childhood and college friends. Third, she set the timer on her phone for one hour, opened her favorite word game app, and lost herself in letter combinations until the timer buzzed. Fourth, she made dinner—grilled cheese on whole grain bread because it was Thursday—and ate at her beat-up coffee table while watching a show on her laptop. Number five, she cleaned up her dishes. Numbers six through eight, she got ready for bed: washing her face, brushing her teeth, and changing into a sleep shirt. Number nine, she lay down in bed with a paperback. Number ten, rather than read, she picked at the eczema on her heels until it bled.

The compulsive act didn't deliver relief tonight. The clock had begun ticking on her long-dreaded twenty-ninth year. With effort, she stifled her mind's desire to wander into hypotheticals of what form this year's tragedy would take. She had little control over the outcome—she was ruled by fate, God, karma, or some other unseen force or deity. She sighed and shuttered her eyes, only to see a vivid close-up of the dead squirrel. The ghoulish image and her fear of the coming year's misfortune weighed on her soul like a damp, moldy blanket. Peeking through a moth hole in the blanket, unrecognized by Charley, was the subtle glow on her shoulder where Xander touched her.

CHAPTER 2: BAGGAGE

Charley wasn't one bit surprised to see Xander with a young woman on his arm. This was the third date he'd brought into the store recently.

The first was an allergy-riddled brunette who didn't even like to read. Charley led her to the audiobooks section and left her in Xander's care.

The second was last week, a striking blonde who worked the morning shift at a local bakery and could barely keep her eyes open. She'd humored Xander and picked out a pastry cookbook so she could go home to bed.

Today's catch was a petite thing with round blue eyes and wavy brown hair who chomped on her gum as if battling it for dominance. Xander wore blue jeans and a T-shirt—his standard wardrobe, apparently. Today's shirt was olive green with a light green silhouette of a tree.

Charley sighed and walked up to them.

"Xander. How are you?"

"Energized," he replied, rising up on his toes and settling back down, his final height about six inches taller than Charley. "You?"

Charley merely nodded.

"I require the services of my bookstore goddess again. My good friend Sherrie desires a reference book on computers. She's applying for a new job and must learn Excel." He scratched his beard and beamed as if this interaction would surely be the highlight of Charley's day.

"Xander promises me it's easy," Sherrie said, "but I don't know. I'm not even very good with Microword."

Charley stared for two beats. "The computer books are that way." She pointed to a spot several aisles over. "Can you find it on your own? I have to go relieve Dale at the register so he can take his break."

"Affirmative. Thanks, Char."

Charley went to the front and told Dale to take his break early. In between customers, she doodled on a pad of paper.

Ten minutes later, Xander and Sherrie landed at the checkout counter with a copy of *Excel Essential Skills*, which he plopped on the counter while she snapped bubbles with her gum.

"Sure you don't want the For Dummies version?" Charley mumbled.

Xander raised an eyebrow. "What?"

"Nothing."

Charley sighed in relief as Xander and Catch of the Day left the store. A minute later, Xander sauntered back in alone.

"Charley," he said, his face serious, "I do believe you disparaged my friend earlier."

Charley blushed and stared at the counter. "I'm really sorry," she said quietly. "It was rude and unprofessional."

Xander said nothing until Charley looked at him. He grinned. "And that's exactly why I like you!"

"I really didn't mean to offend your girlfriend."

Xander waved his hand as if shooing a fly, the knotted ends of a number of beaded and leather bracelets tossing from the motion. "Don't fret, she didn't hear a thing. She was too enraptured by the pretty pictures on the back of the book. And I don't currently boast a girlfriend. But I do like to bring friends in for their birthdays and procure them a book even though most of them—between you and me—haven't cracked open a hard copy book in years. And in the process of my altruism, I provide much-needed support to an independent local business. It's all good, yes?"

Charley's shoulders relaxed. "I appreciate the support. And it's a great idea to bring your dates here. Maybe I could do a promotion around that. Bring your date to the bookstore instead of catching a movie."

"Sherrie's not a date. We're merely old friends."

"Hm. But the others were dates?" Her hand floated up to the mole under her lip.

Xander bounced on his toes a few times, studying her. "Yes, the others were dates."

Charley lowered her hand to her side. "Well, I would go broke buying books for presents if I had as many friends as you."

Xander chuckled. "Life is fleeting, my friend. Drink the wine, eat the dessert, and buy the books. Listen, I should go. But might we sit down and engage in genuine conversation sometime instead of continuing this ephemeral discourse?"

Charley fiddled with the pen in her hand. His eyes narrowed, and he cocked his head. "Something tame. Minimal commitment. You must take breaks during the day, yes?"

Charley nodded.

"We can simply rest here in the café and converse about nothing."

Charley shook her head. "That won't work. I've tried sitting in the café during breaks, but people see the name tag and keep asking me questions."

Xander put his hands on the counter's edge and pushed himself up a few inches. Charley noticed the muscles tensing in his forearms. She pictured his feet leaving the floor and landing again. "Here's a fanciful idea. Are you ready?"

He waited until Charley nodded.

"Take off the name tag. I know, it's heretical. But wouldn't it feel good to be bad, just for a spell?" He grinned slyly.

Charley had to smile. "Okay. The next time we run into each other, I'll take a break—if I can—and we can sit in the café. Okay?"

"Spectacular. Let's plan to run into each other tomorrow at two o'clock. Yes?"

"Yes," Charley said.

"Excellent. It's a date." He bounded out of the store after Sherrie.

***

After Dale relieved her at the check-out counter, Charley returned to the children's section to finish a re-shelving project. Sitting on a stool, she pondered the vague emotion Xander stirred up. It wasn't tough to identify once she gave it a minute's thought. She had been a virtual recluse since Nathan moved out a few years ago. She doubted her college or childhood friends even remembered her. She avoided social media rather than be bombarded by the anniversary photos Facebook insisted on shoving onto her feed, reminding her of better times best left forgotten. Obviously, she simply wanted a friend. And Xander was the first person she had connected with in any meaningful way in years. Still, he was merely a customer, and she would do well to remember that.

Reaching inside her shoe, she scratched her eczema through her sock until the skin stung with relief, then turned her attention back to the children's section.

***

Xander came the following day as promised, and Charley removed her name tag and sat with him in the café as promised. She learned about his job at the Wilderness Protection Society's regional headquarters in an outer borough of Wrighton and that he set his own hours, hence his ability to pop into City Books at any given time of day. She learned that he grew up in a working-class area of the city. And she learned that the concept of a new friend felt pretty good.

Xander took a breath and leaned back. "I'm doing the majority of the talking here. Enlighten me with a tidbit from your life."

Charley shrugged. "Like what? There's not a lot to me: a bookstore manager who lives in an apartment upstairs. Not very exciting."

"What about your parents? Where might they reside?" Xander sipped his coffee and waited.

Charley swallowed. "I don't have any. I've been orphaned a lot. You could say I'm a professional orphan." Her eyes widened at how quickly the words spilled out of her.

Xander was quiet until she chanced a glance at him. "And what does that mean?"

Charley sighed. "I've been orphaned twice. By my parents when I was fifteen and then by my grandparents when I was twenty-two. All of them accidents." She absentmindedly ran her fingers over the mole under her lip and then her whole mouth before regaining control of her digits.

He reached across the small table and clutched her hand, his fingers warm against her cool ones. Fine blonde hairs glinted on his tan arm in the fluorescent lighting. "I am so sorry, Charley. Truly."

She squeezed her eyes closed and nodded, sliding her hand out of his grasp.

"New subject?" he suggested.

"Yes, please." She sipped her mint tea. "So, you actually arrange protests and rallies and marches as part of your job?"

Xander nodded. "You should come to one sometime. It's simultaneously empowering and humbling."

Charley grimaced. "I don't know. A protest is so . . . public. With so many . . . people."

Xander laughed loudly. "That does go with the territory." He leaned forward. "It is an incredible feeling, though. You're there as yourself, as an individual, standing up for what you believe in. But you're also part of this larger entity—all the people who share your beliefs. It's heady stuff, the sensation of solidarity. You start to believe we can really change the world if we try."

"I get how that's attractive to someone like you."

He waited and watched.

Charley's mouth twisted to the side. "I mean, you're passionate and enthusiastic, and it's people like you who do change the world. But some of us aren't cut out for that."

"Hmm. Well, just bear in mind, if you stand by while people are treated unfairly, whether it's minorities or immigrants or gay people, you are—if you'll pardon the use of a cliché—part of the problem."

To steer the conversation away from her deficiencies, she reached for the first new topic that entered her head. "You didn't bring a date with you. I was looking forward to seeing the latest catch of the day." She pulled her lips in and bit them with her gums, wondering if that sounded snarky.

He smiled slowly. "You're amusing when you lower your guard. You should do it more."

She half-smiled and looked away.

"You're not impressed with my selection of women?"

"You mean Sneezy, Sleepy, and Dopey?" She viewed him tentatively with one eye.

He laughed so loudly that she startled in her chair. She smiled unsurely.

"Yeah, I see how those labels apply. Wait until you meet Happy, Grumpy, and Doc." He perused his mug. "What about you? Boyfriends, past, present, or unaccounted for?"

She hesitated only a second, wondering what magic this man practiced that encouraged her to open up so freely. "I lived with my boyfriend Nathan for a few years, but he left a while ago."

"A while ago, as in months or years?"

"Years. I don't remember exactly how many."

"Pray tell, what happened?"

Charley hesitated, unsure what Nathan's leaving said about her. She'd never had anyone to discuss it with, so she'd never worried about what such a person might think. She groped for a sentence that would tell the story of the entire relationship in one go. "He just up and went, leaving me with three months on the lease and Baggage."

"Baggage? He left you with baggage. Literally or figuratively?"

"Literally. Baggage is the cat."

Xander's blue eyes squinted. "The cat's name is Baggage."

"Technically, its name is Beauregard, and Nathan called it Beau, Bogie, Baggy, and a bunch of other nicknames. But aren't those terrible names for a cat?" Xander said nothing. "Baggage fits better."

"Hmm. I hate to end on that unsatisfying note, which begs all sorts of questions, but popular opinion notwithstanding, I do have a real job and must get back to work." He stood up and stretched.

"I should go too. Those books won't unpack themselves." She winced at her lame words.

They parted at the store's entrance, Charley fearing she'd already ruined the potential friendship since he didn't say anything about getting together again.

***

Back in the spare room that functioned as the store's warehouse, Charley sat on an unopened box of books, her elbows balancing on her thighs and her head resting in her hands. She couldn't remember the last time she'd talked about Nathan, to a near stranger of all people.

At one point, he'd been her lifeline. They dated all of their senior year in college. She assumed the attraction was mainly one of convenience, so was shocked when he asked her to move in with him after they graduated. Initially, she'd said no because she planned on living with her grandparents for a while. She owed them that. She'd been living with them since her parents died at the start of Charley's freshman year of high school. Gram and Gramps weren't in the best health, and she wanted to be around for whatever time they had left. She told Nathan they could keep dating, though, since they'd both be moving to Wrighton. Nothing had to change.

And then.

She would kick herself until the day she died for not talking longer with Gramps when he'd called the day before the fire. Exhausted from studying for final exams and distracted by the tantalizing nearness of the long-awaited freedom signified by graduation, she barely focused on the conversation. She remembered him saying he had moved one-hundred-thousand dollars—her parents' entire nest egg—into her bank account so she'd have easy access to it. But she remembered nothing else from the call except his excitement about attending her graduation.

She'd hung up with a yawn, saying she'd see him and Gram soon.

Then they died.

Nathan had stepped in, propped her up, and propelled her through a graduation she could not remember.

"You'll move in with me," he stated after the ceremony. Her grandparents' house had burned to the ground with them in it, so there was no house to go back to. Charley had nodded, and that was that.

Looking back, she couldn't figure out where four years of cohabitation went. Their first months in the city were clouded by much alcohol, which Nathan supplied readily at first but with more hesitation as the weeks plodded on. She remembered Nathan pleading with her, as if from behind a translucent shower curtain that blurred his features and muffled his voice, to get help—a chorus he sang intermittently throughout the years.

"You're depressed," he said, over and over, the notes echoing in her mind but never forming a recognizable song.

A few months into that first year, Nathan refused to go to the store for more coffee and tequila unless she came with him. Charley needed coffee to trick her mind into waking, and tequila to tell her mind to rest. Not much happened in between, but somehow the cycle of liquids convinced her she was living a normal life, even if she wasn't yet working like most of her friends.

"Why do I have to go?" she'd whined from the couch.

"Because I can't look at you stagnating on that couch for another minute. I'm going to lose my mind. And for all I know, you've already lost yours. So, suit yourself. But I'm not going to the store unless you come too." He sat down beside her and crossed his arms over his chest.

Charley stared into space for an unknown period of time. Eventually, it occurred to her that Nathan had wanted something from her. She turned and looked at him. He returned the look, defiance in his eyes. Maybe it was the fact that defiance was not a normal look for him. Maybe it was the caffeine withdrawal headache flicking at her temples. For whatever reason, Charley stood and said, "Okay."

Nathan helped her change into jeans and a clean shirt and led her a few blocks away from their apartment. He steered her through a door into a space that her injured soul slowly registered as something other than the grocery or liquor store. Those were books, not vegetables, and over there were magazines, not meat.

Nathan gripped her arms. "Charley, look at me. We're in a bookstore. Remember how much you love books?"

"Why are we here?" she whispered, vaguely wondering why he spoke to her as if she were a child.

"Because they are hiring a part-time person, and you're going to apply." Her eyes widened. "I know you think you're not ready. But you have to be, or we're not going to make it. Do you understand me?"

She nodded fuzzily, not understanding him at all.

"I want you to walk around this store until something happens. . . something slips into place, or out of place—I don't know—but you are going to hang with these books until you can talk coherently like the intelligent girl I know you are. Do you understand?"

"Yes," she whispered.

"Then go. I'll wait here in the café. Take as long as you need." He pushed her away.

Charley blinked and stumbled toward a table of books where she stood for a long time, scanning covers until her eyes focused. This cover showed a house on a cliff. *Would that house burn down?* Charley's chest screamed as if pierced and retracted by a rib spreader. She bent forward from the pain, not noticing how it rent the bank of fog in her brain and sent a severed wispy tendril out and away.

When the pain subsided, she looked at a cover with a man and woman embracing. Nathan was a man and she was a woman. Nathan was good to her. What would she do without him? The image of her boyfriend waiting in the café registered in her numb mind. She closed her eyes to capture the sensation of the mental connection.

"Mommy, wait," a child cried nearby, startling Charley. She turned to watch a small boy toddle up and into his mother's arms. Another tendril of brain fog broke away.

She ran her fingers over the embossed letters on the cover of a vampire book, tracing the letters and sending messages from her fingers to her brain. Another tendril slipped aside. She opened the book and ran her hand down the page. As a girl, she used to pretend she could feel the letters, as if they were embossed like the book's cover or in Braille. A full finger's worth of fog evaporated. Charley lifted the book to her face and inhaled. New book smell wasn't as tantalizing as an old book in a childhood attic, but it was something.

Growing up, she had treasured the attic in their old, brick-walled, ivy-adorned house. The warm unfinished space cradled a faded armchair with stuffing poking out of a gash in its deep red fabric, uneven blocky towers built from corrugated cardboard boxes, armies of books lined up on a staunch wooden bookcase, and a phantasmagoria of cobwebs. Her mother told Charley not to go up there because it was dirty and unsafe. But, drawn by the secrets sandwiched between the book covers, she snuck in when her parents taught late afternoon classes—her dad was an English literature professor at the local college, her mom an Economics professor. The lone bulb dangling from the ceiling shed meager light, but Charley learned to shift the red chair back and forth between the windows so she could read at any hour.

Once, she lost track of time and her father surprised her in the attic.

"Here you are," he'd said.

"Don't tell Mom, she'll be mad!" Charley pleaded. "She doesn't love books like we do."

"Don't worry. I'll take care of it. Stay." He caressed her hair awkwardly before descending the stairs. Charley dove back into her book.

Several chapters later, lighter footsteps tapped up the stairs and Charley's mom appeared, extending a glossy red and green apple to her only child. "Here. I always loved munching on an apple when I curled up with a good book at your age."

Charley smiled at her mother and accepted the apple. As her mom descended, Charley kissed the fruit's smooth skin and held it to her chest briefly before sinking her teeth in.

That scene remained one of Charley's favorite memories in the days when she allowed herself to remember. Her erudite parents were not particularly demonstrative but, on that day, she felt truly loved.

Her attention gradually came back to the bookstore. A passing man studied her and she wondered how long she'd been standing there in a daze. To reassure him, she scanned the bookstore as if in search of a particular section. As the man moved on, she walked on wooden legs to the nearest bookcase. For an hour, she browsed—smelling, touching and seeing. She noticed the colors on the covers and the fonts of the titles. She thump-thumped her palm along a row of spines. She feathered her fingers along the top of a line of books, the uneven edges tickling her skin. She whispered the names of the books to accompany the sounds in her head as she read the titles. She consulted every sign hanging from the ceiling, denoting a section of books. She visited each section. By the time she reached History, her brain fog had scattered save a few tiny tendrils, which would hang around for the long-term, generally resting quietly but reawakening and asserting themselves to cloak fear or anxiety in blue moments.

She closed her eyes and breathed in as much air as her lungs could hold. She exhaled months of melancholy. She breathed in deeply again, savoring the tugging sensation as her lungs stretched to capacity. Exhaling, she turned her head this way and that, soaking in all the sounds, colors and movements the store offered.

Nathan. She found him in the small section of the store that served as a café.

Charley's elbow slipped off her thigh, jolting her out of her reverie. Nathan had always been too good for her. Now was not the time to replay their breakup. She had work to do.

***

That night, she didn't wait until bedtime to start picking at the eczema that marred her feet. She put down her phone after reaching level 6,825 of her favorite word game, half an hour still on the timer. She stripped off her shoes and socks and inspected the sections of scaly red flesh covering her heels and part of her soles, the thick tissue crisscrossed by white canyons in some places, dotted by scabs in others. She picked at a flap of dead skin and peeled it away, taking fresh skin with it. She continued peeling bits of her skin until the sting and burn drew all her focus and calmed her mind.

Walking barefoot on her tender feet, she made dinner—pasta because it was Friday—and washed the food down with a hefty helping of self-loathing because she had picked at her feet again and, even worse, strayed from the schedule that regulated her emotions.

CHAPTER 3: BULLIES

"A turtle. A fucking four-inch turtle."

Liam Flammer's lead outside attorney, Marty Murkowski, couldn't tell if his client spoke in anger or awe. The two were often intertwined when it came to Flammer. Anybody or anything worthy of his awe had somehow beaten Flammer at his own game, so the awe quickly mutated into anger, sometimes of an extreme nature. Like most successful businesspeople, Flammer did not like losing.

"Let's get out and walk. I'm too pissed off to sit here." Liam eased his six-foot-one, sixty-seven-year-old frame out of the Town Car and told his driver to wait for them. He stretched his shoulders up and back, smoothed his ample brown hair with both hands, and strode ahead, his unbuttoned suit coat flapping in his wake.

Marty, seventeen years younger and seven inches shorter, scooted around the far side of the car and caught up with Liam at the padlocked gate to the construction site. A large particle board sign hanging on the chain-link fence shouted, "Stone Circle, an All-American Development & Construction project. Office – Retail – Residential. Coming soon!"

Liam unlocked the gate, pocketed the key, and walked through. Marty hustled after him—past the forty-foot-high dirt hill dubbed Flammer Mountain by the locals and the media—to the edge of Long Lake, where the real estate developer stopped and crammed his hands into his pants pockets. Liam stared, frowning, across the marshy edge and sparkly blue center of the lake to the thick woods of the City Edge Nature Preserve on the far side.

Marty breathed through his mouth rather than inhale the fetid swampy air. He noticed with annoyance that Liam wore construction boots. Had he known they were stopping by the site, Marty would have changed out of his Italian leather shoes, which were sinking into the muddy bank with an eerie squelching sound at such an alarming rate that an irrational image of quicksand formed in Marty's mind. Thankfully, the squelching and sinking stopped before the mud reached the laces of his sienna brown derbies.

"I can't believe we lost this one, Liam." Marty tried to appear professional and authoritative, but it wasn't easy with your most important client looking down on your bald spot and your mud-encased shoes.

Liam sighed and ran a hand over his hair again. "Stone Circle was going to be my most significant project in a long time. Instead, it's been a five-year time and money suck."

Marty braced himself for a rant.

"After all the crap we went through with the local community, carving out low-rent office space, promising them seventy-five percent of the retail jobs, throwing in sidewalks and streetlights that weren't even on my land." Liam's face darkened from annoyed pink to angry red like an algae bloom.

"And let's not forget changing twenty of the condos to affordable housing," Marty piped in.

Liam smirked at his counsel. "Little did those idiots know that by cutting the unit size, adding the square footage to the condos, and upping the condo prices, we more than made up the difference." His harsh laugh made Marty flinch and squelch further into the mud. "And little did they know, the cut-rate apartments and offices were only guaranteed for two years. After that, we could've demanded top-dollar prices for all of it. See ya later, 'local community.'" Liam closed his eyes as if savoring the imagined victory. "All the money we sank into this," he mused. "All the time. All the environmental reviews. All the hearings. All the community outreach. All successful. Until that goddamn bog turtle entered the picture." He turned on Marty. The edge returned to his voice. "What the hell happened, Marty? Why didn't you know about the turtles?"

Marty swallowed with difficulty. "Liam, no one knew about the turtles. They've never been found in this area before. We hired the best environmental consultants and sailed through the review process. The hydrologist, the soil specialist, the wetlands expert—they all came through. The fact that the EPA didn't deem this wetlands and require a permit made the project feasible. We managed it all perfectly." He swallowed again. "You know that," he added tentatively. Sometimes, standing up to Liam calmed him down. Other times, it fired Liam up more and earned you a humiliating drubbing in front of the rest of the team.

"Relax, Marty, I know you did the job right." Liam patted Marty on the shoulder. "And the right campaign donations didn't hurt either." He shook his head. "A multi-million-dollar project stymied by some little girl finding a cute little turtle-wurtle in the woods...."

His attempt at a little girl's voice grated on Marty.

Liam sighed. "Now I have to decide if I'm going to play hardball and hang onto the land just to irritate the tree-huggers or call it a day and sell them the land for market value."

"Hm, when have you ever sold property for market value?"

"Never," Liam shouted, "and that was the right answer!"

Marty smiled at his minor victory. "Of course, you could play nice guy and donate the land for the tax write-off and the—"

"Stop right there. I don't give a shit about the tax write-off on this one. I'm going to get full market value and then some to make up for the money I've lost on this project. And to make up for the headache of pretending to kowtow to the minority neighborhood. I know it's the price of admission for city development these days, but it still turns my stomach having to play ball with anyone who raises their stinking voice."

Before he'd finished his sentence, Liam was dialing on his cell phone. "Jay, we need some quick-hit wins to make up for this bog turtle debacle. Projects we can fast-track with minimal community review.

Low-hanging fruit." He paused for two seconds. "Put a few of your brightest on the job. Maybe that hottie you keep telling me about, the one with all the potential." He paused and listened while pulling his lips back in a gesture faintly resembling a grin. "Tell them to have a list of viable properties on my desk in two weeks. That's all."

He slipped the phone into his suit coat pocket and strode back toward the entry gate.

"Nice of you to leave the community a souvenir at least," Marty said with attempted wit as they passed the massive dirt pile in the middle of the site. Sixteen months had gone by since excavators dug up the topsoil and piled it in a heap. Two weeks after breaking ground, construction had halted when the threatened turtle species was discovered on the site.

"Ah yes. Flammer Mountain," Liam said, with a humorless laugh. "I hope the locals enjoy the view, and the muggings and drug deals that are going to return to their vacant lot that could have been turned into an amazing asset to this city."

Marty nodded, even though it wasn't the community that derailed Stone Circle but the environmentalists at the Wilderness Protection Society, who managed the adjacent preserve. Liam knew that, of course. But it didn't matter to Liam who officially stole the project from him. Anybody who stood in the way of an All-American project at any point in the project's development earned Liam's undying scorn.

***

After his driver dropped Marty outside his downtown office, Liam phoned his daughter April.

"Sweetie, I want my next quarterly donation to go to the Wilderness Protection Society. But wait until they've started fundraising for the capital to purchase the land next to the lake. Make sure it goes toward that."

"Daddy, the Stone Circle site?" April asked. "Really? Why don't you just reduce your sale price by twenty-five thousand?"

"For the same reason I have you make the donations in your name: I can't let my opponents know I support environmental initiatives. I'd lose all my negotiating power if the cities and towns and neighborhood groups and do-good nonprofits knew I believe in global warming and care about the world my grandchildren inherit. In fact, don't even use your name on this one. Make it anonymous."

"But—"

"I have to go. Kiss the kids for me."

***

Terrance's hybrid glided into his hometown like a ghost. His last trip home was seven months ago, right before he started the job at the Wilderness Protection Society. Even though he phoned her weekly, his mother never missed a chance to remind him he now lived twice as far away, as if that somehow correlated to him loving her half as much.

Even though he knew his mother would be waiting, he swung into the local cemetery first. Reflexively, he checked his fuel efficiency—fifty-one miles to the gallon for the four-hour trip—before getting out of the car and starting a slow walk to the twelfth row.

The older headstones—mostly gray slabs of rough, muted granite—leaned into the earth as if they, like the bodies they memorialized, were slowly returning to the soil. Newer headstones popped in shiny black, glossy brown and pearly white. The thirteen-year-old stone that he could find blindfolded gleamed in light rose, dressed with etched roses connected by swirling vines accented with pointed leaves. The headstone always made Terrance smile. Its over-the-top style compared to the drab grays and serious blacks around it so matched Tito's own flair.

Terrance rested his palm on the top of the headstone. "Still miss you, brother."

He bowed his head and prayed.

***

"Every time I come here, the yard looks smaller," Terrance said to his mother as she emerged from their side of the two-family house with a glass of iced tea and a beer. Mary Washington wore dungaree shorts and a white sleeveless blouse. Her short, salt-and-pepper hair capped cherubic features that echoed the trace of baby face her son was stuck with for life.

"Really? To me it seems bigger without the toys and sports stuff." She sat down at the dimpled, glass-topped table on the back patio. "Still like the new job?"

Terrance braced himself for the requisite maternal inquisition—a regular feature of visits home regardless of the number of phone calls in between. If only Jasmine were here to join in the fun. "I love it. It's important work and I'll be in a great position to apply for the national communications director job in a year or two."

"That's my boy. I know you'll make me proud."

"Mama, you should already be proud. Wilderness Protection is a major organization and we're doing good for the world."

She clapped her hand over his where it lay on the table. "I am, I am! Although with all the hurt in this world, why you're protecting animals is beyond me."

He flipped his hand over and clasped hers, shaking it for emphasis. "I'm trying to save the environment. What bigger cause is there? Racism, sexism, you name it—none of those will matter if we destroy the planet and everybody on it."

She sighed as if unable to fathom that concept. "Have you got a new girlfriend yet?"

"No, still trying." He swigged his beer, already warming in the heat.

Mary stared over his shoulder and smacked her tongue against her palate—a familiar sound that meant a lecture was coming unless he cut it off at the pass.

"Mama, trust me—I want a wife and family as much as you do. The right person will come along. Give it time." He thought about letting her in on the list of qualities he was seeking—ranked by "must have" and "nice to have"—but decided it was safer, on balance, to drop the subject.

She sighed and returned her gaze to him. "Are you going to church?"

"Every Sunday, and praying every night."

"Got enough money?"

"Yes. And I've got sixteen-thousand saved toward a down payment on a house."

She smiled but winced, and he knew she was wondering what city and state that house would be in. "Being cautious?"

Terrance studied his mother for clues to the intent behind her question. With her, being cautious could mean anything from looking both ways before crossing the street, to wearing a condom, to not joining a gang.

"Yes, ma'am. I'm staying true to the docile boy you raised. Don't make trouble. Stay alive."

She slapped the side of his head lightly and lovingly, but her voice rang strident. "Don't sass me. You have no idea what it's like to give birth to a Black boy. Motherhood is supposed to be the greatest joy a woman can feel, but when you give birth to a boy, all you are is scared. I was scared then and I'm scared now."

Terrance bowed his head. He'd grown up in the shadow of his mother's omnipresent worry, but she'd never explained the root of her fear so bluntly and personally.

"What about Jasmine?" he asked quietly. "Don't you worry about her?"

"Of course, baby. But for different reasons. Too many people see a Black man as a threat, and I live in fear someone will take action against you as a result." She scanned his six feet of height and broad shoulders and shook her head as if his size either incriminated him or was not nearly protection enough.

Terrance picked at a loose corner of the beer bottle's label. "It's the Black boy with the least courage who stays alive, you said to me once. Remember?" Mary didn't respond. "I was so mad 'cause I thought you were telling me to be a wimp."

Mary's eyes narrowed and saddened at the same time. She opened her mouth to reply but was interrupted by the back door banging open. "Where's my baby brother?" Jasmine sang out.

They embraced, Jasmine standing almost as tall as Terrance in her wedged sandals. Her braids reached her waist, and her face glistened in the afternoon heat. From the bright red toenails peeping out of her sandals to her canary yellow shirt, Jasmine was all about color, in contrast to Terrance's deep black T-shirt and faded black jeans.

She turned puppy-dog eyes on Mary. "Can I steal him, Mama? Please?"

"I'm not going to fight you over him," Mary said, pretending to be exasperated. "I've got a chicken to cook anyway." She took her glass and the beer bottle into the house.

"Come on, let's walk," Jasmine said. "Check out the old 'hood."

Terrance raised an eyebrow. The old neighborhood wasn't much to see. While the houses on their block were neat and painted, the more steps they took away from their home, the more visible became the poverty and neglect.

As usual, Jasmine dominated the conversation, which was fine with him. His big sister's mere presence flooded Terrance with unnamable waves of emotion that left him feeling cleansed and secure. She regaled him with news of her job, her marriage, her two-year-old daughter and the one on the way—all things that made their mother proud.

"Don't pout, little brother. She'll be just as proud of you when you marry a good woman and start cranking out kids." She shook her forefinger at him while imitating Mary's voice: "Just make sure she's Black."

Jasmine elbowed him as they passed a blocky, tan building—the Montessori school they'd attended. She hummed the first few bars of "The Twelve Days of Christmas," then switched to singing: "Two African-Americans, two Asians from somewhere, one Puerto Rican and a partridge in a pear tree." She pealed with laughter at the song they'd made up as kids to describe the racial demographics of their school's student body.

Terrance chuckled. "At least Montessori wasn't racist. I got bullied because I was a nerd with glasses who didn't say boo to anyone, but no one called me names or anything." His sister turned her most skeptical look on him, mouth half-smirked, head cocked, hand on hip. "Except Joey Russo and Jeffrey Tan," he said, to get back in her good graces. "They were definitely racist."

Jasmine wrinkled her nose. "I know all about Joey Russo and that time at his house."

Terrance's step faltered and resumed. "You do? I never told anyone."

"School wasn't that big. I heard."

Residual shame flushed Terrance's neck and face. He hadn't made any real friends in his first three years at Montessori, so Mary was pleased when Joey Russo invited Terrance over to play after school. Terrance harbored a healthy skepticism of Joey—the eight-year-old version of the quintessential Italian tough-guy—but Jeffrey Tan was going too, and he seemed okay.

"You can join our club if you want," Joey had announced after they washed their hands, ate cookies and were shooed into the backyard by Mrs. Russo. Joey led his small flock to the far edge of the yard. His middle-class suburban house stood in a long row of similar-looking houses that backed up onto the backyards of another row of similar-looking houses. Terrance couldn't tell where each yard began and ended. "But there's an initiation. Kind of like being blood brothers. Are you in?" Joey asked.

"Who's in the club?" Terrance dared to ask.

"Just me and Tan so far. But if you pass our initiation, you can help us decide who else to invite."

Terrance's heart-wings fluttered a bit. Inclusion teased his veins like a drug.

Joey smiled the first friendly smile Terrance had ever seen cross his face.

They took off their sneakers because Jeffrey reminded Joey that was step one. They blindfolded Terrance with a navy-blue-and-white paisley handkerchief, because they were taking him somewhere secret. Terrance pushed aside his mother's voice demanding caution and let his hope rise up. Giddiness threatened to escape from his throat as a giggle.

"Follow my voice."

Terrance, smiling big, obediently took baby steps in the prickly grass toward Joey's voice. He turned a few times to catch up with Joey's voice, losing all sense of direction. "This way, dummy," Joey said more than once. Terrance started to flounder, swinging his arms in front of him as if to latch onto the void.

"No, here," Jeffrey pitched in, grabbing Terrance's arm and correcting his course. "This way. That's it. Right. Here."

Terrance's foot landed on something squishy that oozed up between his toes. Joey and Jeffrey roared with laughter. Terrance tore off the blindfold to see what he already knew from the vile, sweet smell. They'd led him straight into a pile of dog poop.

"What's the matter, Washington? Did you step in something? I can't see anything except your shitty brown skin." Joey laughed so hard it looked like he might croak.

"I smell it though," said Jeffrey. "It stinks! Just like you!"

"Dog shit boy. Dog shit boy," they sing-songed.

Terrance stepped back with each hurtful chant before finding his legs, turning and running. Partially blinded by tears, he ran and ran, stopping only when back in Joey's yard. He pawed his foot on the grass but couldn't dislodge all of the brown matter. He spied an outdoor spigot beside the back door and hopped to it on one foot, not wanting to smear dog poop on the Russo's patio. Hanging onto the spigot for balance, he positioned his right foot under the flood of cold water. The sticky residue slowly broke off in malodorous clumps and washed away in the torrent. Terrance jumped back from the stream on the patio bricks, lest he be soiled twice.

"Terrance, what are you doing over there?" Mrs. Russo asked from the next house over, her hand shading her eyes from the afternoon light. "That's not our house."

Terrance's humiliation tumbled and bounced up even bigger, like a snowball rolling downhill. He wiped at his wet face with the back of his hand, turned off the spigot and trudged to the Russo's yard. "I don't feel so good," he mumbled.

Mrs. Russo retrieved his sneakers and called his mother, who was home because she worked the late shift at the hospital. On the ride home, Mary didn't force the issue when he said his stomach hurt. Terrance was sure she could smell the stinky toe jam lingering inside his sneaker. The stench was seared into his nostrils.

He barely ate his supper, and Mary suggested he take a shower and go to bed early because he looked like he might be coming down with something. For once, he didn't complain.

She wasn't as patient a month later when he declared he wanted to go to the local public school instead of Montessori.

"Do you know how hard it is to get into Montessori?"

"But I don't have any friends there, Mama. And some of the kids are mean to me."

"It's true, Mama, Terrance doesn't have any friends, except the teacher." Jasmine was quickly silenced by a glare from Mary.

Mary inhaled and exhaled noisily. "Terrance Washington, you listen to me. Did you know a sixth-grade boy was just expelled for dealing drugs at the city school? Is *that* where you want to be? This Montessori school is your best chance to stay safe and make something better of yourself. And you will make the most of it."

Terrance didn't know what better self waited out there for him. He was already stained with dog shit. His young soul feared that's all he'd ever be. So, night after night, he curled up in bed, knees nearly butting his chin, a fist in his mouth blocking his sobs, and accepted his fate.

He couldn't know his tears were matched on the face of his mother, who methodically rocked herself on a stationary kitchen chair in the blue light from the stove's digital clock. Her keen maternal ears picked up the muffled crying from her baby's room. Her heart cracked, but her resolve to steer him safely and possibly successfully through life hardened even more, like a layer of copper being electroplated onto a steel core to prevent weakening or corrosion.

***

Jasmine pulled Terrance into a hug which he quickly rejected as a small group of teenagers in front of a sub shop stared and laughed. "Hey, kids of every color have some jerk do something mean to them as a kid, right?" she said. Terrance nodded absently while noticing through the shop window that the same beady-eyed manager as when he was a kid still worked the register, no doubt continuing to fix his evil eye on every Black or Brown teen who entered.

"It's fine, Jas. Not a big deal."

"I guess not. I mean, look at you now," she said, sizing him up with narrowed eyes from across the arms-length he'd put between them. She made approval noises before weaving her arm though his and resuming the walk. "You were just a late bloomer," she said. "But tell me, aren't you tired of the all-black ensembles? Add some color, please."

CHAPTER 4: ANIMAL OMENS

Charley unlocked the bookstore's old, green wooden door and let Xander in, the Closed sign swaying on its suction cup hook. She pretended not to see his approving glance at her purple tank top and black leggings.

"Come on, my car's parked in the back." She relocked the door behind him and led the way, long ponytail swaying.

Thirty minutes later, they arrived at State Park. Although not the state's only park, it was the closest to city-dwellers and therefore the only one that mattered. To them, it was The State Park.

Xander steered Charley right at the fork onto his preferred hiking trail. She sped up to keep pace, enjoying the sight of him in shorts, his long legs well-muscled but not bulky.

They continued in silence for a quarter mile or so. Charley usually drove to State Park on her days off and jogged the flat trails, but she'd never climbed the one small mountain. It was as if she'd entered an entirely new world: the earth's perfume, the chorus of birdsong, and the stout evergreens standing sentinel were unfamiliar in their new configuration.

Xander peered up at the tree cover. *"Jade leaves and saplings, white birches slashing the green, shooting to the clouds."* He looked at Charley, smiled warmly, and returned his attention to the trail ahead.

Charley followed him up a short set of crumbling wooden logs fashioned into a rudimentary staircase. "What was that? You sounded like you were in a trance, or someone was speaking through you."

Xander laughed, presumably at her melodramatic observation. She joined him, thrilling in the simple forgotten pleasure of laughing at oneself. "While I prefer your interpretation, the truth is much more pedestrian. It's a haiku. I make them up as I meander through life."

Charley scratched her nose. "Haiku. I remember those. I'm terrible at poetry, but those were so short, they weren't as intimidating."

"Yeah, that's why I like them. They're not intimidating."

She was pretty sure he was making fun of her. She stopped to stick her finger into her running shoe for a quick dig at her eczema and to adjust the band-aid on her heel. "Why do you like them then?"

"They're elegant in their structure and, properly executed, deeper than their simple surface would suggest." He smiled at her encouragingly. "Give it a try. Five syllables, then seven, then five."

Charley grimaced and shook her head. She watched her feet for a while, her light blue running shoes stirring up dust clouds with each step.

Xander cleared his throat. "*Friendship is precious. Like a brook soothing pebbles, it sings and moves us.*"

Charley stopped and stared at him until he halted. "What?" he said, bouncing on his toes.

"That's really pretty. You have to remember that one. Write it down."

"Why?"

"So you can keep it. And go back and enjoy it. And let other people enjoy it."

"Nope, not necessary. They're meant to be savored fleetingly and by whomever I am with, and perchance the universe if it's listening. Writing them down would diminish their essence."

She couldn't tell if he was messing with her. "How very Zen of you," she said finally, resuming the walk.

"Have you heard tell of the mandalas Buddhist monks create? They construct these massive, byzantine designs that depict the world in divine form. They tessellate them from sand, literally one grain at a time. It can take a team of monks weeks to complete one mandala. And when they're done? They demolish it. They sweep up the sand and cast it into a stream to bless the universe." He whooshed his arm in front of him to emphasize the point.

Charley gasped. "That's why you don't keep your poems—to bless the world?"

"Please," he said, "I'm not that worthy." He slowed his pace and watched the ground before him for a few steps before turning to Charley. "Each step I take disappears in an instant. Each step eats up another small piece of the Earth and my time on it. And we're content to let each step go. We move on. So the haiku, and the mandala, are like steps upon the Earth that we are content—no, grateful—to have taken, but do not need to dwell upon."

Charley furrowed her brow. "I think maybe haiku are beautiful because they distill the world's chaos into a few manageable images."

He nodded and smiled. The trail climbed steadily now, and they concentrated on their upward progress for a few minutes.

"*Life is full of death*," Charley intoned as the path leveled, eyes focused on the dirt trail. "*Dead parents, dead grandparents. Everyone leaves me.*" She smiled wryly.

Xander grabbed Charley and enveloped her in a tight hug. She froze. His body heat and salty odor oozed through her clothes and into her flesh and bones, coaxing her into a relaxed, liquid-like state. As quickly as he'd initiated the embrace, he let go and continued climbing.

Charley's mind wanted to ask why he did that, but her heart said let it go, like their steps on the path. For the first time in years, she listened to her heart.

***

After cresting the mountain, they rested while taking in the view: the woods and marshes of State Park encircling the hill like a lush cowl, the city unfurling like a quilt of Lego blocks beyond that to the northeast, and in the other direction, Long Lake twinkling in the sun.

After a few minutes of contemplation, Xander bounced on his toes as if his body were humming to get moving again. "Shall we?"

"Sure." Charley started picking her way down the trail. "Why didn't you bring your dog? Fred, right?"

Xander hopped onto and off a boulder in the path. Charley worked around it. "He's rambunctious and requires constant supervision to protect himself and the wildlife, so I wouldn't have been able to give you my complete attention." His matter-of-fact delivery of this pronouncement minimized the awkwardness those words should have created in her.

"I love dogs. I had one growing up."

"Do tell. I adore a good pet story. I hope it has a happy ending."

Charley frowned but forged onward. "My dog as a kid was named Chaucer."

"How literary of you. You must have been a precocious child," he joked.

She ignored the ache in her chest. "My dad named him. He was an English professor." She kicked a rock in the path. "As a puppy, Chaucer was always eating shoes, and the name Chaucer comes from the French word *chausseur*, which means shoemaker." Charley smiled, surprised at how natural it felt, even on the heels of a painful memory.

"What breed was the aptly named Chaucer?" Xander's utterance of the dog's name made Charley feel she had allowed him through a door to her childhood.

She pretended to focus on the roots and rocks strewn throughout the trail for a minute. "He was a mixed-breed—some Lab and we weren't sure what else. Tan and brown. Nothing special to look at, but the biggest heart you could imagine. My mom and dad got him as their trial run for parenting. Which was successful, because about a year later, I showed up."

"And the world was made a better place." Xander nodded, as if his saying it made it so. Charley was learning that many of Xander's statements required no response.

"He was my dog from then on, meeting me when I got off the school bus every afternoon, sleeping at the foot of my bed, watching over me."

"No siblings?" He grabbed her arm and steadied her as her foot caught on a root.

Charley shook her head.

"Mm. So what happened to Chaucer?"

Charley inhaled as deeply as her lungs allowed. "I went to a friend's house one day—her mother picked us up at school—and when I didn't get off the bus, Chaucer freaked out. He chased the bus like the driver forgot to let me off. He was running up the middle of the road when a car came around the corner from the other direction and—that was it."

"Hm. Losing a dog is always excruciating, no matter how many times you experience it. How old were you?"

"I was eight, and Chaucer was nine."

"If it makes you feel better, at least fifty percent of large dogs succumb to cancer by age ten. He was likely approaching the end of his life anyway. No other dogs after that?"

"My mother refused to get another one. She said—" Charley winced—"I was too distraught for her to go through losing another one."

Xander leaped over another rock in the path. They continued silently for a minute.

"I've been curious, since you told me about Baggage—why do you refer to the cat as 'it' instead of 'he' or 'she,' when you clearly have an affinity for animals?"

Charley shrugged. "I don't know. It's just not my cat, and never will be."

"I know cats can be aloof, but one never knows. He might be as— he might be lonely and more willing to be a sociable companion than you think."

"Okay," Charley said, more to end the conversation than from agreement. She was pretty sure Baggage hated her.

They reached the bottom of the mountain and wound their way back to the dirt parking lot, where they leaned side by side against

Charley's Mazda and shared water from Xander's stainless steel bottle. Xander poured a little water on his messy curls and shook his head, spraying Charley in the process. She didn't react; she merely pushed back the sweaty strands of hair escaping from her ponytail and stared at her feet.

"You've suffered more than your fair allotment of tragedy, haven't you? Your parents, grandparents, Chaucer." He busied himself loosening and tightening the top of the water bottle.

Charley considered answering Xander's kindness with complete disclosure about her seven-year curse, but she feared ridicule or an attempt by him to dissuade her of the curse's existence. Instead, she took a leap of faith and offered him a lesser confession. "You're a nature person so you may not think this is weird."

He shrugged and waited.

"I believe in animal omens. Lots of times when I see an animal—usually in the wild—I feel as if it's telling me something." His silence encouraged her to continue. "The day before I got the call saying my grandparents died in a house fire, my boyfriend and I were driving back to campus after having lunch downtown, and a cardinal flew right in front of our car and disappeared. I was so upset I made Nathan stop. I was afraid I'd find the bird plastered to the front of the car."

Xander swigged some water. "And did you?"

"No, but there was one red feather stuck in the radiator grill." Her hand moved as if plucking the stuck feather and bringing it to her eyes for perusal.

"So maybe that was a good omen. The bird survived and left you something beautiful."

Charley lowered her hand. "No. Think about it. A red feather and, that night, my grandparents die in a fire. It took a while, but I put two and two together. My parents—our last summer, we were camping up north and there was a dead moose in the lake near our campsite. The carcass was bloated, literally falling apart when the campground staff tried to pull it out." Charley shuddered and refused the water bottle Xander offered.

"And you think that forebode your parents' deaths?"

"I know it did. Just two weeks later, the small plane they were in crashed near a waterfall in the Brazilian rainforest." Her voice dropped to a whisper. "That came out in pieces, too."

Xander looked skyward. "But you can have good omens, too, yes?"

"I guess," Charley said.

"Then look," Xander said, pointing up. "I just spied two hawks. Wait . . . here they come." Charley looked east and saw two birds soaring in large circles, their wings outstretched and still. Occasionally they crossed paths as if dancing with each other to the sound of the wind. "Aren't they incredible?"

"Yeah, beautiful," Charley said to reassure him. She didn't ask if he'd seen the dead frog in the parking lot between their car and the trailhead, its skin stretched by the wheel of a car or mountain bike to its maximum potential length, its height reduced to a few millimeters, its internal organs squashed into oblivion.

"That's enough death talk for today," she said, her light tone masking the ache inside her. "Let's go back. I've got to do my grocery shopping." She lied, since her shopping for the week was done, per her usual schedule. But she was tired and wanted to be in her apartment alone.

CHAPTER 5: JESSICA'S WHEELHOUSE

Jessica Delgado had a choice to make: which of her three standard breakup reasons to give Thomas—a sought-after investment banker, one of the city's most eligible bachelors and her Caribbean holiday companion for the last ten days.

Just as they touched down on American soil, Thomas casually announced he wanted to make their thirteen-week-old relationship exclusive. Jess had busied herself with her carry-on items, as if suddenly her pocketbook and computer bag had unorganized themselves. Now, options revolved in her head like the baggage carousel she and Thomas stood before. She calculated having twenty minutes at most to make her decision. Not ideal for someone used to digesting numbers and facts *ad nauseum* before recommending a course of action.

Telling the truth—that her focus remained solidly on her career for two more years minimum—had proved frustratingly ineffective with the last few men, who acted as if they knew her better than she knew herself. Right. Telling the man she simply wasn't ready to commit was futile. He would say he'd hang on until she was ready. But she refused to continue a relationship in which the parties' objectives weren't aligned.

That left option number three, the strategy with the highest success rate of late.

"I've met someone else," she blurted as her brown-and-black patterned suitcase plowed through the heavy plastic fringe separating outside from in. Thomas turned to her, mouth open, eyes hurt, luggage forgotten. She jutted out her lower lip and blew a puff of air up to shift her long side-swept bangs out of her eyes. "What I mean is, I ran into an old boyfriend right before we left. I can't stop thinking about him. I'm so sorry, I didn't plan this. You're an amazing person who will make someone else very happy. Very soon."

She stepped away to retrieve her suitcase from the carousel.

"Can we talk about it?" Thomas asked.

"I'm sorry. There's nothing to talk about. Thank you for coming. This was a great vacation." She rolled her luggage outside while Thomas tactfully ducked into the men's room to avoid an awkward wait together at the taxi stand.

Fifty-two minutes later, she arrived home to the apartment she shared with two roommates. Rifling through her pile of mail, she was accosted by two wedding invitations from high school friends and a baby shower invitation from a colleague.

Why, she wondered, did people insist on spending three percent of their wedding budgets printing and mailing invitations when an evite would suffice, freeing up cash to be funneled into other aspects of their events while doing something good for the planet? Unlike the brides-to-be, whom she'd grown up with in one of the city's more affluent suburbs, Jess prided herself on demonstrating more economy. She bought her fine-quality clothes at discount stores and websites. Rather than rent a posh high-rise apartment closer to downtown, she lived here, in this cheaper but less convenient neighborhood that allowed her to bank two-thousand dollars a month toward a down payment on the city center condo she planned to buy in the near future.

At least the reason for the hard-copy shower invitation was clear, if annoying. When Jess opened the card, a flurry of pastel pink and blue confetti in the shape of baby booties and rattles spilled all over the floor.

"Fred, no!" she cried at Xander's dog, who licked up a few pieces of confetti before Jess towed him away.

She tossed the invitation onto the table and collapsed on the couch. Other than Xander and Sunny, all her friends were married, getting married, pregnant, getting pregnant, or recently pregnant. Jess flicked a tenacious baby blue bootie from her leg. She did want a husband and kids someday. Just not yet.

Thirteen hours later, Jess was back at the job she loved like some people loved friends and partners. She'd planned on easing into things in her cubicle on the seventeenth floor in one of the financial district's most desirable high-rises. Instead, she and one other accountant in the commercial department were asked to scope out potential investment properties anywhere in the city they chose. The head of the company— Flammer the Hammer as employees called him with admiration and critics called him with scorn—wanted some quick-hit wins to take the sting out of the recently tanked Stone Circle project out in South City, the one Xander helped derail.

Adept as she was at financial analysis, Jess knew she had to exhibit visionary thinking as well if she wanted the promotion to accounting manager when her boss Rodney retired. And want it she did. It represented a major milestone on her road to becoming a chief financial officer. So even though her first day back after vacation was hijacked by this project, landing her here, walking the streets of Wrighton instead of at her desk, the assignment couldn't have been timed better.

Cruising the city to uncover forgotten jewels was in her wheelhouse. She'd grown up taking regular trips intown with her father. During summers, and school vacation weeks if the family wasn't away, she'd go with him as he traversed the city's formal districts and informal neighborhoods to meet with clients. All those years ago, the city had reached out and anointed Jess as one of its own.

Most people visiting Wrighton smelled croissant shops or exhaust. Jess smelled success. Others heard street sweepers and crossing walk signals and car horns. Jess heard money changing hands. They sensed the flutter of pigeon wings and the rush of buses barreling by. Jess sensed opportunity poised and waiting to be grasped. Where others saw historical and present-day social ills, Jessica saw numbers: square footage, rent, taxes, revenue, overhead, profit, loss.

With her knowledge of the city, she was sure she could identify a number of viable acquisition targets. She'd decided to scout between the historic downtown center and the cultural district. Small businesses sprang up regularly in this no man's land, and one-point-five out of three failed within two years. Surely, she could find one or two owners looking to sell.

She turned onto Canal Street and scanned the block stretching before her. An optician, a deli, a vegan cafe, a florist, a realtor, an Asian grocery store, and a bookstore. She knew the first building on the right was a non-starter. A prominent inner-city leader leased it at below-market rates to organizations like the legal aid service and community watch association situated there now.

Next to the corner building stood the bookstore, occupying the ground floor of a standalone three-story. The curtain and lamp in the second-story window suggested living quarters, and the smudged third-floor windows suggested unused space. Jess shook her head. Leaving an inch of city real estate empty was like heaving money out the window. Checking a paper pulled from her bag, she scanned her property list. Her finger stopped at City Books, owned by Georgina O'Hanlan. She buttoned her blazer, smoothed her short, asymmetrically cut brunette hair, and marched through the propped-open, green-wooden door.

The store was well laid out to make the most of limited square footage with a small café section on the left, a checkout counter to the right, and a table of new releases and discount books straight ahead. Beyond that, she saw a tiny, circular information desk and rows of bookcases. She smiled at the man behind the register and asked to speak with the owner.

CHAPTER 6: LOVE OF THE LIST

Xander stepped through the door of City Books and leaned against the checkout counter as if resuming an ongoing conversation.

"You haven't brought in a birthday girl in a while. Did you run out?" Charley quipped, pleased that whatever small amount of wit she possessed was intact after years of neglect. Exercising it released endorphins as if she were engaging in physical exertion.

"Would you believe it's no one's birthday today? At least no one with whom I am acquainted." He shrugged.

"I guess you don't have as many friends as I thought," Charley replied, immediately worrying her sarcasm had gone too far.

Xander grinned. "I come because a friend invited me and several others to his family's summer house next weekend, and I'm hoping you'll come with. It's right on the water. Should be an entertaining escapade."

Charley's palms began to sweat. "I work weekends. That's our busiest time."

"Noted. But I suspect you haven't taken a weekend off in years, and you determine the schedule. I changed mine—I'm forgoing a protest planning meeting that weekend to get away."

"But Dale always has Sunday off to spend with his family."

"You deserve to have Sunday off, too, once in a while. Can't someone cover your shift?"

"I won't know anyone there except you. You should invite someone else instead."

"I don't want to invite someone else. What I do want is to introduce you to some of my other friends. You'll love them, and the feeling will be mutual."

Charley sighed. "I'll think about it." She looked away from his piercing blue eyes.

"I have never worked so hard at being friends with someone."

She stared at the cash register.

"Never mind. See you later, Charley."

"Xander, wait." He stopped, but she had nothing to add.

He shook his head. "Come if you want. Don't if you don't want."

The cheery bell over the shop door mocked Charley as Xander waltzed out of the store.

***

In bed that night, the jester of friendship courted Charley. He leaped, he twirled, he frolicked around her, teasing and cajoling. When she'd first met Xander, she wondered if his interest in her reflected a desire to collect more friends like some people collected Instagram followers. The quality didn't matter, only the quantity. What else could explain his interest in her?

Regardless of his motivation, laughing and bantering with him revived something in Charley. The allure of his visits grew more intense each time. She accepted this fact as proof of her innate weakness, although surely there were worse addictions in life than to one friendship.

But she felt compelled to reject this invitation, tempting though it was. She couldn't quiet the voice reminding her that making friends, forming relationships, maybe even loving people, was dangerous—for her and the others. She didn't know why she was toxic. She could only guess it was somehow tied to her apparent inability to love in whatever was the right way.

Saying "no" was the responsible answer. She couldn't bear to bring tragedy down on yet another.

***

Driving home on the interstate Sunday afternoon, having given up on getting the intermittent setting of the windshield wipers to align with the capricious sprinkle of rain, Terrance focused on the to-do list waiting for him: Send his landlord the rent money, check his work emails to get a jump on the week, and pick up a few groceries plus a new sharpie for marking his food items since one of his roommates didn't understand the rule, "If you didn't buy it, don't eat it."

Terrance loved a list for its clarity of expectations and sequence. If your boss approved your list of priorities, you could pursue those projects with abandon. If your girlfriend wanted more quality time, you defined the list of actions that constituted quality time and established the desired frequency. He inherited his love of the list from his mother. Mary's most important collection of instructions was the Staying Alive List, which evolved as Terrance grew. She drilled the first version into him at age twelve after a Black boy playing with a toy gun was shot by police in a park halfway across the country. Terrance could recite the list in his sleep:

1. Don't travel in groups of more than two.
2. Don't carry anything besides schoolbooks in your hands.
3. Don't wear hoodies.
4. Avoid/don't start confrontations.
5. Do not even think about breaking the law. If someone dares you to, say, steal a pack of gum, you smile, say you're not that stupid, and walk away.
6. Keep receipts for anything you buy as proof you paid.
7. If a police officer stops you, be extra respectful and polite and say 'Yes, sir. Yes, ma'am.'

At twelve, Terrance knew Black kids got stopped by the cops for no reason, but he refused to believe such a thing could happen to him. He was a good kid, bordering on boring and shy. Trouble couldn't find him if it tried. He said as much to his mother to reassure her, only to be accused of sassing.

"Some things will happen for sure in your life, Terrance Washington. You will eat and sleep. You will go to school and get an education. You will keep growing. Someone will call you hurtful names you don't deserve. And someday, someone will say you did something you didn't and that someone may be a cop. It's not right. But it's going to happen."

Over the next three years, Terrance was questioned by the police twice, once after trash-talking with some White boys, and once when they were looking for a suspected robber. So when he entered high school, Mary wrote an updated Staying Alive List all about what to do *when* he was stopped by the police.

"Your number-one goal when you're stopped is to get home safely, you understand?"

Terrance's fifteen-year-old brain had been fixated on how he might manage to talk to the new girl at school. Mary seemed to accept his wandering mind and stopped talking. But the following day, instead of a plate of food, she slammed a sheet of paper onto the dinner table.

"Read it. Out loud."

He quietly repeated the original seven instructions he'd memorized at age twelve, then read the new ones.

8. Don't resist the police. If they order you out of your car, do it. Do not resist arrest, even if innocent.
9. Do not run.
10. Keep your hands in plain sight.
11. Don't make sudden movements.
12. Do not argue.
13. Stay calm. You can't control the situation, but you can control yourself. Wait until you get home to show emotion.

"But Mama, what if my life is in danger—do I run then?"

Mary breathed in sharply. She consulted her lap, her hand rubbing her forehead.

"If your life is in danger from the police, I guess you'd have to." Her face contorted as if she'd agreed to send him to an early death. She let loose a five-minute rant about respecting yourself, your family, your neighbors and even those unworthy of respect, leaving Terrance's head spinning as he wondered how they got there.

He shook his head as he drove across the state line. Be respectful but don't expect respect back. Be strong but not bold. Take your time to marry smart but don't wait too long. Be proud of being Black but don't be too proud. His mother's contradictory advice sometimes left him befuddled at how to manage life's more confusing aspects. For years, he blamed her for making him compliant and conformist. It was only after Tito died that Terrance forced himself to admit it was unfair to blame Mary for his reserved ways.

Tito had a way of building Terrance up—making him more than he was, belittling anybody or anything that troubled Terrance, and slyly encouraging him to exercise his potential by couching suggestions in good-natured insults. *Go out for basketball—maybe your God-given height can make up for your total lack of coordination. Give up the contacts that make your eyes water—girls love nerdy guys in glasses. Tell your guidance counselor you want to be in National Honor Society— maybe you can fool them into thinking something actually goes on in that head of yours.*

Terrance realized he needed Tito's firm hand on his back to get anywhere in life because yes—at heart, he was docile, like his mother always wanted. Without Tito by his side, where would he end up? Nowhere is what he decided. Between his mother's constant battering to keep his head down and his natural reserve, he'd have a mediocre life at best.

In the most decisive moment of his sixteen years, he decided he would not defile his best friend's memory by back-tracking down the road Tito steered him onto. He would be more assertive. Assimilate— that's what he would do. He'd abide by the Staying Alive List because he didn't want to inflict on his mother the agony forever etched on Tito's mother's face. But he would be his own man. He'd get invited to any party or gathering on his decent looks or the charisma Tito insisted he possessed if he'd only let it fly. He would shine and make all walks of life embrace him—high school teachers, college professors, classmates, colleagues, and bosses. He would succeed, and on his own merits. But if a company had a diversity goal he could help them reach, he would grab the opportunity with both hands and not apologize.

Terrance pulled into a rest stop and cleaned his glasses with the microfiber cloth from his pocket. Walking up to the double glass doors of the restaurant-restroom-store combo, he saw his reflection and said a silent hello to Tito. After Tito's descent into the earth, Terrance had copied his friend's blonde hair as homage, remembrance, encouragement, and penance.

He was doing all right. Tito would be proud. His career was on track. If only he could find the right life partner. He wanted to build a family unit to make his mother proud. He'd be a major presence in his kids' lives, not like his own father, who'd disappeared after the divorce. Terrance and his wife would speak openly to their children, educating them as Mary did but with a lower fear factor. They'd tell them they can be anything they want to be, not like Mary who scoffed when he'd come home from first grade bubbling over a future as an astronaut or Nobel Prize winner. She'd said people would always try to knock Terrance down and his father had gotten annoyed, saying Terrance was too young to have his dreams crushed. Mary replied it's never too early to learn how society works, and she was more concerned with him being alive at fifteen, and eighteen, and twenty, than being an astronaut.

Cold hard truth was a medicine best delivered in age-appropriate doses. Terrance knew his future wife would get that. They would form an indivisible team. With the kids, they'd cohere into a solid unit strong enough to withstand anything, be that a racist comment or action, workplace harassment, or glass ceilings should he have daughters, or homophobia should any of his kids be drawn to their own gender. And they would, all of them, revere and protect the earth.

Yes. His dog shit days were long gone and over for good.

***

"She's akin to a wounded animal, Sunny. She lost her parents, and then her grandparents, and she's got no one unless you count her crotchety boss. Strike that—I'm not sure the boss even likes Charley. Or anyone."

"But now she's got you, Xan," Sunny said, their voice as smooth as warm honey. They weren't surprised that a damaged soul was Xander's latest project. He'd been on a crusade to save the world and all the people and animals in it since the day they'd met at college in freshman year.

Xander wasn't done. "She needs to be pulled kicking and screaming into the realm of the living. I believe she's existed in a state of suspended animation for years now."

"You've been able to draw her out some, right? So, she must want friends. Maybe she just doesn't know it yet. You really think I can help?"

Xander snorted. "This from the person who dragged my sorry drunken posterior out of the gutter after that frat party, cradled me in their arms, and convinced me I would not only survive, but flourish." He tugged on the long tail of the orange paisley scarf Sunny wore like a headband, set back a few inches from the forehead. The cloth divided their four-inch-long Afro into a narrow, sleek band in the front and a cloud of black fuzz in the back, like a smoke tree in bloom. "Yeah, I think you can help. Radiate your luminance on her like you do with everyone else."

Sunny put a tawny index finger in the center of their lower lip and used their thumb and middle finger to squeeze the lip, folding it inward on itself. Xander recognized their thinking pose and remained silent as the two of them reached the bookstore and stopped outside. "Maybe you came on too strong. You can be overpowering, you know."

"Hmph. I merely conveyed that it would be a highly entertaining weekend with a coterie of extraordinarily stimulating people."

"That's not too strong for you or me, but maybe too strong for her. Let's make it sound like less of a commitment."

"Can you be more specific?"

"Just follow my lead," Sunny said, entering the store with a jingle.

***

Sharon, one of the store's sales associates, hung onto the frame of the office doorway. Charley was donning a hoodie because the air-conditioning requested by the constantly moving café employees left her chilled. "Your friend Xander's here. He said to tell you he wants you to meet Happy. He said to make sure I told you that's Happy with a capital H."

Joy and dismay jostled for position as Charley pondered her options. She couldn't ignore him. It wouldn't be professional. The fact that he had brought in another girlfriend boded well. Maybe their relationship could revert to the friendly store manager/customer rapport of the early days, before he coaxed her into walks in the woods and breaks at work. But was he still annoyed with her?

She tugged down the hoodie and went to find him.

Nearing the store's doughnut-shaped customer service desk, which was so small the hole in the middle only accommodated one, Charley hesitated, staring at a woman on the far side. The woman's stunning, heavy-lidded, almond-shaped eyes were offset by a round mouth that made Charley think of childhood innocence and puppies, a connotation that intensified when that mouth stretched into a disarming smile at something her companion said. A row of tiny gold hoop earrings traveled down the helix of her coppery left ear, glinting from within her Afro.

Charley noticed with a start that Xander stood beside the woman, his back to her. This was Xander's Happy? She seemed much more substantial than Dopey, Sneezy, or Sleepy.

Charley walked into the open center of the circular desk and said hi, her hand covering the mole under her lip. Xander made introductions and advised Charley that Sunny was nonbinary and preferred the pronoun 'they,' but Charley barely registered anything he said after the name.

"Your name is Sunny?" She widened her eyes at Xander, who snickered.

"Not Happy, but remarkably close, right?" he said.

Sunny didn't react, leaving Charley to wonder if she—*they*—knew about the seven dwarves joke or not. She hoped not.

"Xander says he invited you to come with us next weekend." Sunny's voice was so comforting it made Charley want to burrow inside it, if that were possible.

"You're going to be there?"

Sunny nodded. "You should come. It'll be fun. Do you like to cook?"

"No. I can do pasta and burgers and that's about it." Charley's face flushed at her limited culinary skills, which suddenly felt overwhelmingly inferior.

"Perfect. You can have all your meals prepared for you for a few days. Won't that be nice?"

Charley stared but didn't nod.

"What's your favorite cocktail?"

Charley scratched her cheek. "Margarita."

"Frozen?"

Charley shook her head.

"Rocks? Salt?"

Charley nodded.

"Perfect. I make a mean one. Do you like to swim?"

"A little, I guess, if it's hot enough. I'd rather run though."

"Perfect, Jess is a runner too. You guys can run along the water together." They clapped their hands together. "Are you tempted?"

"It sounds fun but—" Charley stopped short because she didn't want to disappoint Sunny, who was trying so hard and so adorably.

"Listen, don't decide right now. But it's going to be totally casual. You can spend the whole weekend in your PJ's if you want. And oh—I have a good idea. Why don't you drive your own car so you can take off early if you want? Consider it a Friday night out with friends and you can go home after if you're not having fun."

Charley was mute, torn between preserving her state of solitude and expanding her tree of friends beyond the one branch of Xander.

"This is not a big commitment, Charley," Sunny said lightly. "At the end of the weekend, we'll all go our separate ways."

"Please consider it, okay?" Xander asked, reminding Charley he was there at the edge of her vision.

Sunny reached across the circular counter, making Charley stiffen. They tugged gently but persuasively on the drawstring of Charley's hoodie, which was perilously short on one side. "Oops, you almost lost your string. That's better." Their hand patted the hoodie twice and withdrew, brushing against Charley's chin in the process.

Xander bounced on his toes once. "Let us know, okay?"

They said their goodbyes, leaving Charley reeling at the customer service desk. The sensation of Sunny's touch lingered on Charley's chin and chest. For some reason she couldn't begin to fathom, her chest ached a bit, and the ache inched up toward her throat. She swallowed hard to stop its progress.

She wanted to shout after them that of course she would go. Instead, she yelled, "Wait—aren't you here for a book?"

Sunny turned and beamed. "It's not my birthday. But I'll come back and get one soon."

＊＊＊

Outside, Xander put his arm around Sunny and pulled them close.

"What if she'd said she did like to cook?"

"Easy. I would have said, 'Perfect, you can be chef for one of the meals. We're taking turns. And that way we won't have to eat Xander's cooking so you're doing us all a solid.'"

He grinned with a head shake, leaned in, and kissed their cinnamon-toned cheek.

***

By morning, Charley's newfound willingness to go away for the weekend was smothered by a fresh pile of doubts. Jogging through State Park, she poured all her attention into her leg muscles and the pounding rhythm of her steps. Faster and faster, she ran until a stitch in her side forced her to stop.

After catching her breath she walked, fixated on the section of path a few feet in front of her. *Whoosh!* The hairs atop Charley's head lifted as a large brown bird swooped over her from behind. Her eye reflexively followed it down the path and up into the trees where it disappeared in a towering oak. Heart pitter-pattering with excitement, Charley approached the bird's landing zone. Only a hawk or maybe an owl had that much mass. Standing near the bottom of the oak tree, she spied the brown form resting on a branch high above. On a whim, she *hoo-ed* twice like an owl. The bird slowly rotated its head around to look at her. Pure joy filled Charley's troubled mind as she marveled at seeing an owl in the daytime and at such close proximity. And it had reacted to her! She laughed out loud. When the owl swiveled its head back around, she floated down the path.

The owl's unusual behavior had to mean something. It was as if it had targeted Charley, flying into her line of vision to force her attention up and away from the path in front of her. Charley's head bobbed up and down in understanding. It was time for her to look beyond her small bubble of existence, to explore a bit of the larger world around her.

She changed her mind again, for what she knew was the last time. She would go away with Xander and his friends.

PART 2:
THE WEEKEND

CHAPTER 7: CLIFF-JUMPING

The apartment door flung open. Charley's eyes were wild.

"I'm not ready yet—I'm sorry! I'm such a loser, I know! I just need five more minutes."

Xander pressed on Charley's shoulder with one hand while tightening up Fred's leash with the other, thwarting the dog's attempt to wriggle into the apartment. "Steady there. We are masters of our schedule and there is no deadline." He waited until Charley stilled. "Is Baggage in a safe place?" Charley nodded, so Xander released Fred into the apartment. The dog bombed toward the kitchen, drawn by crumbs from human and feline meals. "Do whatever you need to, and we'll await here patiently." Xander walked past Charley into the living room, Sunny on his heels.

"The cash register was acting up and I had to help Dale figure it out before I could go and I know I said I'd be ready at six sharp—"

"Shhh," soothed Sunny, "it's all good. Do you want some help?"

Charley's face twisted. "No, I just need to throw a few more things into my backpack."

"Great. We'll hang here until you're ready. Believe me, we're in no hurry to get into rush hour traffic," Sunny said.

"Oh, I'm sorry, it's my fault we couldn't leave after lunch." Charley's fists bunched at her sides.

"No, I had a customer site visit that went until five-thirty anyway. We're fine."

Charley stared, then nodded. "Okay. Um, make yourself at home." She turned toward her bedroom. "Don't worry about breaking anything. There's nothing of value here," she said over her shoulder before disappearing.

"Wow," Sunny mouthed to Xander. "That girl's got a serious lack of self-worth."

Xander nodded and began exploring. The small living room held a couch of a blue color that could only be characterized as blah, two wobbly wooden chairs, and a coffee table that looked like a rescue from the side of a very downtrodden road. He stopped at a small bookcase holding a lone framed photo of an older couple on the top shelf, a few cookbooks on the middle shelf, and a lopsided pile of newspapers sliding off the bottom shelf.

"I expected a miniature bookstore from a bibliophile employed at City Books," Xander mused as he scanned the unadorned walls. "It's sparse to say the least."

"There's not one personal touch, except for this," Sunny whispered, picking up the five-by-seven photo.

Charley re-entered, a tan backpack over her shoulder and a lumpy cloth shopping bag in her arms. "Okay, I'm ready." She smiled sheepishly, looking from Xander to Sunny to Fred. She dropped to her knees, depositing the canvas bag at her side. "Fred, it's so nice to meet you finally."

She rubbed his black ears, one of which flopped down as if in defiance of the other, which always stood at attention. The rest of Fred was white splattered with black bits, including a large black circle covering much of the right side of his face like a misshapen pirate's eyepatch. "I'm glad you conquered your barking problem."

Fred wagged in agreement, then tried to lunge past Charley down the hallway toward her bedroom before Xander grabbed the leash and pulled him up short. "Turns out he merely required more exercise."

Sunny laughed. "The apple doesn't fall far from the tree."

Xander made a face at them and turned back to Charley. "Are these your grandparents?" He pointed to the photo in Sunny's hands.

"Yep." Charley picked up her bags and keys and rushed out the door. After double-checking the door locks, the trio headed down to the tiny parking area behind the building, Xander and Sunny each grabbing the cooler and backpack they'd left at the bottom of the stairs.

Busy blue-gray clouds buffeted the sky, promising to finish their dance by morning and usher in a gorgeous weekend. At ground level, a warm gust blew past Xander's bare legs, depositing tiny grains of gravel in the open toes of his Teva sandals. Charley, he noticed as he shook his foot, wore canvas shoes that seemed heavy for the summer heat.

He arranged their belongings in the rear of the blue hatchback, a process Fred observed with his butt wiggling as if he expected to be packed in there too. Xander nudged the last bag into position and stepped back. "So, I see you're a minimalist in the decorating arena."

Charley shut the hatch door. "I don't need much since it's only me."

"Not even books?" Sunny asked.

"Books are too important to store in an apartment. What if something happened?"

Charley settled in the driver's seat with Xander beside her, Sunny and Fred in back. Fred immediately lolled his head out the window as if he knew a breeze was coming.

Charley glanced at Sunny in the rearview mirror. The woman—*Was she allowed to call them that? If not, what was the right word for a nonbinary person?*—practically vibrated in their Kente-patterned shirt of yellows and oranges, making Charley feel dull by comparison in her plain, light green jersey. She steeled her shoulders and started the ignition.

Once they turned onto the highway, the cityscape whizzing away behind them, Charley listened to the lazy chatter between Xander and Sunny that filled the space in the car. Fred gulped air for a while before lying down next to Sunny with a sigh.

Ninety minutes later, Charley exited the highway and Fred resumed his high-alert stance. A fine mist speckled the dusky air as she pulled onto a two-lane route edged with a cluster of small houses on one side and a heavily wooded section on the other. Charley watched her speedometer until it dropped to the speed limit. Looking back up, she gasped as a deer appeared in her peripheral vision followed instantly by the doe's head right in front of the windshield, as if it might turn toward Charley and start a conversation.

A nauseating thud resounded through the car. Charley shut her eyes reflexively while jamming on the brakes. A second thud echoed soon after. The car inched to a full stop.

"Oh my God, I hit her twice! Is she hurt? Is she dead?" Charley's heart raced erratically. Deep dread seeped through her like fingers weaving through thick hair. She barely registered Fred barking and lunging at his window.

Sunny leaned into the space between the two front seats. "Charley, it was two deer. Small does. They went up there." They pointed to a small, overgrown field backed by thick evergreens.

"I hit two?" Charley's hand flew to her mouth. "They're—they're gone? Were they bleeding? We have to find them and make sure they're okay!"

Xander put his hand over hers on the steering wheel and turned it toward the road's edge. "Pull over, Char. I'll assess the situation." He got out, studied the front of the Mazda, and followed the deer's path through the field to the edge of the woods.

"It's all good," he reported after getting back in the car. "There is no bloody trail or stray tufts of fur, so it appears they merely got bumped; they're fine and they're most likely returning home now." He squeezed her trembling shoulder.

"How is that possible?" Charley whispered, "I hit them both."

"Deer are extremely springy and resilient," Xander said. "You were driving slowly, so I think you simply tapped them and they continued on their way. It's fine. Nothing to worry about." He stared into her eyes. "It wasn't your fault. Deer are known for catapulting in front of cars. Fred didn't even notice them, they advanced so rapidly."

Charley looked Fred's way but didn't actually see him, not even when he noisily slurped her face.

"Why don't you let one of us drive? You could use a break anyway."

Charley nodded and walked to the back seat on wet noodle legs as Xander and Sunny met at the driver's door.

"I'm driving," Sunny said with enthusiasm.

"Why can't I drive?" Xander said.

"Because, you hardly ever drive." Sunny sat in the driver's seat, lifted their bum to adjust the fabric of their shorts, and looked back at Charley. "He's never even owned a car."

"Hmph. Some friends would assert that's a fine reason to let me drive, so I can practice," he said through the open window before trudging dramatically back to his seat in the front passenger side. "How are you doing back there, Char?" He patted Charley's knee as Sunny pulled the car back onto the road.

"This is a mistake," she whispered to Xander. "You don't want to be my friends. Everyone I love dies."

"Eh, let's not rush things. Calling us friends may be premature. We may not even like you after this weekend."

Sunny laughed airily. "Or you might not like us," they added.

Charley managed a wan half-smile. "I'm sorry, I'm being stupid."

Sunny shook their head vigorously. "Not stupid. Superstitious maybe."

"And therefore illogical. Animals don't exist to guide our lives." Xander drummed his fingers on his thigh. "Plus, that was two females, so it's also illogical that they represented me and Sunny, if that's what you're surmising. And even if in some plane of existence, those animals do represent us, it says you might bump us around, but it will take more than that to extirpate us; we'll bounce right back and carry on with our quotidian lives."

Charley looked at him, wanting to believe. She nodded with a tight smile.

"Go head. Bump me."

"What?"

"Hit me. Right here on my arm." He twisted his upper body into the space between the front seats and extended his arm. Charley realized he was serious. She tapped his bicep with her fist.

"Harder."

She pulled back about a foot and punched him with slightly more force. Fred stopped panting and watched.

"Harder."

She yanked her fist back to her shoulder and rammed it into Xander's arm, smiling for real at how silly she felt. Fred growled softly until Xander shushed him.

"See?" He rubbed his arm. "Still standing. Or sitting, as the case may be." He looked at Sunny and mouthed, "Ow!" while pointing at Charley.

Charley's smile faded and her arm embraced Fred, who leaned into her.

Sunny stopped at an intersection and moved their hand up and over the back of their seat, fingers wiggling. Fred immediately stepped in Charley's lap and gave Sunny's fingers a lick.

"Charley, assuming that wasn't you, give me your hand."

Charley stared for a second before awkwardly grasping Sunny's fingers, which felt warm and strong in Charley's cool ones, and a touch slimy thanks to Fred's contribution. A hint of calm moved through Charley's hand to her arm.

"All good?"

"All good," Charley lied, hoping that between Sunny's warmth and Xander's ability to make her laugh, she might make it through the weekend after all, omens or no omens.

Like a recovering addict, she committed to taking it one hour at a time. Leaving the shelter of her rigid routine felt like a long-awaited jailbreak and a perilous jump off a cliff at the same time. But really, her routine wasn't all that rigid. She bent it all the time, jogging in two different parks, eating different meals each night of the week. Plus, she'd only been relying on the stability of a structured schedule for a few of her twenty-nine years. Surely, she could be spontaneous for a weekend.

****

Charley's jaw dropped as Sunny pulled into a long, crushed stone driveway and parked behind a white BMW and a dark gray Jeep. The long home before them boasted at least twice the square footage of any home they'd passed on the way. The house's white trim popped in contrast to the weathered-gray shingles, and a white railing surrounded a second-floor balcony with French doors.

"Buwan Bakunawa!" Xander exclaimed as a sprightly figure with bronze skin, short black hair, and a huge smile burst from inside with a bang of the screen door. A Chinese-looking dragon tattoo emerged from the sleeve of his black T-shirt, encircling much of his left arm, and tattooed bracelets of various geometric designs encircled his right forearm.

"Xander, my man," Buwan said, white teeth gleaming and dark eyes sparkling. "How are you?"

"Anticipatory," Xander said with a fist bump. He indicated his companions. "Meet Sunny and Charley."

"Your place is beyond beautiful," Sunny said, shaking Buwan's hand.

Charley extended her hand. "How do you guys know each other?"

"We went to the same high school," Buwan said. "I was two years ahead so I didn't get to know him until—"

"Until he saved my ass. A couple of loathsome seniors were giving me a hard time and Bu, Mr. Popular, came to my aid and told them to cease their execrable behavior."

Charley's eyes grew. "You were bullied in high school?"

Xander ran his hand down his purple T-shirt with a flourish, like a game show hostess showing off the prizes. "I wasn't always the fine specimen of manhood you see before you now."

Sunny snorted, then covered their mouth and laughed.

"Freshman year, I was scrawny, gangly, and one giant zit. I was forced to become erudite to survive. But then I was bullied for being too scholarly."

Sunny laughed again. "When you use words like scholarly and erudite in high school, what do you expect?"

"Hey," sang out an attractive woman with short, asymmetrical brown hair and a huge smile as she descended the steps to the driveway. She wore a sleeveless red blouse and black Capri pants.

"Roomie," Xander called while Sunny said, "Jess!"

"Good to see you survived the trip with these two," Jess said to Charley.

Charley wasn't sure how to react. "What do you mean?"

"A moment of Zen is all right. But you had miles and miles of Zen." She looked from Sunny to Xander. "Plus, keeping him locked up in a car for two hours is usually a test of patience."

Xander leaned toward Charley. "What she's really insinuating, dear Char, is that she is the bore-ring one," he said, drawling out the insult in childlike fashion.

Jess snickered. "You love me and you know it."

"Guilty, though most days I have no idea why." Xander kissed her on the cheek and moved up the stairs. "I'm taking my belongings inside so I can accompany Fred to the water posthaste."

All five plus Fred traipsed into the kitchen where coolers and backpacks were deposited.

"I put sticky notes on the bedroom doors so you know where you're sleeping," Jess said. "X, we've got you bunking with your work friend T. S, you and I can share the room with two twin beds. And C, you get the room with the full bed."

Charley squinted and asked Sunny, "Is she talking in code?"

"Jess likes to save syllables wherever possible, so she calls us by our first initials."

Jess blew a breath up to shift her side bangs out of her eyes. "It's about efficiency. And this is perfect, having Charley and Terrance join. We don't have any other C's or T's."

Xander smirked. "Choosing friends based on the alphabet? That's calculating even for you, Jess."

"At least I don't have a phobia of clichés like you. Or some weird need to use the biggest words I know. Which makes you sound like an old man, by the way."

Xander turned to Charley again. "It's true I am admittedly grandiloquent, and I dread the use of stock phrases and uninventive word choices, but for good reason—there are more than a million words in the English language, each awaiting its turn in the spotlight."

Sunny moved a bowl from a cooler into the fridge and sighed. "Jess is all about efficiency. Xander's all about equality, even for words. Now stop bickering, you two."

After storing their things, the gang convened in the living area where massive picture windows offered panoramic vistas of the water, underscored by a modest strip of beach. An expansive lawn connected the beach to a raised porch running the entire waterside of the house, its rocking chairs and chaise lounges begging for company. Studded across the lawn were a modern teak picnic table, a paved patio with a row of heavy wooden lounge chairs, and another patio with a firepit and six Adirondack chairs.

"Water!" Xander shouted, a yellow Frisbee in his hand making Fred bark and jump.

"Let's go!" Sunny said, reminding Charley of a sprinter ready to jump out of the starting blocks.

Xander flung open the screen door and he, Sunny and Fred thundered across the porch in a tornado of purple, orange, and yellow, down the steps, across the lawn, the beach, and into the shallows. Buwan followed, resembling a little kid trying to keep up with the big kids. Sunny and Xander stopped where the water hit their knees, Sunny squealing. Xander whipped the Frisbee into the deep water for Fred to fetch. Buwan hesitated when the water reached the top of his red-and-black swimming trunks, then dove in, T-shirt and all.

Charley shook her head at the display of sheer life force. She noticed Jess watching her. "Are they always like that? Exuding joy?"

"X and S? Yeah, the two of them can be overwhelming with their energy. I call them the Celestial Twins. But don't worry. I balance them out. I'm the sane, grounded friend."

Charley was referring only to Sunny, who seemed to gush happiness and peace, but decided not to clarify.

"So, what do you do, C?" Jess sat in a white wicker chair with a light blue cushion, crossing her legs and leaning forward, black thong sandal bouncing. Charley wanted to head outside with the others but didn't want to be rude. She looked around the white-walled, open-concept living area, which was divided into a dining space dominated by a chunky, light-colored wooden table that would easily accommodate twelve, and the tastefully decorated sitting area full of understated couches and chairs with cushions in various shades of gray, light blue, and light green. She chose a light green chair across from Jess, sinking deep into the cushion.

"I work at a bookstore in the city."

"What's your title?"

Charley pushed aside annoyance at the job interview tone. "I'm the manager."

"Nice!" Jess smiled sincerely, wiping away Charley's annoyance. "Do you like being in charge? I know I would."

Charley covered her mole and considered the question. "I do. I pick the titles I like, I set the prices, and even decorate the store how I want, as long as Georgina's willing to shell out the money. And she let me move into an apartment upstairs, so the commute is awesome."

Jessica's eyes darkened. Her eyebrows nudged severely inward. "Georgina—is that your boss's name?" She plucked at a sprig of wicker poking out from the arm of the chair.

"Yeah, she's the owner of City Books. How about you? Where do you work?"

Jess gave her head a tiny shake as Xander, Sunny and Buwan burst into the room, Bu holding a towel around his waist, his wet T-shirt clinging to his torso. Fred whined from the other side of the screen door. "I'm a CPA in All-American Development & Construction's commercial real estate division. I work in the financial district."

"Jess works for the Evil Empire." Xander flashed a wise-ass grin in Jessica's direction.

She shot him back a smarmy, fake smile.

Xander sat on the arm of Charley's chair, his thigh brushing her arm. "How's Liam Flammer faring after his brutalizing defeat on Stone Circle?"

Sunny groaned. "You guys are roommates. Haven't you already covered this at home?"

"I hardly ever see X. I've been working a lot, and he doesn't exactly keep regular hours," Jess said. "Anyway, it's no big deal. You win some, you lose some in real estate development. It's on to the next project," she said with a yawn. Charley wondered if the yawn was real or meant to display a lack of concern.

"And what jewel of the city will Flammer apply his hammer to now?" Xander asked.

"Nothing that concerns you," Jess said. A knock rattled the driveway-side door, punctuating the finality of her statement.

***

"Anybody home?" The voice filtered through the screen door into the living area.

The party is complete, Buwan thought with glee.

He ran to open the door for a tall Black man wearing a dark gray T-shirt and black cargo shorts, juggling a large cooler, a shopping bag, and a duffel bag.

"Come on in. I'm Buwan. Terrance, right?"

Terrance nodded as they shuttled everything into the kitchen, glass clinking from within the bag and the cooler as rain began to spatter outside. Buwan followed Terrance into the living area with five beer bottles gathered in his arms, which he distributed all around.

"Not partaking?" Xander asked.

"Naw, I'm on some medicine and I'm not supposed to mix," Buwan said, rather than tell the more complicated truth, which was that he'd actually stopped his medication a few weeks before and drinking alcohol might trigger a manic episode. He'd put his prescription away after making plans for this weekend with Xander, first because he was tired of feeling sluggish and foggy-brained, and he missed the power of creativity rushing through his veins; second, because Xander had said he'd bring a few female friends, and Buwan needed his sex drive back to normal, just in case.

Terrance gave a small wave. "Hey everyone, I'm Terrance. Work friend of Xander's." He smiled, his cheeks nudging his glasses up and transforming what Bu thought women would call a handsome face into a boyish one. "So, you've all known each other how long?"

Sunny answered, but their words were drowned out by high-volume drumbeats and hand claps introducing an Imagine Dragons song. "Sorry!" Buwan yelled while fiddling with a tablet and turning the music down to mere party level.

Voices rose as Xander and Terrance went off on a loud tear about some sports team while Sunny showed Jess a photo on their phone of a new solar energy system they'd recently sold. Charley sat back and closed her eyes. Bu sat still for the first time all day and studied her, sketching the lines of her face in his head. When she opened her eyes and found him staring, he smiled with a little shrug.

He wondered what he'd got himself into by inviting Xander and four of his friends out for the weekend. But, he also thought, anything was better than being alone and in a fog. Now, he wouldn't be either.

CHAPTER 8: TWO KINDS OF PEOPLE

Terrance placed the platter of steaming grilled sirloin, portobello mushrooms, onions, and peppers in the middle of the long wooden table in the dining room. "They call me the grill master for a reason," he said with a satisfied nod, wondering if his culinary skills impressed any of the women.

The beauty of all three had struck him when he'd been introduced earlier. Jessica had intense brown eyes and subtly highlighted short hair that reached to the bottom of her earlobe on the left and to her chin on the right. Olive skin, strong eyebrows, a perfect nose, rosy lips, and a cleft in her chin combined for a striking visage. Charley appeared made of porcelain with long silky hair and stunning emerald eyes. Sunny— gorgeous in a waiflike way, with big almond-shaped eyes and a round mouth—was the darkest, with an unusual, orange-brown skin tone. They all had solid careers, based on what he'd gleaned so far, and if they were friends with Xander, they must also be environmentally minded.

Everyone sat, all but Buwan bringing margaritas in hefty tumblers with salted rims. The steaks were flanked by Sunny's vegetarian options—their signature potato salad sprinkled with fresh parsley and cilantro, a green salad, and a bowl of spiralized zucchini-and-carrot salad.

Occasional breezes wrung a few remaining raindrops out of the air and tossed them against the picture window as Xander raised his glass at the head of the table, opposite Buwan. "Before we eat, let's toast. *Water, earth and sky. Essential elements all. Friends, love and romance.*"

"Cheers," said Terrance, Buwan and Charley.

"Romance?" Sunny echoed, eyebrow raised.

Jess speared a steak from the platter. "Is the meat organic?"

"No, sorry. It was more than twice the price," Terrance said, wondering how Jessica felt about men with glasses, then reminding himself it didn't matter.

"Understandable," Jess replied with a nod.

"The more we buy organic, the cheaper it will get," Xander said.

Sunny rested a serving-spoon-wielding hand on the table. "Organic food shouldn't be the 'other food,' if you think about it. We should say 'real food' and 'food with chemicals.'"

Buwan laughed.

"Good point," Charley said.

Bu cleared his throat. "So not to be weird or awkward, but the variety of hues in the skin tones around this table are amazing."

"Buwan's an artist," Xander said. "The man knows his colors."

Bu reached for Sunny's forearm and stopped. "Can I?" They nodded. His bronze thumb rubbed Sunny's skin in an almost scientific way. "I'm trying to figure out what color it is."

Terrance also fixated on Sunny's arm, ignoring the clean, yeasty aroma of fresh rolls wafting before him, making his stomach growl. "I would call it warm brown with an overtone of rust."

Sunny smiled like a child unwillingly indulging overly attentive adults. "Xander calls my skin fulvous. He promises that's a good thing. I call it half-Black, half-Indian. Mix those together and you get me." They shrugged, retrieved their arm and scooped potato salad onto their plate.

Buwan sat back and crossed his arms over his chest. "I would call it raw sienna."

"Jessica, what's your background?" Terrance asked, thinking her olive skin could reflect one of a dozen different heritages.

Jess stopped mid-sip. "Me? American. Born and raised right here." She set her tumbler down on the table with a thump and licked salt from her upper lip.

"I just meant, do you know where your ancestors are from? I mean, it's pretty clear where mine are from."

Xander raised his index finger. "Not necessarily. Could be Africa, but it could also be the Caribbean."

Buwan cut into his steak. "There are two kinds of people in this country. Those who acknowledge they're immigrants or their ancestors were, and those who don't."

"Well, plus the Native Americans," Xander said.

Jess stretched her shoulders up and back. "I'm not denying my heritage. It's just not relevant to everyday life. My parents immigrated from Colombia in the early nineteen-eighties so my father could set up a law practice here." She sipped her margarita.

Buwan pursed his lips. "You don't meet a lot of Colombian immigrants. I think you're the first I've ever m—sorry, the first person I've met with Colombian ancestry."

"There are a lot of Colombians in the U.S., but most people here couldn't name one. Except for Sofía Vergara, maybe. I guess that's better than when a drug lord was the most famous Colombian."

"And at least your family chose to come here. Some of us can't say the same," Terrance said, getting a fist bump from Sunny.

Xander read from his phone screen. "Colombians are the fourth largest group of undocumented residents in the U.S. The first Colombians immigrated here in the 1800s."

"I can top that," Buwan said. "The first Filipinos came to the U.S. in 1587."

Xander punched away on his phone. "Who knew? Are there many here, though?"

"We're right up there with the Vietnamese, Chinese, and Korean," Bu gave a short laugh. "I know this 'cause my moms liked to make sure I knew I wasn't the only Filipino-American around."

Jess's fork stopped halfway to her mouth. "Moms?"

"Yeah, I've got two moms."

"The Philippines has the twelfth largest immigrant population in the U.S.," Xander reported.

Sunny hmph'd. "Yet no one freaks out about Filipinos or Colombians coming here. Why are they different from Mexicans and Salvadorans and Guatemalans?"

Terrance put down his margarita. "Well, wait, we don't know how many Filipinos are coming in illegally versus legally, but we know a lot of Central Americans are illegal."

"Right," Jess said. "And we know illegal immigration is a scourge on this country." Jess flinched slightly under Sunny's stare. "What? It's in the numbers. It costs 10,800 dollars to deport one person. One night in a detention center costs taxpayers 180 dollars. So while I'd like to say immigration isn't my problem, it's everyone's problem."

"How can it cost so much for a mat on the floor in a chain-link cell?" Sunny asked.

Xander hummed a few bars of the Eagles' "Hotel California" before breaking into song, "Welcome to the Hotel Immigration. You can enter any time you like, but you can never leave."

Buwan reached for his water. "Sometimes you gotta wonder why people say America is the land of dreams."

Xander's fist landed lightly on the table. "More to the point is why they come—what they're fleeing—crime, corruption, and poverty. Rape is a given, kids can't play outside for fear of being kidnapped into gangs, and corrupt governments extort as much as the criminals. Many immigrants are literally running for their lives."

"That's total exaggeration," Jess countered. "They can't all be at risk of death if they stay. They come here because they want our good jobs and public services."

"First of all, Jessica, when's the last time you competed against a Mexican or Salvadoran for a job?" Jess was silent. "I thought so. Second of all, think about how horrendous your existence would have to be for you to up and leave your country and trek hundreds of miles to cross a raging river and enter the U.S. illegally with no certain prospects."

"It'd have to be pretty bad," Charley said.

Jess fingered her gold hoop earring and thanked God her parents and her childhood nanny-slash-second-mother Bertie were in the U.S.

legally. "None of that changes the fact that illegal immigration costs us taxpaying citizens something like fifty billion a year. That's a serious drain on our coffers. And there's the financial and social cost of the crimes they commit."

Sunny put down their fork with a clatter. "It's really hard to be your friend when you say things like that, Jess. All immigrants are not criminals."

Xander cleared his throat. "Actually, it's well-documented that higher immigration quotas would *reduce* crime because then they could obtain better-paying jobs and not have to resort to crime to sustain their families. And they commit far fewer crimes than Americans on a per capita basis."

"Plus, a lot of undocumented immigrants pay taxes, even though they can't collect Social Security or other benefits," Sunny said.

Heavy silence weighed on the table.

Sunny sipped their margarita. "On other fun topics, Xan, do you know if anyone's organizing a protest about the nightclub shooting?"

Charley gasped. "What shooting?"

Jess peered at Charley, wide-eyed. "Been living under a rock?"

Charley shrank back into her chair.

"Tactful as always, Jessica," Xander said. "It only transpired yesterday, Charley, several states away, so not everyone has heard about it. Eighteen people murdered at a gay club, so the shooter was unequivocally targeting gays and lesbians."

"And everyone else in the LGBTQX alphabet soup contingent," Jess said. Sunny lightly slapped their friend's arm. "What? I can never get the acronym right," Jess complained. "Anyway, does that call for a protest about gun control or gay rights?"

"Yes," Sunny said, standing and grabbing their glass. "Time for another round. Charley, want to squeeze the limes?"

Charley scrambled up with her glass.

Xander stood and stretched. "Let's clear the table while we're at it."

"Wait—everyone freeze," Jess said. "I want to bring up another serious subject. This has been bothering me a long time." All eyes focused on her. "Don't you think X should shave the beard off his neck? It looks like a small animal growing there. A beard is facial hair, not neck hair, am I right people?"

Xander's hand flew to his neck as if a razor were already shearing the ample growth there. Charley and Sunny cracked up. Terrance and Buwan traded glances, unsure which side to take.

"Do I qualify for a vote in this matter?" Xander asked.

"No. You are the crux of the issue." She panned the group. "Who thinks X should shave his neck hair?" Jess and Sunny raised their hands; Charley followed. "Who thinks X should continue to sport that affront to humanity?"

Buwan and Terrance communicated with their eyes. "We're abstaining, man," Terrance said while Buwan nodded.

Buwan headed for the kitchen with a few plates and forks. "That's settled. Let's do the dishes."

***

Quiet murmurs floated back and forth between Charley, Xander, and Sunny on the couch and Jess, Buwan, and Terrance at the dining room table. Xander drained his margarita, stood, and declared he was going to bed.

Charley deflated a bit. Beside her, Sunny took Charley's hand. Charley noticed for the second time that day how their soft, dry skin transferred warmth directly into Charley. She resisted an unexpected urge to trace the fine ridges of Sunny's metacarpal bones and the softer slopes of vein.

"Char, I hope I'm not butting in, but Xan told me a little about your life. We've all been hurt one way or another by our age, but you've had it especially rough. So, I want to say, you're one of us now. We're here for you, whatever you need. Okay?"

"Okay," Charley whispered as her chest tightened. Sunny placed their arm around Charley's shoulders as casually as if Charley were an old friend. Charley stiffened, then gradually softened into the security of Sunny's embrace, sliding into sleep after a few minutes.

A burst of laughter from the dining room startled Charley awake. She rubbed her eyes. Sunny was gone. She stumbled to the bathroom, where she perched near the front of the toilet so her pee trickled down the front of the bowl instead of rushing noisily into the water. On the way to her bedroom, she peeked into Xander's room and saw him and Sunny cuddled together on the bottom bunk, a faint after-smell of weed in the air. A pang of jealousy ripped through Charley's chest, stunning her with its strength. Why did she think Xander would choose her, when Sunny was so amazing?

She trudged back to the dining room and told the others to re-think the sleeping arrangements. After a discussion complicated by too much tequila and the late hour, they agreed Jess and Charley would share the room with the twin beds, and Terrance could take the full bed, since he refused to sleep on the top bunk over Xander and Sunny. Terrance offered to share the room with the twin beds with one of the women and give up the big bed to the other, but his offer was declined.

Charley tumbled into bed, realizing she hadn't thought once all night about the deer or the curse or about returning to her routine in the city. Now, her eyes were scratchy and tired, but her mind moved nimbly from thought to thought as she replayed the past few hours. She'd socialized more today than in all the previous year, the lively conversations stimulating dormant sections of her brain. And she'd gone from one friend to five in the course of a few hours.

The door creaked open and Jess stumbled in, banging something in the process. "Ow," she whisper-yelled.

"You okay?"

"Sorry, I was trying not to wake you."

"It's all right. I'm awake."

Charley heard clothes peeling, a bag unzipping, and more clothes flapping. "'Night," Jess whispered, climbing between the sheets, which rustled as she got settled.

Charley really needed to get some rest if she was going to jog in the morning. She had to unwind. She turned away from Jess, curled up on her side and bent her leg, running a finger over the fresh scabs on her heel. No, she didn't need that. Plus, she didn't want to risk bloodying the sheets. Instead, she raked her nails across the inside of her arm, moving from spot to spot so as not to leave a mark. When she tired of that, she brought both hands up to rest flat between her cheek and the pillow and closed her eyes.

***

In the other bed, Jess was being dragged into the past instead of the deep sleep she'd hoped for. Meeting Buwan was like seeing a ghost, one capable of firing a bullet between the eyes. He reminded her so much, physically and personality-wise, of Ozzy. Both had bronze skin, short jet-black hair, and fearless grins. Both stood about her height, so a tad shorter than most guys like to be. Ozzy was a bit goofier than Buwan, though, and his voice was different, although she couldn't define how, so she had focused on those differences and thoroughly quizzed Buwan on his life to further separate this new friend from the specter of Oz.

She peeked over at Charley, who lay still.

If she were alone, she would touch herself to stop the flow of thoughts. Instead, she rested her left hand low on the crease where her thigh met her torso, her pulse bumping against her fingers. She actively relaxed, feeling the pulse slow with her breath, until she dropped off, free of memories.

***

Buwan lay on the living room floor, trying to lure Fred into play. Fred stood, stretched, yawned, and padded down the hallway where he nudged Xander's door open. Buwan heard the dog settle on the floor inside with a grunt.

"Traitor," Buwan mumbled while pacing the living area. His energy had increased throughout the day, his long-suppressed vitality returning in an ebb and flow pattern, and now he was jazzed. Giving in to the house's silence, he retreated upstairs to his parents' room, where he flopped onto the bed and lay spread-eagled, his eyes tracing the swirled architectural detail on the ceiling.

He'd been mildly depressed when his parents first suggested he invite friends out to their summer home for the weekend more than a month ago. Then he ran into his old high school friend Xander before a therapy appointment in the city, and he'd asked Xander to come to the summer house basically to make his parents happy. But over the next few days, Buwan repeatedly flashed back to how stable and strong he'd been in high school, and he got excited about the weekend, thinking it might bring some surety back to his life. Excitement turned to frustration when he realized merely thinking about his better years wasn't going to return him to the physical and mental state of that time. In particular, his weight bothered him; he fluctuated from paunchy when taking his meds reliably to skinny when the mania was stronger than the meds. Reliable muscle tone was a thing of the past. Convincing himself he would stop the meds only long enough to lose a few pounds and regain some energy before the weekend, he went cold turkey. Sure enough, a few days ago he'd felt life surging through his body, albeit still sluggishly and in bursts, and his appetite abated. His brain cleared, his thoughts crispened. His confidence returned from the dark closet where it had been biding its time.

And now, man, he had so much energy. He jumped off the bed and moved to the master suite's spacious sitting room, which his parents had re-purposed as a studio with a daybed for him. Both the studio and bedroom pulled the water view in through massive picture windows in daytime. At night, the studio window resembled a gaping, pitch-black abyss, until Buwan flicked on the light and tamed the view. He picked out a primed, four-by-five-foot canvas from a stack in the corner and set it on his easel. He wheeled over two small tables, one holding palette paper, his favorite palette knife, and a clean rag. The other held dozens of acrylic paint tubes, several large tin cans full of brushes, and a glass jar, which he filled with water in the bathroom before replacing it on the table.

He selected a large brush and faced the easel. The nighttime window reflected the back of the easel and canvas, and Buwan, paintbrush hovering in the air. Susurrant water sounds filtered through smaller, open windows to the sides of the picture window. He closed his eyes for several minutes. Upon opening them, he tore off his T-shirt, revealing a series of moon tattoos trailing down his spine, starting with a waxing crescent at the top, building to a full moon in the middle, and ending with a waning crescent.

His tattooed arms took off in a frenzy of sweeping motions like a symphony conductor guiding his musicians. The sinuous dragon on his arm rippled as if it were a muse guiding the creation. Buwan blazed broad trails of color across the canvas, jabbed blobs of paint as accents, and slowed to a concentrated pace to refine hue, line, and intensity to his liking.

Three hours later, arm and wrist muscles throbbing, he dropped face first onto the daybed, paintbrush clutched in one hand. The paintbrush dropped, smearing an inch of rich black paint on the light gray wooden floor. Drool slid out of the corner of his mouth as he snored, smiling, into the sheets.

CHAPTER 9: SURRENDERING

After their morning run—during which she casually and unsuccessfully tried to interest Charley in a career beyond City Books—Jess gave Charley first use of the shower. Under the guise of cooling off, she wandered until she found a suitable spot to be alone with her memories.

In the woods off the side of the driveway, she perched on a flat-topped rock, surrounded by birches, oaks, and evergreens. She lifted her face to the sky. Pockets of sun slipped through the leafy cover and dappled her skin with puddles of gold.

She'd sprinted the last bit of the jog to escape the image of Ozzy huffing and puffing alongside her, as he'd done so many times. As young kids, they ran simply for joy. In later years, they ran to condition themselves for school sports.

As usually happened when she couldn't blockade the memories, Ozzy's ups and downs presented themselves in Jess's head like a bulleted list, as if she were reciting a resume of his life: Moved here with his parents from Guatemala as a toddler, just before Jess was born. Grew up in the carriage house on the Delgados' property when Jess's dad hired Ozzy's father Al as a driver, landscaper, and general handyman, and his mother Bertie as a cook, housekeeper, and sometimes nanny. Excelled at soccer, displaying more natural talent than Jess, although she was a smarter and more aggressive player. Stupidly hurt his back jumping off a bridge into the river, ending his soccer season and ruining his senior year of high school. Relied on painkillers to function while his fortitude atrophied with appalling speed. Managed to graduate, barely. Never got his driver's license. Didn't go to college. Blew the job Jess's dad got him at a landscaping company through tardiness and absence. Took up drugs. Got busted for dealing, although Jess's dad managed to fix that situation somehow. Disappeared, breaking three hearts: Jessica's, Bertie's, and Al's. Returned years later only to drop his illegitimate, two-month-old, nameless daughter on his parents' doorstep. Disappeared again. Summary: Squandered his opportunities, made nothing of himself, and crushed the people he left behind.

The only thing worse than dwelling on Ozzy was attempting to quantify the pain Ozzy's mother must feel. Bertie, over the years, had become a second mother to Jess, although they didn't bond until Jess was in first grade. Jess had been in a sullen phase, annoyed with her father for pressuring her mother into taking college classes, let down by her mother for giving in to her father, and disgusted with her baby brother Philip for willfully settling into Bertie's ample lap as if he'd forgotten their mother completely when she was at class or studying.

The sullen phase ended the day Jess stepped out of her seven-year-old head and saw the world as a place bigger than herself, filled with other people who sometimes needed help.

Both English and Spanish were spoken in the Delgados' house because Michael knew being bilingual was an asset in most careers. Jess knew Bertie and Al grew up speaking Ixil in a barely there village in the mountains of Guatemala, and that Bertie didn't even know how to read. Al also spoke fluent Spanish and passable English when they arrived in the U.S. Bertie, however, spoke little Spanish and no English so for the first few years, she communicated through gestures, smiles, and her husband's interpretations. By the time Jess's memories started, Bertie had a rudimentary understanding of English and Spanish, but she mixed them up a lot. She still got embarrassed and clammed up when she got it wrong, and she especially struggled with reading.

Jess had been on the way to her bedroom to change into shorts after school when she saw Bertie sitting on a child-size stool in Philip's room. About to giggle, thinking Bertie looked like an elephant balancing on a circus stand, she noticed the book in the housekeeper's lap. It was a board book teaching the Spanish words for familiar items like dog, cat, shirt, and hat. Bertie's round face was screwed up, her fingernail sliding up and down the gap between her two front teeth.

"PING-in-no. Pin-GOO-no." Bertie softly tried different pronunciations for *pinguino*—Spanish for penguin. She let loose an enormous sigh and closed her eyes.

"Pin-GWEE-no," Jess said from the doorway. Learning languages came as easily to her as math. Both were puzzles to be solved by moving things into the right places.

Bertie's face lit up as it did every time she saw Jess, regardless of the girl's mood. "Pin-GWEE-no," Bertie repeated. "Gracias. Thank you."

Jess went to Bertie's side and sat on the floor beside her. She put the book in her lap and pointed at the next picture. Page by page, they covered the correct pronunciations. Every few pages, Jess covered the letters with her hand and quizzed Bertie on the words.

The final word was burro, which Bertie spoke confidently with a natural rolling of the 'r'.

"Burrrrro," Jess repeated, extending the roll as long as her tongue allowed.

Bertie laughed, her bosom shaking. "Good, Jessica!" She trilled her tongue to make sure Jess knew she was referring to the rolling of the 'r.' "Smart girl," she said, tenderly patting Jess's hair.

Jess's memory jumped from Bertie's grateful laughter that day to the anguished, heart-stopping wail the housekeeper made the day she learned Ozzy had been arrested. *What happened to you, Oz?* Jess asked for the millionth time. What happened to the boy who used to race her up trees and down stairs? The boy who taught her how to steal fruit from the local orchard without getting caught? What happened to the teenager who trained side-by-side with her every summer so they'd be sure to make varsity?

She dropped her head onto her knees to catch a few tears, then raised it to dry her cheeks in the sun.

***

Terrance strolled the property, trying to dislodge the cobwebs spun in his head during the alcohol-infused late night. He noticed a flash of royal blue amidst the green, black and brown landscape and slowed, not wanting to scare the person as only a tall Black man surprising you from behind could do. Inching closer, he realized it was Jessica. He decided not to disturb her and circled wide. A sharp sniffing noise stopped his retreat. Turning toward the sound, he side-stepped behind a wide oak and watched.

Gone was the fiery, self-possessed woman from the night before. Her eyes were closed, her face seeking the sun. The cleft in her chin resembled a smudge of dirt from a distance. Her neck looked achingly vulnerable and sensuous. Her skin shone light green as if reflecting the leaves and mosses surrounding her, and she seemed smaller, her knees hugged to her chest, her arms wrapped tightly around her shins. Terrance's heart stopped for a second, shifted in his chest, and started up again. He didn't feel the reset, so neither did he recognize that a fundamental alteration had occurred inside him.

The scene should have been peaceful, but to Terrance it emanated sadness. A momentary sparkle as the sunlight connected with a tear on her cheek confirmed the mood. Resisting the urge to catalog potential causes of her angst, he looked away and snuck off.

***

Xander followed the powerful smell of hefty, dark coffee into the kitchen, Fred at his heels. "Java. You are a lifesaver, Buwan."

Buwan pulled a mug out of the cabinet. "It's rocket fuel. That okay?"

Xander blinked sleepily in reply. Buwan handed him a steaming cup.

"You messed up the sleeping arrangements last night," Buwan said with a sly smile. "Did you enjoy your moment in the sun?"

Xander stared blankly at Buwan until the uncouth nature of his remark sunk in. "Bu, I never pegged you for a swine when it comes to women." He took a throat-searing gulp of coffee.

"We could make eggs for breakfast. Do you like yours sunny side up or did you have that last night?"

"Seriously, man, cut it out."

Bu's grin faded. "Sorry. Sometimes I go too far."

"Yeah, we're a tad old for this lowly discourse."

Charley entered the kitchen, rubbing her long hair with a towel. "Did I hear something about Sunny? Where is she—where are they anyway?"

"Meditating, in the bedroom," Xander said.

Bu swung open a cabinet. "My moms stocked up on all kinds of breakfast stuff. Let's make a gigantic breakfast."

"I'll prepare eggs and bacon if you guys manage the rest," Xander said.

Charley poked around in the cabinet. "I actually know how to make pancakes. If there's a mix."

Charley and Xander got to work, occasionally bumping into each other and rubbing arms. Once Xander grabbed Charley by the waist and lifted her out of his way, forcing her to remind herself he'd slept with Sunny last night and not to harbor hope.

Terrance entered via the waterside door. A minute later, Jess walked in from the street-side door. "Caffeine, my old friend," she said to the coffee pot, filling herself a cup. "Exercise endorphins needing a little help today."

"Our morning banquet is almost ready," Xander said. "Will you summon Sunny?"

"Sunny, breakfast!" Jess yelled down the hallway.

"I have to brush my teeth. Then I'll help," Terrance said.

Xander raised his mug. "That window has closed for me. At this stage, I'll wait until after our repast to brush."

"That's gross, not brushing first thing," Jess said. "I wish I didn't know that about you, roomie."

"Yeah, man, you have to brush when you wake up," Terrance chipped in, watching Jess from the corner of his eye.

Xander rolled his eyes at the conversation. "We'll be eating in two minutes. I promise I'll brush after that, Mom and Dad."

"Hmm," Buwan murmured from his seat at the island. "There are two kinds of people in the world. Those who brush when they wake up, and those who wait until after breakfast." He crossed his arms and nodded.

Xander pulled a broiler pan full of bacon from the oven. "The man has spoken. There is no right or wrong."

Jess ferried the coffee pot and a trivet to the dining room table. "Clearly you didn't have a dental hygienist for a mother."

"Here comes the sun," Buwan announced as Sunny floated into the kitchen. He raised an eyebrow at Xander in question.

"I'll allow that," Xander said. He pecked Sunny on the cheek. "*Sunny oh Sunny. My golden pixie dream love. Sprite of my own soul.*"

"Morning to you too, haiku king," Sunny said, the row of gold hoops on their helix glinting in the fingers of awakening sunlight stretching into the kitchen.

"Does anyone want anything to drink besides juice?" Bu said. "We could make Bloody Marys."

"Ugh, no, B. I need to pace if we're having another late night tonight," Jess said.

Terrance returned, rubbing his hands together. "Let's eat."

They settled around the big table. Buwan plopped a beer in front of his plate.

Sunny cringed. "Bu, for breakfast?"

"I'm coffee-d out. I can't drink milk. I'm lactose intolerant. And I hate orange juice." He shrugged.

"Didn't you say you can't mix alcohol with your prescription?" Terrance asked.

Buwan smirked. "I don't always do what's best for me. Cheers." He raised his beer bottle to the group. Everyone else raised coffee mugs or juice glasses.

***

Charley rubbed her fingers across the back of her neck, near the hairline. "Hey, can someone tell me what this bump is?"

"Let me see," Sunny said as the others cleared the dishes. They pulled Charley's light brown hair aside, the brush of their hand sending a subtle shiver through Charley. "Ew, it's a tick!" they cried, dropping Charley's hair and stepping back. "I'm sorry, that was rude, but I can't stand ticks. The only thing in nature I truly don't like. What purpose do they even serve?"

Charley, for once, wasn't interested in Sunny's opinion. "I'm sorry to be a pain but can someone else help, please?" she pleaded, trying not to picture the arachnid nestling into her flesh.

"I've got this," Jess said, her dark eyebrows angling in as she frowned at Charley's neck. "It's way in there. We need a needle or something super sharp. And rubbing alcohol. And tweezers."

"On it," Buwan said, bounding to the bathroom and back while Charley lay on the pale blue couch, her head on Jessica's lap. Putting herself at another's mercy was embarrassing, but she didn't have much choice. Jess seemed unfazed by the close contact.

Jess tried pulling with the tweezers but soon switched implements. She dipped the needle in the alcohol, smoothed Charley's hair away from her neck, and began to dig. Charley steeled herself against the pricks and tugs and clamped her mouth shut. "Sorry," Jess said. "It's really stuck." After another minute of botched surgery, Buwan came to Charley's side, his phone in one hand and a bottle of lotion in the other.

"Let me try." He put down his phone and switched positions with Jess, his thighs cradling Charley's head. "This takes longer but works better."

"What are you doing?" Charley asked, as his finger lightly touched her neck a few times.

"I'm going to suffocate it. They breathe through holes near their back legs so if I cover them up, it should back out on its own."

"I've heard that isn't the best way," Terrance said from the kitchen.

"I already put the lotion on. We might as well see what happens," Bu said. He hummed and stroked Charley's hair while they waited. Charley forgot about the tick, closed her eyes, and remembered how her father used to stroke her head while he sat in an armchair reading, Charley on the floor leaning against his legs. A long-forgotten feeling of security eased over her.

"Got it," Bu said with the smallest of tugs as Charley was on the edge of dozing off. She struggled upright through her memories, surprised that the warm sensation remained, and that it was not accompanied by the devastating regret and pain that came with most remembrances of her father.

****

"Xander, hoops?" Terrance asked as he shut the dishwasher. "There's a court on the far side of the house."

Xander lifted his faded pink T-shirt and rubbed his belly. "I'm far too full. I could partake of some HORSE or something less strenuous, though."

"Wimp. Okay, you're in. Anyone else? Jess?"

Jess caught Terrance's eyes running over her curves, amply displayed by her jogging shorts and racerback top. "I was going to shower but what the hell. I can do it after."

Terrance sniffed and grinned. "You are a little ripe, now that you mention it."

Her dark brown eyes stared him down. "You're on, then, T. I'll be sure to guard you so you can enjoy my ripeness even more."

Terrance's grin widened. "Let's go. We need a fourth though."

"I'll play," Buwan said, swinging his arms front and back. "I'll grab a ball and meet you there in two seconds."

Courtside, Jess finished applying a fresh coat of sunscreen. Terrance attached an elastic cord to his glasses and adjusted the fit. Xander and

Bu stretched their limbs on the tarred court, a row of evergreens forming a backdrop.

"Hurry up, old men," Jess said. "How much warming up do you need?"

Terrance perused the group. "What are the teams? Should we go by skill or size?"

"There are only four of us. Does the division of talents truly matter?" Xander said.

"Why X, I do believe your hangover is making you irritable."

"I'd be fine if we were playing HORSE like I suggested. But no, you all have to show off and play two-on-two."

"Don't be such a baby," Jess said.

Terrance scanned the group, Xander almost matching his own six feet, Jess and Buwan about the same at roughly five-foot-eight. "Let's go with height. I'll take Bu, and Jess, you're on Xander's team." He picked up the ball and started dribbling in place. "First team to twenty-one wins." He beckoned Xander toward him with a serious look on his face.

Jess started out defending against Buwan one-on-one—barely keeping up with his quick bursts around the court—while Xander guarded Terrance, but she told Xander to switch to a zone defense when Terrance blew past her sluggish teammate for the third time in a row.

"Think you can stop me?" Terrance asked her, one eyebrow raised. She smirked. "Try me."

Terrance drove past her to the hoop as if she were mere air, diamond stud sparkling, brown eyes twinkling. He alternated layups with jump shots, leaving the others in his dust. Jess got more fired up the further behind she and Xander got. Eventually, her team sunk a few baskets, fueled by sheer determination more than talent.

With the score six to fourteen, sweat streaming, Terrance called time out and struggled out of his sticky shirt. His well-defined chest and arms resembled an ad for an exercise machine if it featured a once-fit thirtyish man softened somewhat by hours at a desk.

Jess dragged her gaze from Terrance to Bu. "I guess it's shirts against skins now if you're stripping too, Bu."

"Nah," Bu said, patting his gray T-shirt where it clung to his slightly protruding gut. "I'm good."

Jess found herself looking forward to defending Terrance, who increasingly dribbled directly at her instead of around, forcing skin contact. Jess snuck glimpses of his graceful athleticism when he wasn't looking. Despite it rising in volume throughout the game, she managed to keep at bay that rolling itchy feeling schoolgirls get when their crushes pay attention to them.

CHAPTER 10: WORD GAMES

After breakfast, Charley escaped to the beach near the edge of the Bakunawa's property. She contemplated driving back to the city, thinking she'd pushed the envelope enough for one weekend. She could slide back into her regular Saturday night schedule. Would they care if she left? Xander wouldn't, that's for sure.

She decided to not decide for at least an hour. Pulling out her phone, she opened up her word game app and let the predictable process of forming words from seven specific letters soothe her unsettled mind. She didn't notice Buwan—clothed in swimming trunks and T-shirt—run and dive into the water farther down the beach. She didn't hear him splashing as he swam, alternate shoulders rising out of the water to fling an arm ahead where it speared the water like a heron diving for fish. She didn't see or hear him leave the water and approach her.

"Level 7,205," he said from behind Charley, causing her to jump and drop her phone in the sand. "Nice."

Charley blushed as if caught writing in a diary. "Hey," she said, the word dying in her throat. She repeated it more loudly.

He picked up her phone, brushed off the sand particles and handed it to her, his hair dripping rivulets around him.

"No towel?" she asked, for something to say.

"Naw, it's so hot. Don't need one." He plopped down beside her and leaned back on his arms.

She fought to resist the draw of the word game. "What's everyone else doing?"

He shook his head, spraying sparkly beads left and right. Charley flinched but said nothing.

"Sorry, water in my ear. We don't have to talk, you know. I've talked more the past twenty-four hours than the whole week before," he chuckled.

Charley nodded and started drawing a horse in the sand with a stick. Suddenly, she tossed the stick away, too insecure to draw in front of an artist. She inhaled deeply and turned toward him. He was cuter than she'd thought at first. Funny how perceptions of attractiveness shifted as you got to know someone. His teeth were a touch big, his eyebrows a tad bushy, his forehead a smidge too high. But his dark brown eyes were alternately warm and devilish, and his smile was big enough for two people. Besides, who was she to rate someone's looks?

"Must be hard for an introvert being around those high-energy people all the time," Buwan said.

A genuine smile tiptoed onto Charley's face. "Are you an introvert, too? You don't seem like one."

He sat up straight and brushed his sandy hands together, scattering the grains. "There are two kinds of people in the world. Those who recharge by being alone and those who recharge from being with people."

"Meaning?"

"I'm not really an introvert. I like being around people. I only like being alone when I'm in my studio. But technically, I go both ways, social and anti-social. High and low. Officially. Medically." He paused. "Don't you want to know what I mean?"

"Okay," she said, mentally kicking herself for being a poor listener.

Buwan gathered himself with a deep sigh. "I've got a mood disorder—bipolar one. So I swing between being manic with shitloads of energy and a depressed state, when I'm ... "

"Depressed," she filled in, which made him laugh for some reason. Not knowing why, she laughed too. "Do you do anything for it?"

"Mm-hmm. Therapy and medicine. But it's hard to get the drugs right. I hate how they mess with my system. I don't swing as much between the highs and the lows, but I still swing. And I lose other stuff when I'm on my meds."

"Like what?" she asked with real concern.

"Creativity. Thinking clear. Energy."

"But you have lots of energy."

"Yeah." He looked away. "I guess I'm in a good phase right now. Anyway, sorry to bore you with that. But it feels good to tell someone. I'm not hiding it or anything," he said, staring at his hands fiddling in his lap, "but I don't think the rest of them would know how to react. Terrance would ask me a million questions, like he could find a cure when no doctor can. Jess would tell me statistics on the best cost for my medicine. And Sunny—I guess Sunny would try to heal me with crystals or something."

They laughed together. "They do have pretty distinct personalities, don't they? What about Xander?"

"Hm. He'd say ignore it and keep on living. Go to a protest or something."

They disappeared into their own thoughts. The water sheen on Bu's skin evaporated. Charley absentmindedly doodled with the stick again.

"I sort of had depression once," she said, eyes on her doodle.

"Tell me." He leaned back again, out of her view.

She jammed the stick in the sand. "My parents died in a plane crash when I was fifteen, and my grandparents died in a fire when I was twenty-two. After my grandparents, I disappeared into a funk for a few months. I didn't do anything. Not even read."

"How'd you get out of it?"

"I don't know. Maybe it just ran its course."

"Hmm. What did it feel like?"

Charley closed her eyes and thought back. She never revisited those dark days; it felt like tempting fate. But Buwan had opened up. She would do the same. "This is the best way I can describe it. When I was little, I used to play dress-up with these old fancy dresses my grandmother had in a big trunk in her spare bedroom. One of them was made of really thick, navy-blue velvet, almost like a curtain or something. It was so heavy, I had to put it on the floor, step into it and pull it up around me. So I wiggled into it and managed to get it over my shoulders. But the sheer weight of it pulled me down to my knees. I felt trapped in all the folds of cloth and I panicked, making it worse. The dress got all twisted up with my legs and arms. Then I was afraid I would suffocate. Finally, I gave up and lay down in the middle of this huge dark velvet pool. I stopped resisting and waited for someone to find me."

She looked at Buwan and saw not pity in his eyes, nor confusion, but understanding and sadness.

"So it was kind of like that. At first, it was scary, but then I got used to it."

"I get it." Buwan patted her knee awkwardly. "And it sounds like your depression was trauma-induced, not something you were born with. So that's good."

Charley shrugged.

"Who wouldn't get depressed after losing two sets of parents?" he said. "Too bad I didn't know you then. I could have loaned you one of my moms."

Charley snickered.

He stood up. "Hey, I'm dying for ice cream. Wanna walk to the store with me to get some?"

***

Buwan and Charley set out for the small general store in the town center, leaving Terrance and Xander making sandwiches, the suggestion of which made the other four groan and question how those two could eat so much and not get fat. Sunny had tried to get someone to sunbathe with them, but Jess begged off for no explicit reason. Charley used the ice cream run as her excuse when in truth, she didn't want to bare her crusty, scarred feet to her new friends.

A bell over the store's door jingled as they entered, reminding Charley of her bookstore. This was the longest she'd been away from it. Ever.

"You can check out the tacky souvenirs if you want while I pick out the ice cream."

"I think I'll look at the books," Charley said, spinning one of two circular racks of paperbacks near the front of the store.

"What flavor do you want?"

"Oh, I'll eat anything," Charley said, unwilling to risk a bad decision for the group. She stopped the rack's spin in a random spot and began noting titles while Buwan headed back toward the freezer section.

Charley looked over at the man behind the register to ask if he knew which book distributor the store used. The fiftyish man had a friendly round face and a round beer gut stretching the limits of his polo shirt. He was fixated on something down the aisle toward the back of the store. Charley stepped over and peeked to see what had his attention. The only customer there was Buwan, studying the ice cream selection, one hand on the handle of the closed freezer door.

Charley wandered to Buwan's side. "I think the guy working the register knows you. He's staring at you."

Buwan turned and faced the cashier. "Nope." He turned back. "How about something with lots of chocolate, something with cookies, and a basic vanilla?"

Charley's upturned nose wrinkled. "Even I don't like vanilla and I'm pretty boring."

"Ha ha," Buwan said with no humor. "Okay, let's get this instead." He grabbed a half-gallon of strawberry. "On second thought, we need more." He grabbed two additional containers without looking at the flavors.

At the register, Buwan presented his debit card seconds after putting the ice cream on the counter. The cashier's movements seemed sluggish in comparison. He stared at Buwan. "Why don't you go back where you came from?" he growled in a tone at complete odds with his amiable countenance. Charley thought she heard him wrong.

"You gonna ring me up or what?" Buwan said in a strained voice.

The cashier broke his glare long enough to scan the ice cream and run Buwan's card. He pushed the purchases back toward Buwan.

"Oh my God," Charley said, "can you put them in a bag please?"

The cashier turned to Charley for the first time. "Sure thing, miss." After doing as requested, he slid the bag over to Charley. "Here you go."

Charley froze.

"Come on," Buwan said, grabbing the bag and tugging her arm.

Charley searched herself for any available courage, remembering Xander's words from their first real conversation. She pulled her arm away from Buwan and faced the man, her heartbeat throbbing in her ears. She vaguely heard the bell over the door jingle.

"Why would you say that?" Her voice sounded meeker than she'd intended.

"Morning, Ed," a policeman with a tan face and active eyes said from the doorway. "How is everyone today?" He took a few steps and extended his hand toward Bu. "Mr. Johnson, good to see you. Here for the week?"

Buwan shook the cop's hand. "No, just the weekend."

"How are your mothers?" he said. The cashier did a classic double-take at the officer's words.

"They're fine, thanks. Not here this weekend. Just me and some friends." Buwan straightened his shoulders.

"Well, have fun. No loud parties, okay?" The policeman chuckled. "And say hello to Anne for me."

"Will do, Stan, thanks." Buwan left the store.

Stan stepped toward the cashier. "That young man is part of the Johnson family that owns most of the waterfront here and has put three family members in the state legislature. Make sure you treat him with courtesy."

"I thought he was a foreigner," Ed grumbled. "He looks Mexican, don't he?"

Charley joined Bu on the sidewalk.

Five silent minutes later, walking down the side of the small road, Charley asked what she hoped was a safe question.

"Why did he call you Mr. Johnson? I thought your last name was Baku—Bakawana?"

Buwan gave a short laugh. "You just answered the question. Most people can't remember the name. If they do, they can't say it. It's Johnson-Bakunawa."

"Oops, sorry," Charley mumbled.

"No biggie. Like I said, people get it wrong all the time, just like they get my nationality wrong." He shrugged. "There's another reason too. My Mom's family has been big in this area for generations. They might as well call it Johnsonville."

"Hmm. So why did your parents go for the harder name? I like it; I'm just curious."

Buwan recounted the story his moms had told him and his younger sister many times. His Mom was Anne Johnson from a prominent family that was a fixture in state politics, commerce, and philanthropy. His other mother, Mamalay as the kids called her, was Layla Kaminsky. She married a Filipino man, also named Buwan Bakunawa, at twenty-four, divorced him two years later when she realized she was lesbian, and married Anne a few years after that.

"They wanted to have kids but needed some help with that. Layla goes to Buwan, her ex-husband, who says he'll be the sperm donor on one condition: the baby has to have his last name. Layla says yes. My moms argue about it for a few months, then settle on Johnson-Bakunawa."

Charley kicked a rock in front of her. "It's a cool name. Do you like it?"

Buwan shrugged. "Sure. Some kids called me names, but it's hard to turn Bakunawa into something bad, so they came up with other stuff."

"Like what?" She stepped on a small, sharp rock and lost her balance, falling slightly into Buwan before righting herself.

"Well, in sixth grade, we did a heritage project in social studies. When the other kids realized lots of Filipinos speak Tagalog, they had a field day with that—" he laughed quickly at his unintentional school pun—"and started calling me things like 'Two-Mom Tagalog.' Could have been worse."

Charley nodded, as if she had an inkling of what it felt like to be mocked for your heritage or parentage. "So does your sister have the same name? And father?"

"Same last name—we're all Johnson-Bakunawa now. Different father—my dad died of cancer." He crossed himself. "Mom had *in vitro*. They picked a donor with dark skin, but Carrie is the spitting image of Mom and as pale as you."

They walked in silence, Buwan whistling, Charley thinking that maybe having your parents die when you're fifteen, while tragic, wasn't such a big life complication after all. Then she decided to tell Buwan about her curse.

CHAPTER 11: NEVER HAVE I EVER

Jess raised her glass of pinot grigio. "Here's to X shaving his neck, and here's to good friends. Thank God we have each other, because we're the only ones left not married with kids." The six friends reached across the picnic table and clinked with gusto as the sun prepared to set over the water.

The table was piled with grilled chicken and portobello mushrooms, salads, and several bottles of wine. The exuberant bhangra-hip-hop-jazz fusion sounds of Sunny Jain and Red Baraat burst out of Xander's solar-powered Bluetooth speaker, mixing with the evening's muggy air and settling around them like a dance club's edgy embrace.

"Xander, we need a haiku," Terrance suggested as he refilled his glass and Jess's. The others tapped utensils against their wineglasses in cheery support of the idea.

Xander cleared his throat. "No, wait. Not ready. Too many conflicting emotions." He stroked his bare neck and pretended to be on the verge of tears. "Someone else inspire us."

"I'll try," Terrance said. "*Xander, Jessica,*" he started, ticking off syllables on his fingers. "*Sunny, Charley, good new friends. Buwan, Terrance too.*"

"Boo," Xander shouted while the others cringed and laughed.

"'That was terrible. I can't believe you work with words for a living," Jess teased.

Terrance flinched and frowned. "Jess. That really hurts."

"I'm sorry, T, I was joking! I didn't mean it."

"Show me. Come give me a kiss." He tapped his cheek, brown eyes twinkling.

"You ass. In your dreams," she said with a click of her tongue, a tad mortified. No one ever fooled Jessica Delgado.

"Someone else try," Xander said, but was met with silence.

"There are two kinds of people in the world. Those who can write haikus on the spot and those who can't," Buwan said.

Sunny groaned. "There are two kinds of people in the world," they said. "Buwan and everyone else."

Buwan downed his glass of wine. "I'll drink to that." Only Charley noticed the touch of hurt in his eyes from Sunny's good-natured jab.

"Let's hear a haiku from Jess, since she's so quick to criticize," Terrance challenged.

"Fine. I'll have a go." Jess swiped her bangs back, closed her eyes and placed her fingers on her temples. "Okay," she said, opening her eyes. "*I don't like haiku. Don't make me write poems for you. You will regret it.*"

Terrance smirked while everyone else booed.

"Are you protesting the act of writing a haiku by writing a haiku? Or is that really the best you can do?" he asked her.

Jess rolled her eyes. "Does it matter?"

"Further," Xander said, "*poem* is technically two syllables, so your count is off." He stood, wine glass in hand. "Okay, hear ye, hear ye, I will now haiku. *Plates of steaming food. Crystal goblets of white wine. Endless feast for all.*"

Cheers erupted and glasses clinked again.

Fred let loose an enormous grumble and sigh from where he lay near Xander's feet, prompting another round of laughs. "Buwan is officially the first person to outlast Fred at Frisbee, by the way." Xander reached down to pet his dog's head. "You've met your match, Freddie my boy."

"You do have crazy energy," Terrance said to their host. "Where does that come from? I wish I could bottle it."

"And Bu's the oldest one of us," Jess marveled.

The setting sun highlighted a gleam of satisfaction in Buwan's eyes just before it dipped below the horizon.

***

Sated, they lounged around the firepit, the lively music replaced by the occasional crackle and hiss from the flames and the early song of crickets warming up for their nighttime concert. Occasional *zaps* sounded from the solar-powered bug lights Terrance brought with him. Empty wine bottles lay scattered around while several full ones waited in a cooler.

Xander scanned the circle of friends and gave himself a mental pat on the back for assembling the group. Terrance and Bu were eminently likeable, so their acceptance by the others was not unexpected. And Charley—she seemed to have forgotten about hitting the deer and was proving to be the smart, funny woman he'd glimpsed in their first conversations.

Jess swirled her wine in its glass, then leaned forward in her Adirondack chair. "I know what we should do now. Let's play Never Have I Ever."

"Yes, perfect!" Sunny said, their rounded lips giving them the air of an enthusiastic child.

Buwan pulled a bottle of wine from the cooler at his side, refilled his glass, and passed the bottle to Terrance. "Play what? I've never heard of it."

"Never Have I Ever," Jess repeated. "We take turns naming something we've never done. Anyone who *has* done that thing loses a point. We start with ten points and the first one out of points loses, obviously. So, for example, if I said 'never have I ever been pansexual,' S would lose a point."

Xander smiled as Charley and Buwan traded confused looks.

"Because I am pansexual," Sunny clarified with a self-assured smile.

Terrance held up his wineglass. "Are we keeping score or playing the drinking game version?"

Xander gave a small hiccup. "We're a mite old for drinking games."

Jess sipped her wine. "Yeah, I've got a nice gentle buzz that I'd rather not screw up."

"I'll go first, with an easy one," Sunny said. "Never have I ever kept a secret from my parents."

Buwan screwed his face up. "Isn't it supposed to be true?"

"It is true. You haven't met my awesome parents," Sunny said. "But I bet it's false for everyone else."

"Guilty," Bu said as the others nodded.

Terrance held up a hand. "Wait—how are we keeping track of the score?"

"You're supposed to count on your fingers. But that sounds like a lot of work," Jess said.

"Blasphemy coming from a professional bean counter!" Xander said.

"Funny," she said with an eye roll.

Bu dashed into the house, returning immediately with a deck of cards. After Sunny took ten cards and everyone else took nine, they resumed the game.

"I'm next," Jess said. "Never have I ever majored in environmental studies."

"Whoa, that's a targeted strike if ever I saw one," Terrance said as Xander and Sunny each tossed away a card.

"Predictable, Jessica," Xander said. "Char?"

"Um, never have I ever attended a protest."

"Good one," Buwan said, giving Charley a high-five as Xander and Sunny tossed in another card each.

"Terrance, seriously? You've never even seen fit to participate in an Earth Day protest?" Xander said.

"X, not everyone has the stomach you have for protesting," Jess pointed out.

Terrance narrowed his eyes at Xander. "Let's just say your right to protest is more protected than mine. When I attend a protest, I become a target. That's a conflict I'd rather avoid. Doesn't make me bad."

"Point taken," Xander said, inwardly chastising himself for his lack of sensitivity.

Buwan shifted forward in his chair. "My turn. Never have I ever lived with one of the people here." Xander, Jessica and Sunny tossed cards away. "Oh sorry, Sunny, I knew those two were roommates but—"

"Yeah, Jess and I were roommates at college when she transferred over sophomore year."

"And living in the freshman dorm was so fun," Jess said, widening her long-lashed eyes.

"I'm up," Terrance said. "Never have I ever left my computer on overnight." The other five all tossed cards away. "And that, my friends, is how it's done." He smiled smugly and brushed a hand over his tightly coiled blonde hair.

Jess squinted at him. "You have to tell the truth, T."

"Hey. I am *religious* about turning off my computer. I even turn off other people's computers."

"Okay, okay. Just checking, Saint Terrance."

"And I am disappointed in you," Terrance said to Xander.

"We all have our weak moments. Try not to judge me too harshly, dude."

Xander's phone chirped. He swiped to read a breaking news story while the others refilled their glasses and thought up new statements. A few states away, a Black couple—Mr. and Mrs. Rindge—had been accused of shoplifting, apparently falsely—and then were injured by local police. Cell phone videos showed the cops roughing up the man and forcing him to the ground. The wife, yelling that her husband had a heart condition, tried to intercede. They both ended up in the hospital, the wife bloodied and bruised, the husband in critical condition.

Xander's eyes, bloodshot from wood-fire smoke and wine, sank down in despair. He circled his head this way and that, stretching the cords of his neck. Clenched his teeth as rage boiled in his gut. So many formidable enemies stalked the world, with racism—overt and institutionalized—currently at the top of the list.

Sunny touched his forearm. "You okay?"

Xander hissed air through his teeth and scanned his circle of friends. Sunny had always been at his side, standing up for justice and change. But the others—despite his love for them, their indifference to the state of society was frustrating. What would it take to open their eyes? Prompt them to act? He felt a moral obligation to light a fire under them.

He rubbed his hands together and grinned as if feeling jovial. "Okay, ready? Never have I ever been made to feel different because of my skin color."

"Ouch, Xan, really?" Sunny said.

From the corner of his eye, Xander saw Terrance glaring at him.

"This is war, my dear, and you guys have been pummeling me." He pointed to his five remaining cards. Sunny, Terrance, Buwan and Charley tossed cards aside. "Really Charley?" Xander said.

"The mean kids at school called me the Ghost Bride." She giggled self-consciously. "You said to be honest, right? Look how pale I am compared to all of you." Her smile dissipated and she receded into the cool shadows where the firelight didn't reach.

"At least you've never been called an Oompa Loompa," Sunny said with forced good cheer. They moved forward to the front edge of their chair and scratched their head through their short Afro. "My turn. Never have I ever . . . worried about getting fat." Buwan, Terrance, Charley and Jess tossed cards away. "Don't say I never gave you anything," they said to Xander, who gave them a mock tip of the hat.

"Don't get too comfortable, X, 'cause I'm going with never have I ever slept with a woman," Jess said.

"Jeesh, that's getting personal," Buwan said with a grimace. He, Terrance, Xander, and Sunny each lost a card.

Charley averted her eyes from Sunny and leaned forward. "Never have I ever been stopped by the cops."

Terrance threw a card away. "Unfair. You know people of color are stopped way more often than White people."

"Oh, I was thinking of speeding or things like that. Sorry?" Charley said, fanning smoke away from her eyes.

Sunny shot a supportive smile Charley's way. "All's fair."

Buwan, Xander, and Jess each tossed a card away.

"At least she didn't say 'never have I ever been stopped by the cops for nothing,'" Bu said to Terrance. "That probably would have left just you and me."

Terrance jerked his head in assent, his eyes darkening.

Bu leaned forward. "Since everyone else is getting personal, never have I ever slept with a man." Charley, Sunny, and Jess tossed cards aside. Bu's eyes shot open as Xander also threw a card away. "Am I the only one here who's straight?"

"No!" Terrance, Jess, and Charley said at the same time.

Sunny and Xander exchanged taken-aback looks and laughed. "Well, that was a strong reaction," Xander said. He turned to Terrance. "You're up. Something provocative, please."

"Never have I ever been called a terrorist," Terrance said, his voice cold as the firelight flickered over his face. "How's that?"

Bu's soft face hardened. He and Sunny threw cards away.

"This game got dark real fast," Sunny muttered.

Xander rested his hands on his knees. "Never have I ever been watched like a hawk in a store." Terrance, Buwan and Sunny threw cards away. No one made wisecracks or grumbled.

Sunny lowered their head. "Never have I ever been shot because of my sexual orientation." No one moved. "I thought we needed something a bit lighter."

Buwan stared into the flames and flicked a card away without looking. "Never have I ever been told to go back where I came from."

"But Bu, that's not—" Charley shivered in her hoodie. "Never mind."

"Are we still keeping score?" Jess asked, her voice edgy.

Terrance held out a card. "Never have I ever wished I were White or that I had White privilege." He dropped his card.

Sunny tossed one away. Xander reached for their hand.

Terrance stared at Jess. "Seriously, Jessica? You've never wished for lighter skin? Been told to go back where you came from? Had a racial slur used against you? That beautiful golden skin of yours doesn't exactly say European."

Xander noticed Terrance took pains to sound curious not angry, but that subtlety was lost on Jess, as was the compliment woven into his last statement. Jess grabbed the nearest wine bottle. "You guys are messing up the rules," she said.

Sunny fiddled with their headband. "Why did we start this game? It sucked the life right out of the party."

Xander leaned in toward the fire. "We should modify the name from Never Have I Ever to Who's the Most Oppressed. Or the Suffering Olympics. But you know, we can sit here and bitch or we can attempt to do something about the inequities plaguing the world."

Terrance surprised Xander by leaning in, eyes intent. His words surprised Xander even more. "We should all commit, right now, to doing more. What do you guys say? Charley?"

Charley chewed on the end of her hood's drawstring. "I just don't know what I can do. I'm only one person."

"Char, every body counts," Xander said, emphasizing each word. "Literally. Every single person who stands up in protest makes a difference. Simply by being there, you help."

She nodded, releasing the drawstring and biting on her lip.

"Buwan?"

"Sure, I'm in," he said excitedly, his earlier scowl replaced by a grin as if he'd been asked to see his favorite sports team play.

"Jess?"

"Look, I support the planet and women's rights." Her face seemed to waver through the flames of the firepit. "That's all I can do. There are way too many causes out there. I can't support them all."

Charley nodded. "I think so too. Maybe we should split them up? Each take one?"

Sunny turned toward the two women. "That's not enough. Big changes require a *lot* of people to stand up and say the status quo is wrong. If we're serious about this, we should start by all going to the next protest." Xander silently thanked Sunny as they turned back to him, "What's next on the calendar, Xan?" they asked.

"The annual Women's March is coming up rapidly, and there's an immigration policy protest, and a Black Lives Matter rally soon after that."

"I didn't know there were so many protests in this city," Buwan said.

"They're not difficult to find if you get your head out of your studio, your bookstore, or your ledger," Xander said impatiently, looking at Buwan, Charley, and Jessica in turn. "And don't fool yourself that these issues don't affect you if you're not one of the disenfranchised or oppressed. Social injustice affects all who exist in this society."

He saw Charley flinch at the edge in his voice.

"Xan," Sunny chided gently, "get off your soapbox."

He downshifted from critic to coach. "Never underestimate the power of a lot of little steps," he said in a more measured voice. "It's like thinking globally, acting locally on the environment. What we do in our little spot of the world matters. How we treat each other matters. We can make the world better by standing up and starting right here."

He rose unsteadily, a violent hiccup nearly throwing him off-balance. "And now, I have to relieve myself, if you'll excuse me."

Sunny rushed to his side. "Actually, I think it's time to get this one to bed." They steered Xander toward the house. Their shadowy shapes—Xander's taller, shaggier one leaning on Sunny's willowy one—disappeared from the firelight's reach.

"Do you think they're coming back?" Charley asked.

Jess shook her head. "Xander's passed the point of no return drinking-wise, and Sunny will stay with him."

"So, Terrance, you're really in?" Bu asked. "You'll go to the next protest?"

Terrance closed his eyes for a second. "Yeah, I'll give it a shot."

The dwindling flames in the firepit leaped to attention, spitting sparks into the dark night before dying down into an otherworldly glow of red cinders.

***

After Sunny and Xander left the firepit, Terrance and the others managed to reclaim the mood, getting silly on wine and non-controversial topics like bad teachers and sibling rivalry. Terrance and Jess got past their moment of tension during the game and resumed an easy flirting repartee.

Nearing midnight, Terrance left to hit the bathroom. Jess followed a minute after.

"I'm coming back though," she slurred to Charley and Buwan, "so don't leave!"

She bumped into a shirtless Terrance at the bathroom door.

"Oh, sorry," he said, shirt in hand. "I was thinking of hitting the hay. Don't tell them I'm bailing." His head tilt indicated the friends by the fire. "I don't know how they can stay awake this long two nights in a row." He rambled, trying to ignore the desire wafting off Jess. Or maybe she merely reflected what he felt. "Does that make me sound old?"

"Shhh, you don't sound old. You don't look old." She placed her palm on his chest and leaned into him.

Hormones shot through Terrance's body. This strong-willed, gorgeous, intelligent, and sometimes annoying woman was wending her way into his psyche, that much he knew. He looked down into her intense eyes and brushed her bangs aside. His finger trailed down the side of her cheek.

"Damn, you're beautiful," he whispered before kissing her.

Their kisses moved from tentative to teasing to tantalizing. Jess grabbed his hand and moved toward his bedroom. Terrance hung back.

Their arms stretched between them, creating a chasm he was unwilling to jump. "Jessica, no."

Her eyes registered hurt like a child who skins a knee only to be reprimanded for being careless. All traces of desire evaporated from her face. "Yeah, no problem. It's a bad idea." She stumbled to her bedroom and shut the door.

Terrance ran his hand over his mouth and bare chest. He went into his room where he sat on the edge of the bed, staring into space.

Why did he rebuff her? He studied his dark-brown hands, the black lines etching the joints, the vulnerable-looking pink nails, as his thoughts settled into an orderly list. First, any relationship with Jess other than friendship would mess up their group dynamic if they dated and things went badly. Second, she was drunk, and he didn't want to take advantage. Third, he respected women too much to embark on a one-night conquest. And fourth, at the top of his list, was that at twenty-nine, he didn't have time to waste with someone who wasn't a potential wife. And Jess didn't fit that bill.

Only a Black woman could understand the jagged contradictions in a Black man's soul. The sheer effort required to retain pride in race when society tells you otherwise. The bold ambition to reach career heights undreamt of by his parents and the sobering recognition that even in this day and age, he might have to work twice as hard as his White colleagues to get there. Despite her immigrant heritage, Jess would never appreciate the hypocrisy and ludicrousness of fellow Americans claiming racism is gone and all are equal.

He lay down and tossed around for a while, wondering which food from dinner was giving him heartburn.

CHAPTER 12: UNWANTED WAVE

Sunny watched Xander's nose twitch as the morning sunbeam sifting through the bedroom blinds tickled his sleeping face. Awe at how deeply they loved him pulsed through them, followed by bewilderment at why they didn't love him more.

Sunny and Xander had been each other's soft place to land since the day they met. He was their soul mate and sometimes savior. Friday night, the nightclub shooting painfully fresh in their minds, they sought each other out as they had off and on over the years in between boyfriends and girlfriends. But Sunny knew the carnal reunion was most likely temporary, and they were okay with that.

Sunny so wanted marriage. Friends liked to say Sunny had it made with such a big pool of potential mates to choose from when truth be told, the people in that pool who could love a nonbinary, biracial pansexual were few and far between.

Sunny wanted children. They craved pregnancy, childbirth, and motherhood intrinsically, and hoped to nurture one child in the womb plus guide another out of the foster system.

Sunny wanted love, the sweetness of which they'd tasted twice only to have it turn stinging and salty. A two-year relationship with a man ended when their political differences became unsurmountable. A two-year relationship with a trans woman followed, but the first forever talk scared her right out the door. Sunny smirked. Heterosexual women who think hetero men in their late twenties are scared of commitment should try building a long-term relationship with someone marginalized into believing their wants aren't as legitimate as everyone else's. It's hard to commit to another person when society isn't committed to you.

Xander stirred. Sunny debated asking him if they were officially a couple again. Then they decided to let sleeping dogs lie.

***

Buwan perched at the kitchen counter. "Looks like we're all up with the sun," he said as Sunny meandered in.

"Was that a bad pun? 'Cause I've heard all the bad sun puns out there," Sunny said, retying the fabric belt of her blue floral romper.

"Hey, is that what you call a sun belt?"

Sunny screwed up their face and punched Bu in the bicep. "No, *that's* what I call a sun belt."

"Ow," he yelled in mock pain. "So, would you be mad if I said I'm a sun worshipper?"

They grinned despite themself. "Bu, did you know there are two kinds of people in the world? Those who make up bad puns, and those who have to suffer through them."

"Touché," he said.

"Can you guys keep it down?" Jess whimpered from the couch. "I've got a first-class hangover going here."

"Same." Sunny massaged their head with both hands.

"Did someone say hangover?" Xander groaned as he entered the kitchen, his hair sticking out in numerous directions. "Why did you let me imbibe so much?" he said to no one in particular.

"Is it just me or do you guys get hungover really fast these days?" Sunny asked.

"Same," Charley said from a padded chair in the living area, where she absorbed the morning light through the windowpane and closed eyelids.

Terrance walked through the screen door from the porch. "Every few years, my alcohol tolerance drops another notch."

Charley opened her eyes and shaded them with her hand. "Where did you come from?"

"I was sitting on the porch, listening to everything you all said."

"Did you hear the part about how loud Terrance is?" Jess mumbled from the couch.

"Go back to your hangover, Jess." Terrance went to the kitchen island and refilled his coffee.

"Getting old sucks," Jess said.

Bu smiled impishly. "Yeah, but it's still better than the alternative." Charley flashed him a supportive smile.

"Please, people, collect yourselves," Xander said. "Haven't you heard of aging gracefully? And I'd venture to say we're all in better-than-average shape for the cusp of thirty."

"Thirty-one," Buwan interjected.

"Be at peace with your aging and you're likely to live longer," Xander answered sagely.

Sunny laughed. "Says the one who complains about his aching back every morning."

"Hey, thanks for not having my back." Xander bumped into Sunny good-naturedly. "But look at us. We're all managing with aplomb. And not one of us is bald yet."

"But the wrinkles," Charley said from the living area, "you know they're coming."

"Like a freight train," Jess contributed.

Buwan shook his head. "Man, what a miserable bunch. Do you guys wanna eat something?"

Jess rolled off the couch and walked unsteadily toward her bedroom. "I'm going to pack."

The reference to packing descended on the friends like an unwanted wave from real life. The gorgeous, breezy day mocked their impending departure as they quietly packed their things.

***

"Oh, hey," Jess said, opening the door of her used BMW and tossing in her bag.

Terrance leaned back against his black Prius and studied her discomfort. "Hey."

She cleared her throat, "So . . . about last night."

"No idea what you're talking about."

Jess nodded. "Okay, good." She slammed the car door shut. "Thanks."

To his surprise, she approached him, brushed stray pine needles off the roof of his car and then leaned against it right next to him. Did she have something else she wanted to say? Was she hoping to bond one-on-one, despite last night? He cleared his throat but she remained silent.

"So, you work at All-American, Flammer's company?" he asked, to break the awkward silence.

"Yeah, I do," she said with an intent, unsettling gaze. "Do you call it the Evil Empire, too?"

Terrance stifled a yawn. "No, I'm not as hard-core as Xander. Our economy depends on a lot more than just nonprofits working to save the world."

Jess's eyebrows shot up. "That's right."

"Are people there bummed about losing the Stone Circle project?" Terrance asked.

She hesitated as if debating how much to tell him. "I'm sure it won't surprise you that the people I work with think this turtle thing got blown way out of proportion. It's wrong to stop progress for one little turtle. And seriously, did they need to kill the entire project? Couldn't they have put aside part of the land for the turtles?"

Terrance struggled to hide his amusement. Jess was obviously a smart woman but—like so many smart people—incredibly naïve or willfully ignorant when it came to the environment. "A lot more than turtles are being protected by this decision. Other animal species, plant species, the air we breathe, and the water we drink."

"Hmm, I could say the same on my side. Responsible development is about more than profits. It's an economic engine that generates jobs. And tax revenue for public services. And it revitalizes parts of the city that sorely need investment."

"Point taken. But why dig up virgin woodlands when so many brownfield sites exist?" She didn't answer and Terrance worried he'd sounded strident. "Anyway, I'm not against all development like Xander. If he had his way, we'd all be living in communes growing our own food and paying for services with chickens and pebbles."

Jess laughed—a gentle, musical sound like a girl's laugh, unlike the sharp-edged laugh he'd gotten used to over the weekend.

"And I know your guy Flammer is a big philanthropist. That's something."

Jess inched closer. "Agreed. And he's a visionary with this crazy ability to make money from any plot of land."

"It must be fun working in a company where you're building things instead of fighting all the time."

"Hmm. You don't have to stay in nonprofits, you know. You could come over to the Dark Side. That's another Xander-ism."

Terrance nodded, "Oh, I know. And believe me, I think a lot about going corporate. I'll always believe in helping the planet, but I also want to raise a family someday, and I want to make career decisions based on what's best for them, not just me."

Jess shifted so their arms grazed. "Can I tell you a secret?"

"Don't tell me you secretly want to work at the Wilderness Protection Society."

She laughed and again, a girlish chime overlay her mature laugh. "Nope. But I need to tell someone this, and I feel like I can trust you."

Her tone made Terrance hope he didn't regret giving her tacit permission.

"When the Stone Circle project was killed, my boss said Flammer wanted a few smaller, faster projects to make up some of the money we lost on that one. I'm one of two people in the finance department they asked to scout around and find properties."

"That sounds great," Terrance said. "What's the problem?"

"One of the properties I identified for Flammer to buy is the bookstore Charley manages."

"Oh." Terrance removed his glasses, held them to the sun for a quick inspection, and replaced them on his nose. "I'm sure she can get a job at another bookstore."

"She also lives in an apartment upstairs . . ."

Terrance wrinkled his nose as if trying to dislodge an itch. "People lose apartments all the time in this city. I heard Sunny tell Buwan they've got to move out soon because their apartment building is being converted to condos."

Jessica exhaled. "Right? That's what I thought. I don't need to feel guilty about this, do I? I didn't even know her when it all started."

Terrance shrugged minutely. "It's not like you were targeting her or anything."

"Do you think I should say something?" She watched him as if his answer mattered. A lot.

"Is the project definitely going forward?"

"No. I can't even put odds on it yet. But I'll be the one doing the financial analysis on it."

Terrance scratched his cheek. "It's not like you can throw the match, so to speak. That would damage your credibility at work."

"Exactly! So, I'm a little torn about this one."

"And I bet that's an unusual feeling for you," he said with a smile.

Jess smiled back. "I've known Xander more than ten years, but you already understand me better than he does."

Terrance ran a finger along his lower lip while gauging her and the situation. "I guess you could keep it quiet for now. If it looks like it's going to happen, then you can tell Charley."

"Okay, that's what I thought, too." She stretched her shoulders up and back.

As the others filtered out of the house toward the cars, Terrance put aside his discomfort at having been appointed secret-bearer. He'd navigated worse over the years in his quest for maximum inclusion, and he'd navigate through this one too, hopefully continuing to earn Jessica's trust in the process.

***

Car doors creaked open and slammed shut as bags were deposited in trunks and back seats.

Terrance let loose a huge yawn. "I can't believe I'm looking forward to the work week so I can get some sleep. It's supposed to be the other way around."

"Buck up, Terrance. Giraffes only sleep twenty minutes a day, so you're awash in slumber by comparison," Xander said.

"If only I had a giraffe's responsibilities to go with it," Terrance said sarcastically.

Xander shrugged. "Maybe snails are more your speed. They can sleep for four years."

Terrance closed his eyes sleepily in reply.

Sunny raised their arms to the sky, inhaled deeply, then floated their arms down to their sides. "I feel like I'm leaving a really great summer camp at the end of the season. You know that achy letdown you get when something special comes to an end?"

Xander bounced once on his toes. "So, let's not let it end. We can re-group soon, possibly at the café in Charley's bookstore. That's a relatively central location."

Jess jingled her car keys. "Sure, let us know when. I'm heading out, B, thanks for an amazing time." She blew their host a kiss and climbed into the driver's seat. "X, you coming?"

Xander hugged and fist-bumped his goodbyes and climbed into Jess's passenger seat. He rolled down the window to yell, "Don't forget about the protest. I'll text the details," as Jess drove down the driveway. "It's up to us to change the world," he shouted as she turned the corner.

After hugs all around, Sunny got in Terrance's car. Charley was driving solo; she'd said she had errands to run on the way home. In truth, she was on emotional overload and needed decompression time.

"Bye, Bu, see you soon," Charley said as she pulled away, feeling unsettled but pleased. She'd not only survived the weekend, she'd enjoyed it. Maybe hitting the deer wasn't an animal omen after all. Maybe she hadn't cursed her new friends with her presence. Still, the numbness of her routine beckoned like a drug. She could glide back into it for a fix and then return to this new life of hers. Use the routine less as a permanent sanctuary and more like a safe port for occasional visits and re-charging, like a normal introvert.

She peered up through the windshield, smiling at a family of hawks dipping and soaring overhead. When they vanished from view, she turned on the radio and sang along.

PART 3:
ATTACK OF THE ARROGANT

CHAPTER 13: AS AMERICAN AS YOU

"Did you hear about the latest ICE raid?" Dennis said by way of greeting as Jess entered the seventeenth-floor kitchen in All-American's suite of offices, which spanned three floors of a sandy-rose-limestone-clad skyscraper. Dennis and two others from the finance department huddled around the coffee machine, watching it drip.

Jess set her coffee cup on the counter. "No."

"Two-hundred Mexicans being sent back where they belong. That's the biggest haul yet." Dennis raised his empty mug in a toast. Steve joined him. Carl did the same but with an unsure look Jess's way. "Delgado what kind of name is that again?" Dennis asked with a touch of smirk. "You're not Mexican, are you? Passing as White?"

Jess rolled her eyes to convey incredulity at the supposition when what she really wanted to do was grab Dennis by his chubby face and shake him. "Seriously, Dennis? Are you going to ask me that every time there's a raid?" She was running out of flippant answers to the question. She stubbornly refused to discuss her heritage at work for fear of being labeled an immigrant, even though she was one generation removed. One time when Dennis lobbed the question at her—its biting nature cloaked in a good-natured veneer—she'd told her colleagues to guess at her name's nationality, and gave a knowing nod when they said *Spanish*, thinking they'd accepted the answer.

But today, she sensed a need to nip something in the bud. All-American, for all its status and opportunity, existed as a microcosm of conservative America. Despite maintaining the lightest skin possible through copious amounts of sunscreen and limited outdoor time, and despite the actual truth that she was not an immigrant, she knew she'd have to answer for her olive skin someday. And apparently that day was today. Anti-immigrant fever climbed a few degrees with every new raid, and the issue was polarizing Wrighton like many U.S. cities. She wasn't going to let a pissant like Dennis whispering behind her back impact her career's forward momentum.

The coffee pot belched a final gurgle and came to a rest. Jess reached for the pot and filled everyone else's mug before her own. Still holding the pot in one hand, she turned to face Dennis, her dark eyes boring into his pale blue ones.

"Look, I was born here. I have the birth certificate to prove it. My parents are also U.S. citizens. My *ancestry*, if you go back a bit, is Colombian. Want to know which box I tick when asked for my race? Caucasian. Clear?"

Dennis stared, his mouth slightly open.

"Colombian?" Carl asked. "That's cool."

"Like Sofía Vergara?" Steve asked. Jess nodded.

"Wait, I think I see a resemblance," Dennis said, having relocated his equilibrium.

Jess replaced the coffee pot on its burner with a clunk. "Not all Colombians look alike, Dennis. See you guys later." She turned on her heel and left.

Back at her desk, she steamed. She'd labored through five years of education and two years at a CPA's office before landing a budget analyst position at this company. A year later, she was promoted to cost accountant, ahead of schedule. The position of accounting manager for the commercial development division dangled within reach. All she had to do was best Dennis—her main in-house competitor for the promotion—and it would be smooth sailing to the next rung on the corporate ladder.

She opened a spreadsheet on her computer but instead of reviewing it, she stared into her coffee as her eyes unfocused and her memory sharpened.

With his deep bronze skin, Ozzy—her best friend for years, her "brother from another mother" as they used to say—had attracted many racist comments. So when Terrance asked if she'd been on the receiving end of prejudiced barbs, his gut wasn't wrong. She shared Ozzy's pain every time someone called him a foreigner or a terrorist or a wetback or worse. Her memory of the first instance unfurled itself with clarity. Eight-year-old Oz had been so confused by the other kid's taunt at the playground.

"What do you mean, go home? I live there," Ozzy had said, pointing down the street.

"Go home to Mexico, you lazy illegal alien," the kid recited in a tone suggesting he had heard and memorized the insult at home.

Ozzy's fists clenched and his dark face flushed darker with red. "I'm not from Mexico. I'm from Guatemala."

"Then go back to Guatemala, before we make you."

Jess stepped toward the bully. "Cut it out. You're being a jerk."

"You go home, too!"

Jess found her hand fisted like her friend's but knew better than to incur her dad's wrath by throwing a punch. She puffed out her smooth chest. "I'm American. So if I'm going home, I'm walking six blocks to Merry Lane. Why don't *you* go home?" She grabbed Ozzy's arm. "Come on, let's go," she said. "Jerk," she threw over her shoulder, ensuring she got the last word.

That night, she'd gone to her father in his study after dinner.

"I'm American, right?" she asked in a tentative voice.

Michael put down his pen, rubbed his eyes and turned to his daughter. "Yes, Jessica. American through and through."

"And what are you and Mommy?"

"We're American citizens now. We were born in Colombia and then moved here. Some years after that, we took a test and became citizens." He rested his hand on the crown of her head. "We've told you this before. Why are you asking?"

"Some stupid boy told Ozzy to go back to Mexico today."

Michael withdrew his hand and picked up his pen. "You know he's not Mexican—not that that is a bad thing."

Jess nodded, her big brown eyes confused and concerned. "Daddy, can they make Ozzy go back to Guatemala? They can't, right?" She had no idea who 'they' might be, but knew that if these unidentified people truly held the power to send her best friend back to his home country, her dad would know about it and be able to stop it.

Michael turned back to his paperwork. "You don't need to worry about that, Jessica. The Lopezes are good people who came here soon after your mother and I did, so they are practically as American as you and me. This is their home now."

Jess relaxed. Ozzy—in words, actions and attitudes—definitely seemed as American as her. His parents still spoke with strong accents and sometimes looked out of place, but her father said they belonged here. That was good enough for her.

In her room that night, she propped her chin on her stacked hands on the windowsill beside her bed, looking across the large lawn to the carriage house where Bertie, Al, and Ozzy lived. She wished she could see Ozzy's window from here, so they could send secret messages back and forth, but his room was on the other side.

****

Instead of plodding through her normal Monday morning routine, brain on autopilot to block out thoughts of what might go wrong that day, Charley dared to savor life's sensations: the muscle burn and flow of sweat during her pre-work jog in Founders Park, the warm shower stream engulfing her, and the crisp feel of her blouse.

Most Mondays, she extracted the crossword puzzle from the previous day's newspaper, put it aside for her day off and tossed the other sections of the paper onto the bottom shelf of her bookcase for eventual recycling. Today, she plopped the entire paper onto the table and flipped through the national and local sections while she ate.

She finished, folded the paper back up, shook her head and frowned. "Baggy, the amount of bad news in the world is mind-boggling."

Baggage perched on the sofa's arm cleaning his coat, uninterested in anything Charley had to say.

No wonder people kept their heads in the sand, Charley thought. Outrage about parents and children severed from each other by U.S. government officials at the southern border. Another shooting of a Black man by a White police officer several states away. Tainted water in a smaller city the next state over. A court challenge to a solar energy policy. An attack that put two gay men in the hospital.

Her newfound commitment to paying attention, maybe even engaging with the world, proved troublesome later that morning when Georgina told her to keep an eye on the woman with the hijab, as if the customer might hide a paperback under her scarf before slipping out of the store. Georgina made such comments on a regular basis, usually about a Black or Brown person. Charley tried to ignore the comments, classifying them as the prejudiced views of a different generation. And truth be told, she did keep an eye on the sketchier looking people Georgina pointed out, because inventory control was one of her managerial responsibilities.

Although she berated herself for her inaction, she didn't push back on Georgina's directive. Georgina was her boss after all. Charley turned the page in the distributor's catalog and circled another new release of interest.

***

"Can crows be mad at you?" Charley blurted out to her new friends a few days later. They were gathered at City Books after closing, drinking wine out of coffee mugs from the café. Charley had had the day off, but came in after closing and let her friends in. Georgina lived outside the city and would never know her manager was using the café as a living room.

Charley had been mildly freaked out since her weekly run in State Park that morning. It all started when she climbed into her car behind the bookstore and a crow on a nearby second-story windowsill cawed at her. When she got out of her car in the park and began stretching her quads, another crow emitted a series of rapid-fire raspy caws while staring right at her. To her horror, a few more crows joined the first, their cacophony giving Charley chills. Was she insanely paranoid or were they targeting her?

She'd broken into a run and lost the crows on the wooded trail. After, she snuck out of the parking lot without being noticed by the bird brigade.

Xander's mug stopped halfway to his mouth. "Crows? They're highly intelligent and display emotions, so maybe."

Buwan chuckled and asked, "Have you pissed off a crow lately?"

Charley shuddered. "It seems like they're following me, and that seems like a bad omen. I mean, they're dark and scary and they eat roadkill."

Jess fiddled with her earring. "I remember in Greek mythology, the crow symbolizes bad luck."

Charley flinched.

"Hang on," said Sunny. "Hindus see crows as good luck, and Native Americans too, I think. Hindus say when a crow caws, it's their ancestors speaking, encouraging them to ask the most important question about human existence—*Why?* In fact, the Sanskrit word for 'why' is 'ka.'"

"You think the crow was my ancestors speaking to me?" The thought horrified and enticed Charley at the same time.

Xander lifted his chin and scratched his neck. "They possess amazing facial recognition abilities and never forget a face. Assuming you've never been inimical to one…have you ever fed them, perchance?"

Charley looked to the ceiling. "I ate an energy bar after my jog the other day. I was sitting at a picnic table and I tossed the crumbs into the grass for the birds to eat."

Terrance adjusted his glasses. "Try feeding them again next time and see what happens."

"Crows aren't the only animals that demonstrate emotion, you know," Xander said. "Many species exhibit altruism and empathy."

Sunny nodded. "Elephants bury their dead under leaves and grass and visit the grave for years after."

"Yeah, but elephants are super smart," Bu said. "Not all animals are like that."

"I beg to differ," Xander said. "Scientists conducted a study with rats in which they simulated drowning—"

"Waterboarding for rodents? That's disgusting." Jess wrinkled her nose.

"They put two rats in containers, one on dry land so to speak, and one in a small swimming pool with no way to get out. The land rat could free the water rat by pressing a lever or get a food reward by pressing another lever. The majority chose freeing the other rat over the food. Tell me that's not proof of empathy and altruism."

Jess drew her severe eyebrows close. "How do they know it was an actual choice and not a reflex?"

"Because when there was no rat in the swimming pool, the rat didn't press that lever."

"Hmm. Maybe he wanted the other rat for a friend and didn't know he was saving the other guy's life," Buwan said.

"A fair supposition, but also proven false. If the second rat was in a dry area, the first rat made no effort to free it."

"That's amazing," Charley said. "People say we're the most evolved but sometimes I wonder."

"The fascinating part," Xander said, "is that the science suggests empathy in animals evolved to preserve their species, but then the behavior stuck with them."

Sunny brightened. "So maybe prejudiced people can still evolve and learn empathy."

"Or maybe," said Terrance, "human beings have evolved to a point where empathy is no longer necessary for their survival."

Sunny shuddered.

"Let's just hope we don't meet the fate of the Haast's eagle," Xander said, "which went extinct because it fancied only one type of prey and when that species died out, they didn't adapt."

Jess sighed dramatically. "Oh my God, let's lay off the doomsday talk, please. X, tell us a funny animal story. You're always good for one of those."

Xander steepled his fingers together. "Happy to lay some esoteric factoids on you," he said, releasing his hands. "Did you know that same-sex relations have been documented in more than one-thousand animal species?"

The group cracked up. "No way," Terrance said.

"It's true. To wit, one in ten male sheep will only copulate with other rams. Bison bulls have sex with each other."

Charley giggled. "Does that make them bull dykes?"

"No, the bull dykes of the animal kingdom would be bonobo apes. Most of their sex is between two or more females."

Jess laughed. "Maybe we should start calling bull dykes bonobos."

Sunny frowned at Jess. "Maybe we shouldn't call them anything except gay or lesbian."

"I can regale you for hours on this topic," Xander said. "Dolphins have same-sex intercourse using their blowholes, which is equivalent to nasal sex."

Terrance moaned, grinning. "Stop, I'm begging you."

"They also rub each other and penetrate other orifices to create pleasure."

"Oh my God, X, TMI," Jess said, shaking her head. "I feel like a voyeur just listening to you."

Bu wiped a tear from his eye. "Dude, are you reading this stuff in the tabloids? It can't all be true."

"He was a zoology minor in college," Jess explained.

Xander nodded. "And I retained the same-sex animal relations data in particular because I thought it might help me convince my father that bisexuality is normal."

"Did it?" Bu asked.

Xander shrugged and picked at a hole in the knee of his jeans.

"Anyway," Jess jumped in, "these stories make him lots of fun at parties. People especially love the one about the worms that fence with their penises."

Buwan stood abruptly. "Anyone else wanna go for a drink? No offense, Charley, but I don't want to spend what's left of Friday night in a bookstore."

Xander jumped up. "Fine idea. Let's burn off our excess energy."

"Excess what? You've got to be kidding. I'm tired," said Jess, weakly blowing her bangs out of her eyes as if the act took her last ounce of strength. Terrance bailed next, citing his long drive home to his suburban apartment, then Sunny said they promised to swing by their parents' house and watch a new documentary with them.

"Char, come with?" Xander asked Charley.

The thought of quality time with Xander tempted Charley—he hadn't stopped by the store all week—but she reminded herself he was with Sunny now. She claimed fatigue like the others.

On the sidewalk, Bu tried to keep up with Xander. "Man, I couldn't wait to get out of there. All that sex talk was making me horny."

Xander looked sideways at his friend. "I can get your mind off of orgasmic encounters if you like. When a honeybee queen is receptive to mating, she flies up as high as she can, and the male bees follow. The one that ascends the highest becomes her mate. They copulate in mid-flight and when the male climaxes, his genitals rip off with a loud *snap* to be left inside the queen bee while he drifts down to the ground, never to mate again."

Buwan's upper lip rose up, exposing his gums and his large front teeth in a comic representation of horror. "Yeah. That worked."

Xander clapped his hand on Buwan's shoulder as they took the stairs down into the subway station. "You're welcome."

***

Days passed with no word from anyone. On her next day off, feeling extra lonely, Charley drove to State Park, sat on a picnic table, and tossed cracker bits to the ground. More than ten crows gathered to enjoy the buffet, and not one scolded her. When the crumbs were gone, the biggest one looked her in the eye and gave two caws she swore sounded like 'thank you.' Charley's spirits lifted a bit at the display of friendship, or maybe it was simply appetite. Either way, Xander's theory was correct. And at least now, she had the crows for companions.

Thursday afternoon, her friendship funk lingering as she opened a box of graphic novels at the customer service desk, she heard Xander's drawl behind her.

"Excuse me, miss? Might you help my dear friend Jessica acquire an appropriate book to commemorate the anniversary of her arrival into this world?"

"Why, I believe I can," Charley said with a smile, straightening up and marveling at how quickly she and Xander returned to the banter of their early acquaintance. "Happy birthday, Jess."

"Thanks, C," Jessica said with a beautiful smile that erased all her corporate edges. "Time for Xander's annual tradition—buying me a book to celebrate. Jewels, exotic trips, dinner and drinks . . . all great birthday presents. But Xander hangs onto this book thing with an iron claw." She smirked as if expecting Charley to join in on the book-bashing.

"Well, at least unlike some of the women he's brought in lately, we know you can read."

Jessica slapped Xander lightly on the chest. "Ooh, nice burn from Char."

Even better than the surprise visit and Jess's use of a new nickname instead of the succinct "C," Jess invited Charley to meet her and Sunny for a drink later. Now, here she stood at the bar of a restaurant on the edge of the financial district, awkward in her black jeans and coral-colored blouse despite the dressier dangly earrings and silver bracelet she wore in addition to her ever-present nose ring. Jess wore a classy pinstriped pantsuit, and Sunny was assuredly comfortable in navy slacks, their royal blue solar company polo shirt, and a plain yellow headband.

Two men in suits finagled their way into the women's circle. The more handsome one, a Ricky Martin lookalike, brushed ever so slightly against Jess and asked her name.

"I'm Jess, and this is Sunny and Charley. But I should tell you, I like women." She smiled apologetically. "We all do."

His mouth opened but he didn't speak.

His friend tugged on his arm. "Have a good night, ladies."

"Leave some of the women here for us, okay?" said the first one as they left for greener pastures.

"Why did you do that?" Charley asked.

Jess shrugged. "Just didn't want to be chatted up tonight. I'd rather spend my birthday talking with you guys, and that was the fastest way to get rid of them."

"Jess uses that line all the time," Sunny told Charley. "By now, half the men in this city must think she's a lesbian."

Jess drained her drink. "Maybe I shouldn't have sent them away. I need a date for a company thing that's coming up." She sighed. "And look at us. Three successful, attractive people, but none of us has found the right guy—or person—yet."

"What about Sunny and Xander?" Charley asked.

"Good question. S, what about you and X? What's the deal this time? Friends with benefits? Quick detour? Playing it by ear?"

Sunny pursed their round mouth and said nothing.

"What about you, C? Haven't met the right guy?"

"No. I lived with my boyfriend Nathan for four years, but I don't think he was the one, even though he was a way better person than me."

Sunny's soft eyebrows drew together. Jess rolled her eyes at Sunny, making Charley worry she'd said something wrong.

"He asked me to marry him," Charley confessed, releasing a secret she'd had no one to tell until now.

"When?" Jess asked.

"Three months before he moved out; with a ring and a knee and everything." Charley turned inward, unwilling to reveal how bad a girlfriend she'd been. Her response to Nathan's marriage proposal had wiped the eagerness off his face like a tsunami clearing a beach: "God no, married people die!" she'd blurted without thinking. Nathan hadn't said anything else and they'd carried on with their lives.

So his announcement that he was leaving caught her by complete surprise.

"But you asked me to marry you."

"And you said 'no.' Since then, it was just a matter of time, don't you think?"

"Why?" was all she could say.

"Your need me to build you up all the time and tell you that you're a worthwhile person—it's wearing me out. I'm suffocating in Charley. I thought once you started working, it would get better. You would get better. But nothing's changed. I've got nothing left to try."

So, at twenty-six, Charley had found herself with Nathan's apartment and Nathan's cat, but no Nathan. That was when she established her protective and strict routine to convince herself she was in control of her life and didn't need anyone else—a ruse that worked for three years, until she met Xander.

She gulped the rest of her gin and tonic and focused on Jess and Sunny in the bar's dim light. "I said no, so that ended it," Charley said to her friends.

Sunny looked unnecessarily sad. "Do you think you'll ever get married?"

Charley stared at the ice melting in her glass. "I have no idea."

"Kids?"

"No idea."

Jess snorted. "S thinks everyone should want a fairytale marriage and a ton of kids like they do."

"You want those things?" Charley asked, immediately ashamed by the note of surprise in her voice.

"I do. And I'm not afraid to admit it, unlike some people."

"S, this might shock you, but I do want to have a family, more all the time."

"Wow. Did your spreadsheet analysis pinpoint when?" they said with loving sarcasm.

"After my—"

"—promotion to accounting manager, we know." Sunny laughed. "And for the record," they said to Charley, "I don't think everyone needs to be married with children. It's perfectly fine if people don't do either."

Charley interrupted their banter. "You guys, I have to say something." She focused on the logo on Sunny's shirt. "It's just that—I want to say—I really appreciate you being so nice to me and inviting me along and all." She peeked at them from under lowered eyelids. They were trading looks.

"C, we like you. You don't have to thank us. Trust me, I don't waste time hanging out with people I don't like," Jess said.

Sunny played with their lower lip. "Yeah, and if you're suggesting you're not worth being nice to, but we think you are, what does that say about your view of us? Do you think we're bad judges of character?"

"Oh my God, no! That's not what I meant at all. I'm sorry. Forget I said anything."

"Agreed," Jess said. "We'll forget you said anything. Now, we need another round."

Charley opened her mouth to say she'd get it when Sunny's head whipped around. "What are you doing?" they hissed at a tall, skinny blonde guy whose pale hand hovered near Sunny's head.

"Nothing," he said, his eyes shifting away. "Okay, I'm lying." He pulled his gaze to Sunny. "I wanted to touch your hair." He withered in Sunny's stare, but then glanced at his friend and drew himself up. "I wondered what a real Afro feels like. I couldn't help myself."

Jess glared at the man. "Try harder," she said. "They're not merchandise."

The man ignored Jess as if caught in the spiderweb of Sunny's eyes.

Sunny inched backward while staring at the guy. "Then I guess you won't mind if I help myself to a feel of your skinny white ass because I've never felt one and can't help myself," they said. Charley noticed that, thankfully, Sunny's hands remained by their sides. The rolling smoothness of their voice had acquired a knife's edge.

"Hey, no offense intended. I think you're really pretty and I was hoping to talk to you." He confidently looked Sunny in the eye. His gall made Charley want to slug him.

Sunny's usually expressive face was immobile, their eyes narrowed to slits. "Mmm, no," they finally said and turned back to their friends.

After a tense moment of waiting, Jess reported, "He's gone." Sunny's face relaxed. "He didn't give up easily, I'll give him that," Jess said. "Charley, you okay? You look a little nauseous."

Charley's full lips were pulled into a grimace, her green eyes wide. "What is wrong with people?" she whispered.

"Char, it's okay," Sunny said soothingly. "I mean, it's not okay, but you don't need to worry about it."

Charley couldn't help feeling she did need to worry about it. "It's such an invasion of personal space."

Sunny regarded Charley, their eyes deep and unbelievably kind. "It's more than that. There's an oppressive entitlement to it—a throwback to the slave era when we were inspected like cattle."

Charley kept her eyes on Sunny's with effort. "It makes me ashamed to be White."

"This stuff happens all the time. You can't let it ruin your day or every day would suck."

Charley's expression changed from shame back to horror.

"I think we're done here." Jess shepherded them toward the exit. "Let's go hang at one of our apartments."

"If I had one," Sunny said, levity back in their voice. "But good news—Bu says I can stay with him until I find a new place."

"S, you know you belong with me and X. Someday Crazy Carl will move out and you can move in."

Charley fought back a wave of jealousy.

CHAPTER 14: RUTHLESS MEN

"Make love to the camera, people." Xander strutted back and forth across his living room, crouching and re-crouching, smart phone in hand.

"You really don't need to do this," Terrance said, though secretly he was pleased he'd have a photo to capture how stunning Jessica looked.

"Nonsense. You only go to senior prom once. Indulge your father and let me snap a few pictures of you crazy kids."

Jess fluffed the full skirt of her forest green, satin evening dress. "Fine, but hurry up. I need to be there in time to mingle before dinner." The sweetheart neckline of her long-sleeved gown plunged in the front and back. A necklace of what looked like diamonds, three of them in a vertical row suspended on a strand of silver, drew Terrance's attention whenever he could steal a glimpse of the spot midway between her breasts.

Jess's short hair and long bangs were swept back, displaying the contours of her face. Normally, her strong eyebrows and the dimple in her chin dominated her features, but with her hair away from her face, her deep brown eyes, chiseled nose, and high cheekbones stole the show.

When she'd walked into the living room of the apartment she and Xander shared, Terrance had felt like an actor in a corny teen drama. He froze, his appendages turned to jelly, and it took him a minute to start breathing again.

Jess arched her back slightly, rested a hand on her hip and faced the camera from a slight angle. "Let's get this over with. Chest out, gut in, T," she said, flashing her biggest smile.

"Speak for yourself, Delgado." Terrance straightened his bowtie. "I don't have a gut to pull in." He placed his arm loosely around her back, fingers sliding against the satin of her dress.

"Fred, what do you think? Conclude this exercise?" Xander asked after five or six shots. The dog lay on his bed in the corner of the living room, where he'd been banished by Jess after leaving one too many moist sniff marks on her dress. He refused to answer. "Fred says yes, that's a wrap," Xander declared. "Go on now. Have fun. Be safe. Don't do anything stupid."

"You clean up nice," Jess said as Terrance opened the passenger door of her car for her. "But I thought you'd go for the all-black tux."

"I thought I should go traditional white shirt for this crowd. I took out my earrings, too."

"Thanks," she said while Terrance circled around to the driver's side. "And thanks for driving," she said as he started the car and pulled away from the curb. "Driving in four-inch heels qualifies as an unnecessary risk."

"My pleasure."

"And thanks for coming on this non-date. I couldn't bring B—he's too hyper and too short, if I'm being honest. And X would stick out like a sore thumb at a black-tie function."

Terrance focused on the road. "I'm surprised you didn't pick one of the other men Xander says are always after you."

Jess busied herself smoothing her skirt. "Oh. Well. It was short notice and all."

They drove in silence for a few minutes.

"Hey, any news from the marketing agency about the job?" she asked.

"Just a form email saying they got my résumé and will be in touch."

"I would think you'd be a shoo-in for an interview, with your experience. And who knows, if you work on the All-American account, we might even cross paths once in a while."

Terrance grinned. "All I know is, if I get the job, you have to protect me from Xander."

"Hey, not everyone needs to work for peanuts at a nonprofit their whole life."

Terrance kept quiet, knowing Jess wouldn't understand the angst this potential job change gave him. He decided to apply when the headhunter contacted him because the pay increase would be substantial and the prestige even greater since the Barber Finch agency represented most of the city's biggest companies. But he had every intention, if they in fact offered him the position, of demanding to work on some environmental accounts as well as the real estate accounts highlighted in the job description. He wasn't willing to sell his soul completely.

He put aside his mental analysis of the pros and cons of moving to Barber Finch versus a continued trajectory at Wilderness Protection when he and Jess reached the hotel.

As they entered the swanky ballroom hosting the All-American Development & Construction soirée, a number of heads swiveled toward Jess. Terrance observed the blunt stares of desire from the men and jealous appreciation from the women.

At least ninety percent of the people in the glittering room were White, Terrance estimated, and of those at least half were men with gray hair and glasses. With effort, he spied two Asians and three Black people, and one guy in a wheelchair. He doubted there was a single gay person there, at least not one out of the closet.

"I recognize a lot of the exec's, but I hardly *know* anyone here," Jess whispered as they moved toward one of four bars set up around the room's perimeter.

"That's okay, I don't recognize or know *anyone*," Terrance whispered back, making Jess smile.

"Whiskey, neat," he told the bartender, drawing an impressed "hmm" from Jess, which made Terrance think she'd expected him to order something fruity or a beer he could chug.

"I'll have a Cabernet," Jess said, pushing a stray lock of hair back in place over a perfectly shaped ear.

"Ready to mingle?" he asked as they moved into the midst of the cocktail reception.

Jess's slender hand adjusted her necklace. "What does this room smell like to you?"

Terrance inhaled as he looked up and around the room. "Perfume. Candles. Dinner."

"It smells like money to me," she said.

Before he could utter a sarcastic reply, she grabbed his arm and towed him toward a nondescript man in his fifties. "Jay, hi, how are you? Let me introduce you to my friend, Terrance Washington."

"Are you Jess's boss?" Terrance asked.

"Not yet, but possibly someday," Jay said with an anemic laugh. "We all work closely and I'm very familiar with her work. Just like one big family, right Jess?"

Jess smiled but her eyebrows flicked up briefly. "Sure, one big family," she said. "One obsessed with revenue, profit, and risk mitigation," she tacked on with a small laugh as Jay drank from his tumbler. "Any idea when interviews will start for the accounting manager position?" she asked.

Jay made the tiniest frown. "Soon, soon." He sipped his drink again. "Terry, is it? Where do you work?"

Terrance knew from the way Jay's eyes darted around the room the executive didn't care, but Terrance wanted to keep him engaged with Jess as long as possible. "I'm in government relations and communications, and I'm currently considering a number of new growth opportunities." Jay nodded absently. "So tell me, is All-American Development & Construction the parent company or is there another layer above it?" Jay perked up.

"It's the parent. Why?"

"Just curious how all the pieces fit together. You have numerous subsidiaries, yes?"

"Of course. We're into property management, mortgage lending, residential real estate sales, commercial leasing, even landscaping. There are fifteen subsidiaries."

"Registered in Delaware?" Terrance asked.

Jay nodded, now regarding Terrance directly. "Do you know why? Why Delaware?" He smirked at Jess as if they were playing a practical joke on Terrance.

"Isn't it for the corporation-friendly laws and tax rates? Lower disclosure requirements for directors and shareholders, faster incorporation time frame, that sort of thing?"

Jay's smirk disappeared as if he'd lost a sure bet. "Yes, yes, and yes." He leaned in a touch. "And you didn't hear it from me, but we're getting ready to incorporate another subsidiary soon. Number sixteen."

Terrance noticed Jess's entire face flinch. "Anything exciting?" she asked.

Jay shrugged her off. "I should go. I see Liam looking at me."

"Jay, before you go, did you see my email about the landscaping company's quarterly numbers? Something was off. Do you want me to talk to someone about it?"

Jay's vision hovered at a point between Jess and Terrance. "Oh, that. Don't worry about it. You got that info by mistake. It was supposed to go to Jessica DeAngelis in legal." He made eye contact again. "Terry, nice to meet you. Jess, enjoy the night. The food here is absolutely fantastic."

"That's annoying," she hissed to Terrance when Jay was out of earshot. "I can't believe he told you about the new subsidiary before I knew about it."

"Jess, do you really think he'd leak a secret to me? It's probably something extremely innocuous."

A few minutes later, a deep voice startled them from behind. "Jessica Delgado, I presume?"

Jess turned and stared at an older man whose florid cheeks suggested he'd enjoyed a few cocktails already. Terrance recognized Liam Flammer from newspaper photos. He thought the CEO resembled a mafioso henchman—looming height a touch taller than Terrance, slick black hair with a touch of gray, an unremarkable and loose face other than the piercing eyes shining blackly in the ballroom's muted light. Terrance tensed at the territorial manner in which Flammer's eyes devoured Jessica, from her slicked-back hair to the hem of her gown, as if she were a lioness in his pride, there for the taking whenever it pleased him.

"Mr. Flammer, hello. So nice to meet you." In her heels, she stood nearly as tall as the CEO. She extended her hand, which he lifted to his mouth and kissed. When Flammer let go, Terrance watched an odd mixture of approval and annoyance color Flammer's dark eyes.

As Jess introduced Terrance, Flammer's eyes flickered with some emotion too fleeting for Terrance to name, followed by casual dismissal. He shook Terrance's hand, releasing his grasp after one shake. "Jay told me I could find you here," he said to Jess, who raised her eyebrows, a professional smile in place. "He says you and Dennis somebody are vying for Rodney's position in commercial development. That's actually why you were both invited tonight. I'm always interested in meeting our ambitious up-and-comers." He smiled coldly.

Jess nodded. "Yes, I'm very interested in the position. I think I can offer a lot."

"I salute your confidence."

She released her most engaging smile. "Someday, I'd like to run your entire financial operation."

Liam stared for a good five seconds before erupting in a chesty laugh that turned a few heads. "You've got balls, young lady. Pardon my expression."

"Oh, I don't mind. Not at all," she said with a direct look, the professional smile still in place.

"Yeah, I guess you wouldn't."

Jess sipped her wine. "While I've got you, what do you think of my analysis on the Stone Circle replacement projects?"

He guffawed again. "Is that what we're calling them?" Terrance froze to remain as inconspicuous as possible now that the project derailed by Wilderness Protection had entered the conversation. "If you want to get ahead here, Jessica," Flammer said in a creepily intimate tone that raised Terrance's hackles, "you should learn not to mention the losses to the CEO. Once a project is dead, we do not speak of it again."

Jess's cheeks turned rosy in the dim light. "Understood. My apologies."

"Anyway," Flammer continued, "Dennis whatshisname came up with a bunch of viable options, and the bookstore you suggested might be worth something. I gather the owner is an old lady who should be easily bought out." His offhand tone gave Terrance the uncomfortable feeling the CEO was tossing Jess a bone. Liam turned abruptly, ending the conversation. Two steps away, he turned back. "Delgado. You're not by any chance related to Michael, are you? The lawyer?"

Now Jess's cheeks paled. "He's—he's my father. You know him?"

"Know him? He was my right-hand man for five years." His eyes narrowed. "Interesting that he never mentioned that, what with you working here and all."

Jess paused for the shortest of seconds. "I'm sure it's because we made a pact early on—that I would make it on my own. He has a lot of great contacts in the city and wanted to help. But I refused. I'm sure that's why."

"Hm." Liam walked away without another word.

"Your dad worked for Flammer?" Terrance asked, his face composed but surprise evident in his voice. "And never told you?"

Jess didn't answer. Her lips thinned into a slash.

An armada of waitstaff began herding people toward the adjacent dining room, where crisp white tablecloths gleamed and silver candlesticks and cutlery sparkled.

"Time to eat. I hear the food here is absolutely fantastic," she said, sarcastically echoing Jay's comment.

***

"T, you were awesome in there. Smart, smooth, clever. You can be my date anytime."

They waited under the hotel's portico for the valet to bring the car around. The meal, which was in fact absolutely fantastic, plus the wine and engaging conversation with their six tablemates, had brought the light back to Jess's eyes, the bombshell about her father apparently forgotten for now.

"Why thank you. That's high praise. I'm glad I didn't embarrass you," Terrance said with a twinkle in his eye. While they waited, he retrieved his diamond studs from his tuxedo jacket pocket and put them back on.

"I wasn't worried," she said in a tone suggesting she had worried a bit.

In the car, as Terrance navigated up the ramp onto the highway to get across town, Jess sighed contentedly, then sat up straight. "I'm too wound up to go home. Let's get a drink, closer to my place though."

"Sure," he said, "as long as I can lose the bowtie and cummerbund."

"Go ahead. Lose them now." She took hold of the steering wheel with her left hand.

Terrance grimaced at the thought of taking his hands off the wheel. He undid the bowtie with one hand and tossed it over his shoulder. Jess's grip on the wheel appeared firm, so he quickly used both hands to reach back and unclip the cummerbund. "Ah, that's better," he said, relaxing his gut, hands back on the wheel.

"Why Terrance," Jess said, patting his abdomen, "I do believe you've got a little bulge here now."

He prepared to retort it was only a food baby when blue light and a piercing siren flooded the interior of the car.

"Shit, what's that for?" Terrance mumbled as he pulled over. "I shouldn't have let you steer, not even for a few seconds."

Jess drew back as if stung. "Don't worry. I've talked myself out of four tickets."

Terrance looked away from the specter of the approaching officer in his side mirror to glare at Jess.

"Do not say anything. Let me handle this," he said in an armored voice.

It's different with me here, he wanted to explain, but the policeman was already at the car. Terrance lowered the window. "Good evening, officer," he said.

The cop shone a flashlight on Terrance's face. He moved the light to Jess's face and left it there.

"Are you okay, miss?"

She squinted into the flashlight's beam, which the cop lowered to rest on the small jewels of her necklace.

"I'm fine," she said in a voice suggesting surprise, Terrance thought. It was hard to tell through the rushing water sound in his ears. He watched the officer's pudgy face. A shadow suggesting hair emerged from the edges of his cap.

The officer's eyes roved over Jess as if looking for a secret sign. "Are you sure?" he asked, spacing out the words.

"Yes. I'm sure," Jess answered. "Why wouldn't I be fine?" Terrance turned to see Jess blink several times. "Do you think I'm being kidnapped or something? By a man in a tuxedo? Seriously?"

"Easy, Jess," Terrance said under his breath.

"What did you say?" the officer shone the light on Terrance. "Step out of the car," he demanded. He switched off the flashlight and returned it to his duty belt. "Get out of the car," he repeated in a steely voice. "Now."

Terrance undid his seatbelt, moving one inch at a time. He stepped weakly out of the car. The cop stood about six inches shorter than Terrance. A second policeman, a tall but slight man with a reddish-gray mustache, appeared beside Jess's door.

"Hey look, Hardy," the first cop said over the roof of the car, after taking in Terrance's height, blonde hair, and diamond earrings. "It's Dennis Rodman." He gave a short, mean laugh. "Stand back against the car," he barked at Terrance. "Where's your license?"

The officer assumed a wide-legged stance four feet away, his right hand resting on the pistol in its holster. The thought *Napoleon complex* formed loosely in the back of Terrance's mind as he focused on keeping his face respectful. He slouched, let his shoulders sag and lowered his head.

"It's in my wallet, in the car. On the center console, sir."

"I got it, Vignetti," said the tall officer—Hardy. "Registration," Hardy said curtly. Terrance heard general rustling behind him as Jess handed over the vehicle registration paper.

"I don't think his name is Jessica Delgado, do you Vignetti?"

"It's my car," Jess said, exasperation seeping into her voice.

"I'll check it out." Hardy walked back to the cruiser.

Terrance used the brief transfer of attention from him to Jess to breathe deeply and will his body to stay calm and his brain clear.

"Where'd you get the tux?"

"Excuse me?" Terrance asked, caught off-guard by the unexpected question.

"Where'd you get the tux, I said."

"I rented it, officer. We're coming back from a work function for Jessica's company, sir."

"It's true," Jess said from inside the car. "I work at All-American Real Estate Development & Construction. As a CPA."

Vignetti smirked as if he found all their answers highly improbable. "Turn around and put your hands on the vehicle," he ordered Terrance.

Terrance did, vaguely wondering if the guy was merely filling time while his partner ran the registration. He called on every ounce of control he possessed to remain still as Vignetti patted him down. The cop pulled a roll of breath mints and a valet parking receipt from the tuxedo jacket's pocket and dropped them. Terrance watched the mints roll under the car. The receipt jerked in an unfelt breeze before flattening on the asphalt.

Hardy returned to the passenger side of the car and handed Jess the registration and driver's license. "They're clean," he announced. "What kind of name is Delgado anyway? Mexican? Puerto Rican?"

"Colombian." Exasperation coated the word. "Officer Hardy, do I have a taillight out or something I need to fix?"

Hardy spoke to Terrance over the top of the car. "Tell Jennifer Lopez to shut up."

Terrance squeezed his eyes shut. Jess went silent.

Hardy moved around the car to join Vignetti behind Terrance. "On the ground, Rodman," he said with a snarl.

Terrance heard a soft gasp from Jess. He slowly pivoted away and dropped to his knees. As his body lowered, his heartbeat moved up into his head where it threatened to burst his skull.

"All the way. Face down. And hurry up," Vignetti growled.

All Terrance wanted, in that moment, was to keep himself together mentally and physically so he didn't drop to the ground too suddenly.

"Hurry up." Vignetti said.

This is it, Terrance thought as he lowered his chest to the ground. *I'm sorry, Mama. I did everything on the list, I swear.*

His torso on the ground, he stopped, head and shoulders raised. "Officer, I'm going to take off my glasses. Is that okay, sir?"

"Give them to me." Hardy snatched the heavy black frames from Terrance's face and tossed them into the driver's side of the BMW.

"Now down!" Vignetti yelled. Terrance laid his cheek on the asphalt. The remainder of the day's heat held captive by the highway surface warmed Terrance's skin and he silently thanked God for that bit of comfort. Small sharp bits of gravel bore into his face and he thanked God for the sensation keeping him connected to the here and now. He thanked God for the life he'd lived and prayed for the chance to keep living it. He wanted to say so much more to God but was unable to build any more coherent prayers in his head. He began to recite the lines from Psalm 86 that he often called upon in troubled times, his lips moving ever so slightly with the words in his head.

The arrogant are attacking me, O God; a band of ruthless men seeks my life—men without regard for you. But you, O Lord, are a compassionate and gracious God, slow to anger, abounding in love and faithfulness—

Terrance grunted as Vignetti's knee drilled into his back. How much time had elapsed while he prayed? Ten seconds? Two minutes?

Why? Terrance wanted to ask. *Why am I here? Why are you doing this?* But he knew to speak would invite worse things. And he knew there were no good answers.

He ground his cheek into the gravel on the pavement, the only available outlet for his anguish.

The radio in the cruiser came to life, blaring unintelligible words. Vignetti's knee went deeper into Terrance's back as Hardy's footsteps sounded away.

"Marty, all units, let's go!" Hardy yelled as the dispatcher continued dispensing staticky instructions over the radio.

Vignetti unplanted his knee and released Terrance. Terrance remained on the ground, relief and hope whispering in his ear, his body melting into the asphalt.

"Get up," Vignetti demanded, as if it had been Terrance's idea to lie down. "Get in your car. You can go." Terrance watched the cop's legs move away toward his partner at the cruiser.

Terrance stood. The fear that consumed him hardened into anger as he watched the two officers confer, as if at a backyard barbecue debating whether the burgers were done. A piece of gravel dropped off his cheek. He wanted to brush off his face and the tuxedo but knew sudden movement was still dangerous.

Vignetti looked his way. "Get in the car. Hurry up."

Both cops watched him climb back into the car, put on his glasses, start the car and pull away. Soon after, their cruiser sped by, siren ear-splitting and lights blinding.

Terrance pulled over to the shoulder on an overpass and stopped the car. He stumbled out and walked to a metal barrier at the edge of the highway. Below him, a cluster of access roads snaked in a seemingly random pattern. The lights of the financial district shone without emotion, a ribbon of haze separating the cityscape from the jet-black sky.

What an imbecile he'd been to think Wrighton might become his city. A place where he could succeed despite the color of his skin. As if this city were any different than the smaller one he grew up in. It didn't matter which city formed the backdrop of his life because he was who he was. He looked like he looked.

His hands tingled with fear and helplessness, but his aching, heaving chest stilled. He placed his palms on his forehead, fingers pointing up. Pressing inward, he slowly ran his hands up and over his scalp, down his neck and across his shoulders. His legs found their strength. He bent each knee twice and wiggled his weak fingers. He brushed the remaining gravel bits from his cheek and the gray road dust from the front of his tuxedo.

Back in the car, he finally looked at Jessica. Two trails, slightly darker than the rest of her face, wormed down her cheeks. The streetlight shining over them cast garish shadows on the planes of her face.

"I'll pay for the tux if they charge you for any damage," she said, her eyes watery and pained. Her pain pissed him off. "I mean, I'm sorry. That was terrible. I'm sorry."

He held her gaze with eyes hard as stone and hollow as the wind. "When I am stopped by a cop," he said, his voice low and slow, "my options are not ticket or no ticket. I don't have the luxury of being annoyed or asking questions. My options are live or die. If I'm very, very lucky, like tonight, I get to drive away."

And so he did. They both watched the road and spoke no words all the way to her apartment.

Once parked, he saw her turn toward him, in his peripheral vision. He refused to face her. His jaw muscles worked under the skin and his chin tipped up in slight defiance. His shoulders jerked as he remembered he was in Jess's car. He handed her the keys, went to his car, and drove away without words.

Only at home, showered and in bed under his comforter, sheet pulled over his head as if he were a child, did Terrance invite his body to release its tension through tears. But the tears would not oblige. The sheet—usually soft and reassuring with a whisper of weight on his face, chest, and legs—probed his mouth and nostrils on his inhale, a blanket of impotence suffocating him. He thrashed and tore the sheet away, damning its new manifestation: a gauzy veil mocking his powerlessness.

CHAPTER 15: BERTIE'S STORY

Xander and Buwan hugged Jess when they arrived at her parents' home in the suburbs the following weekend, five minutes after she did. To Jess's disappointment, Terrance ignored her, busying himself with the straps they'd brought to tie down the couch in the back of the blue, beat-up pickup truck Buwan borrowed from his parents. The sun had burned through a morning mist on its upward trek away from the horizon, promising a hot and dry day.

"Where might the couch be, Jess?" Xander asked. "Let's accomplish our task so we have ample time to get to the festival."

"Jessica, introduce me to your friends," said a thin woman coming out the front door. She had large brown eyes, long, thick black hair with a widow's peak, and pinched features that broadened into a delicate elegance when she smiled. She exuded class despite a simple outfit of dark blue capris and a sleeveless pale-yellow blouse.

"You met Xander at graduation, remember?" Jess said.

"Of course. How are you, Xander?"

Xander swept his arm out to indicate the lush yards and widely spaced houses of the neighborhood. "Feeling bucolic," he replied.

"And these are my good friends Terrance and Buwan. Guys, this is my mom, Valerie."

"Pleasure," Valerie said. "Let me show you the monstrosity also known as our old couch. Thank you for taking it off my hands," she said in a rich, slightly accented voice as she led them into the detached garage of the four-bedroom Tudor home.

Xander inspected the huge brown leather couch, not a scrape or scratch on it. "Monstrosity to you, spectacular find to us. I'm quite sure it will be the finest furnishing in Charley's bookstore, and certainly more comfortable than the rickety metal chairs she has now."

Jess left the guys to do the loading and snuck off toward her father's study, knowing he'd be there squeezing in a few hours of work as he did every Saturday morning.

On the way, she stopped in the kitchen where Bertie bustled about, murmuring to herself in her native Ixil. Jess stooped to give Bertie a warm hug, feeling—as always—like a protected little girl in Bertie's soft embrace, despite the fact that she towered over the family's housekeeper/former nanny.

She detached from Bertie and went to her father's study, the dark wooden double doors resting open. Michael sat at his computer, wearing his typical weekend work outfit of pressed slacks and button-down shirt; he'd once explained to Jess he couldn't think like a lawyer in shorts and a T-shirt.

From the doorway, Jess watched him scroll through a document on his screen. His eyes were animated under strong, dark eyebrows. A full head of silver hair swept back from his broad, deeply tanned forehead and lightly lined face. His high cheekbones sloped down to a square jaw with a cleft in the chin. He was, without a doubt, the most handsome man Jess knew, and ever expected to know.

"I met Liam Flammer last weekend."

Michael startled, pushed his chair back from his mahogany desk and turned to face her. He blinked twice. "That's surprising. He doesn't usually mingle with rank-and-file employees." His deep voice carried a trace of a South American accent.

"Is that why you didn't think I'd find out you used to work for him?" She stepped closer, face blank.

Michael regarded her, his face also neutral. "That's what I was hoping. It's not a period of my life of which I'm proud."

She crossed her arms over her chest. "Why not?"

"No one thing in particular. Liam hired me soon after I passed the bar. I worked on his in-house legal team and he liked my work, so I rose through the ranks quickly. But I didn't like how he cut corners—financially, operationally, ethically—so after five years, I left and started my own practice."

The annoyance clouding her eyes cleared a tad. She was well aware of Liam's corner-cutting tendencies. "Because you're more honest than he is."

"Essentially, yes. In addition to my personal ethics, I feel what is perhaps an irrational responsibility to represent all Colombian-Americans as trustworthy and hard-working."

She nodded sharply. "Understood. Why didn't you tell me this before?"

Michael's mouth twitched like the mildest of shrugs. "Liam was angry when I resigned, and he holds grudges. I thought our connection might hurt you. You had your heart set on the job and I knew you would learn a lot quickly, so I advised you to get in and get out in a few years, as you'll recall."

"But the accounting manager position—" Jess started.

Michael kept talking. "My advice *today* is to get the manager position you want so badly, put in a year, and then get out. If you don't get the promotion, get out sooner."

"You make it sound like a cult or a prison."

Michael shrugged his shoulders in a rare physical gesture. "You're too good for them, Jessie. You can do much greater things than be a cog in Liam Flammer's wheel."

She uncrossed her arms and nodded. "Dad, you ran a landscaping company before I was born, right?" Michael nodded. "So, you would know if something was sketchy in the financials for a similar business?"

"Probably. Liam bought my landscaping company when I started working for him—a signing bonus, if you will. The deal included the provision that he keep the current employees for at least five years and then he was free to run it as he pleased."

"So that's *your* business he runs now?"

"It was. I expect it looks nothing like the company I built. Tell me what troubles you."

Jess sat on the edge of the desk. "I saw the quarterly report for our landscaping subsidiary and the wages line item was really low. I could have sworn there were a lot more staff than that number could possibly represent. So I went through some employee newsletters and found a photo I remembered that showed a huge group of at least a hundred happy workers at a company cookout." Michael nodded. Jess knew he trusted her memory of anything numbers-related. "But I don't work for that division, and I couldn't dig into the numbers. So maybe there's a valid reason for the discrepancy."

Michael shifted in his chair. "They could be using contractors, not actual staff. But I gather you didn't see a line item supporting that theory?"

Jess shook her head.

"Then they could be underreporting the staff numbers so the payroll reflects the minimum wage."

"Oh." Jess said. "Of course. Right. I should have thought of that."

"That's the type of practice that made me leave. And you should too, when the time is right," he said again, in a rare beating of a dead horse.

Jess ignored the horse. "But wait—what kind of person even works for less than minimum wage?"

"The kind that has no other choice. Undocumented immigrants mostly."

"Hmph. I guess that's the choice they make when they decide to come here illegally."

Michael's head pulled back on his neck and his eyes on Jess went still, almost blank. She knew this look, for she'd been on the receiving end of it throughout her childhood every time she disappointed her father.

"Jessica," he said, looking down his razor-straight nose, "immigrants are not to be disparaged. You should be more sympathetic. Don't forget, Valerie and I are immigrants, and you are only one generation removed. We were fortunate to come here via petition and to have education and family money at our disposal. The only difference between us and many others is the slip of paper that that good fortune put in our hands."

"But you came—"

"Jess, you in here?" Xander stuck his shaggy head into the study. "The truck's loaded but Valerie and Bertie insist we stay for lunch."

Michael stood up. "Lunch sounds like a good idea."

"B and T want to stay, too?" Jess asked.

Xander grinned. "Buwan's already at the table."

***

Bertie shooed everyone into the eat-in kitchen, bright with white modern furniture and lemon-yellow curtains. "Come, sit, eat."

Bertie's three-year-old granddaughter Dacey left Bertie's side and scurried to Buwan, pulling on his black basketball shorts. He leaned over in his chair, stuck out his tongue and wiggled his fingers next to his ears, eliciting a glissando of laughter and making the girl's big blackberry eyes sparkle. She babbled in a combination of Spanish and English, which Buwan answered in baby talk.

Bertie scooped her granddaughter up to her chest. "I'll take Dacey home for lunch and come back to clean the dishes."

"Nonsense, Bertie," Valerie said. "Sit down with us. There's plenty of food. I'll get the booster seat."

Before Terrance could sit, Jess grabbed his arm and flicked her head toward the kitchen's back door. Terrance remained stone-faced and unmoving.

"Please," Jess mouthed.

Terrance blinked slowly behind his glasses, then strode to and out the door.

They faced off on a large patio under the intensifying sun, Terrance waiting for her to speak.

"I lost a lot of sleep the past week."

Terrance made a *tsk* noise. "Poor thing."

"What I mean is, I'm sorry and I feel like crap for anything I did to make it worse. I thought I was just answering their questions. But I realize now it's not that simple." The steel in his eyes softened a touch. "And I'm worried about you."

He looked away. "I'm fine, Jess, and there's nothing you can do to help."

Her heart stuttered. The possibility that she'd lost another good friend forever had tormented her all week. The day after the police incident, she'd defiantly blamed the cops and only the cops. But over the ensuing days, she'd acknowledged the unwelcome truth that she had not helped the situation. Her regret burst into full-fledged shame.

"I really am so sorry I made things worse." She looked at his hand hanging by his side. "Do you want to talk about it?"

He sighed so heavily Jess thought it must have reached his toes. He stretched his shoulders back against the boundary of his black polo shirt. "Let's forget about it. I forgot about our little encounter at Buwan's summer house when you asked. Now you can forget about last weekend, for me."

"Agreed. Does that mean you forgive me?"

Terrance sighed again. "I will, in time. You didn't know about the Staying Alive list. You didn't grow up Black. How could you know that the best strategy was complete submission?"

Jess looked away from the shame in his eyes, resisting the urge to ask about this list. "Terrance," she said to a point on the patio in front of her blue canvas slip-on shoes, "you are an amazing, talented guy and you have an amazing future in front of you and no one—not even racist cops—can stop you. You are so much more than what happened that night."

She met his eyes, relieved to see the coldness retreating.

"Let's go eat," he said, "I can't take any more of this inspirational crap. Put it on a poster."

She stared, unsure, until a small, sad smile touched half his mouth.

"You're making fun of me, aren't you?" She linked her arm through his as they moved toward the house. He withdrew his arm and opened the kitchen door for her.

"You just stick to working with numbers and leave the words to me."

***

Bertie sprang up from the kitchen table when Jess and Terrance entered, although at five-foot-one-inch she wasn't much taller standing than sitting. She moved quickly despite her squat, blocky build. "Eat, eat," she said, gesturing at the counter bearing a platter of assorted cold-cut sandwiches, bowls of potato salad, and green salad. "It's not much, but I didn't have time to make more." She looked approvingly at Terrance and patted Jessica's hand. Bertie's smile revealed a considerable gap between the front teeth and lifted her entire face, squeezing her eyes into half-moons. A thick, black bob framed her round face and her summery dress exploded in abstract shapes of primary colors.

As Terrance and Jess loaded their plates, Bertie sat back down, smiling and watching everyone eat. Next to her, Dacey sat in a booster seat, banging a spoon on the plastic mat in front of her and splattering bits of yogurt into the short black curls framing her round, brown face.

"Buwan," Bertie said, as if tasting a new food. "I like your name. I like that you didn't change it to something else," she said with her heavy accent.

Buwan wiped mayonnaise from his mouth with the cloth napkin. "It's Filipino."

"Bertie," said Valerie, "do you not like your nickname?"

Bertie shrugged. "Everything is fast in America. Even names."

"Tell them your full name," Jess encouraged. "And Al's and Ozzy's." Immediately, she regretted mentioning Bertie's wayward son, but Bertie didn't appear upset. But then, she rarely displayed any emotion except good cheer.

"Yeah, tell us," Buwan encouraged.

Bertie sat up straighter. "My name is Rigoberta de Leon. Here I become Roberta and then Bertie. My husband Al is Abilio Lopez and my son Ozzy's true name is Hermenegildo." Unlike the clumsiness affecting Bertie's pronunciation of many English words, the names of her family floated from her like the lyrics of a song.

"Wow, those are beautiful names," Terrance said between bites, "but how do you get Ozzy from Hermen—Hermenegildo?"

"When he was a baby, he was cute and fat like the teddy bear, so the priest called him Osito. His friends here changed him to Ozzy." She studied the half-eaten sandwich on her plate as if debating whether or not to eat more.

"Where are you from?" Bu asked.

Bertie pushed potato salad around her plate with a fork. "A small town in the pine forest and the clouds of Guatemala. The jungle and many waterfalls were my neighbors. And *también* a volcano if you walked two days."

"Wow. Sounds very pretty."

"It was the top and the edge of the world."

"What was your house like?" Buwan asked.

Bertie squirmed but soldiered on. Jess noticed she focused only on Buwan as she spoke. "It was not a house like this," she said. "It was with no windows and one room."

"Cool. What did your family do? Were you farmers or ranchers?"

Bertie giggled. "No ranch in the mountains. My family had one goat. We were farmers when I was a little girl. We grew corn and beans and made food like tortillas."

"You said when you were little. What about after that?"

Bertie's face stiffened. "Those were bad years. Guatemala had war for thirty-six years."

Gasps escaped from her audience.

"A civil war," Michael said from the head of the table, "from 1960 to 1996."

"This war was very bad for Maya people. When I was fourteen, our home was burned," Bertie said in a hushed voice.

"Those were called the 'scorched earth' years," Michael said. "Indigenous people were targeted and driven from their homes."

"*Si, tierra quemada.* So, my family, we went up higher in the mountains and lived like animals."

"Why didn't the government protect you?" Jess said, while asking herself why she had never asked Bertie these questions.

"Jessica, it's the government who burned our villages."

"Hm. I dare say that makes the U.S. government look a scintilla less evil," Xander said, drawing reproving looks from Jessica's parents, whose loyalty to their adopted country did not waver. He ignored the looks and continued. "Of course, it's rumored the CIA trained the Guatemalan military in those scorched earth tactics, so I guess my point is debatable." He shook his head.

Bu patted Bertie's shoulder. "Do you still have family in Guatemala?

Bertie nodded. "One sister and one brother, and their families."

Valerie shifted in her seat. "I don't think Bertie will mind me telling you this—she and Al send most of what they make to her sister. Poverty is rampant in Guatemala with few avenues for making money."

"So, then what happened? After you moved higher up in the mountains?" Buwan said, his eyes bright as if waiting for the next episode of a compelling TV drama.

Bertie's eyes lowered to her lap. "You do not want to hear about that," she said in a voice that clearly meant, *I do not want to talk about that.*

"Lucky for us," Michael said quickly, "Bertie and Al came here to live. They might look like our housekeeper and gardener, but they're so much more than that."

Valerie took Bertie's hand and squeezed. "They're family. Bertie is the sister I never had."

"Are you glad you came to America?" Bu asked.

Bertie hesitated, surprising Jess who expected her to answer with an unequivocal 'yes.' "America is the dream," Bertie finally said. "Life is better here." She did not sound convincing.

Terrance reached for his iced tea. "What about social issues like sexism and racism? Are those worse here?"

"I am Maya. I know about *racismo*," Bertie said in a low but fierce tone. "They take our land. They push us out. We do not go to school. We do not have doctors. We have no way to live. Why?" She thumped a fist against her chest. "Because I am Maya. Here is better. Here *los niños* go to school and see doctors. There is much that is bad here, *si*. But much is good, too. In Guatemala, only family is good. And the land. The rest—it is bad." Her chest heaved as if the short speech tired her.

Bu patted her hand. "It must be hard, coming from another country and having us Americans change your name and make you speak English and everything."

"Bu, you've touched on the conundrum for any immigrant," Xander said, his drawl slower than usual for Bertie's sake. "This question of how quickly and to what degree immigrants integrate into a new society fascinates me."

Michael sighed, drawing all eyes his way. "Integration is an age-old problem. And as with most age-old problems, there is no easy answer. Most people aim to honor their heritage *and* adapt to the new country's ways—and usually end up somewhere in the middle. Sometimes you feel you are neither one nor the other. Sometimes you feel homeless, having given up your past—your roots—too readily, but never completely at home in America. But you carry on and make the best of the choice you made." Jess put down her fork and watched her father, who focused on his wife. "You forever wonder if you did the right thing by encouraging your children to assimilate as quickly and wholly as possible." He dabbed an imaginary crumb from his lip with his napkin. "Roots take time to grow."

Xander nudged Jess out of her fascinated consideration of her father and flicked his eyes to the wall clock.

Jess stood. "We need to get going. The guys and S are—the guys and Sunny are taking me and Charley to a reggae/reggaeton festival for our birthdays."

"A music festival?" Valerie asked with a smile of approval. "We should do something different like that sometime, Michael."

"Sure, *mi reina*. But reggae?"

Jess was willing to bet Valerie wouldn't know reggae from rap if presented with the two. "Mom, if you want to do something different, you should go to the Women's March next weekend. A bunch of us are going."

Valerie put an index finger to her lips. "Hm. Bertie, what do you think? Should we go hold signs and protest for women's rights with the young people?"

Bertie grimaced. "Ah no, Mrs. Valerie, a protest is no place for me." She shook her head.

"No, of course not," Valerie said. "You can represent us, Jessica." She stood. "Did you gentlemen get the two chairs out of the garage too? The ones Jessica dragged off the street as if she were a common vagabond?"

Xander chuckled. "Not to worry, Mrs. Delgado. The offensive chairs have been removed, never to sully the premises again."

The group moved outside into the baking circular driveway, Bertie toting a squirming Dacey in her arms while beaming at Buwan. "Next time you visit, I will make you my special tamales and *pepián* stew."

"Sounds great, Bertie, thanks," Bu said. "It was really nice meeting you." He leaned down and kissed her round cheek. She awkwardly patted his shoulder, her eyes misty.

Bertie turned to Valerie as the young people drove off, Dacey rubbing her eyes with small brown fists. "I'll put Dacey to bed for her nap and come back to clean the dishes."

Valerie shook her head. "No, you take a break and come back in a few hours. We'll make dinner together."

Bertie nodded, grateful for the chance to lie down. Walking to the carriage house, she rubbed her eye with the heel of her hand, echoing Dacey's movement but with a much deeper sense of fatigue, one pierced by loss.

CHAPTER 16: NATURE VS. NURTURE

Three hours later, the furniture successfully unloaded into the bookstore's café, the six friends plus Fred settled on blankets on an expansive sloping lawn overlooking an outdoor stage. The lawn filled steadily with bodies, color, laughter, and the odor of weed. Auditorium-style seating near the stage cradled people standing and swaying to the throbbing bass lines of the current act. A huge banner with a pot plant emblazoned over bold stripes of red, gold, and green festooned the back of the stage.

Everyone but Charley shed their shoes. Terrance stretched his toes and turned to Buwan. "So, Bu, does your name mean anything in particular?"

The friends scooched themselves into a tight semi-circle to hear better over the music.

Buwan nodded while drinking heartily from his beer, a drip running down his chin. "Buwan means 'moon' in Tagalog, and in Filipino mythology Bakunawa is the name of a serpent or dragon."

"Like the one on your arm?" Charley asked.

"Uh-huh. My moms told me a bunch of stories about the Bakunawa when I was growing up. Wanna hear one?"

"Yes, of course!"

"Okay." He stretched his legs out in front of him and leaned back on his arms. Fred squeezed into the space between Xander and Charley and lay down on the blanket. "There are a few versions of the Bakunawa legend. Sometimes the Bakunawa is a 'he,' sometimes a 'she.'

Sometimes it's a dragon or sea serpent. Sometimes it's a *diwata* guardian spirit and sometimes it's a *naga,* which is part human and part cobra. I'll tell you the story I like the most, because it has both my names in it. It goes like this.

"The Bakunawa lives in the sea and has purple iridescent scales, huge red wings with gold underneath them, and a long, super powerful tail with fins at the end. Her tongue is bright red and forked. She has lots of sharp teeth, and she has enormous strength and a temper, so she can be dangerous, too. She's got gills so she can breathe underwater, but she breathes in the air, too. The Bakunawa lives deep in the sea but comes to the surface every night to see the moon, which she thinks is beautiful and precious and she longs to touch it or see it up close."

Fred exhaled a body-length sigh, dropped his head onto his paws and closed his eyes.

"Meanwhile in the Philippines, for hundreds of years, people thought there were seven moons. Buwan is a minor god and the boy version of the moon. There aren't a lot of pictures of Buwan so I pictured him looking like me as a kid."

Terrance nodded. "Artistic license. Seems fair," he said.

"Buwan the moon boy heard the most beautiful song one day and was drawn out of the sky and down to the earth to find out where it came from. The sound came from the sea, from the mouths of some gorgeous mermaids—"

Xander chuckled. "That's why you're partial to this version of the leviathan myth—the presence of the gorgeous mermaids," he said.

Buwan's eyes flicked to Charley and back. He laughed. "Busted. So Buwan goes into the sea to swim with the mermaids. He's so busy having fun with them, he doesn't see the Bakunawa swim over to see what all the excitement is about. The Bakunawa, she gets mad and jealous because she thinks Buwan is ignoring her, so she devours the moon boy and causes an eclipse." He motions with his hands as if beating on a drum. "The people bang on pots and pans to scare the Bakunawa into giving the moon back, but she doesn't listen. Finally, Bathala—the creator and ruler of the universe—gets involved and talks sense into the Bakunawa, so she spits out the moon and Buwan goes back into the sky. The end."

"I love it," Sunny gushed. "Folklore explanations are way more interesting than scientific ones."

Xander frowned, lying back on his blanket. "Eh. Personally, I think science is exquisitely captivating in its own right."

"But Bu," Terrance said, "there's a conflict between Buwan and the Bakunawa. Your first name means moon and your last name is the moon eater. Talk about an identity crisis!"

"Yep. You could say I'm destined to self-destruct," he said with a sad smile.

Charley leaned into Bu with a gentle nudge. "Or you could say a myth is a myth, and nothing more. Meanwhile, you have two very interesting names."

He lifted his arm and wrapped it around her, pulling her close and kissing the top of her shiny hair. She pulled back with a look at Xander, while Buwan stared at the tattoos on his right forearm as if he'd never seen them before.

Sunny looked up from the tiny braid they were plaiting from Xander's locks. "Besides Bu, you couldn't possibly have a devil like the Bakunawa inside of you. You're too kind for that."

"Hey, speaking of kind," Bu said, "Charley and Sunny, you guys have got to meet Bertie, the Delgados' housekeeper. She was your nanny too, right Jess?" Jess nodded. "She's awesome! Like a little Guatemalan gnome. In a good way. It must have been sweet having her around when you were growing up, Jess. Not like my babysitter—Angela, the Filipino Antichrist. Did you know there are two kinds of babysitters in the world? Those who like kids and those who don't."

Terrance's eyelids slipped to half-mast. "Has anyone else noticed weed makes Buwan talkative?"

Charley turned to Jess. "Did you like having a nanny?"

"Mm. At first I was mad because I saw my mother less. But Bertie became like my second mother. She got me through some rough times."

The band finished its set, sending a thick hush over the lawn. As if by unspoken agreement, Sunny, Terrance, and Charley reclined, joining Xander. Jess re-applied sunscreen and offered some to Charley who replied, "I'm good. I put on some fifty SPF earlier."

"Jess is afraid of vitamin D," Sunny muttered.

Jess capped her sunscreen tube and lay back, hands behind her head.

Buwan frowned at the group. "Anyone wanna go for a walk?"

"Maybe later," Terrance said from his face-down position on the blanket.

"Well, I'm going," Buwan said, jumping up. Fred rose as well, watching Buwan with bright eyes and wagging tail. "I'll be back in a while."

"Bring more beer," Xander mumbled, reaching out to pull Fred back down beside him and double-checking his grip on the leash as his eyes closed.

***

Buwan picked his way through the throngs of people on the lawn.

"No woman no cry," he bellowed as the classic Bob Marley song burst through the stage speakers. On the stage, roadies broke down the previous band's equipment to make room for the headliner. "No woman no cry." His enthusiastic rendition drew laughs from the people he passed. The lines at the beer tent were twenty-people deep so he cruised over to the shorter lines at the T-shirt stand.

"Ants in his pants," his Mamalay used to say when, as a kid, his excess energy blew out of him, making him run or shout at inappropriate times. Now, he felt ants under his skin everywhere, traveling up and down his arms and legs and encircling his torso, generating heat that made his limbs feel like they were on fire. He studied the dragon tattoo on his left arm, half-expecting the black and gray flames spurting out of the Bakunawa's mouth to turn molten red and orange.

"Dude, you're next." The woman behind him gave him a gentle push.

Samples of long-sleeved jerseys and T-shirts in numerous colors were pinned down to the tables separating buyers from sellers.

"I'll take a medium, long-sleeved one in white, and give me a minute to think about what else I need." The sales guy handed over the shirt and turned to the person beside Buwan. Bu tucked the shirt into the back of his shorts waistband and pretended to peruse the goods on the table, his legs twitching. He took one tentative step back.

"Hey. I know what you're doing," the woman behind him said. He pulled the shirt from his waistband and turned. She was cute—wavy blonde hair and an impish smile. "Go for it. I won't say anything."

His ache for a thrill turned to shame.

"I'm not a thief. Watch." He turned back to the sales guy and ordered five more long-sleeved shirts in various colors.

"Two-hundred-ten," the guy said as Buwan handed over a gold card.

Rather than order her own shirt, the blonde followed Bu out of the line. "I'm Cara."

Once past the press of people in the merchandise line, he stopped and looked at her.

"What are you gonna do with all those shirts?" she asked. Her azure eyes were eager now, the lips she licked a deep rose. Her short shirt exposed a swath of downy skin.

"They're for my friends. I would have bought you one if you wanted."

"Aw, that's really nice. What's your name?"

"Buwan."

She squinted at the unfamiliar sound.

"You can call me Bu."

"Cool. I like it! Bu, who are you here with?"

"Some friends, but they're all taking naps up there." He tilted his chin up toward the rolling lawn. "I've got energy to burn." He didn't dare say how much energy, or that he'd only been sleeping a few hours a night. Or that moments of edgy panic had started forcing their way into the waves of mania-induced creativity and clarity he'd been enjoying. Or that he'd started to roam the city streets at all hours in search of outlets for his energy when painting, pacing his studio, and playing video games didn't do the job.

"I've got tons of energy, too!" Cara said, eyes wide and pupils dilated. "Let's do something crazy. Want some coke?"

Buwan pushed his lower teeth up over his upper lip and thought. "Okay. Or do you have weed?"

"Both. Come on." She clutched his hand and led him to a small, wooded area at the edge of the lawn where a handful of older festivalgoers stayed cool in folding chairs they'd brought from home. Bu and Cara snuck into the trees, stopping behind a wide oak to sit with their backs up against it, bare arms touching, the pile of T-shirts tossed at their feet. After smoking a joint, Cara put her hand on Buwan's crotch and pressed. A premonition of sweet release soothed the ants in Buwan's body as he reached behind her head, pulled her forward and kissed her while pushing her down with his body.

Ten minutes later, she stroked his damp forehead as he lay on his back, eyes closed. "Want some food?"

Buwan rolled his head side to side. His appetite for food had up and left him the past few weeks. "Beer maybe?"

"I'll get it. You stay here." She stroked his forehead one last time and then silence.

Bu opened his eyes to see her disappearing behind a trailer, her arms full of his shirts. "Shit," he said to the empty space around him. A blip of anger welled up behind his eyes but receded when he realized he didn't care about the theft. She probably needed money more than him. And he still felt the lump of his wallet in his shorts' back pocket; she hadn't taken that.

His mania temporarily abated by the tryst, he scrambled up and brushed the pine needles and dirt flecks off his shorts and tan T-shirt. He left the wooded area, ignoring the judgmental stares from some of the old people in lounge chairs and the grins of support from others.

He pushed past the food and drink stands where the sour smell of spilled beer mixed with the aromas of piquant sausage and sweet onions. Back at the merchandise line, he took one look and knew he would lose it waiting in the long line, even in his current state of equilibrium. He inserted himself between people and worked his way to the front of the line, drawing exclamations, cusses and a few sharp elbows.

"Remember me?" he said to the sales guy.

"Yeah, dude, you bought a crapload of T-shirts. Want more?"

"Yup. I'll take ten more." He reeled off his order—choosing colors to fit each friend's personality, charged three-hundred-fifty dollars to his credit card, and moved up the hill bellowing "no woman no cry" against feedback from the stage, where the roadies tested the microphones, guitars, and drums for the next band.

***

Bu was doling out shirts to his surprised friends and explaining his color choices—red for passionate Xander, green for nature-loving Charley, blue for spiritual Sunny, turquoise for dynamic Jess, and yellow, which he said was a logical color through and through, for Terrance—when Terrance interrupted. "Xan, grab Fred," he said sharply. "I don't like the looks of the pit bull coming this way."

Xander jumped to his feet and snagged the leash as Fred growled at a muscular dog dragging a short, round person of questionable gender on its leash. The person gained control and steered the pit bull away. Fred's growl dropped to a barely audible rumble, then disappeared as he turned to Xander, wagging his tail.

"I know it's prejudiced, but pit bulls scare me," Charley said. "How much of their behavior is nature and how much is nurture?"

"Behaviors can most certainly be bred into dogs," Xander said.

Bu nodded and sat beside Terrance, leaning into the group to speak above the noise from the stage. "One of my uncles is awesome with dogs. He has two that are the same breed, but totally different. The female's from a farm and she's a herder. Super gentle. And the male's from a guy who breeds guard dogs and attack dogs. That one goes crazy if he sees a guy in a van or wearing a hat or holding something sketchy that could be a weapon."

Jess chuckled. "Talk about jumping to conclusions."

"The point is, the one from guard dog stock acted way different than the other one, even as a puppy. He wasn't taught it. It was in his blood."

"Or," Xander said, "his genes." His bloodshot eyes brightened. "Bu's stating an important point that relates to oppression and racism."

"Enlighten us," Sunny said.

"When you treat generations the same over time, certain behaviors become natural to them. Innate. When Lyndon Johnson signed the Civil Rights Act in 1964, he said something like we can't expect Black people, or Negroes as they were called then, to suddenly move past generations of prejudice, Jim Crow laws, and general victimization. It would take time for the vestiges of slavery and oppression to dissipate and for Black people to become as successful as Whites."

"Truth," Terrance said with a head nod.

Jess squinted. "Seriously, T? You're fine being compared to dogs?"

"That's not what he's doing. Look past the symbol to the point he's making. Here's another analogy. When a kid grows up in an abusive home, and then finally gets removed from that environment, no one expects the kid to be completely normal right away. It takes time for the psychological wounds to heal and for the kid to become stable, if it even happens at all."

Sunny sat up tall. "And that's damage from one lifetime. Think about repairing the damage inflicted over generations, all while the abuse—institutionalized racism—continues to exist." They stood and stretched as the headliner band took the stage to a roar from the audience. The bassist grabbed the crowd's attention with a throbbing, hard-to-resist, swinging reggae beat. "But we're at a music festival, guys," Sunny said. "The only way we're going to make the world better today is by dancing." They pulled Charley and Jess up from the ground.

Charley took the leash from Xander's hand so Fred could dance with them. He leaped and twirled, making them all laugh.

By the end of the song, the six friends and the majority of the people around them on the lawn moved their bodies to the hypnotic reggae groove, some dancing and some sitting, some animated with emphatic steps and fist thrusts and some mellow with eyes closed and faces turned skyward, some in sync with the rhythm and some not.

CHAPTER 17: EDUCATING CHARLEY

Charley peered out her Mazda's open window but couldn't spot a house number anywhere. All the homes were variations on a theme: slightly taller than wide, two floors plus a smaller third floor nestled by gable roofs, wide clapboards in muted colors with white trim, small open or enclosed porches. She braked, seeing Sunny's silver Prius parked beside a dark greenish-gray house, then reversed and swung into the long driveway.

Sunny threw the front door open as Charley scanned the names under the doorbells. "Charley! Did you find it okay?" They enveloped her in a loose embrace, orange forearm resting against Charley's silky long hair.

Charley held a bakery box out to the side. "Careful, don't crush the cupcakes."

Sunny let go and took the box, round mouth pursed in appreciation. "Ooh, Giovanni's. Perfect. Daddy will be thrilled."

They led Charley through the entryway to a modern kitchen with stainless steel appliances and Shaker-style cabinetry in an unusual, deep teal color.

Sunny's mother—a stocky woman with shoulder-length black hair and a round, deep russet face divided by tortoiseshell-rimmed glasses—smiled from her position at the stove. She stirred something in a pot, sending garlic, cumin, and cinnamon curling through the air.

Sunny's father was a tall, lean man with short black hair, a graying goatee and soul patch, and medium brown skin. He leaned against the fridge, swirling the deep red wine in his stemmed glass.

Charley braced herself for hugs from strangers but both parents offered hands to shake instead, introducing themselves as Fatima and Earl.

"We're having Indian, since you said you love it," Sunny said.

"It smells amazing. Can I help with anything?"

"No, no," Fatima said with a bouncy accent. "It's all ready. Go ahead and sit." She motioned with her wooden spoon toward the eat-in kitchen's table, which sported a teal, navy, and white paisley-patterned tablecloth.

"This seems like a nice neighborhood," Charley offered as they filled their plates with what Fatima identified as green moong dal, chicken dum biryani, and dosas.

"Mama and Daddy picked this area because it's so multi-cultural. We've got every color under the sun here." Sunny laughed. "In kindergarten, I drew a rainbow with black, brown, tan and yellow bands. It wasn't pretty but it was representative."

Fatima nodded. "Being a Brown and Black couple, it was very important to teach our kids about tolerance and prejudice early on. Being in this neighborhood helped."

Charley cleared her throat, surprised at how casually they addressed this sensitive subject.

Sunny picked up their wine glass. "Dealing with prejudice was one of our safety lessons. Over the years, they taught me and my brother and sister how to cross the street, how to use a kitchen knife, how to drive defensively, how to protect your body against an attack, and how to deal with racism—those lessons started in kindergarten."

Charley's eyes widened. "You dealt with racism that young?"

Fatima and Earl shared a knowing glance that embarrassed Charley before Fatima looked back to her. "We don't expect you to know what it's like," she said kindly. "But it could be rough. We had a nightly tradition. During dinner, Earl and I asked the kids to name the best and worst things that happened to them that day.”

Earl gestured with his fork. “That let us keep a handle on what they were experiencing, and it let them get things off their chest instead of letting them fester. Our hope was they wouldn’t internalize the insults and microaggressions, even though that’s a tall order.”

“It must have worked. Sunny is the most well-adjusted person I know,” Charley said, regretting her simplistic analysis when sadness crossed Sunny’s eyes.

“It wasn’t all easy,” Sunny said, playing with their lower lip. “And growing up in two cultures was hard sometimes.”

Earl chuckled, surprising Charley. “We have a delicate balance of Indian and African-American heritage symbols around the house.” He looked at his wife. “Both sets of our parents worried that their culture was being lost on our kids.” Charley noticed that Earl’s deep rolling voice was an older, male version of Sunny’s thick, warm voice.

Fatima smirked. “We have photos of Martin Luther King, Jr. and Gandhi on the mantle. When my parents come, we put Gandhi in the middle. When Earl’s parents come, we put MLK in the middle.”

All three Winstons laughed heartily.

Fatima reached behind her glasses to scratch near her eye. “I don’t know why people can’t celebrate our cultural differences, and our different races, instead of mocking them or using them as weapons.” Her pained look made Charley think she spoke from personal experience. “When you combine many ingredients in a recipe, each one contributes to the flavor. Picture every race as a vegetable, and you put them all in a soup. Each vegetable retains its identity, but the total is so much more than the individual flavors. That’s how we should view America.”

She stood and retrieved the bakery box from the counter. “Anyway, time for those gorgeous cupcakes Charley brought.”

“Oh my, my,” Earl muttered when Fatima opened the box to reveal a rainbow of frostings. “Cupcakes aren’t as straightforward as in the old days. It used to be just chocolate and vanilla.”

"Just like people!" Sunny said with glee. Charley shook her head, amazed at the return to uncomfortable topics. "Lots of new flavors, and each one different, but equally delicious."

When the cupcakes were reduced to a pile of crumbs, Sunny surprised Charley by suggesting it was time to call it a night. Charley could have stayed in the comfort of the Winston home for hours more.

"Mama, you'll see Charley again at the Women's March on Saturday, right?"

Fatima squirmed in her seat. "*Noori*, I told you before, I am not a protestor."

Earl watched his wife's discomfort with amusement. "*Maahru*, we can't teach our children to stand up against injustice if we're not willing to do it ourselves."

Fatima threw an annoyed look his way. "I'm too old for protesting. I don't have to be there to support the cause. I can donate more money, okay? Plus, women's rights are fairly well established." She trailed off.

"As a husband and father, I beg to differ," he said, his brown eyes serious. "Women's rights are always at risk. I'll be there."

"Of course you'll be there. You're a cop. It's not the same thing," Fatima said.

"But if I weren't working, I would go and march."

Fatima's eyebrows shot up, then lowered to scowl level. "I'll think about it." She stood up to end the conversation.

On the way out, Fatima gave Charley a hug and said, "Visit us again soon."

Earl hugged her gently and quickly, his tall, wide frame reminding Charley of her grandfather. "Be safe."

Charley followed Sunny, who toted a lumpy, plastic shopping bag toward the back door. In the mudroom, Charley stopped to study three childish paintings, framed and hung in a row. "Sunny," "Dash," and "Dharma" were written in neat adult penmanship in the lower right corners.

"Dash and Dharma are my sibs," Sunny explained. "Mama insists on keeping up some of our elementary school artwork. But I guess all parents do that."

"No, they don't," Charley said, unable to remember a single piece of childhood art being displayed in her home, not even temporarily on the fridge. "My mom wasn't into impractical things. One time, I gave her a little vase because I thought it was pretty. When she opened it, she said, 'Oh, good. Something else to collect dust.'"

Sunny's nose twitched. "Some people don't like frilly things."

Charley moved toward the door. "I used to think my dad was unromantic because he gave Mom appliances every Christmas. Then I realized that's what she wanted." She followed Sunny into a tiny backyard.

"Let me just dump this compost," Sunny said, emptying the contents of the bag into a large wooden container and tucking the bag behind the screen door. "I brought my food scraps here since Bu doesn't compost. Is that weird?"

Charley giggled. "Most people bring laundry when they visit their parents, but for you, Sunny, no—that's not weird." Sunny didn't smile. "I mean that in a good way. I say it with love," Charley added, afraid she'd hurt Sunny's feelings. Sunny smiled as if caught in an illicit act and started down the narrow path alongside the driveway.

"Let's sit a minute before you go," they said, walking to the front steps. They reclined in the waning sun. "Do you have any brothers or sisters?"

"No. Mom couldn't have any more after me." Charley's voice caught. She stared at her hands in her lap and picked at a hangnail.

"I know I hug people too much, but can I hug you?" Sunny asked, their velvet voice unnaturally high. Charley nodded. She stiffened under the long embrace but eventually gave in and relaxed.

As Sunny let go to sit back, a strand of Charley's long hair snagged one of the tiny gold hoops on their ear.

"Wait—I'll get it," Charley said. She moved her head back as far as possible and ran her fingers along the strand of hair until it hit Sunny's helix. She teased the hair out of the earring bit by bit. "There. I hope that didn't hurt. You're free now."

***

Her normal evening routine disrupted by dinner with the Winstons, Charley poured herself a glass of wine at home, even though it wasn't an official wine night.

She also broke routine by picking up the photo of her grandparents, blowing dust off the top of the frame, and re-familiarizing herself with the lines of their faces. She wished she felt Gram and Gramps watching over her, but she felt nothing. For seven years, they'd been her stand-in parents, and those were the best years of her life. Slender, angular Gram was infinitely practical but also soft and loving. Yes, Charley had to do her chores or homework first, without fail, but often there'd be freshly baked chocolate-chip cookies at the end. And always a hug. Gramps loomed over Edith and Charley but with a gentle manner designed to offset the intimidation factor of his six-two height and broad frame. Charley never figured out how this sensitive, affectionate couple produced Jane, Charley's mother. Jane had twice the angles and twice the practicality of Edith, and not a hint of the softness. Charley's parents had applauded her achievements and attended some of her school events, but Charley hadn't truly known familial love until she moved in with her grandparents.

Before tonight, she'd never thought about parenting styles. Dinner with Earl and Fatima felt like a master class in how to raise children. But it was pointless and selfish to want what she didn't have, when what she did have got the job done. And despite the story she'd told Sunny about her mother mocking the small vase, Jane apparently had treasured another of her daughter's gifts, although Charley didn't discover this until after she died.

The dean of the college where Charley's parents taught asked her to visit him. Fifteen and awkwardly shy, numbness from her parents' deaths cloaked the anxiety she would have felt had the circumstances been different.

"Miss Byrne—may I call you Charlotte?" Dean Stanwick had asked. Charley nodded, unable to summon the energy to explain no one called her Charlotte anymore. "On behalf of everyone at the university—professors, staff and students—I offer my condolences about the—the situation."

He focused his watery, wrinkly eyes on her. His saggy cheeks quivered.

Charley cleared her throat. Twice. "Thank you," she muttered.

"I understand you'll be moving away to live with your grandparents. But I imagine you'll want to attend college when the time comes, given that Jane and Eamon are—I apologize, were—both academics." His eyebrows drew inward and he looked down momentarily. "Tuition to our fine establishment is free for children of faculty and staff. I proposed to the board of trustees, and they approved unanimously, that we extend that offer to you *ad infinitum*. It pains us to know the trip to South America was taken in part so Jane could attend the economics conference on behalf of the college. You are welcome to matriculate here, at any point in your adult life, free of charge."

He waited for a reaction. In the back of her mind, Charley knew she wasn't being responsive enough. She nodded and croaked "thank you" again.

"Right, then." Dean Stanwick stood and brushed his hands together, as if he'd started to clap before realizing the inappropriateness of the gesture. "Would you like to see Eamon's and Jane's offices? You're welcome to take any of their personal things with you. Here's a box to get you started, and we have more if you need them."

Charley stood. Charley followed. Charley nodded when he pointed out Eamon's office down the hall before leaving her in Jane's office. He promised to return in twenty minutes should she need assistance transporting anything to the car that, driven by a TA, would take her back home—the home she had four days to vacate to make room for one of the replacement professors and his or her family.

Charley rotated herself around three times as if on a spit, attempting to distinguish her mother's personal belongings from the college's. Selecting mementos by which to remember the two people who created her began to feel like a fool's errand. What could possibly encapsulate fifteen years of family life, such as it was, or a collection of memories already feeling slippery and elusive?

She walked the perimeter of the small office, her eyes grazing the tall, dusty windows and the dark woodwork. Stepping behind her mother's desk, she saw it. There, on a low knob on a tall cabinet behind the desk, hung the small decorative pillow she'd bought at a silly holiday fair and given to her mother the Christmas of fifth grade. *I Love Mom* and a border of vines and flowers were stitched into blue velveteen. Twisted rope cord outlined the rectangular pillow and looped loosely at the top for hanging. Charley's eyes searched the office for other sentimental items but found none. The pillow was the sole impractical item.

When the pillow disappeared from the house soon after Christmas, Charley assumed she'd made a mistake in choosing another dust-collecting, useless present. But here it hung. Hidden from the view of office visitors, but in plain view of her mother on a daily basis.

Charley unhooked the small pillow from the drawer pull, held it in both hands and caressed the stitching with her thumbs. She pressed it against her nose and breathed in the light but recognizable smell of the sandalwood soap her parents shared. She put the pillow to rest in the box provided by Dean Stanwick and padded down the hall to the door marked *Prof. Byrne, English Dept.*

Charley collected two photos from her dad's desk: one of Jane holding Charley in the hospital the day she was born, and one of the three of them at a country fair—Charley, age six, perched on a pony, her parents flanking her on each side, smiles tentative. She placed the photos in the box on the desk, next to the *I Love Mom* pillow, and walked to the first large bookcase. Unlike a good daughter, she had no clue which novels, memoirs, or anthologies were her dad's favorites. Except *The Canterbury Tales*, which she knew he loved teaching, in part—he would say—because its variety of narrative forms and mixture of bawdy and spiritual concerns so confounded the students. She extracted the old book with gold lettering on faded blue cloth from its slot on the shelf and placed it on the scarred wood floor. She turned back and, with a sudden need to be done, pulled a dozen or so hardcover books from random locations in the bookcase as if filling a shopping bag for five dollars at a flea market or church sale.

Breathing heavily after her flurry, she stacked the books in the box. When done, she turned to see the round-shouldered Dean Stanwick in the doorway. He approached and peered into the box.

"Don't you want more than that?"

Charley shook her head. "This is all I can carry right now," she'd replied before walking out of her father's office and her parents' workplace for the final time.

Charley poured another glass of wine, swallowed half of it in one go, and pictured the pillow and the photos and the books lying fallow, still in the same box, stuffed in the back of her closet. How much dust had that box gathered since Charley packed it all those years ago? The only reason it hadn't gone up in flames with Gram's house was because Gram insisted Charley take the mementos to college with her. "You mustn't forget them," she'd said. Gram didn't know Charley never unpacked the box in any of her four years away.

Baggage purred and rubbed his ribs against the kitchen table leg. Charley watched the cat slink between the table leg and Charley's own leg, leaning into the former, avoiding the latter.

She went to the bedroom and collapsed onto the bed. She scratched the insides of her arms, watching, satisfied, as a web of red trails crisscrossed the soft skin. When one raised trail threatened to bleed, she stopped and stared. She rubbed her arms as if erasing her actions. She tore off her shoes. The eczema was healing. She had to dig and scrape with ferocity to draw forth two startlingly red droplets and piercing relief.

PART 4:
ACTING UP

CHAPTER 18: SECRETS

"I feel so decadent. Going to dinner and a movie on a weeknight," Jess said to Terrance as they strode through the city's tourist district, caressed by the early evening sun and a smooth summery breeze. Terrance stopped and used his thumb and forefinger to lift a water bottle from a sidewalk trash can and place it in the adjacent recycling bin. He laughed when Jess wrinkled her nose in distaste and smiled in approval at the same time. "But let's try to catch the seven o'clock movie, so we're not up too late."

Terrance's smirk quickly turned into a self-deprecating smile. "I can't even give you shit for how lame that sounded because I feel the same. In fact, we could skip the movie and go straight to dinner. Then we can be home in bed at a reasonable hour."

Jess raised an eyebrow, making Terrance realize the unintended innuendo of his words. He cleared his throat and shifted direction away from the cinema.

Twenty minutes later, she raised her martini at a small seafood restaurant favored by locals because its dull, weathered gray exterior and location off the beaten path kept the tourists at bay. "Cheers, T. To your new job," she said over the animated chatter of the other diners.

"To my new job."

"What did your boss say when you quit?"

Terrance shrugged. "She seemed disappointed but understood the opportunity. I swore her to silence until I can tell Xander."

"I'm surprised you didn't do that first."

Terrance's eyebrows flicked up. The idea of telling a friend before his boss was a breach of protocol he'd never considered. "I'll tell him at work tomorrow. Or at the march on Saturday." He sipped his drink without taking his eyes off her. "How's it going with your secret?"

Jess's shoulder twitched. "I finished my detailed analysis of the three properties that made the cut. I hate to say it, but the bookstore has the best numbers. Mainly because that area is kind of rundown so we can buy it cheaper than the other two buildings, which are in prime downtown territory. The CFO is looking at the proposals now."

Terrance studied her. "Thought any more about telling Charley?"

Jess swirled the liquid in her glass. "Don't you think our plan still makes sense? Don't say anything unless the deal actually goes through?"

"Just remember it would suck for her to hear it from someone else."

Jess leaned in. "So, I have to let you in on another secret. I'm not going to the Women's March this weekend. Are you definitely going?"

"Yeah, I'm marching for my sister and my mother."

Jess ran her finger around the edge of her martini glass.

"Why aren't you going?"

"I just—I've been extra busy at work because of this special project, which is over and above my regular work. That cuts into my time to get my personal errands done. I know Xander will give me a hard time, but I can't support every cause all the time."

Terrance tilted his head. "No need to get defensive. I get it. My interest in marching and chanting isn't that high either. Sometimes I doubt sixty seconds of TV coverage changes anything. I'd rather help change things in other ways."

"Like what?"

"I don't know. Volunteering, maybe. And to be honest, Xander's constant harping on me to get more involved in Black Lives Matter is offensive sometimes. He has no idea what's right for me to do."

Jess leaned back as the waiter placed steaming dinner plates before them. "One fish stew and one fried clams," he announced.

Jess nodded at Terrance. "I feel the same way every time he bugs me to get more involved in women's issues. But I've known him long enough to know this: he doesn't pressure me because of my gender or you because of your race. He pressures everyone to be more involved in everything, all the time. All causes and all people are the same to him."

"Hmph. I try to tell myself that, but sometimes it still rankles." He peered at his plate and sighed. He picked up a batter-coated clam with his fingers and dangled it before Jess. "Anyway, this place has the best fried clams in town. Taste?"

Jess inhaled the thick odor of fried food while spreading her napkin across her lap. "My pores and my arteries are clogging just looking at that. But what the hell. No one can say Jessica Delgado doesn't know how to live dangerously." She opened her mouth and accepted the offering. "Mmm," she said while chewing. "Okay, that was worth it."

Terrance grinned, licked the grease from his fingers and wiped his fingers on his napkin. His phone wiggled and vibrated on the table. He looked at the screen. "I've got to take this. It's the new boss."

Jess shooed him away from the table, watching him go.

***

"Georgina O'Hanlan? This is Marty Murkowski, lead counsel for All-American Development & Construction. How are you this fine day?"

"I was starting to think you weren't interested. It's been ages since your girl came in." Her raspy voice squawking through the phone made Marty's teeth hurt. "I've got other offers, you know."

He emitted a puff of annoyance and impatience. "We're prepared to make you a generous offer for your property. We have concerns, however. For example, the general state of the building—various systems need updating, and the location isn't prime for the city, of course."

Georgina chuckled. "Cut to the chase. This is prime real estate and if I don't like your offer, I'll go elsewhere."

Marty sincerely doubted she had other suitors. He smiled ingratiatingly into the phone. "I see you're a tough negotiator, Ms. O'Hanlan. Let me tell you what we're prepared to offer." He spoke a number into the phone and when Georgina did not answer, he repeated it.

"Hmph. I'll need to think about it," she grumbled.

Marty hung up and chuckled. He returned his fountain pen—decorative only because writing with those damn things was impossible—to its desktop holder. *Like shooting ducks in a pond*, he thought. He had her. He knew it. And for a lowball price bound to increase his stock with Liam. He hadn't even needed to go see her in person.

Marty inspected his manicured fingernails. One or two more of these quick-hit wins and Stone Circle would be but a footnote in All-American's annual report.

***

When Buwan barged out of his bedroom holding a fluffy gray towel around his lower half, he had no idea the most shameful and painful episode of his childhood was about to be laid bare.

Charley and Sunny stood chatting near the loft's main door. The chatter stopped the second they saw him. Their jaws dropped.

The towel slipped from Bu's grasp and floated to the floor.

His friends' eyes remained fixed on his torso.

Bu stared to the side, toward the kitchen. "Didn't—I—I thought you went to a yoga class."

"I ran into Charley on my way out," Sunny said woodenly, as if hypnotized, "and decided I'd rather come back and visit with you guys. I can go to a class tonight."

Charley averted her eyes. "Bu, you dropped your towel," she said in a hushed voice.

Sunny took a hesitant step toward Buwan. He scooped up the towel from the floor and fled to the bedroom in one movement.

***

They staggered to Bu's L-shaped burnt-orange couch and sank down, tears filling Charley's green eyes and Sunny's chocolate brown ones.

"What do we do?" Sunny whispered.

Charley struggled for the answer. "I'll ask." She walked to his door and knocked. "Bu, should we go? Or stay? And maybe talk?" She squeezed her eyes shut at her own suggestion. Knowing a bit about his mental health did not qualify her to play therapist.

"Stay," Bu said, the door muffling his voice. "I'll be out in a minute."

Sunny gave a strangled sob. Charley went to them and shook her head.

"Don't cry. We have to be strong."

Sunny nodded and wiped away a tear before it spilled over onto their cheek.

Bu bounded into the room wearing off-white painter pants and a brown T-shirt. "Hey, you guys." He plopped into a chair facing them. "So, what's up?"

Sunny stared at the coffee table. Charley pulled a hardcover children's book from her bag and handed it to him. She forced a smile. "I brought you a present. It took a while, but I found a book on Filipino myths and legends with the Bakunawa in it." Bu flipped rapidly through the pages. "Do you like it?"

"I love it. What's the occasion though?"

"None," Charley said, knowing that in her mind, the gift of the book would forever be associated with the day she saw Bu's naked chest.

Sunny and Charley traded unsure looks and waited.

Buwan fiddled with the tool loop on the side seam of his pants.

Charley cleared her throat. "So, Bu. Will you tell us what happened?"

His eyes flitted to hers and away again. "You mean the scars?"

"Yes."

His eyes rested on Charley. "On one condition." Charley nodded. "We have drinks while we do it."

Charley tossed her day's scheduled routine to the wind. "Of course."

"Great idea."

"Better make it a pitcher."

They pulled the vodka, gin, rum, and tequila from Buwan's cabinet and OJ, Coke, and lemons from the fridge, and mixed Long Island iced teas. They bustled about and joked as they worked, as if convincing themselves everything was normal.

"Mm, perfect," Sunny said, taking a sip as they resettled in the living room, the pitcher on the coffee table.

Buwan drained half his tall drink and leaned forward, clutching the glass with both hands. "Okay. So I guess after seeing that, you deserve to know what happened."

"No, Bu," Charley said, "you don't *have* to tell us. Only if you want to."

Buwan forged on. "I've told this to three therapists in my life, and it gets easier every time. In a way, it feels good to tell people. You'll be the first friends I've told." He paused for another hearty drink. "Sunny knows what it's like to grow up with skin that makes you feel different. Right, Sun?"

Sunny raised their glass in grim acknowledgement.

Charley frowned, unclear where he was going with this.

"The first time I knew I was different," Bu continued, "was at my fifth birthday party. My moms tried to make me feel normal growing up, even though everyone else in my family was female and had white skin. They invited Black and Brown kids over all the time, even before I went to school.

"So anyway, the party. This lady looks at me standing between my moms and says, 'It's like you and Layla are Wonder Bread and Buwan is your Nutella!' The friend points at Mom's pregnant belly and says, 'Will the next one be Nutella, white bread, or something else, do you think?'"

Sunny stirred ice cubes around their glass with a metal straw. "People are so clueless."

Buwan shrugged. "I probably only remember that because I loved Nutella. That night, I looked in the mirror and saw how different I was. I started to think my dark skin was bad."

"Oh, Bu! Didn't your parents tell you it wasn't?" Sunny asked.

Bu frowned. "They couldn't change the cartoons where the bad guys always wear black. They couldn't stop people from saying stuff when my moms, my sister, and I were out together."

"What did they say?" Charley asked.

"Things like, 'Oh, did you adopt him and then conceive your own child?' and 'How dark does he get in the summer?' I started turning all the comments into negatives, even if the person didn't mean it that way. Then I decided my moms would love me more if I was White like them. Maybe that's why they called me Moon Boy, I thought, because the moon is white and white is good."

Sunny grimaced. "Did it get worse when you went to school?" they asked, in a tone suggesting they knew the answer.

"The girls in elementary school used to giggle and ask where I was from. They'd guess Mexico or Puerto Rico. 'I'm from here,' I'd say. They'd say I couldn't be. 'Not with that funny name. And you're dark.'"

He stopped abruptly, re-filled his glass and sat back, his eyes unfocused.

"But clueless girls weren't the problem. Angela is the devil in my story."

***

When Bu was seven years old and his sister Carrie was two, Layla went back to work as a computer programmer. She and Anne were so excited to find a Filipino woman in the next borough to watch the kids after school. Angela had lived in the Philippines most of her life and had skin almost as dark as Buwan's. Her pageboy haircut and bangs and high, round cheeks, suggested an air of youth and cheerfulness completely at odds with her tired and cranky, passive-aggressive nature. But she was a very good actor, and her true nature only revealed itself when she chose.

Unbeknownst to Anne and Layla, Angela taught Buwan his skin color was ugly, dirty, and bad. His immature brain translated that into him being ugly, dirty and bad.

"You're too dark. Spend less time in the sun," she'd say, forcing him inside the house while she and Carrie stayed out in the sunshine and fresh air. "It's a good thing you're in America because in the Philippines, the girls only like light-skinned boys. Here, you have a chance. But no point making it worse than it is."

The more he thought about it, the more he hated his dark skin and the more he thought his mothers did, too. They constantly discussed how sensitive Carrie's fair skin was, their concern reinforcing his belief that white was more valuable. They made him wear white shirts in family photos, saying he looked so handsome in white. It became clear to him. They were embarrassed by his brown skin and wished he were White like the rest of the family.

Meanwhile, his brain synapses started doing cartwheels and jumping jacks, at the mercy of a chemical imbalance that revealed itself through temper tantrums at home and frustration-induced angry outbursts at school. His teacher—the same one who said, "Aren't you lucky, being adopted and living here?" on his first day of second grade—threw her hands up after a particularly bad outburst, asking what happened to the well-behaved, eager boy who'd started out the school year. Her disdain fed his increasingly loathsome self-image.

By the time he was eight-and-a-half, Buwan made a decision. If dark skin was bad and white skin was good, he would make his skin white.

Angela said once that dark Filipinos used bleaching products to lighten their skin. One night when he was supposed to be doing homework, he researched how to get some online. He quickly realized he couldn't buy anything on his own and he couldn't ask Angela to help—she'd laugh and say he deserved to be dark, or it wasn't worth the effort or something equally disheartening.

The next night, when his moms were watching a Disney movie with Carrie, he said he wanted to read in his room. Instead, he snuck into the basement laundry room and lugged a gallon bottle of bleach to the utility sink. He plugged the stopper in the drain and watched the lemon-lime-tinted liquid flow into the sink with giant glugs.

Bu scanned the laundry room, found a clean white washcloth with little purple flowers on it, and removed his shirt. He smiled to the sink full of salvation. He dropped the washcloth into the bleach and squeezed out some of the excess, the harsh smell making his eyes and nose tingle. He laid the washcloth over his chest and patted it. A loose stream escaped and trickled coolly down his chest to be absorbed by his waistband. He removed the washcloth and checked his chest. No change. He dipped the washcloth again and rubbed it forcefully over his chest, as if scrubbing away the brown skin. The resulting sting assured him it was working. He repeated the process three times, covering his torso from the neckline to his pants. He laughed, picturing a whiter body with the private parts still dark. Maybe he should bleach down there too.

He scrubbed a few more rounds on his chest and stomach and moved to his arms. By the time he completed the third coat on his arms, his chest stung harshly, which he accepted as the price of attaining purity. His resolve weakened, though, when he peered down at his fiery red skin. Welts were rising. The pain made his head swim and his stomach turn somersaults.

"I am the Moon Boy, and Bakunawa has breathed her dragon flames on me," he said, trying to convince himself he could stand the burn. But when the pain intensified to an unbearable level, he gave up and turned on the water in the utility sink, thrusting his arms under the stream. He tried to splash water onto his chest but found he couldn't bend his torso over the sink. His head felt fuzzy. He clutched the edge of the utility sink, fighting dizziness, until he could walk.

He hobbled up the stairs into the living room and stood behind the couch, only the tops of his parents' heads visible.

"Mom," he said faintly.

Anne's head spun around, drawn by the strong smell of bleach before he even said her name. "Jesus, Mary, and Joseph! What happened, Buwan? Tell me what happened!" She flew to his side and inhaled. "Is that bleach? Did you spill bleach on yourself?"

His face had paled two shades. On his chest and stomach, patches of violent red, putrid pink, and sickly white obliterated his normally golden bronze skin. Heartless blisters practically formed while Anne stared. She reached for the back of the couch to steady herself.

"Water. Buwan, come with me now!" Layla commanded. "Anne, call 9-1-1."

Layla scooped up her son, heedless of any bleach contacting her skin. She set him in the bathtub, pants and all, and turned on the water, detaching the showerhead nozzle from its hook for better control. She applied the cool stream to his red chest. Buwan screamed, making Layla shiver.

"It hurts, Mamalay, it hurts," he sobbed.

Layla adjusted the stream to a gentler setting and flicked moisture off the lens of her glasses. "I'm sorry, Moon Boy, I'm sorry, but we have to get the bleach off before it does more damage." She watched, aghast, as the water stream bounced off the unyielding blisters on her son's skin, as if the blisters were winning a battle of the wills.

Anne rushed into the bathroom, eyes wild, cell phone in hand. "Cool water and mild soap," she yelled. "For twenty minutes."

"What else did they say?" Layla asked. Anne caught the unspoken question: *Will he be all right?*

Anne's shoulders rose and fell slowly in a weary shrug. "The dispatcher said to flush it with cool water and mild soap for at least twenty minutes," she repeated. "An ambulance is coming," she said loudly as Bu's cries ramped up again.

"Should we drive him ourselves? It might be faster."

"No, they said the water is more important right now. Do you want me to take over?"

Layla nodded, her usually stoic stomach writhing. She handed the shower nozzle to her wife and kneeled beside the tub.

Anne avoided looking directly at Buwan's enraged skin, focusing instead on the tile wall behind him as she alternated spraying and soaping his skin. His screams died down to long, slow, heavy sobs as he shivered and burned at the same time.

"Don't!" Layla cried as he raised a fist to wipe his eye. "Don't touch anything, Bu!"

Stung by her reprimand, he closed his eyes and let the lids squeeze out more tears.

"Why, Bu?" Layla asked in a tortured voice. "Did someone dare you? Was it like when you jumped out of that tree because Josh dared you?"

Bu's lower lip trembled like a toddler's before they dissolve into an ear-splitting wail. He hurt too much to think up any answer beyond the truth. "I want to be White like you."

The showerhead stopped moving in Anne's hand. Layla's mouth hung open until accumulating saliva made her close it. Even worse than the words, even worse than the damage on his body, was the pleading, heart-stopping look in his eyes that declared he still craved white skin, even now.

Anne began moving the showerhead again, mechanically. "But Buwan, you have such beautiful skin. We love you just the way you are."

"Keep washing," Layla said with bitterness. "We'll wash the Filipino right off of him, if that's what he wants," she said.

Anne glared at Layla but softened at the immense sadness on her wife's face. This was new territory for them all. She turned to Bu, keeping her eyes on his still-beautiful face. "Mamalay's not mad at you, Bu. She's just mad that this happened. But we're not mad at you."

Layla clutched the wavy hair on top of her head and pulled. "No, sweetie, of course I'm not mad at you. I love you so much." She stood. "I better check on Carrie," she said, leaving the bathroom.

By the time the ambulance arrived, Buwan's skin looked worse, not better. Quarter-sized blisters exploded from his mottled chest. His arms were blister-free and less inflamed than his torso; the color of the burned brown skin there resembled dried blood.

The paramedics calmly rushed in with a stretcher. "What happened, little man?" asked the male paramedic. "Tell José."

Anne and Layla exchanged guilty looks, wondering for the first time if they might be accused of negligence.

"I got some bleach on my skin," Buwan said, his voice faint, his sobs slowed to occasional hiccups.

José scanned Bu's skin and nodded. "Okay, well we're going to fix you up. I hope you weren't trying to lighten your skin or anything stupid like that. 'Cause us beautiful Brown boys, we need to stick together and be proud of our skin. When you get to be my age, you'll learn that the girls love us Brown boys," he said with a wink.

Bu's bloodshot eyes widened and he looked quickly at Anne to see if she'd picked up on this man-to-man discussion.

"Can you stand up?" José asked after confirming how long the parents had flushed his skin. Bu obliged, screaming as the movement sent stabs of pain through his chest and fresh tears to his eyes. "That's it, little man. I'm going to lift you up and put you on this cool traveling bed, okay?"

Bu nodded.

"And pain is good, in this case. Remember that. Pain is good."

Bu blinked at the man, unable to make sense of what he said.

Anne climbed into the back of the ambulance with Bu and José, the empty bleach bottle in her hand per the paramedic's request. Layla and Carrie followed in the car.

As the ambulance careened through the streets, José cut off the boy's soaking-wet pants, underwear and socks. He checked the boy's vitals, apologizing in advance for causing additional pain, and started an IV. He tore open multiple packages of white dressings and wet one with sterile water from a jug.

"I'm going to wrap you up in these white bandages. You know what a mummy is? Like for Halloween?"

Bu nodded.

"When I'm done, you're going to look like a mummy. How cool is that?"

Bu's eyelids drooped.

José gently wound the wet sterile dressing around Buwan's arm, then another, and then another, until his arms were encased in white. Anne held her son in a sitting position while José wrapped the torso.

"Almost there," he said, looking at his watch.

Anne nodded and squeezed Bu's foot, her chest tightening and throbbing as if experiencing the burn of bleach on her own vulnerable skin.

***

"Later, when I was feeling better, I was mad that Mom didn't take a picture of me with all those bandages on me like a mummy. But after that day, they didn't do anything that might make me feel like white is better than dark."

He laughed, but Charley and Sunny didn't respond. Both were picturing the jumble of pink bumps and raised white lines they'd seen desecrating Buwan's chest and stomach, the cords of scar tissue layered at arbitrary angles against a backdrop of damaged skin more pink than brown. Charley's first thought upon seeing his scars had been house fire; Sunny's had been racial attack. Knowing Buwan did this to himself increased the tragedy tenfold.

"How long did it take you to get better?" Charley finally asked quietly. "You know, for the burns to heal."

"I don't know. I was in the hospital and out of school for a while."

"Something like that has to give you some PTSD," Sunny murmured, reminding Charley they weren't aware of Bu's bipolar disorder.

"Yeah, my parents put me in therapy after that. The therapist said I had ADHD because that comes with non-suicidal self-injury sometimes," he related in a clinical tone. "But I wasn't trying to hurt myself. I was trying to make myself better."

"But—you never tried again, right? Were you okay with your skin color after that?" Charley asked.

"Yeah, I guess," he said, shaking his head. "No, if I'm being honest, my dark skin still bugged me—but I learned my lesson." He sat back in his chair and placed his feet on an ottoman. "It helped when I realized lots of girls in sixth grade wanted skin my color. They'd spend hours tanning to get bronzed like me. And then I got popular in high school 'cause I was good at sports." He grinned like he'd won the lottery, neglecting to mention he took major ribbing for never removing his shirt in the locker room, not even to shower after a game.

Sunny unwound their legs, rose and approached him. "Hugs," they requested.

Bu stood and embraced Sunny. Charley joined them.

"Nothing heals like a cuddle puddle," Sunny cooed.

Sunny released a minute later and left the other two hugging, Bu hanging onto Charley like a lifeline, his face burrowing into her hair.

CHAPTER 19: EVERY BODY COUNTS

Xander woke with his promise to the world's disenfranchised populations echoing in his head: *Today, I will make a difference. Today, I will do my part and demand change and equality.*

His participation in the afternoon's march and rally was mandatory in his mind. The more individuals who turned out, the greater the mass and the more powerful the impact.

Every body counts had been his mantra since attending his first protest at age sixteen. His social studies teacher had taken a small group of students to Washington, D.C. for a protest challenging a bill that would classify undocumented immigrants and those who helped them as felons. As he chanted with the other protestors, something fresh and meaningful stirred in him. The awkwardness and insults that defined high school melted away, replaced by the passion and courage required to demand change and the confidence required to think you can make a difference. Gone for the moment was the angst attached to his bisexuality and the imagined reaction from his father if he ever dared to come out, pushed aside by a keen worldview and more holistic sense of purpose.

The bug got hold of him and never let go.

He arose, stretched his wiry arms to the ceiling, ran a hand through his unruly dirty blonde curls, and combed his short brown beard with his fingers. The familiar buzz he lovingly called protest fever began to surge in his veins. He grabbed his shorts and headed to the bathroom.

***

"Come on. Let's stake out our position," Xander yelled over a squawking bullhorn that issued unintelligible instructions to the throngs gathering for the Women's March. He plunged into the mass of bodies, Terrance, Sunny, Charley, and Buwan trailing closely behind.

People of all genders, ages, and races milled around the block cordoned off for the march's assembly point. The crowd sparkled in every possible color with a predominance of bright pink pussy hats, continuing the trend that took off in 2017. Parents hoisted kids onto their shoulders for a better look and removed them when their shoulders tired, like a human version of whack-a-mole. Music and the odors of kebab and freshly baked pretzels wafted on a breeze. Near Charley and Terrance, a frail-looking, silver-haired couple perused all the people and leaned into each other. Charley gasped to see the woman's hand resting on a cane, but the woman caught Charley's eye, smiled, and nodded.

A boisterous man pushed past Charley, knocking her off balance.

Terrance squeezed her shoulder. "We can do this, right? Then maybe Xander will get off our backs." He grinned, his brown eyes warm and reassuring.

Charley returned the grin as if she, too, wanted Xander off her back.

Terrance looked over Charley's shoulder and groaned. "Lord help us, someone's got a megaphone and it's coming this way."

"Equal rights now! Equal rights now!" yelled a large woman into the megaphone. The people nearest her joined in. Sunny chanted with a beatific smile and Xander and Buwan punched the air while chanting. "Pass it on!" the woman yelled before handing the megaphone to an upraised pair of hands which passed it to another set of hands.

When the megaphone reached the vicinity of their group, Buwan pushed his way past two people and lunged up, wresting the megaphone away like an overeager bridesmaid claiming the bouquet.

"Aaaaarrrrgh," Buwan screamed into the megaphone, causing people to cover their ears.

Xander, laughing, took the megaphone from Buwan. "Why are we assembled here today?" he projected across the crowd. The closest protestors turned to listen. "Are we here for justice?"

People responded with a jubilant cheer.

"I have a wish," he said with a wink at his friends. "It goes like this. *Make your voices heard. Embody change together. More strength in numbers.* What do you think?"

The crowd cheered again.

Terrance scratched his head. "Wait, was that a—"

"A haiku! Yes!" said Sunny.

The friends roared with laughter.

"Make your voices heard!" Xander said again.

"Make your voices heard!" the crowd repeated. Sunny and Bu shouted their replies. Terrance and Charley looked at each other and tentatively mouthed the words.

"Embody change together!" Xander directed.

"Embody change together!" people yelled, some messing up the first word.

"More strength in numbers!"

"More strength in numbers!"

Xander passed on the megaphone when he sensed bodies moving forward. The Women's March had begun.

It started with a series of stutters as people tried to find the right spacing and pace, but soon settled into a rhythm. The five friends, side by side, took up half a row as the march journeyed down the wide streets leading downtown.

"When did you make your signs?" Charley asked Bu and Sunny.

"Last night," Bu said. "You like?" He turned the wooden post so Charley could read the bold black letters on the fluorescent green poster board, which read: *Women Are The Majority.*

"And mine?" Sunny turned their magenta poster board toward Charley and Terrance. *Our Bodies, Our Minds, Our Power* it read, with a clenched fist. "Bu drew the fist for me."

Before anyone answered, a chant rippled through the marchers, gaining volume as it progressed through the rows. "What do we want? Equality. When do we want it? Now." Sunny, Buwan, and Xander immediately added their voices to the cry. The chant matched up with the marchers' steps, each left and right beating out the words like a military cadence.

Terrance tested the words in his mouth. When the chant started a new round, he spoke the words in sync with the others.

Charley watched her footfalls and tentatively said the words in time, her spoken voice somehow louder to her ears than all the chanters put together. She lifted her head and saw marchers smiling and laughing, others shouting, faces determined. A sudden desire to be one with them erased any self-consciousness. Her singularity melted away as she raised her voice and blended in with the others in word, step, and spirit.

Sunny grabbed Bu's arm to interrupt his chant, which had risen to a yell. They leaned toward his ear. "You might want to stop yelling so you have some voice left for the rally."

He stared as if surprised to see Sunny there. "Good idea." He resumed chanting at a lower level and redirected his excess energy to his sign, which he jabbed in the air in time to his steps.

When the chanting faded, Xander leaned around Sunny to get Terrance's attention. "So Terrance, when were you planning to inform me of your impending career move?"

All the friends' heads and eyes swung to Terrance.

"What? Are you leaving Wilderness Protection?" Sunny asked.

Terrance met Xander's gaze. "Who told you? Jess?"

"Affirmative. Last night, she asked if you talked to me at work. I told her we barely saw each other all day, so she backtracked and pretended it was an innocuous inquiry. I dragged it out of her of course."

Xander and Terrance stared at each other for eight footsteps.

"So? What's the deal?" Xander asked.

"I told Sarah on Thursday, and I wanted to tell you myself but didn't have a chance."

"Text? Email?"

Terrance ignored the jabs. "So, you think I'm selling out?"

"Would someone please tell us what's going on?" Sunny pleaded.

"Terrance has been abducted by the dark side. Corporate America."

"Sunny, I got a new job at Barber Finch. It's the biggest marketing agency in the city." His eyes found Xander. "And that's why I didn't tell you. Because I knew you'd react like you just did."

Sunny beamed. "It sounds like a great opportunity. We're happy for you. Aren't we, Xander?"

Xander swung his head in figure eights, eyes peering up. "Yeah, yeah, we're all happy for you." He stopped swinging. "Really. If that's what you want, then good for you, man."

Terrance nodded his blonde head. "Thanks. I appreciate that. Here's the funny part. One of the agency's clients is All-American Development & Construction, so I might end up working with Jess's company."

Xander's face contorted as if the shift in allegiance caused him physical pain.

∗∗∗

One hour and many chants later, the marchers arrived at Founders Park. The street-wide current of people flowed into the park and toward the stage. Like so much flotsam, the friends bobbed back and forth for a minute, trying to hold their position, finally stilling as the current moved sideways up the park's gentle slope and to the outer reaches of the green.

Ten or so women and two men marched onto the stage, drawing the eyes and ears of the thousands of spectators in one giant whoosh. Bodies swelled forward to be inches closer to the speakers. As if planned, a flock of birds shot over the stage, their breasts a rush of orange-spotted silver. Charley's chest pulled up and forward as if she could fly with them.

A famous actor from the city served as MC. For forty-five minutes, she and the other speakers inspired, educated, motivated, sobered, and re-inspired the audience.

When they finished, an all-female band broke into a cover of No Doubt's "Just A Girl," the slashing guitar and soaring vocals capturing the event's energy in musical form.

The friends staked a claim on the grassy hill. Buwan stayed standing as his friends sat and pulled water bottles and apples and cheese from the soft-sided cooler Terrance had worn as a backpack. A musky hint of weed weaved into the air from several directions.

"That was amazing!" Bu shouted, his eyes bulging. "What are we gonna do next? How can you guys sit down? Who wants to walk around with me?"

Xander extended his shorts-clad legs and kicked off his hiking shoes. "Jesus, Bu, chill out. Sit and savor the quiescence."

Sunny patted the grass beside their long, folded legs. "Yeah, Bu, the frantic part's over. Now we relax and enjoy this beautiful afternoon."

Buwan inhaled and exhaled forcefully. "Fine." He sank to the ground. "But let's plan another fun day. I'm so pumped and we need to do some crazy shit before we're too old."

Terrance looked up from the cheese he was slicing. "Whoa, when did this become a conversation about us getting old?"

"Well, we are. You know it. Let's go skydiving or bungee jumping before it's too late. Something scary and—and invigorating."

Charley grimaced. "Clubbing is scary and invigorating enough for me."

Sunny smiled at her in agreement.

Bu gritted his teeth. "Come on, you guys. All we do is sit around. We sit at protests and concerts and we talk, talk, talk. It's driving me mad."

Xander sighed. "I might be into skydiving at some point. But I'll be extremely busy at work for the foreseeable future because we'll be short-staffed, and I've got four protests to attend in the next two weeks, unlike you socially unconscious types." He grinned to convey he was at least partly joking.

Terrance gave a puff. "Nice, Xander. You dissed me for quitting and dissed all of us for not being as active in social justice causes as you, all in one breath."

"I know. Impressive, right?" Xander held out his fist until Terrance reluctantly bumped it.

"And by the way, I gave three weeks' notice, so you won't be rid of me for a while."

Charley swallowed a bite of an apple. "Xan, are all those protests here in Wrighton?"

"No, some are out-of-town."

"It's like you're trying to single-handedly save the world," she said reverently.

"Eh. I do my part but unfortunately, saving the world without buy-in from the oppressors in power is not feasible."

"What do you mean?"

"Well, for example, women would not have achieved the right to vote absent the support of some men. Acknowledging this aspect of achieving equal rights doesn't make us weak. It makes us smart."

Sunny polished an apple on their shirt. "Xander has a theory on this," they said.

Xander leaned into their circle, resting his elbows on his bent knees. "Shall I share?"

Terrance arranged crackers and cheese on a cloth napkin. "Knock yourself out."

Bu sighed dramatically and lay back on the grass.

Xander cleared his throat. "For discrimination to end, against any disenfranchised population, oppressors must travel along a spectrum of change. The spectrum has five stages. The first is *awareness* that the oppressed population exists." Elbows still on knees, he pounded his right fist into his left palm. "That leads to stage two, when the oppressors *understand* the impact of society's laws, policies, and attitudes on the population. Third is *empathy*, when outsiders start to care about the disenfranchised as real people. Empathy is what turns oppressors into allies. It often requires a personal connection to the disenfranchised, but news coverage of a particularly egregious act can also move people to this stage. Fourth, after empathy comes *outrage* and, finally, the *fight* for protections and equality."

Xander stopped to scratch his beard. "Protections of people with disabilities are an example of a fight that's made some progress with the American Disabilities Act, but still has a long way to go. In the case of women's rights, we're quite far along the spectrum in some areas but not others. Women won't achieve true equality until the oppressors acknowledge the travesty of the current situation. So, when others strike an acidulous tone and say shut up, you're being petulant—"

"Use real words," Bu interjected.

"—when others criticize the woman or the gay person or the minority for speaking up, we need to push back and emphasize that we *have* to stand up and demand attention or the discrimination will never end."

***

Having heard Xander's theory about the spectrum of change on the road to equality numerous times, Sunny tuned out. They noticed how intently Charley watched Xander—hanging on his words and absorbing every movement, little smiles teasing her lips and eyes. They also noticed that Bu regularly stole longing looks at Charley.

The equilibrium of their group was out of whack. How had they missed this? Bu wanted Charley. Charley wanted Xander. And Xander wanted Sunny.

The dynamics of a six-person group are not under my control, they told themself.

They studied Charley again, their heart flopping about. Sunny's affection for Charley was real and growing by the day. Therefore, they wanted her to be happy. A benevolent person would put aside personal desires and help someone they cared about get what she wants.

***

Bu heaved a huge sigh, prompting amused looks. "I gotta go walk around. Maybe I can find my moms somewhere." He sprang up and trod off on his own.

Sunny peered at their phone. "Speaking of moms . . ." They sent a text, stood up, and started waving and jumping.

A minute later, Fatima walked up.

"Mama!" Sunny cried, bouncing and hugging their mother at the same time and nearly knocking her over. "You came! I'm so proud of you."

Fatima separated from her child, smoothed her hair, said hello to Xander and Charley, and shook hands with Terrance. "You were right, Sunny, I'm glad I came."

"Did you like the speeches, Fatima?" Charley asked.

"Yes, very much. It's a bit daunting, hearing about all the challenges we face. But I also came away with some hope that we can make things better." She beamed at her child as if Sunny were responsible for the entire movement's commitment and progress.

Xander smiled and nodded at Fatima. "And that's what it's all about. Sit down. Partake of our humble fare."

"Oh no, that's all right. I'm going to look around, then head home. I'm not required to stay to the bitter end, am I, *noori*?" She smiled sweetly.

"No, Mama, of course not. Thank you for coming. I love you." Sunny kissed Fatima on her russet cheek and watched her leave like a proud parent on a child's first day of school.

***

Buwan cruised the information table area but ignored the posters and pamphlets. Instead, he perused the people he passed, looking for an ally to expend some energy with. The ants were moving under his skin again, making his fingers twitch. His scalp tingled as if being zapped with minute electrical pulses.

Away from the tables, farther into the park, shouts grabbed his attention. He found a handful of men and women watching—some with amusement, some with horror—as two middle-aged women wearing bright yellow T-shirts emblazoned with *Marriage = 1 man + 1 woman* faced off with two young women in sundresses.

"Real women love men and only men!" screamed one of the Yellow Shirts, a stout woman with gray hair and red cheeks.

"Women loving women is natural too," one of the sundress women replied emphatically but without yelling.

"No, it's not. It's an abomination against nature."

Buwan stepped between the two women, stopping the vitriolic volley. "What's going on?" he said, as if he'd run into friends on the sidewalk.

Sundress One addressed Buwan, her face anguished. "She's crazy. We were just walking by and she shoved her sign in my face. I told her to back off and they both got ugly."

The gray-haired woman spat at the feet of the sundress women, indifferent to the growing group of bystanders.

"Hey, stop that," Buwan said, his arms twitching.

"What do you care? Are you a lesbo-lover?"

"Lesbians are a disgrace," her cohort chimed in.

Buwan drew himself up to full height, eye to eye with Gray Hair. "Okay, now you're getting personal. You need to stop right now."

"Come on, let's go," Sundress Two said to Sundress One, pulling her by the arm.

"Yeah, go. Nobody wants you here." Gray Hair lunged after Sundress One, her sign extended like a lance as if she intended to spear the other woman. Buwan again stepped between the two factions, wincing as the wooden post of Gray Hair's sign banged into him and dragged his beige T-shirt across his chest.

"Ow!" he cried, reflexively grabbing the poster board sign and tearing it in two. His bronze face reddened. "That's what I think of your sign."

Gray Hair glared at him, the sundress women forgotten. She pushed the signpost into his chest with more force. "Mind your own business," she said.

Bu's voice rose to a shout. "Gay women are my business." He took hold of the post with both hands and pushed back hard. Gray Hair stumbled and would have landed on her ass except her friend caught her from behind. Bu stomped up to her and screamed in her face. "You have no idea what you're talking about! Don't judge other people until you know what you're talking about!"

Both Yellow Shirts backed up, but Buwan kept advancing. "Are you listening? Do you hear me? 'Cause I don't hear you answering!" His face deepened into an angry purple and the whites of his eyes showed all the way around his brown irises. Sweat popped out on his forehead.

"Break it up, folks, break it up," commanded a police officer wading through the small ring of people into the center of the action. He waved his billy club at Buwan and Gray Hair.

"Buwan!" A woman with wavy brunette hair and intense dark eyes behind frameless glasses rushed up to Bu. "What's going on? Are you all right?" She reached his side, stroked his hair, and stared into his eyes. "Breathe, honey, breathe."

"Ma'am, please step away," the cop said.

"He's my son," Layla said, never taking her gaze off Bu. "I've got him now."

"He's a bully, that's what he is," Gray Hair said, acting the part of an old, pitiful woman. "He knocked me to the ground!"

The cop focused on Layla. "I need to question him. We're trying to keep this event peaceful."

A tall, expensively dressed blonde woman joined the crowd. "Layla, there you are! I thought you were waiting for m—Bu?—what's going on here?"

The cop considered the woman, who seemed vaguely familiar. "You know these two?" He gestured toward Buwan and Layla with his billy club.

"That's my son." She walked close to the policeman, her diamond earrings flashing in the sunlight, and said quietly, "He has a minor mental health issue. If he was out of line, I apologize, but he's in my care now and I assure you it won't happen again." Her steady gaze invited the cop to acquiesce.

"It wasn't his fault," yelled a bystander. "He was trying to help. Those two started it," he said, pointing at the Yellow Shirts.

The cop moved away from Anne. "Okay, fun's over. Ma'am, are you all right?" he said to Gray Hair, who sniffed and held up her ripped sign.

"Come on," her friend implored. "Let's go."

"Yeah, I'm fine," Gray Hair muttered, walking away.

Anne and Layla each took one of Buwan's arms—Anne the tallest, Layla and Buwan about the same height. They moved a short distance away where Bu's parents stopped and turned to him. "Do you want us to take you home?" Anne asked, her blue eyes searching and tentative.

Buwan shook his head vigorously. "I'm okay. I promise."

Sundress One and Two stepped in front of them, holding hands. "I'm sorry to butt in, but that woman was a total bitch," Sundress One said. "He was trying to protect us." She smiled at Bu.

He smiled back, wondering how he could find them later.

Anne and Layla exchanged subtle nods and silent words. Layla looked at Bu. "Are your friends here?"

"Yeah, come on. You can meet them."

CHAPTER 20: FACE VALUE

Xander wondered if the universe was trying to tell him something. Negativity was piling up around him at a frightening rate.

Another police shooting stole the life of another young Black man in the very next state. ICE raided a factory outside Wrighton, rounding up hundreds of immigrants for deportation. And last night at his apartment, Sunny informed him they would no longer hook up. "It's not healthy. We're twenty-eight years old. We have to stop being each other's security blankets," they'd said.

Teary-eyed, they'd assured him the end of their physical relationship didn't affect the emotional and spiritual ones. Apparently, Sunny didn't realize that physical and spiritual intertwined inextricably for him. Then there was their cryptic message: sometimes you find what you're looking for right in front of you. They left in a rush, not even staying for one last night together.

And now tonight—the community meeting he expected to be a celebration of sorts had spiraled into a shit-show. He gulped his whiskey, the taste barely registering on his tongue, the burn unnoticed by his clenched throat. He yanked the bottle from the kitchen cabinet and poured another double. This time, he left the bottle on the green laminated countertop next to his hands, which gripped the counter's edge.

He had walked into the conference room of the South City Community Center excited to share the Wilderness Protection Society's plans for the new nature preserve with the president and vice president of the neighborhood association. The parcel of land where the preserve would be created—the former Stone Circle site—fell in Wrighton's South City borough. Flammer's project notwithstanding, the largely minority neighborhood had been neglected for years and continued to suffer from higher crime and lower investment rates than any other part of the sprawling city. By all accounts, the residents felt ignored or even disrespected by local leaders and were frustrated with the eyesore known as Flammer Mountain.

Terrance had warned Xander not to expect a hero's welcome, and their boss Sarah refused to define expectations for the evening because so many of the community meetings she'd presented at over the years went in a different direction than expected. Still, all three were caught off-guard when they entered the room and found not two but roughly twenty people seated around a large square table and in chairs lining the white walls of the room. The space pulsed with body heat and something intangible and concerning.

As they sat opposite Deiondra Ray, the association president, Sarah nodded at Terrance and Xander on either side of her with a look saying she would stay the course with their prepared, informal presentation.

"Thank you for inviting us to tell you about our plans for the new preserve, which for now we're calling the Bog Turtle Preserve, in honor of the little guy who brought the land under our umbrella," she said. "We're incredibly excited to add on to our existing conservation land and to become a next-door neighbor to South City. We look forward to cleaning up the site and creating a pristine community resource.

"With me is Terrance Washington, our communications director, and Xander Wallace, our regional campaign manager. I'm going to turn this over to Xander, since he led the charge to get U.S. Fish & Wildlife to designate the site as a Critical Habitat for the threatened bog turtle. It was his good work that ultimately led to Liam Flammer and All-American Development & Construction abandoning their hideous, super-sized project."

Due to his years as a grassroots organizer, Xander possessed significant skills at reading a crowd, but he still wasn't sure what agenda the stone faces around this room brought to the table. He forced a smile in Sarah's direction and then around the room.

"Forty percent of the turtles in this country are in danger of extinction, and we have an opportunity to help one of those species. Our win against All-American and—"

"Win? You call it a win?" said a young woman at a volume that made Xander reflexively sit up and back in his chair. Her dark hair was constrained in a severe bun, *Power to the People* emblazoned across her maroon T-shirt. "Tell us why this is a win for the people of this community." She glared at the guests, her wide eyes seeming to take in all three at once. "Go on. We're listening." She sat back and folded her arms across the word Power, as if that pose were somehow inviting of free speech.

"Miss—what's your name, may I ask?" Xander said.

"My name is Tani Rice and my family has lived in South City for three generations. So we know what constitutes a win here."

"Okay, Miss Rice—"

"Please. We don't have time or patience for formalities. Just call me Tani," she said, with what felt to Xander like a mock attempt at hospitality. "Everyone else does."

"Sure," Xander said. "Maybe I'm wrong, but I was under the impression the South City Neighborhood Association was exasperated waiting for All-American to do something with that vacant lot. We thought you'd be happy that something productive is finally going to occur there."

"Well, you're right on that. We do want something to happen," Tani said, while Sarah squirmed and Xander wondered if this brash woman would dominate the entire meeting. "For almost two years, we've been looking at that forty-foot-high dirt pile and that ugly construction fence. After that pile was made, nothing else on the site budged, no matter how many calls we made to our city councilors and the mayor. Now, we'll just skip over the fact that you people are the main reason the project came to a standstill for so long—"

"Technically," Xander said, "we're not the reason the project stalled. We neither sought out nor spotted the turtle. And Flammer could have moved that pile of dirt. He just chose not to."

Tani narrowed her eyes until Xander stopped talking. "Let's look to the future," she said. "Are you going to do something about that dirt pile?"

"Of course," Sarah jumped in. "We've already got drawings of how the new preserve will look, if we can show them—"

"*When* will you do something with that dirt?"

"Tani," Deiondra interjected. "Let's give them a chance to answer one question before we hit them with the next one." Deiondra's words caused shuffling and whispers in several corners of the room.

When the noise subsided, Xander dove in. "Can I ask, would you like to know about our plans at this stage?" Responses came from several directions.

"You people don't know what this neighborhood needs," said a young man beside Tani. "We don't care about your plans!"

"Why should we trust you after we've been lied to for years?" a very dark-skinned man with an accent lobbed from one side.

"We want this blight on our neighborhood removed yesterday!" an elderly woman shouted.

Xander, Terrance and Sarah traded concerned looks as the chorus of voices rose and ebbed. Then Terrance cleared his throat. "Can I point out, respectfully, that we are not responsible for Flammer's lack of attention to the site? We have nothing to do with All-American."

"Oh, we know you don't," said the man to Deiondra's right. Xander believed this was Eric Tate, the association's vice president. He was in his early thirties, bald presumably by choice, with well-muscled neck and shoulders. "That is abundantly clear," Eric continued. "Did you ever stop to think maybe we *wanted* Flammer's development?"

The silence and dead stares from the Wilderness Protection trio answered the question.

"That mixed-use project came with a lot of benefits to our community. Jobs—"

"With all due respect," Terrance said, "those construction jobs would have been union, and the Black community isn't well-represented in those trades."

Eric talked over Terrance. "Jobs in building management and the retail shops. Flammer committed to hiring seventy-five percent of the building's employees from the community."

Xander suppressed a smirk. Unless Flammer had planned on managing the twelve stores at the base of his own mixed-use development, he wouldn't control who was hired to work there. That was up to the store owners. More B.S. from the slimy developer.

Eric went on. "His project came with affordable office space for locally owned businesses. Plus, new sidewalks and street lighting throughout the neighborhood, not just on his property."

"And quality affordable housing," Tani added. "He wanted condos, but we insisted on apartments, some of them for lower-income families."

Xander couldn't believe all these people were buying into everything that snake promised. Or, more likely, they were merely using the concessions they'd wrangled out of Flammer as leverage.

"We're very willing to collaborate with you, too, to ensure the community benefits from the new preserve," he said, extending a verbal olive branch.

"Now how are you going to do that?" Tani nearly shouted. "Turtles for everyone?" She laughed heartily, joined by many around the room.

Xander said nothing, just drummed his fingers on his thigh under the table.

"We can set up educational programs for the local schools," Terrance offered. "Free of charge."

"And have free admission for neighborhood residents one day a week," Sarah added. "Maybe even every day, but that's something our board needs to approve. Deiondra, maybe we can meet in a few weeks, and I can tell you what we're able to offer to invest the community in the Bog Turtle Preserve."

Deiondra nodded and Xander prayed the meeting would end there, on that note, but Tani wasn't done with them. "Which one of you thought up that campaign to 'Save the Turtles, Save the City's Kidneys'?" she asked. Xander pictured sarcasm dripping in heavy globs off the air quotes she made with her fingers.

"That was me." Xander kept his voice level and resisted the urge to correct the campaign's name or clarify that it was replaced by the "Looking Out for the Little Guy" theme. "You see, by saving the bog turtle, we protect the wetlands, and wetlands are to nature what the kidney is to a human body. They extract toxins—"

"You can stop," Tani said, her words lashing at Xander, "I read the fine print in your materials. What I want to know is, why do you think our neighborhood needs cleaning? Are we toxins to you?"

Tani's twisting of the intention behind his words stung him into silence.

"Those words were not describing South City," Terrance said. "I think you might be misunderstanding—"

"And you!" Tani slung at Terrance, raising a finger at him. "Mm-hmm," she said with a slow head shake but no more words. Terrance's eyes widened in disbelief as his body shrank in on itself.

An elderly man with white kinky hair and a kind face stood up, offering the Wilderness Protection contingent the prospect of a more kindly perspective. "You come in here all roses and sunshine, but how do we know you'll do what you say you will? We don't know you from Adam." His words strung out across the space between him and Xander like barbs on a wire, reminding Xander of the activist's maxim to never judge a book by its cover. Or its pleasant face or friendly tone of voice. "How do we know you'll move that pile of dirt—that monstrosity that is an insult to every man, woman, and child who lives here? How do we know we have been heard? How do we know you won't forget us and everything you're promising?"

When it was clear he was finished, Sarah cleared her throat. "I'd like to be sure you realize that much as we'd like to, we haven't promised anything tonight. I need to discuss these ideas with—"

"Mm-hmm, here we go." Tani raised her chin and scrutinized Sarah with half-closed eyes.

Sarah looked at Tani and slowly closed her mouth.

"Same old shit," Tani said to Eric, who nodded.

The elderly man shook his head and sat as if let down by the world for the tenth time that day. Picking up on the rising tension in the room, people began commenting at once, making it impossible to determine who said what, and if any response was in order.

"Lies. All lies. We're tired of being lied to."

"What do they think we are, stupid?"

"Who needs a nature park? Do we look like we need a nature park?"

"We need investment is what we need!"

"Same old story. Different players."

"How long will we have to wait this time?"

"We need progress! Real progress!"

Deiondra, who had watched all of this quietly, not once adding her opinion or attempting to restore order, suddenly stood. "That's enough for tonight, folks." She repeated her words as the clamor died down, then turned to Sarah. "Thank you for coming. We'll be in touch." She turned her attention to the pile of papers on the table in front of her.

Xander kept his gaze down as he pushed back from the table, his chair's metal feet screeching against the linoleum floor. Muttered conversations continued around him as he bolted for the door, followed in short order by Sarah and Terrance.

He stopped on the sidewalk, breathing in the dark, muggy night. He pressed his eyelids tight to stem the frustration and aggravation behind them.

"Wow, can you say scapegoat?" Sarah asked in a tone that attempted jocularity but fell far short. "Are you guys okay? Listen, let's walk." One block later, the tension building in Xander over the last forty-five minutes blew out of him like a steam whistle.

"I've never been so blindsided in my life! Or assaulted so unfairly. We didn't do anything to deserve that."

"They just needed to get that out of their system," Terrance said in a dejected, low voice.

"Tomorrow will be better," Sarah said unconvincingly. She veered off to her car, parked at the curb. "Don't take it personally, guys. See you later."

Xander rolled his shoulders back and tried to breathe normally. He and Terrance walked for a minute without speaking. When they reached Terrance's car, Xander planted a hand on the driver's side door before Terrance could open it.

"Drink?" Xander asked.

"Nope." Terrance picked up Xander's hand and removed it from the car. "Later," he said as he climbed in and drove away, leaving Xander on the sidewalk staring after him.

Xander walked the few miles home to cool off. He stumbled into his apartment and headed straight for the kitchen cabinet that held the liquor. Focused solely on his hands moving in front of him, he got the bottle of Jack Daniels and a rocks glass and sloshed the rich sienna liquid to the halfway point of the glass, heedless of the drips trailing down the outside.

Now, two shots later, his brain began to wriggle out of the confusion constricting it like a straitjacket. *What the hell happened?* He couldn't make sense of it. Okay, clearly, the neighborhood residents were incensed at being ignored in general and then jerked around by Flammer, the City and now, they were anticipating, Wilderness Protection. Objectively, he could fathom their anger. But personally, he'd never endured such an undeserved attack. For merely being in the room.

"X, what's happening?" Jess yelled into the kitchen as she let herself into the apartment, juggling a gym bag and a garment bag. She dropped her keys on the hallway table and joined him in the kitchen. "Are you okay? You look like you saw a ghost or a nuclear bomb or something."

"Bad work event." He poured another shot.

"Want to talk about it?" she asked.

He considered the offer but concluded no words could capture the ordeal or how ragged it left his emotions. He shook his head and turned back to the bottle, suddenly craving inebriation—stupefaction sounding preferable to pointless analysis. Sometimes you just had to accept a bad situation and live with it.

***

Xander collapsed at the peak of the modest mountain in State Park as if he'd outrun a demon.

"Man," Charley exhaled, bending at the waist, touching her fingertips to the granite mountaintop and plopping down beside him on a warm slab of ledge. "I'm not sure that counted as hiking. More like running uphill. I thought I was in shape but now I don't know." She wiped her brow with her bare forearm, catching a bead of sweat before it dripped in her eye.

She leaned back, supported by her pale slender arms, and studied Xander. He'd suggested the hike but had hardly spoken two words the entire climb, not even when Charley pointed out two hawks cavorting in the pale blue sky. At least he had smiled when they stopped at the first picnic area at the mountain's base and were greeted by a large crow. Others from the flock gathered as Charley tossed them bits of bread, which she did regularly now. When she tucked the empty plastic bag into the back pocket of her moisture-wicking shirt for recycling later, the big crow had cawed twice before departing.

She picked up a pebble and tossed it at Xander's prostrate form. "What's on your mind, Xan?"

Xander sat up and leaned back, mirroring Charley's position. "I endured a challenging week."

"Mm. Maybe it would help to talk about it," Charley said. "You know what they say." She closed her eyes to count syllables in her head while speaking. *"Don't let things fester. Keeping things inside is bad. Tell it to your friends."*

He smirked. "Self-help haiku. You may be onto something there."

Charley grinned and picked up her hand to look at the small, sharp impressions left by the bits of gravel on the ledge. She sat up straight and wrapped her legs into a cross-legged pose. "We could do some yoga here. It's a great spot for it. As Sunny says, if we all did yoga, everyone would be happy and there would be no wars."

Xander cocked his head and studied her.

"I guess you've heard them say that before."

"Actually, no." He crossed his lean, tan legs at the ankles. "But I like it."

He contemplated her face for so long she jerked her head away to consider the horizon.

"Speaking of Sunny, I may as well inform you," Xander said. "We're not together anymore."

Charley choked on her saliva. Xander thumped her on the back and handed over his water bottle. She chugged until her esophagus calmed down.

"Wow. That's big news." She peeked at him from behind the water bottle. "Are you upset?"

He stared away at Long Lake. Charley followed his gaze and had to squint against the diamond sparkles on the surface. "I was initially, but as per usual, they're right. If we were destined to be a couple, it would have transpired by now. Although they made a quizzical comment about how I should look—" He clammed up.

"Should what?" Charley prodded.

Xander blinked. "Regardless, they'll always be my soul mate. Any future partner will have to be copasetic with that."

A glimmer of hope snuggled into Charley's heart. She handed his water bottle back, its silver surface winking in the sun. "I'm sure you'll find someone who gets it."

"Right." He screwed the cover onto the water bottle. "How's your week going?" He ran his hand through his bangs and up over his head, distributing sweat among his curls.

"Basic," Charley said. "Except for yesterday's police shooting of the Black teenager, of course. That was horrible. I can't believe it's happened right here in Wrighton."

Xander sighed. "We are no longer immune to the plague of police violence raging across the country. Things are ratcheting up."

Usually such pronouncements elicited passion from Xander but today, he merely sounded weary.

He lay back on the warm rock, hands cupped behind his head, and his eyes closed.

Charley watched him breathe for a minute before lying down beside him, not touching but close enough to feel his body heat.

"Xander?" she whispered, a hand shielding her eyes from the sun.

"Mm-hmm."

"It's my mother's birthday and I've been thinking about her and my dad, and everything I did wrong as a daughter and how I'll never get to fix it." Xander opened one eye to regard her. "And like we were saying, it's not good to keep things inside. So, will you listen if I talk about her?"

He closed his eye and grabbed her hand where it lay between them. Like everything about Xander, his hand pulsed with life, heat, and energy.

Charley closed her eyes and shifted them away from the sun, the orange inside her eyelids turning blue-gray. A bird trilled in a nearby tree, answered by a distant, equivalent call.

"It was terrible," she said softly. She sensed Xander inching closer to her. "My mom had an economics conference in Brazil, so they decided to make a family vacation of it and visit the rainforest. Their classes at the college started a week after my high school classes, and I would have missed the first few days of freshman year. I was a really irritating fifteen-year-old and I insisted it would be no fun for me and I was old enough to stay home by myself. I said I didn't want to go to the stupid rainforest." She licked her lips. "I said that for professors, they were very willing to have me forgo my education, and she said she thought I was smart enough to survive missing a few days at the beginning of the year. In the end, they said I didn't have to go, but I had to stay with a friend. The final argument ended with her shouting that she guessed I was so grown up I didn't need them anymore. She was being sarcastic, obviously. And then, a few days later, they crashed. And I was on my own."

Xander squeezed her hand. "We always regret our arguments, but I'm sure she knew you loved her."

Charley grunted. "How? I never told her. But they never told me either. We weren't that kind of family. I never even said the words 'I love you' until a few years after I moved in with Gram and Gramps."

Xander's finger brushed along Charley's cheek. Her eyes shot open but quickly closed under the force of his penetrating gaze.

"Tell me about your grandparents."

Charley smiled at the mental picture of Phil and Edith. "We lived in a two-family on the southwest side of the city. Gramps owned it. He ran a construction company, she taught elementary school until she retired. I lived with them all through high school and when I was home from college. And even though I could have gone back to my parents' college tuition-free, Gram and Gramps knew that would be hard, so they helped me go to Babson instead, even though it was farther away and cost more."

"They sound phenomenal."

"They were." A smile teased Charley's lips. "She had a classic grandmother cross-stitch in the living room with the golden rule: 'Do unto others as you would have them do unto you.' When I would come home from high school upset because I was getting stares and rude comments from some of the kids, especially some of the Black and Latino ones, she said just treat everyone like you want to be treated. Then she said the Irish were one of the country's first minorities, and that she and Gramps were the product of a mixed marriage because she was Protestant and he was Catholic."

Xander chuckled, then turned serious. "A lot of people think the golden rule solves all discrimination. If only it were that easy."

"Yeah, well, Gram's cross-stitch went up in flames. How's that symbolism for you? That's when I decided I liked George Bernard Shaw's take better: 'The golden rule is that there are no golden rules.'"

"Oh my, Charley. You can be quite the cynic." He let go of her hand.

She eased up from the rock. "Can we move before I start cramping up?"

He stood. "Feeling any better?"

She nodded before realizing she did, in fact, feel lighter than when she started. "You?"

He shrugged. "A little. The world's injustices can be a heavy weight sometimes."

"Well, how about on the way down, we forget about injustice and enjoy Mother Nature?"

And that's what they did, descending at a comfortable pace, taking time to hear overlapping layers of summer birdsong, smell pungent pine and musty disintegrating logs, and feast their eyes on the sharp spines, jagged lines, and soft shadows of nature's canvas.

Back in the parking lot, something shiny on the hood of Charley's car caught her eye. Xander picked it up—a blue, triangular fragment of sea glass, each side about an inch long.

"How the heck did that get there?" Charley wondered.

A large crow swooped down, making Xander duck. "Whoa!" he exclaimed. The crow made a second pass. Xander's eyes narrowed, then he handed the glass to Charley. The crow landed twenty feet away, cocked its head, and cawed once. Charley's eyebrows touched in confusion.

Xander slowly smiled. "I do believe this gift has been bestowed upon you by your *Corvus brachyrhynchos* friend."

"Really?" Charley fingered the smooth glass, turning it over in her hand. The points of the timeworn object were muted and the edges velvety other than one sharp spot.

The crow cawed again. "Thank you," Charley said to the crow, feeling foolish. His black eye appeared to wink before he collected himself and vaulted into the air. "Wow," Charley breathed in disbelieving gratitude.

Xander smiled at her. A butter-yellow butterfly with ebony-trimmed wings floated by, lingering briefly before continuing on its way. "I can't compete with the crow's token or even that butterfly, but I can offer you this small present: *In the Amazon, butterflies drink turtle tears, better than nectar.*"

"That's beautiful," Charley said, facing him. Her breath caught when their eyes locked. Fervor often sparked his eyes, but this look was new. She rested a hand on her car for balance. He leaned in a few inches and stopped.

"Would it be all right if I kissed you? I don't want to create any awkwardness."

Charley still held her breath. She licked her lips, immediately embarrassed by her reflexive movement. She nodded rather than risk saying something to ruin the moment.

Xander bent his head to close the distance between them. His smooth warm lips melded into Charley's and his mustache tickled, spawning a seed of giddiness in her belly. The combined sensation of affection and laughter tugged her lips into a smile mid-kiss. She regained her composure and focused on their connection. The long and searching kiss was uninterrupted until a loud "caw" nearby broke them apart.

"Man, let's depart before your passerine friend makes another run at me." Xander laughed, his eyes remaining on Charley's face.

They jumped into the car, Xander's mood vastly improved, and Charley free-falling somewhere above cloud nine.

CHAPTER 21: SUNNY'S SACRIFICE

"How long 'til we leave for the vigil?" Buwan asked as Charley let him into the closed bookstore.

Jess consulted her watch. "Thirty-eight minutes," she answered over the short wall separating the entrance from the café.

"Thirty-eight minutes," Bu repeated. "That's plenty of time for these." He flashed his wide grin, fished a dewy six-pack out of a canvas bag and passed a can to each friend.

Charley sat on the brown leather couch rescued from the Delgados between Terrance and Xander. Jess noticed a strand of Charley's hair clung to Xander's shoulder.

Bu's can popped and hissed as he bent back the aluminum tab. "Cheers—to Friday night!" he said so loudly, Jess involuntarily drew back in her chair. He dropped into one of the chairs Jess plucked from the side of the road in her parents' neighborhood: an ivory armchair festooned in a hideous floral pattern of dark-orange tiger lilies and army-green leaves and vines.

"Does this chair make me look ugly?" Bu asked in a high voice. He laughed at his own joke.

"B, I'm not sure you need any more alcohol," Jess said.

"What are you talking about? This is my first one."

Xander raised his beer. "To social justice," he proclaimed.

"To social justice," the others repeated.

"Do you think the vigil will be peaceful?" Charley asked Xander.

"Who knows? It will take whatever form it needs to take."

Sunny frowned. "Not a comforting thing to say to the child of a cop." They curled up in Jess's other rescue—a pale yellow chenille armchair embellished with an embroidered swirl pattern—as if they wanted to burrow into the crevice where the side and back met the seat cushion.

"Sunny, you know I eschew violence, but you have to admit, sometimes peaceful doesn't get the required attention or response," Xander said.

Sunny kept frowning. "What are you talking about? Of course peaceful works. And it keeps the focus on the cause."

Jess noticed tension in Sunny's voice as their eyes dropped to the space between Xander's and Charley's shoulders. Sunny had told Jess they broke up with Xander, not the other way around, so why, Jess wondered, did they seem annoyed with him?

"Well, even though we don't know details," Jess said, "it sucks that a teenage boy was killed."

"It does a lot more than suck," Terrance said with a headshake. "It's tragic."

Jess scowled, feeling unfairly criticized for a weak word choice.

"And that boy has a name—Jamal Cartwright—and we have enough details to know this is another case of the police shooting first, asking questions second," Terrance continued.

"Charley," Xander said, "can you imagine if you and your friends were indulging in a pickup soccer game at the school field and the cops arrived to break up the game?" She shook her head. "If it had been a bunch of White kids, no one would have summoned the cops or insinuated they were dealing drugs. The police would've conversed like civilized people instead of shouting through a bullhorn. And they wouldn't have considered themselves threatened when one of the kids approached calmly to explain they were merely having a pickup game rather than meandering the streets aimlessly. If Jamal Cartwright had been White, he'd be alive today." Xander stopped speaking but his fingers tapped against his thigh in a rapid pattern, as if reflecting an ongoing internal dialogue.

"You have to cut the police some slack," Jess said. "Their job isn't easy. They only have a split second to decide how dangerous a threat is."

"Come on, really?" Anger pierced Xander's voice. He leaned forward in his seat. "They had ample time to assess the situation and confirm this was a kid with no weapon. There was no need to shoot to kill. It's repugnant and brazen. It's an epidemic and they must be stopped."

"They?" Jess asked, her voice rising. "If you paint all cops with the same brush, you're being prejudiced too."

Xander sat back, shoulders stiff. "Generalizations are by definition discriminatory to some."

Jess squinted at him. "Listen, we haven't been together in over a week. Let's catch up. First of all, great find, B, on this rocking chair." She nudged the floor, sending the chipped, bright-green-painted chair into a short-lived rock. A sharp edge from the torn rattan seat poked the back of her thigh through her jeans, so she made a mental note to never sit there in her work clothes. "S, tell us—how's work?"

Sunny shrugged. "Still saving the world one solar panel at a time," they said with no emotion.

"X?"

Xander sighed. "Still saving the world one tree at a time."

Jess rolled her eyes at the lack of enthusiasm in the group. "T? Ready for the new job?"

"Ready and willing." He had nothing to add.

"B, any updates?"

Buwan launched out of the tiger-lily chair and walked around the small café, flexing his hands in and out of fists. "Not about a job. Still gainfully unemployed." He gave a hollow laugh. "But I am psyched about a new piece I'm working on. I think you guys will like it."

Sunny perked up. "What's it of?"

"Can't tell you. It's a surprise. And Sunny—no peeking in my studio!"

"Okay," Jess said, "we'll wait with bated breath. As for my job, since no one asked, I'm still waiting to hear about my promotion. They are taking forever to decide and it's killing me."

"You need to say something. They shouldn't string you along like this," Terrance said. "It'd be one thing if you were an external candidate, but if they value you as an employee, they should be more open with you."

Jess blew her long bangs out of her eyes. "I've asked my boss about it so many times, he's getting annoyed with me."

"Can't you ask HR? Tell them the delay is hurting your morale."

Jess fiddled with her earring. "I'm not going to say that—I'd sound like a whiner—but maybe I will visit the VP of HR who interviewed me when I started at All-American. I can at least ask her what's up." She consulted the ceiling and nodded.

"You didn't ask Charley about her job," Xander pointed out. Jess looked at Terrance who hoisted his eyebrows as high as they would go. She quickly looked away.

"C, how is life at the bookstore?" Jess asked.

"Amazing. I know it doesn't make me ambitious to say this, but I love managing this stupid little store. And who knows, maybe I can take over someday when Georgina retires." She gushed with such reverence that Jess assumed the new romance with Xander was tinting Charley's rosy view of the rundown store even rosier.

"Doesn't it get old doing the same thing over and over?" Jess asked, drawing a subtle smirk and headshake from Terrance.

"No, it's never the same two days in a row. Plus, I have a bunch of ideas for improvements if I can just convince Georgina to let me make them."

"Time out—" Xander said, studying his phone, one hand raised in a stop gesture. "Jess, guess what?" he asked with more energy than the entire room had displayed all night. "Crazy Carl is moving out. He says he'll be gone by the end of the month."

Jess stood up to fist-bump Xander where he sat. "Finally!" she enthused. "Hate to be mean, but I will not miss our strange roommate one bit. And Sunny, now you can move in with us!"

Sunny displayed not one iota of the excitement Jess expected. Instead, they stared across the café at the empty display case, devoid of muffins and croissants, and ran their finger along the line of tiny gold hoops adorning their helix.

"It's such a cute place," Charley said, blushing when all eyes except Sunny's turned to her.

"S? Yes?"

"I'll think about it." They focused on untying and re-tying their pale green headband.

Jess raised her eyebrows. Something was seriously off, not just with Sunny. Xander was in his typical focused but high-strung, pre-protest mood, but Charley was infatuated to the point she barely noticed anyone else in the shop. Bu paced the café like a caged lion. Terrance seemed distant, almost cold—she'd thought they were past that.

Xander slapped his hands on his thighs and stood, throwing Charley slightly off balance. "We should depart. We can't be late. By the way, who's in on a gun control protest tomorrow afternoon at the State House?"

Only Buwan responded. "I'll go, dude. I love these protests!"

Jess smirked at the two protest buddies.

Sunny headed for the back of the store. "Bathroom first."

Charley hopped up and followed, as did Jess.

"Sunny, want to do something this weekend?" Charley asked Sunny's narrow back as they walked. "A yoga class maybe?"

Jess noticed Sunny's shoulders sag a touch at Charley's voice.

"Or maybe I could invite myself over to your house for dinner? I'd love to see your parents again. I promise to bring some of the food."

Sunny stopped at the bathroom door. Still facing away, they said, "I don't think I can, Char, but sometime soon, okay?" They stepped away from the door. "You can go first."

"Okay." Charley hung her head and pushed into the one-person bathroom.

After hearing the door lock, Jess pulled Sunny a few feet away. "What is going on, S? Are you upset about Charley and Xander?"

Sunny didn't answer, but their entire face flagged, and tears filled their eyes. Jess hugged them tightly for ten seconds, then released them to study their face.

"If you broke up with Xan, why do you care that he's dating Char—" Jessica's mouth stayed open. "Oh. Ohhhhh," she said, eyes wide. "You have a thing for Charley," she said in her kindest voice. "Am I right?"

Sunny wiped away a tear and nodded.

"Did you have any idea they might get together when you ended things with X?"

Jess expected a hard and fast "no," so Sunny's delayed response took her by surprise. Sunny inhaled with a quiver, shot a look at the bathroom door and spoke. "I've known for a while that Charley liked Xander, and I figured since I lo—since I love her," they said, dropping their eyes to their clasped hands, "I should do what makes her happy." They choked a bit on the final words.

"And Xander makes her happy," Jess said. Sunny nodded. "S, you are the most giving person I have ever known. I hope it doesn't doom you to a life of unhappiness." The bathroom lock rasped and the door squeaked open. "Go," Jess whispered, pushing Sunny toward a bookcase to hide behind. "Man, do I need to pee," she said as she passed Charley on her way into the restroom.

A few minutes later, Jess faced her own hushed inquisition. As the six friends walked in groups of two, down the sidewalk toward the subway station, Terrance tugged Jess back from the others. "Why didn't you tell her? You said it was a done deal."

Jess walked slowly and reached for the low-hanging excuse. "Did you see how happy she is with Xander? I didn't want to ruin her night. Plus, they only have verbal agreement—no signed contract yet. I'll tell her soon, I promise." She turned away from his stare, which penetrated the dusky air like a lighthouse beam in heavy fog.

Terrance suddenly stopped. "I've got somewhere else to go. I'll catch up with you guys later if I can." He veered off in a completely different direction, leaving Jess wondering just how annoyed he was.

***

Several hours later, Terrance hummed in his car, looking forward to an easy drive home this late on a weekend night. He couldn't stomach going to the vigil. Sharing frustration and anguish with hundreds of people, most of his own race, just made him more frustrated and anguished. Through no fault of their own, they couldn't solve the problems they protested—at least not single-handedly. And Terrance was all about solutions.

After leaving his friends, he'd made his way to City Hall. He signed in, asked for directions, and wound his way through the huge building's cool passages to the City Council meeting room. For two hours, along with a gaggle of reporters and other observers, he'd watched and listened.

The ordered process and formal agenda for the special meeting spoke to him. The personalities of the individual city councilors—combative, conciliatory, balanced, firm—played off each other as they moved toward what appeared to be a common goal. Terrance's ability to translate the jargon of governing into real-life terms grew the more he listened.

Discussion of the Jamal Cartwright shooting—the main agenda item—broadened into a general discussion on the state of race relations in the city. The council president managed to keep the group on-track and productive. When the meeting ended, Terrance had a firm hold on the next steps: The Council gave the police department two weeks to come back with a specific report on the shooting, including identification of contributing factors and proposed solutions to prevent similar incidents. In parallel to that work, two councilors would work with an independent commission on a similar report. Four additional councilors would seek input directly from law enforcement experts, union leaders, human rights activists, social service organizations, faith leaders, and other community representatives.

That focused approach, more than the raw emotion inherent in a vigil, gave Terrance hope that maybe, just maybe, solutions would be found to scrape away at the long-festering sore of racism in their city.

CHAPTER 22: BETRAYAL

Terrance scrutinized Charley's paler-than-normal face as she joined him, Xander, and Buwan in the café a few nights later. She dropped to the enormous brown leather couch between Xander and Buwan and stared into space.

Xander took her hand. "Charley, you look positively queasy. Should we send everyone away?"

Terrance wondered if she'd caught the flu rampaging through Wrighton until his mind made a sharp right turn and he realized why she looked so lost. He planted his feet to stop the green rocking chair's gentle movement. "What's wrong, Char?" he asked, afraid he knew the answer.

She opened her mouth, closed it, and tried again. "Georgina's selling the store."

Terrance's burnt umber face hardened.

Buwan's hand flicked toward Charley's free hand next to him on the couch but didn't reach for it. "When?" he asked.

"Soon. I saw her meeting with a lawyer. She told me she's working out the final details."

Xander shifted toward Charley. "She's hardly the ideal boss anyway. Maybe the new owner will represent an improvement. Maybe you'll finally be given the wherewithal to embark upon some of those improvements on your list."

Charley stared at her lap. A nerve jumped under her eye. "Do you think so?"

Terrance cleared his throat so harshly it sounded like he was trying to dislodge a chicken bone. *Time to fess up.* "Jess knew."

"What?" Bu and Xander said together.

Charley's eyebrows drew so close together, the motion pinched her entire face.

"Jess knew. Her company is the buyer. She helped put the deal together."

"What the fuck?" Xander said.

"Oh my God," Charley moaned at the same time.

Bu leaned forward, staring at Terrance as if challenging him to retract the statement. "You're shitting us, right? Just screwing around with us? Jess wouldn't do that."

Terrance's neck muscles bulged. He squared his shoulders. "She identified the store as a potential acquisition target before she met you at Bu's house that weekend. And once the ball got rolling, she couldn't exactly control it." He stopped, unwilling to defend Jess.

Like an apparition summoned by name, a sliver of Jess's face appeared in the store's front picture window, caught between the window frame and the edge of the shade. She rapped on the glass. "Let me in."

Terrance saw Charley grip Xander's hand. She stayed put.

Buwan stood. "I'll do it."

***

Jess swept into the café, her greeting curtailed and her smile erased upon seeing Xander's angry face, Terrance's judgmental one, and Buwan's puzzled one. Charley didn't look at her.

"What's going on, peeps?" She plopped into the pale-yellow chenille armchair, tossing a concerned look to Terrance. He wouldn't look at her. He stretched his jaw, the resulting pop audible to all. *Uh oh—he's pissed.* A tentacle of uncertainty wormed through her.

"Jessica," Xander seethed, shifting to the front edge of the couch, "why didn't you tell us All-American is buying the bookstore?"

Jess's mouth clamped shut. She chanced a look at Terrance for a clue as to how they found out, but his face revealed nothing. *He must have told them. Why would he do that?* She swallowed hard and faced Charley. "I meant to. The time was never right."

"The time was never right?" Xander echoed in disbelief. "Jesus, Jess. This might be another transaction to you. But it's Charley's home. This is callous, even by your standards."

Bu reached over to pat Jess's knee and spoke kindly. "Will she at least get to stay here, at the job and in the apartment?"

Terrance stared down his nose at Jess, nostrils flaring. "Go ahead, Jess. Tell them," he said.

Jess continued looking at Charley, even though Charley wouldn't look at her. "They're going to tear it down. The guy next door is selling, too. Flammer's going to build something new on both lots."

A collective in-breath sucked the air from the room.

"How could you keep this from us?" Xander demanded. "From Charley? How?"

Jess's eyes watered. "I didn't know you, Charley, when I suggested we buy the store, and then I didn't know how to stop it. I decided not to say anything unless it was definite."

"And—?" Terrance prompted.

"And I didn't say anything when it was a done deal because I chickened out." She stood up, briefcase in hand, stiffened her spine and turned to leave. "Thanks a lot, T," she said, her voice laden with sarcasm. Her briefcase banged against his rocker as she brushed past and left.

Terrance ran a hand over his hair. "I tried to get her to tell you sooner."

Charley lifted her head for the first time since dropping the bombshell. "You knew, too. You knew and you didn't tell me, either."

Terrance's breath caught in his throat. "You're right. I was an accomplice." He nodded and frowned. "I'm sorry I didn't say something. I hope you'll forgive me, and I'll try to make it up to you."

Sunny came through the doorway and peered over the short wall between the entrance and the café. "What's wrong with Jess? She just blew past me and didn't even stop."

Terrance removed his glasses and began cleaning them. "All-American is buying the bookstore and razing the building."

Sunny's face sank. "Oh my God, Charley—your job, your apartment, your passion. This is terrible. What can we do?" They dropped their daisy backpack and went to stand before Charley. Charley remained seated, precluding a hug. Sunny moved to the tiger-lily armchair and sank in. "Come on, guys—there must be something we can do," they said.

Xander moved his arm around Charley's shoulder and pressed her into his side. "There's no environmental implication on this one. It's not a historical building. It's a simple real estate transaction. There's no leverage for challenging Flammer."

Charley narrowed her eyes. "Or Jess," she said flatly. "There's nothing to challenge Jess on. This is her project. This is what she wants."

Sunny's almond-shaped eyes rounded. They looked to Xander who confirmed Jess's involvement with a nod.

"Sunny, tell us something good. How was your day?"

Sunny's eyes drooped. "Not great. You know that old homeless woman shot by the police? Queenie? The Mayor is blaming her for being homeless, for hurting that man, and for not getting mental health support. He's turning her from a person into a stereotype. And the policeman who shot her isn't being held accountable."

The pain in Sunny's voice drew Charley up. She walked to Sunny, tugged their arm, and eased them to a standing position. They leaned into each other, chests rising and falling.

"I don't know why our esteemed mayor traducing the reputation of an innocent woman should surprise you," Xander said as his phone chirped. He studied the screen. "We should go."

"What?" Charley and Sunny asked together as they released their embrace.

"An impromptu protest is starting outside City Hall. We should be there."

"About Queenie?" Buwan asked.

"Queenie. Jamal Cartwright. The Mayor's indifference. All those."

Charley peered at Xander as if trying to translate a foreign language.

Xander stood. "Come on. It's an exigent matter. And it will be beneficial for all of us. Forget our personal problems and focus on the greater picture."

Sunny wiped a palm across their face, leaving an incredulous look in its wake. "Does this really seem like a good night?" They cocked their head toward Charley, who stood still except for a subtle trembling. "Take a night off from saving the world, Xan, and take care of Charley."

Xander shoved his water bottle into his backpack. "Char, come with? Get your mind off your troubles?"

She was immobile.

Xander walked to her and embraced her with one arm. "Why don't you go upstairs and soak in a long bath or something then? We'll survive without you for this one protest."

"How big of you," Sunny sneered, making Bu frown.

"You could sit this one out too, Sun, unless you want to come pay tribute to Queenie." Xander's legitimately innocent face suggested he had no idea how his words stung.

"Gee, thanks for the free pass," Sunny spat. They sank into the tiger-lily chair. Xander poised on his toes, looking from his friends to the door and back. Sunny waved Xander off. "Go. Go save the world."

"Wait for me." Bu stopped to give Sunny and Charley quick hugs before bounding after Xander.

"Terrance, you coming?" Xander yelled through the open door.

"No," Terrance bellowed back. He hugged Sunny for a long time, and then Charley. "If there's anything either of you need, you'll call or text, right?" Neither looked at him. "Right?"

"Sure," Sunny said. "Thanks, Terrance."

***

Sunny led Charley out the back and up to her apartment. Baggage scooted up to Sunny and rubbed his black-and-gray tabby coat against their shin. Sunny scooped up the cat, who started purring although his head remained stiff and alert.

Desperate to draw something out of Charley—a word, a tear—they put Baggage down and sat beside her on the blah blue couch. "Are you mad? At Jess? You have every right to be."

"Jess. Terrance." Charley's eerily neutral voice gave Sunny chills. "Xander." Her voice hitched on his name, but her face remained blank as she stared, unseeing, across her apartment. She blinked and looked at Sunny, her green eyes cloudy. "You can go, Sunny. You don't need to stay."

"But I want to."

Charley shook her head. "You can go."

***

Charley didn't cry at the inevitable. What had she expected? Her friends didn't really care for her after all. Or at least Jess and Terrance. Xander was more attached to activism than to her. Sunny confused her— standoffish one minute, affectionate the next. *Well,* she thought, *I'm completely unfettered now; no friends, no job, nowhere to live.* She could move anywhere she wanted. Start fresh. No ties to anyone or anything except Baggage. Maybe Sunny would take the cat. They seemed to like each other.

She thought about making a snack. She thought about a bath. She thought about playing word games on her phone.

Instead, she sat on the living room floor, peeled off her socks and shoes, and stared at her feet. So much healing had occurred since she met Xander and the rest that a faint, whitish crust was all that remained of the former eczema patch on her heel. She scratched at the crust with her fingernail, flaking off dead skin cells until she exposed healthy, shiny, smooth pink skin underneath. No rough edges. She twisted her foot and found a thicker section of still-scaly skin on the sole. A little digging unearthed dead, loose skin. She grasped a flake of flesh between thumb and index finger and peeled until she reached live skin. She peeled more, leaving a red, angry path behind. She closed her eyes and shivered, savoring the sharp physical pain. When the pain began to subside, she reached for another loose edge.

***

Jess should've gone to the gym. Working off her pent-up frustration on the treadmill, she decided, would have been more productive than sitting on her bed, third glass of *pinot gris* in hand.

She replayed the evening's short conversation as a form of penance. Try as she might, she couldn't envision things unfolding in a more satisfactory way. Even if she had been the one to tell Charley, the reaction would have been the same.

Her thoughts snagged on Buwan—specifically, the earnest look in his dark eyes when he'd reached forward and rested his hand on her knee. When she'd said that Liam intended to tear down the bookstore, his concerned look faded into a confused mixture of disappointment and fear of her awesome ability to disappoint. She'd seen that look before—in Ozzy's equally kind eyes.

A puff of bittersweet laughter moved her chest as she remembered the day Ozzy first flashed her this look. They'd been playing in the groomed backyard, waiting for the wedding to start.

The Delgados always assumed Bertie and Al Lopez were married, but when Jess was nine, Al revealed to Michael that they hadn't had time to marry before they fled Guatemala. Al had just consulted their local priest and been shattered to find he wouldn't marry him and Bertie because they'd been living together. Al convinced Bertie that being married outside the church was better than not at all. Michael became a temporary officiant for a day, and they held a small ceremony at home.

Jess's mom served as maid-of-honor, Jess was the flower girl, her little brother Philip the ring bearer, and Ozzy the best man. Valerie and Jess wore matching silk dresses chosen by Bertie, except Valerie's was tea green and Jess's was peony. That was the day Jess decided words, unlike numbers, were illogical—a proclamation later reinforced by grammar lessons at school. First off, her mom's dress looked nothing like green tea—Jess had seen the grayish-brown flakes captured in see-through bags in their pantry. And Jess's dress looked nothing like the peonies in their garden. Why couldn't people call them what they were—light green and light pink?

Shooed outside when their pre-ceremony boredom and fidgeting threatened to erupt into the much-vilified running inside the house, Jess and Ozzy retreated to the backyard. Ozzy interrupted Jess's rambling monologue about what they could do for fun without getting in trouble by dropping to one knee before her. He pulled a modest gold band from his suit jacket pocket.

"Put that back! Al gave you that to hold because he knew Philip would lose it."

Osito ignored her. "Jessica Delgado, will you marry me?" He raised his black eyes and grinned his biggest grin—the one that showed his gums and squeezed his eyes into slits.

Irritated at his embarrassing gesture, Jess grabbed the ring and tossed it a few feet into the air.

"Hey!" Ozzy yelled, jumping up from his suitor's stance.

"I've got it, don't worry dummy," Jess said as the ring dropped into her cupped hands.

"Give it back."

"Catch!" she yelled, throwing the ring into the air again, higher this time.

Ozzy threw his head back, hands cupped in front of his face, feet mincing back and forth like a left fielder positioning himself to catch a fly ball. "Got it!" he said as the metal ring found his hands. "I'm going really high this time. Ready?" He reached his arm as far back as it would go, launched it forward and propelled the ring into the sky.

Jess jockeyed for position next to him, arms outstretched. She lost sight of the ring in the sun's glare, forced to shield her eyes with her hand. When she could see again, the ring was gone.

"Did you get it?" Her casual tone suggested nothing less than full confidence in her friend's ability to snag a tiny object out of thin air while blinded by the sun.

Ozzy answered by continuing to scan the sky as if the atmosphere had hung onto the ring for fun and would release it any second.

Jess's stomach turned. "Shoot," she whispered. "That's okay. We'll find it. It's here somewhere."

And that's when Ozzy gave her that horrible look. Shock she would understand. Or anger at her for starting the stupid game. But his eyes said, *You failed me. You disappoint me and I am a little afraid of your ability to always disappoint me.*

Jessica's chest had burned. All that mattered at that second was finding the ring and replacing that look on his face with the look of muted admiration he usually wore. She circled the area, duck-walking and running her dangling hand through the grass. Ten minutes later, she stood up to see Ozzy staring straight ahead, cheeks scrunched up to contain the tears in his eyes.

"Shit," Jess said quietly, the use of the forbidden swear word somehow giving her new strength and confidence—she would find the damn ring. She returned to the spot she'd held when Ozzy swung his arm into the air. She scanned the sky, locating what she thought was the last place she'd seen the ring. In her mind, she drew a line from the sky to the ground. She dropped to all fours at the base of her imaginary line and picked in increasingly large circles through the grass, blade by blade. By now, she felt like Ozzy looked. She inched toward him on her knees, wincing as her right kneecap settled on something hard. Holding her breath, she peeked under her knee and closed her eyes in thanks. Opening her eyes, she plucked the gold band from the grass, wiped off the dirt specks and held it out to Ozzy. Like a spell being broken, his eyes brightened, and his goofy grin shattered his face. His first laugh sounded a bit like a sob but then his normal guffaw took over.

"We found it!" he cried, reaching for the ring.

"Yep. We did."

The back door opened, framing Valerie in her pale green dress. "Osito! Jessica! Come on, we're starting."

The friends ran to the house, stumbling over their laughter.

Jess was so relieved that she didn't even mind when her mother scolded her for the grass stains on the knees of her white tights. In fact, the ebullient invincibility one feels after dodging a bullet made her downright bubbly. She practically skipped down the short aisle between the two rows of chairs, swinging her basket of orange, yellow, and purple flowers—a performance worthy of an approving smile from Valerie.

She didn't remember any of the words Michael spoke as he officiated the ceremony. She thought she remembered a few tears from Bertie when Al kissed her. She did remember Bertie's bouquet because it matched the flowers in her own basket. Having been convinced to wear a plain dress, Bertie declared her love of color in the jumble of flowers she held: bold yellow zinnias, deep purple hollyhock, and bright orange gerbera—all of which looked like daisies if you asked Jess.

But most of her memories of Bertie's wedding day centered around Ozzy. Once in position with the rest of the tiny wedding party, they snuck glances at each other throughout the brief ceremony, trying not to giggle. Several harsh looks from Valerie later, they tried *not* to catch the other's eye, but that produced even more giggles. Bertie hadn't minded. She'd even turned once to beam at Jess and giggle back at her.

Jess patted a hand against her aching heart and heaved herself off the bed to fetch more wine. She knew what she had to do. She had to find the ring.

PART 5:
FALLING APART

CHAPTER 23: PRESUMPTION

"Are you still cross with Jessica?"

"What do you think?"

Xander kneaded Charley's tight shoulders from his position on her couch, Charley having refused to go to Xander's apartment for fear of seeing Jess. He'd had to talk her into letting him come by. Her stiff back conveyed nothing—not even relief when his thumbs broke up a tight spot.

"You're entitled. But I hope you'll give her another chance. Don't tell her I said this, but being a raving capitalist and having a big heart are not mutually exclusive." He massaged between her shoulder blades and waited for a reply.

"But don't you think what she did was wrong?" she asked.

"Char, I hate seeing big business profit at the expense of the little guy more than anyone. But if Flammer had his sights on the bookstore, he would likely have procured it even without Jess's participation. Plus, if you blame her for Georgina selling, and Terrance for not telling you, then you need to blame me, too."

"Why?" she whispered.

"Because if Wilderness Protection hadn't curtailed Flammer's Stone Circle project, he wouldn't have gone in search of other projects. Jess informed me that's how the bookstore came to his attention."

Charley pulled away from his hands. "Thanks for coming over and bringing lunch and giving me the massage. I feel a little better now."

Xander kissed the top of her head. "I'm glad. Are you up for coming out tonight? Food maybe? The Black Lives Matter protest?"

Charley fiddled with her nose ring. "Not dinner. Maybe I'll come to the protest."

Xander stood up and circled his arms a few times. "I could grab a bite with Bu. He's been begging me to do something before the protest. That boy's alacrity is impressive." He bounced on his toes. "Do try to come to the protest. It promises to be even more monumental than the last two nights. Text me and we'll meet up." He picked up his backpack. "Try not to let this apartment become an unhealthy hermitage, even if you feel lousy."

Charley's brow gave the barest of wrinkles. "Assuming hermitage means me being a hermit, how can that happen when my days here are numbered?"

"Point taken. What I mean, though, is try not to wallow in your impending job loss, okay?" He stroked her hair. "It's such a cliché," he added in a joking tone.

Charley frowned. "Just because it's a cliché doesn't mean it's not valid."

Xander welcomed the note of irritability poking through the blank veneer she'd worn all day. He left with a kiss and a promise to check in later by text.

✳✳✳

Maybe Xander liked her some after all, Charley thought. She tried to hang onto that concept, but instead, an absurd image of Jess and Georgina laughing and conspiring against her in the bookstore office insisted on occupying her mind.

She reached for her sock with one hand and slapped her arm with the other, stopping her movement mid-air. She stared at her quivering hands. Shook her head.

Word games. No, a jog. Yes, a jog and then maybe the protest would keep her on track. She'd given into her grumpy mood and skipped her morning run but could make up for it now.

She rushed to her bedroom and pulled dirty jogging clothes from the laundry basket, repeating like a mantra, but one that stubbornly refused to take hold in a distracted meditator's consciousness, "Xander likes me. Xander likes me."

***

Buwan took another plug from a beer bottle encased in a twisted brown bag. "Do you think we look like old winos?"

Through the dimming light of early dusk, Xander studied his friend, the green-slatted park bench on which they lounged, and the block-wide mini-park around them. Car engines revved as the traffic light in the road opposite them changed. Two teenage girls walking the diagonal pathway through the park stared at Xander and giggled.

"Apparently not yet. Give us a few years." He drained his last beer, took Bu's now-empty bottle and put all six beside the trash bin for an enterprising youth or needy adult to return for the deposits.

Bu stood and clapped his hands once. "Liquid dinner complete. Ready to head intown?"

Xander measured his long strides to match Buwan's shorter paces. "How's Charley?"

Xander sighed. "Extremely distraught. She called in sick and I passed the bulk of the day with her." He belched and his head spun a touch, making him lament his deteriorating ability to tolerate alcohol. "Can I confess something?"

"Shoot."

Xander ran a hand through his mop of hair. "I realized something today. While I love Charley desperately, I'm not in love with her. I'm sure you think that makes me despicable. I would have to agree. But as with Sunny, I entered the liaison out of a perhaps misguided belief that she needed me." Xander waited for a retort that never came.

Bu appeared to consult his feet for a few strides before speaking. "Xander, there are two kinds of people in the world: Those who seek the love they need, and those who seek people they think need them."

"Hm. Thanks, I think."

Bu continued. "Wanting to help people doesn't make you bad. But don't forget to think about what you need."

Xander stopped, placed his hands in a prayer position and bowed. "I remain in awe of your benevolence and perspicacity, Moon Boy."

The comment, or maybe the three beers they'd each consumed in half an hour, threw them into fits of laughter.

Xander pointed at a hole-in-the-wall liquor store. "We have some time. Let's stop in here."

Bu pulled a silver flask from the side pocket of his army-green cargo pants and grinned, his eyebrows twitching evilly. "No need."

Xander returned the grin. "Whiskey?"

"Tequila. No limes or salt, but it's a good one so that shouldn't matter."

Xander reached for the flask. "Limes and salt are for the weak. Me thinks I'm a little tanked already, but it's not like I'm organizing the protest or anything." He hiccupped.

Bu bounced gently at the knees as if to a dance beat in his head. "Alcohol doesn't affect me. I'll be designated walker." As he spoke, his eyes skittered from Xander to nearby pedestrians to the pewter clouds dotting the evening sky.

Xander drank from the flask, wiped his hand across his mouth, and resumed walking. "You must be fueled by adrenaline, Bu. I relate entirely though. Protests fire me up as well. And tonight's going to be colossal. I feel it."

"Tonight, we are supermen!" Bu yelled, stepping into the street, arms up, making an approaching car honk as it zipped around him. Bu stepped back onto the curb.

Xander laughed nervously. "Whoa, dude, we're not actually invincible."

Bu eyed his friend. "Don't you ever play chicken with cars? It makes you feel totally alive. Try it."

"No thanks. My self-destructive tendencies revolve around romantic liaisons entered for the wrong reasons and a pathological need to represent at every protest or rally within a hundred-mile radius."

"Loser," Bu joked. "Watch."

He eyed the line of traffic headed their way as the light turned green. He darted in front of a maroon SUV and vaulted onto the median strip as the SUV swerved, its front wheel scraping the curb on the right. "Asshole!" yelled the driver, waving his fist out his window.

Xander pocketed the flask and crossed during a lull in traffic, holding his breath against the gray exhaust lingering behind the last car. He grabbed Bu's arm, hiccups gone. "I'm escorting you to the subway station. Stay with, please."

***

What seemed to Charley like a thousand people milled about City Hall Plaza like restless, displaced insects, thrusting signs into the air that read "Black Lives Matter," "Justice for Jamal," and "Queenie Mattered." Occasional shouts—angry, sharp—punctured the humid, heavy night. Unlike the other protests she'd gone to, there was no rhythm—no speakers, no schedule, no sense of organized chaos. Her earlier jog, despite the impromptu timing, had calmed her. But now, the press of bodies unsettled her.

The police, at least, presented an orderly front—a human border around the plaza, and more cruisers than Charley had ever seen in one place. Ambulances and SWAT vehicles hummed around the edges. Clouds darker than the still innocent night sky scuttled past the stars and obliterated the moon at times, casting somber, fast-moving shadows on it all.

"This is boring." Buwan spoke loudly over the crowd's buzz. "Let's go find some action."

Charley shivered at the thought. Already she questioned her choice to get out of the apartment.

A man broke through the crowd nearby. Charley drew back. "Yo! We got a fight down the street." He grabbed another guy's arm and towed him away.

A flash of moon lit Bu's eyes. "Let's go!"

Xander clutched Charley's hand and started to follow but stopped. He turned back, capturing a burp in his free palm. "You guys coming?"

Terrance's face was a blurry smudge. A cloud shifted and the moon revealed the shadows of his features. "Why would we go *toward* the violence?"

"Because nothing's happening here." Xander's fingers drummed against Charley's palm in his hand.

"Let's go," Bu repeated. His silhouette bounced with impatience, his red shirt indistinguishable from his dark green pants in the cloud cover.

"Come on, Terrance. Engage," Xander said.

A loud *Bang!* from down the street rolled toward them. Shouts followed.

Terrance looked to the sky. "Why are my friends always trying to get me killed?"

Jess stepped closer to Terrance. "T, let's stay here. C, want to stay with?"

Charley hesitated. Xander's hand squeezed hers. "I'll go with these guys," she said.

"Later," Xander said, already moving unsteadily down the street, Bu and Charley close behind.

***

A smattering of cards and flowers rested on the section of blood-stained sidewalk where the homeless woman died. Sunny placed a handmade bouquet of frilly pink and yellow snapdragons, tied with a strand of cork-colored jute, on the concrete deathbed. They bowed their head, lips moving silently, then spoke softly. "I brought you snapdragons because they symbolize grace and inner strength. And presumption. I know you were more than they said. God bless, Queenie."

They moved on toward the subway station to meet the others at City Hall. A wave of people, some carrying signs about Queenie, swept past in the other direction. Curious, Sunny changed course to join, thinking the protestors must be targeting the police precinct they knew was nearby because their dad had worked there a few years before.

At the police station, their stomach soured. Scores of protestors occupied the street in a tense congregation. Fifty or more police in black helmets with clear visors lined the sidewalk in front of the station.

A familiar chorus wafted toward Sunny but offered no comfort. "What do we want? Justice! When do we want it? Now!"

Sunny frowned and pressed on. The heat of the crowd melded with their own body heat. They bumped up against a narrow wall of people, five or six rows deep, running along a makeshift series of temporary wooden barriers separating protestors and police at the sidewalk. Helmeted officers formed an ominous wall, long black riot batons at the ready. Negative energy crawled over Sunny's skin. Body odor and steamy fear wove through the air around them.

"I'm Black and I'm proud!" a man shouted into the lull when the first chant subsided. His eyes caught Sunny's. He wore glasses, a black suit jacket, and white dress shirt. He smiled and stopped chanting. "I am Etufu," he yelled with a lilting accent they couldn't identify.

"I'm Sunny," they said, stepping closer and joining his cry.

The police stood impassive.

Sunny leaned into Etufu as a young woman in a bright yellow shirt with elaborate braids coiled atop her head pushed past. She broke through to the front row of protestors and thrust her fist at the cops. "Stop killing us! When's it gonna stop?"

Sunny cringed as others began taunting the police. A few protestors surged forward. The wooden barriers tipped precariously. The cops maintained position but raised their batons horizontally, as one unit, keeping the protestors on their side of the invisible plane. Sunny held their breath.

A full plastic water bottle sailed overhead, drawing Sunny's eye up. It smacked into a police helmet and bounced off.

Etufu stepped toward the police line, paused, and stepped again. Sunny grasped his arm. He stared, waiting. Sunny could barely hear themself over the crowd's rising taunts and jeers. "Violence is not the answer."

"This is not violence," he yelled. "This is controlled fury born of a lifetime of being marginalized. Of being told how lucky I am to have so little. Come with me or let me go."

Sunny let go.

He nodded and moved away. He shouted and shook his fist at shoulder level, reminding Sunny of a young child tentatively challenging a parent, unsure if it was a smart move.

The woman with the braids backed up, almost stepping on Sunny's toes. She fired a water bottle at the police. As her arm shot back to her side, her elbow caught Sunny's chin. The impact reverberated through Sunny's skull.

"Sorry," she said with a glance.

Sunny cradled their chin with one hand and grabbed the woman's arm with the other. The limb quivered in Sunny's grasp.

The woman faced Sunny. "What?"

"I'm Sunny. What's your name?"

The woman cocked her head and squinted. "Lateisha. Why?"

"This isn't right," Sunny pleaded. "There are other ways. Violence is a crime."

Lateisha's head drew back as she faced Sunny. "You serious? So's murder," she shouted. "What can they do to us? We're in prison already. My skin is my jail. Yours, too."

"You think I don't know that? You think I'm not angry and hurt? But breaking the law doesn't help!"

Lateisha scoffed. "The law *never* protected me. Not even as a kid. Not from my mother's boyfriends. Not from my foster parents. The law doesn't care about me. So why should I respect the law? We got to stand up for ourselves!"

Sunny frowned.

Lateisha shook her head. "You go be the peace police if you want. But get out of my way 'cause I'm here to be heard!" She twisted away from Sunny and shoved her way forward again.

The protestors' momentum threatened to pin the cops against the police station wall. The police breached the barricade and infiltrated the street. They waded in and beat people back with batons. A strange guttural chant rang in Sunny's ears. It finally formed words they could comprehend—the police were commanding, "Move back. Disperse. Move back. Disperse."

Sunny watched Lateisha slip in the crush of bodies and fall to one knee. Eyes wild, she gazed up at an anonymous man in black uniform towering over her. She roared up and heaved all her might against her attacker. The cop rained blows on her shoulders, forcing her back to the ground.

Bile stung Sunny's throat. They inched away through the people surging toward the police. They saw Etufu and stopped. The bespectacled man conversed bizarrely with a policeman who was slowly pushing the man back. Etufu didn't resist. The cop moved him more with body language than baton. Sunny glimpsed a brown neck between the cop's helmet and collar. They stepped closer to hear.

"You're a Judas," Etufu was saying in his accented English. "You are Black first. Cop second." He spoke loudly but calmly as if socializing at a party.

"And don't forget you're more than an angry protestor," the policeman said. "We're not that different."

"But you are part of a racist, oppressive system."

"If we don't work from inside, brother, it'll never change. Now stay back and out of trouble."

The cop placed his hand on Etufu's chest and pushed softly. Etufu froze with hands up, unsure what to do. The cop turned away, reaching up under his visor to wipe his face with his hand. Etufu held his ground silently as the chaos enveloped him.

Sunny hesitated, then moved toward the sidewalk on the far side of the street. A guy clambered down from a metal trash can chained to a lamppost and ran screaming into the surge. Sunny took his spot, using the lamppost as leverage to reach the top of the trash can. They clung to the light pole, their sneakers straddling the hole in the lid's center. Glass crystals crunched underfoot.

Sunny's eyes watered. Their heart tugged with each push and pull by protestors and police. The din hurt their ears. Under the streetlamps' harsh orange light, the protestors looked vulnerable in their light clothing and bare skin, armed mainly with anger. The cops' ominous face shields hid their humanity, but Sunny knew they were like her dad, most of them—good people wanting the right thing. More water bottles bounced off of helmets. Batons rose and fell, hitting flesh with sickening thuds.

"It's too much," they said.

No one heard them speak.

Tears flowed down their cheeks and collected at the jawline, dripping off when the surface tension became unbearable.

They slid their hands down the light pole and slumped into a squat on the trash can.

"It's too much."

***

Terrance and Jess walked single file through the crowds around the edges of City Hall Plaza toward the adjacent tourist district. Some people moved with purpose and others meandered almost lazily. It reminded Terrance of the atmosphere after a concert or pro ball game, except for the constantly changing sky sending eerie shadows in all directions. And the cops in body armor and riot helmets standing guard. Bizarrely, a street vendor hawked hot dogs on a corner, people diverting around his cart on both sides. The smell of steamed meat and human sweat mixed with city dust and exhaust added to the surreal atmosphere.

They stopped and rested against the wall of a small history museum, one of Wrighton's oldest buildings, and watched the chanting crowd from a safe distance.

Jess leaned into Terrance to be heard. "Are you mad at me? About Charley?"

Terrance removed his glasses and wiped them rather than look at her. "I'm not happy that I was the one who had to tell her it was your project upending her life. You know you should have done it yourself. You had plenty of chances."

"I know." She scratched her nose. "But you're not one to talk. You didn't tell Xander you were quitting. He didn't hear it from you."

Terrance replaced his glasses and met her gaze straight on. "That was different and you know it. Me leaving Wilderness Protection meant Xander and I wouldn't be colleagues anymore. I didn't take away his job or his apartment. And if you believe Xander, the store is basically Charley's reason for being."

Terrance didn't care if his words stung. Jess needed to step up and take responsibility for this. Just as he'd finished forgiving her for the night the cops stopped them, she does this—falls short on telling Charley. Sometimes he wondered what drew him to her.

Suddenly, Jess lurched forward. She hit the ground with a grunt. A man with a buzz cut stumbled over her as if playing a clumsy game of leapfrog.

Terrance dragged the guy off by his dark T-shirt, emblazoned across the back with *Moulder's Auto Body*. "Watch out! What's wrong with you?" Terrance put his hands on Jess's waist and helped her up, dismayed both by his inability to protect her and the realization of how much that bothered him. "You okay?"

Jess brushed off her bleeding hands and inspected the rough scrapes on her bare knees, tiny dark pearls emerging from the broken skin.

"Fine." She turned to glare at the man who pushed her, but he was leaving in a hurry. She and Terrance watched Moulder's Auto Body zip away and shove a tall Black man into a White guy. Angry shouts flared between the two men as Moulder moved away. Abruptly, he stopped and yelled, "Death to cops!" before continuing through the crowd.

"That doesn't make any sense," Terrance said.

Jess grabbed Terrance's hand and moved toward the mob. "Let's follow him," she said.

Terrance dragged his feet for two steps, then relented.

Farther down the street, they watched Moulder hunch over a trash can in the shadows, fiddling with something. They reached the trash can as Moulder ran off. Flames licked the top edge of the trash can and *voomed* up with menace as Terrance yanked Jess back. He wrinkled his nose. Some kind of accelerant tickled his nostrils.

"This dude's crazy," he said.

Jess pulled Terrance along Moulder's path. "Come on. Let's stay on him."

Terrance peered through the increasingly agitated crowd. "I lost him. Do you see him?"

"There! I see his ugly skinhead!"

Moulder lobbed a rock at the police. Then another. Then one at the protestors. He disappeared into the crowd again.

Scuffles, shouts, and pushing popped up in his wake. One overly pumped cop lashed out at one overly enthusiastic protestor, and the relative calm splintered. Shouting intensified. Cell phone holders and TV camera crews started filming.

Terrance jerked Jess out of the way as two police officers threw a Black man to the ground right next to them. The shorter of the two cops yanked the man's arms behind his back to cuff him.

"Uh-oh. Here we go," Jess said.

Terrance fixated on the struggle before him.

The man on the ground craned his neck to see the officers. "Listen to me. Just listen to me," he implored.

The taller of the two cops screamed down at the man. "Stop being destructive and maybe we'll listen!"

The man yelled back. "When you start listening, maybe we'll stop being destructive!"

The shorter cop bent over and punched the man in the jaw. Terrance flinched and clutched his own jaw. He shook his head to dislodge the horrifying sound and memory it evoked. He willed himself to stay in the present. *It's not that night,* he told himself.

He tugged Jess back a few steps and surveyed the area. Small fires penetrated the dark in five or six spots now. Small clashes resembling barroom brawls had erupted around the plaza.

Jess leaned in toward him. "Don't they know fighting will get them nowhere?"

He put his mouth near her ear. "Haven't you ever thrown a plate when you're mad?"

Her head twitched. "Possibly."

Terrance nodded and raised his voice. "You've been frustrated, or maybe crazy with grief, enough to throw a plate or punch or kick something. Multiply that feeling times hundreds of incidents over decades of life. Yet people expect protestors to be so balanced and calm all the time."

Jess drew back and regarded him with narrowed eyes. "I thought you were against violence."

"I am. Rioting gives the other side a scapegoat. But I feel the rage. Believe me."

She stared into his dark eyes. "I believe you."

The two cops passed off their detainee to another officer who led him away. They remained, staring at Jess and Terrance, the tall one slapping his baton in his palm.

The short one flipped up his visor. "Hey Hardy, look," he shouted. "It's Dennis Rodman and Jennifer Lopez."

Terrance looked in the hungry eyes of the cop who'd pulled him over that night.

"Don't worry about him, Vignetti," yelled the tall one, lifting his visor, and turning the full force of his mockery on Terrance. "He's harmless. We know that. Let's go find some real troublemakers that need straightening out."

They remained, though, smirking at Terrance.

Blood rushed noisily to Terrance's head. His vision narrowed, gloomy fog pulsating around the supposed protectors of the peace. He squeezed his hands into fists. Closed his eyes. Focused on the rough sensation of his breath in his nostrils. In. Out. In. Out.

"Aw, he's no fun. Let's go."

Terrance opened his eyes to see their backs moving away. What he would give to jump on Vignetti's back, push him to the ground, pummel his face into a bloody mess. Bang his head against the pavement a few times. Knee him in the kidneys and stomach and groin.

"Breathe, Terrance. Breathe."

He slowly focused on Jess. He registered her hands on his straining biceps.

She moved her hands to either side of his face. "That's it."

His eyes locked on hers, finding calm in the least likely of places. He reached up, placed his hands over hers and pulled them away from his cheeks. He held them briefly before letting go.

Jess cleared her throat. "What should we do? Stay here?"

Terrance scanned the scene. The skirmishes hadn't coalesced into an all-out assault. Order seemed to be returning. A fireman sprayed a trash can with an extinguisher; the other fires were already out. For the most part, protestors had remained even-tempered. Police backed off. The two sides re-formed, alert but stable.

"I'm done. I'll walk you to the subway. Text me when you're home safely."

***

The sixteen-year-old was bored. Business wasn't as brisk as he'd hoped. Apparently, tonight's protestors were not interested in diversion by weed, MDMA, or even Oxy. He sauntered from the shadows of the side street for the light and energy of the city's main retail thoroughfare— four lanes of road lined by shops and restaurants that became more upscale the farther south you went. Hundreds of people filled the wide street, many chanting or yelling angrily.

A cute girl with dark hair and a small pink backpack hovering over her round behind turned and smiled at him. "What's your name?"

He smiled back and sidled up. "Call me Calvin. You know, you shouldn't wear a backpack on a night like this."

She shrugged. "Why not?"

He stepped behind her. "Because someone might do this." He grabbed both backpack straps, tore them down and off her shoulders, and ran into the crowd.

He zig-zagged back and forth for two blocks and swung over to a trash can lit by a streetlamp. He looked around, licked his lips. No one paid him any attention. He pawed through the backpack until he found a wallet. Calvin took the cash—a ten and a five—plus a bank card, and scraped through the rest of the pack's contents. He stuffed a pack of gum in his jeans pocket and crammed the backpack into the trash—driver's license, apartment keys, photo of a uniformed brother, asthma inhaler and all.

Three blocks away, a man named Joe Brown and his number-two guy Daryl reclined against a brick building. Joe was squat and hulking in his dark clothes, Daryl taller and wiry. Both carried bulky black gym bags.

Daryl stared straight ahead while talking from the side of his mouth. "Should we start?"

"Soon. Patience." Joe's eyes tripped around the scene, gauging the crowd's agitated mood, analyzing the intimidating police presence. A passing woman held out a joint. "No thanks," he said, his eyes flicking beyond her. He inhaled deeply to center himself and texted his crew. "Start the distractions. Meet in 15, ready to work."

He raised the hood of his sweatshirt, leaving only a dark beard visible. He and Daryl separated. They gravitated toward tense spots based on the crowd's body language and volume. A shouting match developed in front of Joe. *Perfect.* He waited while others gathered, drawn to the altercation, then shoved a woman into another woman, making one fall and the other flail for balance. He faded back as a bystander screamed. A policeman rushed up and raised his baton but then lowered it, unsure where the danger lay.

The shattering cry of breaking glass down the block reached Joe's ears. *Good job, Daryl,* Joe thought. Heads turned toward the noise. Joe plucked a brick from his bag and heaved it into the closest shop window. He stepped back and looked away as the pane shattered. People screamed and reflexively withdrew from the flying fragments, jostling him.

A policeman shoved a mouthy protestor who immediately clammed up, palms out in a gesture of surrender. Joe looked away and hip-checked the protestor into the cop's vested chest. The cop howled and brought his billy club down on the protestor's head. The protestor crumpled to his knees. The cop hit again.

Another crash sounded, closer than the first one. Joe smiled. *Freelancers already. That was too close to be Daryl.*

He strode down the street southbound as chaos billowed behind him. Bullhorns began to squawk. Sirens blared. Crashes, thuds, and screams punched the thick night air. A line of police marched in from the south with rigid, threatening stomps. Dehumanized by full riot gear—shields, helmets, bulletproof vests, shoulder and knee pads, shin guards. Like an echo, a faint clamor of stamping feet approached from the opposite direction. Probably a good block away, he guessed. They were going to squeeze the protestors from both sides—force them off the main retail street and into the side streets. Dispersion by force.

Joe slipped past the advancing line of cops—head, eyes, and hands down—unthreatening. Once past, he hurled another brick—right at a cop's head. The man's face shield cracked. His head jolted.

The battalion of cops reached the main crowd, human tanks plowing into the people. Unprepared protestors shrieked and struggled. Dove out of the way. Shields pushed people aside like flies. Batons worked systematically. Sirens blared from several directions. At the cross street, a string of police vans blew by.

Joe smiled as he jogged to the meeting point. Bedlam achieved.

***

Xander, Buwan, and Charley turned in circles, looking for an outlet amidst the crowd. The action on the retail street was more than they bargained for. Police approached from both sides, squeezing the volatile crowd tighter. Xander watched Charley flinching at nearby sounds—a shout, a body hitting the pavement, a shield making contact—each noise making her smaller.

Adrenaline temporarily quelled the alcohol in his system. He grabbed Charley's arm and gestured to Buwan, who was dodging a baton intended for someone else. "We have to get out of here!" He rushed toward a gap in the crowd. The gap immediately filled with police yelling "Get back!"

Xander turned and pulled Charley in the direction of the nearest side street. Mere steps later—right in front of them—a cop lifted his shield, catching a white-haired man on the forehead. The man's hands flew to his head. The cop stopped as if unsure before moving quickly away. Blood pulsed down the old man's dark face, glistening in the glare of revolving blue lights. He sank to the crosswalk. Blood dripped through his fingers onto the zebra-striped lines.

Xander's mouth twitched. His jaw clenched.

An old White woman pressed a cloth—produced seemingly out of nowhere—to the old man's head. Swimming goggles encircled her neck, and she wore long sleeves and long pants despite the heat. She spoke loudly but in a soothing tone. "Don't worry, Levon. It's not a bad cut. Not like Berkeley. Let's get you out of here." Her frantic eyes made a lie out of her calm voice.

"Do you need help?" Xander yelled, inches from the woman's face.

"We're okay. I just don't know which way to go."

Xander nodded. "Follow us."

He helped the man to his feet. They worked their way past the melee for half a block and then thankfully merged into a cross street with scores of other protestors.

"Do you know where you're going now?" Xander shouted.

"Yes. Thank you. Be careful." The old woman moved off, her skinny arm about the man's waist. Soon the crowd swallowed them up.

"Shit. We lost Bu," Xander cried to Charley. The shock on her face stopped him cold. Her skin was dull and ghostlike. The whites of her eyes showed all the way around her pupils. "Look. It's getting vicious back there. I can't leave Bu. But wait here—don't move from this spot—and I'll be back in a minute." He wedged her against an eight-inch gap between two brick buildings—one housing a clothing boutique, the other a gelateria.

Xander left. A beefy man blew past Charley, bumping her hard, the building's brick corner cutting into her back. Her heart catapulted. She ran after Xander. Thank God he was tall—she saw his head bobbing among the protestors and kept it in sight until he stopped.

She stopped too, a short distance behind him, mesmerized by the scene. The retail street was now a battleground. Cops stationed at both ends of the block. Hysterical protestors in the middle lurching out at anything and anybody. Trying to stay upright. Controlled, unflinching, nondiscriminatory force clashing against long pent-up rage, unbridled frustration, and toxic fear. The resulting infection spreading like a virus through a compromised immune system.

SWAT vans roared in from side streets, forcing protestors to peel back and dive for cover.

Three flashes and bangs exploded near Xander, disorienting him for a second. He ducked reflexively. Straightening, he saw a metal canister rolling on the street. A dense cloud of acrid fog hissed from it, seeking contact with human moisture. More canisters rocketed through the air, white tails whining behind them like fireworks.

"Tear gas!" Xander yelled to anyone who could hear. He tugged a bandana from his pocket and tied it around his face, covering his nose and mouth.

A guy in a red shirt picked up a canister and hurled it back through the rising cloud of smoke. *Buwan.* Xander stormed toward Bu. A padded, black-clothed arm reached through the smoke and grabbed Bu's shirt. A cop, looking like an alien insect in his gas mask, waded through. Wrestled Bu down. Slammed his face into the street. Zip-tied Bu's wrists and hauled him upright. Bu saw Xander and grinned—part of his front tooth broken off, face bloody—and yelled "Avenge me!" as the cop hustled him to the closest black van.

Xander wormed through a gap in the fighting and fled from the tear gas cloud's reach, eyes streaming.

Charley skirted the noxious, sour-smelling cloud and tried to keep up.

As Xander moved, thoughts pinballed around his skull. *Bu. The old couple. People exercising their rights and being beaten. Bloodied. By the people who are supposed to protect. Black lives matter. The oppressors don't see that. Or, worse, they see but don't care.* A surging feeling of helplessness against an apathetic and arrogant oppressor knotted his insides.

Farther down the street—removed from the crush of police and the fog of tear gas—protestors ran freely, shouting and venting their fury on anything and everything. Xander granted the frustrations of the night and of his life free rein. He was so sick of not being heard. So sick of the slow pace of progress. Sick of the ineffectiveness of peaceful protest. Sick of blatant inequality. Sick even of himself, his cowardice in the face of his father, and his meager attempts to save the world.

He banged on the hood of a police cruiser. Its refusal to react mocked him. His anger mushroomed.

Charley watched mutely from behind a corner, eyes smarting.

"Here. Use this." Joe Brown, white teeth flashing in his dark beard, handed Xander a baseball bat, smirked, and moved on.

Xander brought the bat down on the cruiser's hood with all his might. The white metal succumbed. A satisfying crunch filled the air. He brought the bat back. Swung it forward into the windshield. The glass crashed inward—a blizzard of square crystals. *All those years of Little League finally paid off,* Xander thought. He smashed his weapon into the car's side window, a bead of sweat flying from his brow. *Crack.*

Nearby, a plate-glass window exploded in a shower of glass shards. A man used a chair to push out the remaining bits of glass. He stepped into the shop's window bay, immediately followed by other protestors.

Xander moved away from the cruiser and watched. His rage settled into the bottom of his gut, simmering.

A young man brushed past, moving toward the violated storefront. Xander grabbed his arm. "Hey, don't do it. The owners of the stores haven't done anything wrong."

"Back off, man. I'm only gonna take some sneakers or a phone. They're taking lives," he said, pointing his thumb up the street. The man walked in through the store's now open front door with a *whoop*.

Two teens walked up and watched, round-eyed, as a guy and a woman carried a TV out of the next store over.

"Wanna hit it?" one teen asked.

"Naw, man, that's trouble." They walked on.

Sixteen-year-old Calvin emerged from the electronics store, two cell phones in each hand, wishing he'd kept the girl's stupid backpack after all.

Farther south in a quieter block near the street's end, unseen by Xander and most of the protestors, Joe Brown's crew methodically emptied a jewelry store, the property's alarm blending in with the night's cacophony. They heisted everything: watches, necklaces, bracelets, and earrings. Even the silver baby spoons and rattles. Job completed, they bolted out the store's back door, climbed into a gray van, and melted into the night.

Xander retreated from the looting, eyes stinging, and chest tight. He had to get back to Charley. He jogged, ignoring the broken glass, discarded clothing, and trash underfoot. He swerved to skirt a prone, injured body being tended to by another body. Detoured around the cloud of tear gas hanging in the air. Near the main action, he remembered the bat still in his hand. He released his grip. The chunk of ash clunked on the ground. His right arm jerked back, sending excruciating pain through his shoulder and back. He turned toward the pain.

"Wha—"

Handcuffs bit into his wrist. Then the other wrist as a cop wrenched his left arm back. The cop shoved Xander toward the nearest police van.

Xander's blood pressure shot up. His heart pumped furiously. His pupils dilated.

He didn't resist as the cop forced him into the back of the van. But after stepping up and in, he turned and screamed.

Out into the mayhem.

At the top of his lungs.

"Aaaaarrrrrrrrgggggghhhhhh!"

And then he saw Charley through the sweat dripping in his eyes. Stock-still in the pandemonium. Otherworldly in the blue lights and tendrils of tear gas. Unmoving as if shell-shocked. Except her face. With horror, he realized the fear and disgust moving across her pretty features were not for the police or even the rioters. They were for him.

CHAPTER 24: SINKING

Charley watched Xander vandalize a cop car and join a bunch of looters through the nighttime air, ominous and heavy. When he ran from the looting site, she snuck out of view, afraid. But then she followed, equally afraid to be on her own. So she saw and heard him scream when arrested—hair on end, eyes bloodshot—like a savage.

Trembling, she stumbled to the subway station stairs. She made her way down, clinging to the railing, and to the platform. Only two stops and she would be safe at home. *Home.* Such a useless word.

Two men ran down the opposite platform, their footsteps and shouts echoing through the train tunnel. She shivered, coated with cold sweat. The sour smell of the air aboveground stuck in her nostrils, masking the subway's dry mildew odor. Her eyes watered from the mild encounter with the tear gas.

"Sugar, you okay?"

Charley raised her eyes to a middle-aged, matronly woman with a kind face, pressing a tissue against a wound on her forearm.

The woman pointed at Charley's left shoe. "Your foot's bleeding." A walnut-sized spot of red bled through the off-white canvas at the heel.

Charley nodded numbly.

"Did you hurt it at the protest?" Charley had the distant sense the woman wanted to keep Charley conscious, like a concussion victim.

"Yes."

The kind woman had to lean forward to catch Charley's whisper. "Well, it's over now. At least for us, right?" She backed away but remained near Charley until the train came. They boarded together. Charley didn't notice where the woman sat.

Back in her apartment, she landed on the couch and removed her shoes. Her heel stung. The sores were rubbed raw. Dirt-encrusted sweat lines marked her ankles. The clammy sweat she'd felt all night had hardened on her skin.

Baggage wandered into the living room and sat a safe distance away, watching.

Xander terrified her. Jess and Terrance betrayed her. The bookstore—her haven—yanked away. Another "home" lost.

Dully, she realized the curse could manifest itself in ways other than the death of a loved one, a thought she found oddly soothing.

"A chapter in my life has ended, Baggy. I don't know what's next. But it will be different. I just need to get some sleep and then I'll figure it out." Her eyelids fluttered as her body crashed down. She dissolved into sleep in seconds. While she slept, sections of her mind shut themselves down for safekeeping.

Baggage blinked his yellow eyes and licked a gray paw to begin his nightly bath.

***

Getting arrested was the most fun Buwan had had in a long time. Chipping a front tooth sucked. His face wouldn't look tougher with a broken tooth—only goofier. But riding in the police van, getting fingerprinted at the station, having a mugshot taken, and hanging in this holding cell overnight with other hyped-up protestors—that was a blast.

But now, as the lone man awake at four in the morning, with too much thinking time on his hands, he realized something was off.

Hours before, he'd been bouncing around the cell, shadowboxing, jabbering with anyone who'd listen—the drunk tossed in with them around two o'clock was good for that. Then he'd tripped over his own foot and fallen onto a surly protestor who opened his eyes and sneered.

"You're an annoying little prick, you know that?"

Bu frowned. "Yeah. I know."

Replaying the exchange in his head, he tried to laugh it off, but his body wouldn't comply. *Why wasn't he laughing? Why was the stupid comment getting to him?*

Bu sighed and rubbed his thumb over the scar tissue under the tail of his dragon tattoo. He'd had similar conversations with himself over the years, so he knew the answer. His shifting attitude wasn't a conscious choice. That finger of doubt threading into his psyche was not in his control. The stupid finger crooked itself at his insecurities, saying *Come on over and join the pity party. Charley wants Xander, not you. Little blonde whatshername at the reggae festival only wanted your stash of shirts. You're a second-rate artist. An unemployed loser.*

Bu put a hand on top of his head and yanked on his short black hair.

He dreaded the soul-sucking lows. Maybe this would be a quick trip.

He sank to the floor, the unyielding steel bars of the cell door tracking his spine.

CHAPTER 25: BEHIND THE CURTAIN

When Xander couldn't reach Charley for a week after the riot, he assumed she was mad at him and needed space. Jess and Terrance assumed Charley was mad at them about the bookstore. But when no one heard from her in two whole weeks, alarm bells rang.

"She is unresponsive to texts or calls," Xander said to the others as they clustered in an assortment of aging, folding lawn chairs in the suburban backyard of the house Terrance shared with four roommates. The lawn showed yellowish-brown in spots—evidence of a recent dry spell. The clean smell of freshly mown, well-watered grass visited from the neighbor's yard. "I went up to her apartment and knocked but got no answer. I asked Georgina if she'd seen her and she said no, and she was quite unhappy about Charley going AWOL."

Terrance waved a spatula back and forth from his grill-side position. "Did you hear any noise inside?"

"One mere meow from Baggage," Xander replied.

Sunny, too, had reached out, their desire to keep a distance from Charley and Xander overruled by the need to make sure Charley was safe. "She's not returning my messages either."

"I texted her a few times and got nothing," Terrance said. "She must be really pissed off. Who could blame her?" He looked pointedly at Jess.

Buwan—whose mania rebounded after the brief depressive episode in jail—crossed his legs at the ankles, jiggling his foot. His tongue noodled his broken front tooth. "Maybe she's not mad. Maybe she's sad."

Sunny readjusted themself in the saggy lawn chair. "That would make perfect sense. But if she's sad, wouldn't being around friends help?"

"It's not that easy. She might be depressed."

Terrance stopped waving the spatula. "Like clinically?"

Bu shrugged. "If she's depressed, she's depressed."

Jess cleared her throat. "Let's go see her. Drag her out for some fun."

Bu stood and paced around the circle of friends, a behavior they'd grown accustomed to. "You can't just decide you're gonna be happy and then be happy."

"Why not?"

"Because, Jess, it's deeper than that. It's a sickness. When you get a cold, no one tells you to decide you don't have one. They don't say it's the food you eat or your attitude making you sneeze and cough." He frowned at the yard's one tree, a small maple. "But when someone's got a mental illness, people say you should just get over it or decide to be normal. If it was that easy, a lot less people would be depressed."

Xander ran his hands through his messy hair.

Jess blew her bangs out of her eyes.

Sunny focused on Bu. "What do we do?"

Bu sighed. "Give her time, I guess. And let her know we're here for her. Maybe take over some food or something." The others nodded as one. "I'll go over tomorrow and see if she'll talk to me," Bu said.

"I'm coming, too," Sunny said.

***

The occasional muffled noises at her apartment door—knocks, voices, scuffling—receded into the audible woodwork of Charley's existence. Like the city noises creeping through her windows, which remained open no matter the weather, the sounds occurred behind the thick, heavy, dark blue curtain and therefore did not affect her or require attention.

Life was comfortable behind the curtain when you stopped fighting, as she'd learned before. Occasional sharp jolts of loss pierced the veil: the bookstore. Her apartment. Her friends. Xander. Without fail, the memory of him hunched in the back of the police van screaming like a savage sent her mind reeling back to the safety of the void.

So she ignored the noises at the door. She didn't want company. Didn't need it. Didn't deserve it. Couldn't risk it.

She still functioned. Her new routine was simple—only two things to remember: order enough pizza or Chinese food to share with Baggage; and move from the bed to a new setting—the couch—when she wanted to play word games. She convinced herself the latter demonstrated discipline when, in truth, it was the increasingly sour odor of her sheets that drove her into the living room at least once a day.

Emptying the litter box posed an exhausting dilemma at first. She began scooping and dumping Baggage's poop into the toilet even though it's bad for the pipes. It didn't matter anymore since the pipes and the toilet and the bathroom and the building would all be demolished soon.

Her heels were troubling. The tears in her skin used to bring sweet relief from unwanted thoughts and feelings. That relief was elusive now. Some days, she scratched her arms and legs instead, but it was harder to draw blood like that. Some days, she applied band-aids to protect her feet from herself. And some days, she picked anyway as proof of her weak resolve and worthless, unlovable character.

***

Jess tapped on the heavy mahogany door of Lisa Reilly's office and wondered when she'd be ensconced behind a similarly impressive door.

The vice president of human resources ushered Jess in and closed the door. Lisa's wavy black hair and milky skin played off her sophisticated suit of black with white trim.

At her initial job interview with the company, three years before, Jess remembered how Lisa tapped her pen against her lips while perusing her notes. Jess had wondered how many times a day Lisa reapplied lipstick because of this pen-tapping habit.

Lisa had lifted her eyes from the page.

"You put 'White' for race. Is that right?"

Jess cocked her head. "Does it affect my chances?"

Lisa's guarded eyes disclosed nothing. "I can't say, but diversity does matter at All-American or I probably wouldn't be here." Her eyes flicked to the office door and back.

"Ms. Reilly?" Jess asked.

"Originally Martinez. Reilly is my married name. Like you, I'm light enough to pass."

Jess couldn't decide if she felt camaraderie, annoyance, or outright offense. She smiled and gave the tiniest shrug. "I don't really need to 'pass'—I'm an American citizen. I was born here."

"So, your answer is . . ."

"It's fine like it is."

Lisa shrugged. "Okay." Her tone suggested Jess had passed on a winning lottery ticket. "Well, you've still got the woman card," she muttered, consulting her notes again.

Since then, Jess had made a point of chit-chatting with Lisa when she could, and they'd built a tentative relationship based on female solidarity or simply professional respect—Jess wasn't sure.

"Sorry it took so long to get this meeting," Lisa was saying. Jess smiled to indicate she'd suffered no inconvenience. "What did you want to see me about?"

Jess straightened her shoulders. "The accounting manager job in the commercial development division. I don't understand why the search is taking so long. Rodney's retiring next month."

Lisa tapped her silver pen against her lips.

"The wait isn't helping department morale," Jess added.

The phone buzzed. Lisa glanced at the caller ID. "I have to take this. Stay." She picked up the receiver with one hand and patted down the air between her and Jess with the other.

Jess lowered her eyes to indicate a lack of interest and attention, when in fact she took in every nuance of Lisa's end of the phone conversation.

"Lisa here . . . Oh, hi, I thought you were—Mm-hmm. . . . I know. . . . There's no need for concern. The system has worked for years and it's still working now. . . . That's what alm is for. . . It works like all shell companies . . . . I'm doing what you've always told me to do. Alm only hires the ICs . . . . Right . . . . Right. . . ." Jess felt rather than saw Lisa look her way. "Honest Abe," she said in a lower voice. "Hm. . . . Mm-hmm . . . Okay." Jess heard a steady tone coming through the phone line, and then Lisa hanging up.

Lisa cleared her throat. "I assume that call meant nothing to you, but just the same, please assure me you'll treat what you heard with the utmost discretion."

Jess nodded. "Of course." She believed "alm" was "AALM" for All-American Landscaping Management, a subsidiary of the parent company she worked for. "Honest Abe" she'd never heard of.

"Where were we?" Lisa said. "Right, the accounting manager position." She sighed, her bosom pushing against the seams of her fitted jacket. "First off, for me to be candid, I have to emphasize this conversation is off the record." She waited for Jess to nod. "It's taking so long because we're also looking outside the company."

"That's absurd," Jess blurted. "I'm more qualified, or as qualified, as anyone for this job. Even Dennis is qualified. We both know the company. Why would Jay look elsewhere?"

"Jay is doing what Liam wants." She put the pen down. "Look, I hear you're doing a great job, Jess, but I hate to see you get your hopes up. Chances are, it's just not going to happen for you, and you might as well know that now."

Their eyes locked.

"Is it because I'm a woman? Or too pushy? Or Colombian? What is it, Lisa?"

Lisa smiled wanly. "Pick one."

***

Bu worked his way through the bookstore to a small dark office tucked in the back. After his eyes adjusted to the gloom, he made out an old woman at what looked like an equally old desk.

"Georgina, right?" Bu beamed his broad smile.

The bookstore's owner turned toward him, the swivel chair squeaking, her face sour.

Bu's eyes lifted to a plaque on a shelf above the desk. "Whoa, is that an award up there? Wow, did you win that?"

Georgina grumbled. "Independent bookstore owner of the year, 2005," she acknowledged.

"That's amazing," Bu said. "You must be really good at what you do."

Her lips twitched. Her eyes narrowed. "What do you want?"

He stepped closer. "I'm a friend of Charley's. We're worried about her. Do you know if she's even up there in her apartment?"

Georgina snorted and doodled on the desk blotter with a blue ballpoint. "Don't know. Don't care. I do care about hiring someone to replace her. Want a job?"

Bu took another small step forward as if taking Georgina into his confidence. "Maybe if she's up there, we can get her to come back to work."

Georgina stopped doodling.

"She's probably upset about the store being sold," he continued with a half-smile. "But I totally get why you're doing it," he added hastily. He looked at the plaque again. "You've earned it, right?" Georgina nodded hesitantly, as if waiting for a punch line she would not find humorous. "Anyway, if you let me in, maybe I can get Charley to show up for work." His eyes shot open as if a thought suddenly occurred to him. "Man, it's going to be hard to hire someone new if the store's being sold, isn't it?" He waited, eyes round and innocent.

"You want me to let you into her apartment?"

"Or I could just borrow the key. I'll bring it right back."

Georgina sighed, opened her desk drawer and pulled out two keys on a flimsy keyring. "There are two locks—doorknob and deadbolt. I don't know which is which." She handed him the keys. "Don't forget to bring them back," she said, already turning toward her computer.

***

Bu took the stairs to Charley's apartment two at a time.

"Shhh," Sunny said, "you don't want to scare her."

Bu doubted Charley was aware enough of her surroundings to be scared. He remembered the way she described being engulfed by the blue velvet dress of depression. He remembered his own heavy dark days when nothing broke through the invisible, padded walls. But he moved more quietly for Sunny's sake.

He opened both locks, eased the door open, and led Sunny in. Litter box stench assaulted their nostrils with a vengeance.

"Charley?" they both said. No reply.

Bu held Sunny back with a hand on their arm. "I'll check. Wait here. Maybe open the windows wider."

He took the few steps to the bedroom and peeked in through the half-open door. Charley lay on her back, brown hair fanned across the pillow, mouth open, snoring softly. After watching her chest rise and fall a few times, Bu returned to Sunny. "She's fine. Sleeping."

They turned their attention to the small living room and galley kitchen. Empty pizza boxes and Chinese food containers cluttered the coffee table and kitchen counter. A dozen or so dirty glasses, some with crusty residue, were strewn around. A lopsided pile of haphazardly stacked newspapers struggled next to the couch.

Baggage sauntered into the living room, meowed, and pressed his gray-and-black-striped body against Sunny's leg. They didn't react.

Bu patted Sunny's shoulder. "It's okay. At least she's eating."

A clunk drew them to Charley's bedroom doorway.

Charley's eyes were dull marbles in her pasty face. Snarls marred her long hair.

"Charley, hi!" Sunny said in an unnaturally upbeat voice.

Charley clamped her eyes shut and pulled the covers up to her chin.

Bu sat beside Charley on the bed. The blanket and sheet were all twisted. One corner of the fitted sheet had pulled loose at the bottom of the bed. Bu picked up a section of blanket. "My Mamalay calls this scrambled-eggs bed."

Charley opened her eyes and blinked at him.

"There you are." Bu willed his energy down to a normal level. He slowly reached for her and patted her arm a few times. "We were worried about you."

Charley's grip on the covers loosened. "Why are you here?" Her voice cracked from disuse.

"We miss you. Listen, Char—it's okay that you checked out for a while." He stared intently, willing her to hear him. "But you don't want to live there forever, right?"

Charley's face scrunched up as if she might cry. It reverted to normal one muscle at a time. "I don't know."

"Great!" Bu said, as if she'd unequivocally expressed a tremendous zest for life. "Listen, since we're here, how about we help with some cleaning?"

"Okay," Charley whispered. Her eyes scanned the piles of dirty clothes and empty glasses around the room. Bu thought her pale cheeks colored a bit.

Sunny ran a bath and helped Charley to the bathroom. Bu stripped the sheets and bundled them plus all the clothes from the floor into a laundry basket. He left for the laundromat and the hardware store to duplicate the apartment keys.

When he returned, Sunny was tossing food containers into a large garbage bag. Their movements were jerky. They spoke robotically. "She's getting dressed. I washed and combed her hair and got her to brush her teeth. She's lost weight. She wouldn't let me help her get dressed."

"That's good." He started to collect glasses, but they stopped him with a hand on his arm.

"Bu, she didn't want me to take her socks off before the bath. When I insisted, her foot was all bloody. I thought she'd had an accident but—" Sunny stopped as a sob erupted, bending them at the waist.

"But what? She did it herself?" Bu asked.

Tears slicked Sunny's face. "I think so. It didn't look like one cut. It was a mess of torn skin. And the other foot was the same." They wiped their cheek. Their brown eyes met his. "Why?" they whispered.

Bu sighed heavily. "Different people, different reasons. Sometimes 'cause physical pain distracts from emotional pain. Sometimes to have some control in a world that doesn't feel controllable. And sometimes just to know you can still feel something."

"Hey," a small voice said from the hallway. Charley limped into the living room, her feet protected by thick fuzzy socks and soft slippers. She wore the clean, mint green T-shirt and gray sweatpants Sunny had laid out for her.

"Hey, Char. Sit down and chill." Bu led her to the couch. "We're gonna finish cleaning."

Sunny returned to filling the trash bag. Bu loaded dirty glasses and forks in the kitchen sink and added so much dish detergent, bubbles threatened to spill over the sink's edge.

Bu looked over his shoulder, watching Charley. "Baggage was sleeping with you," he said.

Charley's eyebrows knit together. "No. He hates me."

"Hmm." Bu shrugged as if maybe he imagined it.

When the living room and kitchen were picked up and wiped down, Bu left to change over the laundry, leaving Sunny to deal with the scummy toilet and the cat litter sprinkled around its base.

When Bu returned the second time, Charley had moved her laptop onto her thighs. She stared at the screen, noiselessly moving her mouth at times. The laptop's sound was muted. Bu peered at the screen.

"*Wheel of Fortune*?" He smiled. "No word games on your phone?"

Charley continued staring at her laptop. "Battery's dead."

Sunny emerged from the bathroom, deposited a pair of rubber gloves in a trash bag, moved to the couch, and perched awkwardly next to Charley. They took Charley's hand. Charley's eyes left the computer screen and rested on the mix of tawny and milky flesh. She frowned as if trying to place a name to something she'd forgotten.

"It's going to get better, Charley."

Charley didn't move, except to utter "Why?" The word seemed to require great effort.

Sunny swallowed. "Because it has to. Because you have people who love you and need you."

Bu knelt in front of Charley. "It's going to get better because it just does. You have to hang in there. Okay?"

He left one last time to collect the laundry. When he came back, Sunny and Charley still sat side by side on the couch, hands still locked, Charley watching *Wheel of Fortune,* Sunny trying to watch Charley without being obvious. Baggy had snuggled up beside Sunny on their other side.

Bu put the laundry away. He found Charley's phone under the bed and plugged it in to charge. He also found a shard of blue sea glass, one edge tinted with dried, rust-colored blood, which he tucked in the pocket of his jeans. A startling caw sounded outside the open bedroom window. He whirled to see a black streak crossing the sky as a puff of air whispered against his face.

He returned to the living room, closed the laptop and waited for Charley to look at him. "We're going now, but one of us will be back every day or so to help out."

Charley frantically shook her head, the energy surprising Bu. "No! You don't have to. I'm fine."

Bu patted the top of her damp head. "We know. But we're coming by anyway. I need something to do. You know that." He smiled at her until he saw her eyes see him.

Sunny mumbled goodbye and stumbled out of the apartment.

At the bottom of the stairs, Sunny dissolved into weeping. Bu wrapped them in his arms.

"Bu, you're so good with her. How do you do it?"

Bu separated from them and smiled sadly. "I've been there, that's all."

Sunny's knees buckled and their face twisted. "No!" they cried as if their vehemence could negate his statement. "You're like the opposite of depressed."

"That's because I've got bipolar one. Manic-depressive disorder."

"Oh. How come none of us knew?" they asked.

"It's not your fault," Bu said. "I'm good at hiding it."

Sunny's tears tumbled over again. Bu led them to the subway and then home.

CHAPTER 26: LOOPHOLES

"I know how we can save the bookstore."

Jess bounced up from the space-age, puffy beige chair in Buwan's loft and paced back and forth between her chair and the mirror-image chair occupied by Bu. Xander, Sunny, and Terrance studded the long burnt-orange couch at equal intervals like sparrows on a telephone wire. Getting Terrance to come wasn't easy; he was still annoyed about being forced to be the bearer of the bad bookstore news to Charley. But when he heard Jess had a plan to help Charley, he was all in.

Sunny tucked their legs up under them as if to contain their excitement. "How? Don't keep us in suspense."

"Well, there are two funny things going on at All-American's landscaping subsidiary. I saw the quarterly financials by accident—the labor numbers seemed off. Then something the top HR person said got me thinking. So I did some digging." Jess stopped pacing the gouged, polished floorboards and rested her hands on her hips. "I found out the landscaping company is using sketchy practices to hire illegal aliens—"

"Jess, call them undocumented immigrants!" Sunny said. "They're not aliens from another planet."

Jess shrugged. "Whatever. One thing they're doing is hiring immigrants as independent contractors so they don't have to show papers. But there are a ton of loopholes in that scheme. I don't think we can get Flammer that way."

Bu squinted. "Wait—we're going after Flammer?"

Jess nodded. "But I also found out—I think—the company is paying some illegal immigrants cash under the table and hiding it under a pile of subsidiaries, some of them shell companies." She looked at them, wondering why they didn't share her excitement. "Paying people cash under the table means—"

"The company isn't paying taxes on those employees' wages!" Terrance jumped up and fist-bumped Jess, immediately backing off as if her hand burned. He turned toward Xander and Sunny. "Not reporting cash wages you pay to your workers and not paying taxes like Social Security and Medicare on those wages is completely illegal."

Jess grinned. "Tax fraud and evasion, to be exact," she said.

Sunny slowly bobbed their head. "How easy will it be to expose this?"

"Liam's not stupid. The actual company that hires these people isn't an All-American subsidiary. It's called—get this—Honest Abe Personnel Management. Ballsy or what?"

Xander scoffed. "Pardon me if I don't share your fervor for his audacity. I've always known he was a criminal morally. Now we know he's a criminal legally, too."

Sunny fiddled with their lower lip. "I'm lost. How do we get him in trouble if it's not his company?

"I have to prove they're connected," Jess said. "I found contracts between the two companies, and two former All-American executives run Honest Abe." She shuddered, remembering the risk she'd taken, digging deep into the corporate accounts. If someone noticed her computer was used to access certain files, who knew what trouble she'd be in.

"But how will you prove they're using illegal labor?" Terrance asked.

Jess plopped into the chair. "I haven't figured that out yet. None of Honest Abe's accounts show up in our system."

Xander drummed his fingers on his thigh.

Sunny played with the long end of their lavender headband.

Bu stared out one of the loft's six-foot-high windows.

Terrance adjusted his glasses. "You need help."

Jess smirked. "Gee, thanks for that bombshell."

To her surprise, Terrance winced at her sarcasm. "I mean, you need outside help. Like an investigative journalist at the city's biggest paper." Terrance leaned forward, hands on knees. "Let me call my contact in business news tomorrow. I'll also try Brian O'Connor. He's a columnist who covered immigration a few weeks ago."

Xander held up his hand. "Hang on. Can I confirm the goal is showing Flammer pays landscaping crews under the table and isn't paying his fair share of taxes?" Jess nodded. "And if that's proven, his business will suffer and hopefully the bookstore acquisition comes to a grinding halt?" Jess and Terrance both nodded. "What about the multitude of workers who are dependent on those landscaping jobs to feed their families?"

Jess stared at Xander as if he'd spoken a different language. Terrance perused the exposed beams and pipes of the loft's ceiling.

"Right," Jess said slowly. "What about them," she trailed off.

"Seems to me that saving the bookstore and Charley means taking out not only Flammer but what—scores? hundreds?—of hard-working immigrants."

Terrance sighed and nodded at Xander. "It's the classic trolley dilemma."

"Say what?" Bu said.

"The trolley dilemma," Xander said. "It's a morality exercise." He stood and paced the same path Jess traveled earlier, between the two beige puffy chairs. "You're a trolley conductor and something goes wrong. The trolley starts running away and you can't control it. You spy five workers down the tracks who are about to be run over by the trolley. Then you realize you can switch a lever and divert to another track where one person will be killed. What do you do?"

"Easy," Jess said. "Switch the lever. Lose one life but save five."

"A common reaction," Xander said.

Sunny shuddered. "I couldn't handle either. I wouldn't want to be responsible for anyone's death, even if it's to save someone else."

Terrance raised a finger. "Inertia is a decision, too," he pointed out.

"We digress," Xander said. "Let's make the dilemma more pertinent to our circumstances."

Jess took comfort in the fact that ownership of the problem had broadened beyond her to include their whole group.

"This time," Xander continued, "the person who's all alone on the other track is a loved one of yours. You have no relationship with any of the five workers on the first track. What do you do?"

Buwan spoke immediately. "If we don't stand by our friends, we're nothing."

"But X, our situation isn't as dire as in your example. We're not choosing between life and death." Buwan and Sunny exchanged frowns. Jess noticed. "What?" she said. "How bad is she?"

"Bad," Sunny whispered.

Jess turned to Terrance. "T, what do you think? Save Charley or lots of immigrant workers we don't know?"

"There's no easy choice. You could evaluate the pros and cons of both options."

Bu exhaled noisily. "You guys are incredible," he said, his tone not complimentary. "You're looking at the pros and cons of saving Charley's life." All eyes fixated on Bu. "That's what this comes down to, you know. Even if she isn't suicidal, yet, she's not living a real life now. We can help her."

Jess chewed on her lip and stared at her shoes.

"Maybe," Sunny said, "we can minimize the impact on the employees somehow."

Xander stared unseeing at the coffee table. "If an article about illegal immigrants working at the landscaping business is published, ICE will raid the place within hours."

Terrance leaned forward. "So—we insist the paper not publish the story until after work hours. That gives the employees time to hear about it and decide if they want to show up at work the next day or not, in case ICE does raid. Does that work?"

Xander shrugged. "It helps."

Bu peered at Xander. "You don't seem like you're on board with this."

"I have a hard time putting hundreds at risk to save one. We could support Charley in alternative ways."

Sunny winced. "Your broad worldview scares me sometimes." They stood, picked up their water glass, and moved toward the kitchen.

Jess declared, "It's settled then."

Terrance lowered his eyelids at Jess. "It's good to see you fixing the problem you created, but I'm surprised you're good with this plan."

Jess puffed her bangs out of her eyes. "Like you said, I need to fix it. I can't save everyone in the world. But I can save one. So that's what I'll do."

"I actually meant in terms of your job. Aren't you worried about risking your promotion if they find out you leaked the information? Or keeping your job for that matter?"

Jess's head jerked toward her shoulder. She quickly applied a hand to the back of her neck as if massaging a tight spot. "Let's not worry about that."

***

How it got to this point, and so fast, Jess wasn't sure. But here she stood, loitering in the hallway outside the executive suite at five o'clock, waiting for the regular monthly meeting of the top team to break before cocktails were served. What's more, the phone in her suit jacket pocket was recording the still air around her.

When Terrance contacted the newspaper columnist Brian O'Connor, he had been extremely interested in the potential story of Liam Flammer committing tax fraud. Brian brought in the paper's investigative team who, it turns out, had been watching Flammer for months. With more digging, Jess had uncovered payments by All-American to the two executives now at Honest Abe for unspecified consulting services. She'd downloaded that and the other incriminating details she'd found onto a flash drive for Brian.

The columnist had located two former Honest Abe employees willing to talk but not to be named in an article, fearing retribution; they still had friends working at the company. Both spoke at length about the long hours Honest Abe workers logged for minimal pay in cash, and how sometimes they were cheated out of overtime pay. But reporters and editors alike agreed they needed more concrete proof before publishing an exposé. Thus, the secret recording idea was born.

Jess smiled and said "Hi," as Lisa Reilly exited the executive suite, followed by Liam and Jay. Lisa entered the women's room. Jay entered the men's room. Thankfully, Liam held back to check his phone. When he moved to put it back in his pocket, Jess approached and clutched his forearm.

"Mr. Flammer, could I talk to you? Privately?"

His eyes registered no recognition.

"I'm Jessica Delgado, from the finance department. It's about the books. I think you should know what's going on."

"Talk to Rodney or Jay."

She squinted and said *sotto voce,* "I think you'll want to hear this yourself."

He perused her up and down, grunted and said, "Follow me."

Jess's knees wobbled as she trailed him into the executive suite and then his office. She felt the eyes of his blonde assistant and the executives milling around outside the big conference room on her back.

Liam leaned against his desk. He crossed his legs at the ankles and his arms over his chest.

"What's this all about?" He sounded more intrigued than irritated. A good sign.

"First, I have a quick question about the bookstore acquisition. Are we one-hundred-percent committed to the deal?"

Liam regarded her coolly.

"I know it's unorthodox, but my father—Michael Delgado, as you know—taught me to look out for the little guy once in a while—only once in a while, I assure you—and this is one of those times."

Liam frowned. "Who's the little guy? Not the old lady who owns it. Marty says she's got one foot out the door already."

"It's a woman named Charley Byrne," Jess said. "She manages the store and lives over it. She'll lose her job and her apartment if we demolish the building. Maybe we could keep the store instead of razing? There's a market for bookstores that modernize and cater to gamers and students and people who want a relaxing place to sip a latte and read a mag—"

Liam stopped her with a wave of his hand. "That's it? That's all you've got? You want me to kill a nice little money-maker for one person? Who the hell is Charley Byrne and why is she so important?"

Jess's heart fluttered. She leaned toward Liam a touch and smiled to acknowledge she knew he was indulging her. "She's a very good friend."

He studied her for ten seconds. "Request denied. I suggest you start acting like the person who proposed the deal in the first place, Charley whatshername be damned."

Jess nodded and tugged at her earring nervously. "Understood. I figured it couldn't hurt to ask." She hadn't told Brian or Terrance she planned to appeal to Liam on Charley's behalf before going for his jugular. She'd wanted to try to avoid the whole labor scandal and not damage the company she worked for or put the employees at risk. Now that he'd turned her down, all bets were off. She steeled herself. "So, I discovered something strange in our books—a discrepancy in the landscaping subsidiary's accounts. Jay may have mentioned it?"

Liam didn't acknowledge her question so she continued. "I dug into it, in the name of protecting the company. And I realized we've got some creative accounting going on there." She took a step toward him and lowered her voice, even though the door was shut. "Are we doing what I think we're doing on the labor side?"

"What do you think we're doing?"

"I think, Liam, that we're using illegal aliens for cheap labor and paying them under the table."

A hint of a smile touched his lips. "Hmm."

"That's what we're doing, right?

He remained silent.

"I mean, it's genius. First, I found the independent contractor model being used at AADM's residential and commercial businesses. I think you're fully protected there."

Liam smirked. "My lawyers will be happy to hear that from an accountant."

"But the Honest Abe connection—that took longer to put together."

The skin around Liam's eyes tightened.

"Not paying taxes on those wages must do wonders for our bottom line."

"Jessica, I don't own Honest Abe. They're merely one of our vendors."

"Maybe we don't own them directly," Jess replied. "But I put two and two together. Fletcher and Fitzgerald? Formerly executives here, now paid as consultants while they run Honest Abe? Come on, Liam, tell me. We're Honest Abe, aren't we?" She smiled as if in camaraderie.

Liam chuckled drily. "You are your father's daughter."

"Meaning?" She struggled to keep smiling.

He shifted the cross of his legs. "Did you know Michael's the one who opened my eyes to the beauty of using illegal labor in the first place?"

Jess lost her smile. She fought to stay focused, ignoring the pit sprouting in her stomach. "Well, my father is not who I thought he was," she said, to buy time.

Liam uncrossed his arms and let them dangle. "Meaning?" he said.

Jess had to get the ship back on course. *Think!* she yelled at herself. "My father chose to leave All-American. Why would he walk away from a good thing? I'm more ambitious than that."

Liam closed the gap between them in one stride and put an arm around her shoulders. "I think it's time for us to have a real talk. We're not making good use of your talents."

Jess tried not to shrink back from his touch. He still hadn't admitted to anything. "So, it's true, Liam? We are paying Honest Abe workers under the table?"

He chuckled. "Of course it's true. But you already knew that. Now let's talk about your future here."

***

After Jess left his office, Liam called his assistant in.

"Holly, hon, do I know a Charley Byrne? Name sounds familiar."

Holly smiled, her teeth framed by red lipstick so glossy it appeared liquid. She flicked her long blonde hair back over her shoulder. "I'll check, Mr. Flammer."

"Let me know if I do. I'm going back into the conference room. Time for a drink."

Ten minutes later, Holly floated noiselessly into the conference room and handed a slip of paper to Liam who, Irish whiskey in hand, was making good use of cocktail hour by issuing directives to his head of commercial operations. After making his point, he stepped back to read the note. He scanned it, strode to the glass wall overlooking the financial district, and read it again in the natural light from the summer sky. A wicked smile crawled onto his face. Charley Byrne was Phil Parlan's granddaughter. He'd met her at Phil's funeral, which he paid for unnecessarily out of spite; one final jab to his former mentor and ultimate nemesis, if you will. He didn't remember the kid—it was seven years ago, for Chrissakes—but Holly assured him they'd spoken to her at the service, offering Liam's help should she need it in the future.

This bookstore acquisition got sweeter all the time. First, they got it for a lowball price. Second, he had used it to teach the Delgado woman a lesson about priorities. And now, by bulldozing it to the ground, he could punish this Charley for her grandfather's self-righteousness.

Liam took a new whiskey from the bartender, who'd left his station to deliver the fresh drink.

No, he didn't give a shit about Charley Byrne. He was surprised the Delgado woman even made such a weak appeal. And then, to turn around and surprise him with her smarts and resourcefulness, connecting dots no one outside of his inner circle even knew existed. Jessica Delgado. She had balls. And he always needed creative accountants. If she was half as clever as her father, that was plenty to work with. Problem with Michael was, he grew a conscience. Wouldn't it be fun to turn Michael's own daughter into the hard-core, cutthroat person Michael refused to be?

Holly floated into the room again. Phil's funeral took place around the time Holly started, that he remembered. So, she'd been with him seven years already. Hard to believe. She took good care of herself, anticipated his needs and kept him organized, and her memory performed like a steel trap. He would overlook the advancing age until it became a definite problem.

***

Jess called Terrance the second she got home. He was still being distant, but helping Charley gave her a legit reason to contact him.

"Got it," she said when he answered his phone. "Tell O'Connor he can have the recording, but on one condition."

"I'm listening," Terrance said.

"My father can't be part of the story."

"Why would he be?"

"Flammer says he got the idea for paying the landscapers under the table from my dad."

"Jess, I'm sure Flammer didn't need your father to put that idea in his head. But I'll talk to O'Connor about it."

"Thanks. I have to go shower now. Maybe twice."

After settling onto the couch in clean sweats, the distastefulness of bad-mouthing her dad and sidling up to Liam somewhat washed away, Jess revisited the end of her discussion with Liam. He'd assured her she'd get the accounting manager job when Rodney retired, and implied that the promotion represented the tip of her career iceberg. The tantalizing vision of an office with a thick mahogany door like Lisa Reilly's and—more important, prestige and respect—wormed its way into her thoughts.

No, she reprimanded herself. If All-American survived this, she would leave. She didn't want the promotion this way. Her father hadn't needed Liam Flammer and neither did she.

She took out her phone and trimmed the recording, removing the first ten minutes of waiting and her appeal to Liam on Charley's behalf.

***

Charley didn't even turn her head when Xander unlocked the apartment door with the spare keys Bu made. She sat, a lump on the couch, her laptop endlessly playing *Wheel of Fortune*. Occasionally, her lips moved but her eyes remained blank and her body listless.

Xander breathed through the pang in his heart. Sunny had said he didn't need to help Charley change clothes. Her hair didn't look like it needed combing. Her bangs were freshly trimmed, courtesy of Sunny. He was only on grocery duty. He took the two bags he'd brought with him into the kitchen.

A bowl filled with water rested in the sink, an empty Ramen noodle package on the counter.

Reflecting on what he'd learned about depression from Bu, Xander decided this was huge. She had prepared food herself, and had even run water into the bowl after.

He put the groceries away in the fridge and cabinets and stared into the bowl of water, drumming his fingers on his leg. Nodding to himself, he went to Charley. He thought her eyelids flickered when he entered the room, although she didn't look at him.

He sat beside her on the saggy, blah blue couch. "Charley? Can I shut this for a minute?" He rested his hand on the laptop and waited.

She closed her eyes and gave a small nod.

He closed the laptop's lid.

"I know you feel like shit and I'm sorry. I wish I could help more. I'm compelled to ask: Am I responsible for this in any way? The night of the protest, when I got arrested—I saw you and you looked justifiably horrified. With me. With my behavior. I stand appropriately horrified myself and I've been conducting more than a modicum of soul-searching as a result. More important, did my display have anything to do with how you feel now? Did I hurt you?"

Her eyes winced a tiny bit.

"If I did, I'm sorry. Truly." He closed his eyes and inhaled and exhaled. He opened his eyes. "Are we over? You and me?" No reaction. "You are an astonishing person and I love you, Charley, I do. But you and me as a couple—what do you want? Are we over? Is that better for you?"

He almost missed it, but it was there—the barest of nods. His chest ached with the finality of their short-lived romance, even though he knew it was better for both of them.

"Do you need me?"

He sensed she was more responsive than she let on, but not willing to engage with him. He studied her like a hawk for any type of reply. There it was. A tiny head shake.

"Still friends?"

Nothing.

Then Charley's hand inched across the foot of fabric separating them. She found his hand and rested hers on top of it. Gently, Xander rolled his hand over and entwined his fingers with hers.

She still stared straight ahead, so he looked at her feet for signs of self-harm. If she was still hurting herself, the socks hid the evidence. No visible blood. He cleared his throat. "I don't want to wear you out, but there's something important you should know. Jess did something for you."

Charley's eyes gave another tiny wince.

"She's trying to derail Flammer's purchase of the bookstore." Charley's finger fluttered in Xander's hand. "If her plan succeeds, you won't lose your job or your apartment." No reaction. "I'll keep you posted, okay?" No reaction, but her eyes looked shinier than before. Hope? Latent tears?

Xander kissed her hand, let go, and stood. "I'm leaving, but Terrance will swing by tomorrow, and you know you can text me if you need anything."

No reaction.

Swallowing his sigh lest she think him frustrated with her, he left quietly, locking the door behind him.

Charley stared straight ahead. Her lips formed soundless words. "Thank you."

After a minute, she rose and headed to the kitchen to wash her bowl.

CHAPTER 27: THE SERPENT & THE MOON BOY

Panic hummed in the air when Jess walked into the accounting department at work. She'd purposely left at five the night before, for the first time in her career, not wanting to be around when the article hit the newspaper's website. She'd purposely arrived at nine this morning, also for the first time in her career, dragging her feet because she didn't want to come in at all but knowing she had to show up.

She approached the hubbub in Dennis's cubicle where he, Steve, Carl, and two other accounting team members stared at the computer screen. A local news broadcast had broken into regular programming to show the aftermath of immigration raids at Honest Abe and AALM that morning. Jess could hear other newscasts trickling over cubicle walls from other computer screens.

She shifted her briefcase strap to her other shoulder. "What's going on?"

Dennis's pale blue eyes gleamed with excitement or maybe panic. "Didn't you see the article? Or hear the news?" He handed her the morning newspaper. The above-the-fold headline blared, "Company Tied to All-American Accused of Tax Fraud". Jess feigned ignorance of the article even though over breakfast, she'd read and re-read that piece, plus O'Connor's column entitled "The Human Cost of Illegal Labor".

"We're in big trouble," Dennis continued. "Some company called Honest Abe's been using illegal immigrants for cheap landscaping labor, under the table, and we're connected to it somehow. At least that's what they're claiming." Sweat stains darkened the armpits of his light blue Oxford shirt.

Jess frowned mock disbelief. "That can't be. Who's Honest Abe? What does Rodney say?"

"He's not saying anything. He's holed up in his office with the door shut. But I don't think he knows much either. I saw him talking to Jay in the hallway earlier and Jay said to leave him alone, he had fires to put out."

"Hm," Jess mused. "Have we called anyone in accounting at our landscaping subsidiary? We must have a contact over there."

"Yeah. They're as surprised as we are."

Jess watched as the live newscast replayed footage of the two raids. Tipped off by the article the night before, all of the city's TV and news radio stations were in position before dawn and ready to record when ICE showed up around six-thirty. The footage showed workers— mouths and eyes agape— being rounded up by ICE agents as they arrived at work. They were frisked, hand-cuffed with zip ties, and— heads hung, shoulders slumped—herded onto buses. No official number of arrests had been released.

The news anchor interrupted her own comments, holding up a hand. "We have new information. ICE has confirmed the number of people arrested between the two facilities is sixty-five and they have been taken to a temporary detention center outside the city. What happens next, ICE isn't saying."

Jess lowered her eyes. Sixty-five victims, out of more than at least two-hundred workers by her calculations. Could have been worse. She wished it had been better. *Why did those sixty-five people show up for work?* She thought of Charley holed up in her apartment, barely living. She hoped this was all worth it.

Her co-workers dispersed when the newscast ended, but little work was accomplished that morning. Threads of steady murmur wove through the air. Tidbits of information tumbled across the seventeenth floor like whispered wildfire. *Rodney's gone to a meeting of all the company's managers. Honest Abe's website doesn't say anything about*

All-American but it's a rinky-dink site, they don't list their clients anywhere. Someone saw Flammer come into the building and he looks pissed. Someone over at AALM said we do use Honest Abe for our landscaping crews.

By midday, the lack of reliable information and increasing fear about job loss spawned speculation, rumor, and bad jokes. *So much for our claim of using one-hundred-percent American labor. I knew the landscaping company's profits were too good to be true. Of course we paid them cash—who wouldn't, since illegal immigrants can't count? I heard Flammer didn't know anything about it. I heard Flammer knew everything about it.*

So when Carl looked out the window and yelled something about the office being raided, people ignored him at first. "I'm serious. There's a bunch of SUVs and vans with tinted windows and like twenty guys in suits about to swarm the building."

Everyone in earshot ran to the window and watched the unidentified agents sweep under the portico roof protecting the skyscraper's entrance. When the agents disappeared from sight, eyes remained glued to the portico as if something else important might unfold there. Jess's gaze rose to the baby blue sky dotted with several perfectly puffy clouds as she thought what a nice day it was for a corporate raid.

A half hour later, Rodney rushed into the main walkway dividing the department's cubicles and offices into two sides. Strands of gray hair drooped across his forehead as if they'd lost the will to cling to his pate. A man in a black suit trailed him like a shadow. "Everyone is ordered to vacate the building," their boss said. "Now. Leave your computers on. Take nothing with you except your personal belongings."

Jess stepped forward. "And then what?" she asked.

"And then I don't know. I'll be in touch somehow when I know more."

Dennis stepped forward, even with Jess with his shoulders back. "Rodney, what's going on?"

Rodney's eyes skittered to the man in the black suit and back to his employees. "We're being investigated for possible willful and unlawful hiring of undocumented immigrants," he intoned as if reciting from memory. "Immigration and Customs Enforcement and the Department of Homeland Security will be going through our books. This will take at least a few days."

Jess needed to know how strong the case was. "But we're not Honest Abe," she said. "They're only a vendor. I don't get it."

Rodney looked to the agent man, who spoke in a neutral voice. "We have reason to believe Honest Abe is actually a front for AALM, and that the parent company for which you all work was in full knowledge of the fraudulent activities taking place there. I tell you this because if any of you have information supporting or disproving these claims, now would be the time to speak up." He scanned the clump of fidgeting employees. "We'll be set up in your ground-floor conference room. You can stop in there on your way out of the building if you have information. Or you can call me directly if you prefer." He handed out business cards to each person. "You have fifteen minutes to vacate." He noiselessly pivoted and strode out.

"What the hell, Rodney?" Dennis asked, his voice pleading for reassurance. "Does this mean we're all out of jobs?"

Rodney spoke in a low, conspiratorial voice. "If it's true, there's probably going to be a fine. That's all. We'll pay it, and it will all be over."

Sighs passed through the ranks.

Only when Jess had packed her things, left the building, and settled in a nearby bagel shop did she allow a smile and a sigh of relief. She did it. It was in motion. And she was safe. She hadn't stopped to talk to the agents on her way out; she'd done her share already. Whether Flammer's business activities and the bookstore purchase were curtailed or not was out of her hands. If the reporter was true to his word, no one would ever tie her to the exposé and investigation.

She grabbed her phone to text Terrance, then thought better of it and called him instead. A phone call was harder to ignore than a text.

She needed his reassurance she'd done the right thing, and she wanted to ask if he'd look at the résumé she'd updated last night.

***

"Took you long enough. Get in here."

Liam Flammer pulled Marty Murkowski into his office and started to shut the door. He poked his head out of the opening.

"Holly, hold—"

"Holding your calls, Mr. Flammer."

Liam's head retracted into his office like a turtle's receding into its shell.

Marty laid his leather briefcase on the round table in Liam's office and sat in one of the black-leather-padded chairs. Liam sat too, although he acted like it pained him.

"What a clusterfuck, Marty. Tell me what's going to happen."

Marty frowned. "Didn't bring my crystal ball today."

The lawyer's curt reply earned him a glare from his most important client, but he didn't care—much. He was sick and tired of pulling Liam out of the holes he dug for himself, and this hole was so deep he wasn't sure anyone could fix it, not even him. After all, his government contacts didn't extend to the IRS, ICE, or DHS.

Still, he needed to act the concerned advisor a bit longer. "Sorry, Liam. I'm feeling a bit on edge. Let's start by pooling our knowledge of what's actually happened." Liam nodded once and floated his hand in the air like a king granting a peasant permission to rise. "Honest Abe was raided by ICE this morning and forty-two undocumented immigrants were arrested."

Liam interrupted him. "Don't give a shit about Honest Abe. Nothing to do with us."

Marty raised his eyebrows. "Well, we can circle back to that. AALM was also raided, and twenty-three more people were arrested, for a total of sixty-five. Computers were seized at both locations, as well as at All-

American Landscaping, Inc., and of course here at corporate." He paused, knowing Liam wanted to say something.

"If I didn't know better, I'd think you were enjoying this."

Marty frowned and shook his head for good measure. "Just being thorough. Comes with the job. Have you been contacted by your banker?"

"No. Why?"

"That's good. The IRS hasn't moved to freeze the assets yet."

Liam's brow sunk to a new low. "But?"

"But I think they will. Probably after a bit of digging. The IRS has a ninety percent success rate with its tax-related criminal investigations. They like to have a solid case before they go too far."

"What do we do in the meantime? Move the money?"

"It's too late for that. They have all your digital records, so they pretty much know, or will know, everything about your inner workings soon enough."

Liam puffed air out between his lips. "Good thing we put all those layers between corporate and Honest Abe," he said. "We can't be found liable for a contractor's hiring practices."

Marty pursed his lips in a subtle pout but his eyes gleamed. "Not so, sadly. Companies that hire contractors that hire undocumented immigrants can be held liable under federal law."

Liam's eyebrows hooded his eyes. "Why didn't I know that before we got to this point?"

Marty sighed and sat back. "I did tell you. As you'll recall, when you hired me, I recommended curtailing this exact practice." He pulled a sheet of paper from his briefcase and held it up. "On March 2, 2006, to be exact, according to these meeting notes."

A vein throbbed in Liam's temple. "What are we looking at here? For charges?"

Marty cleared his throat. "Charges might include filing fraudulent tax returns—more specifically, neglecting to report wages and to pay federal and state taxes on those wages, knowingly hiring unauthorized individuals, and—if they get creative—harboring undocumented immigrants, which can apply if more than ten such individuals have been hired."

Liam's eyelids drooped, shading his eyes. "And the potential fallout?"

"Assuming you mean punishment, some combination of paying the back taxes plus penalties, and jail time."

Liam stared unnervingly at his lawyer, head swaying like a king cobra preparing to strike. "Jail?"

Marty blinked rapidly, several times. "Federal prison, to be more precise. But it might only be a few months for a first offense, if that."

"Well, praise the Lord for small favors," Liam said sarcastically.

"There's some good news," Marty said. "It's unlikely your business licenses will be revoked."

Liam's harsh squint suggested he was not buoyed by this tidbit of news.

Might as well pile it on, Marty thought. "Of course, even if you can stay in business, the PR ramifications will be significant. Liberals will spurn you for paying unethically low wages to the poor immigrants, maybe even holding back overtime pay, although I'm not saying you did—I'm not privy to those details. Conservatives will feel betrayed that your claims of using all American labor were a sham. So—" He ended with a shrug meant to convey helplessness on his part.

"What do I do, Marty?"

The words made Marty all warm and fuzzy inside. Usually, Liam told Marty what to do. And when he did ask Marty for guidance, he usually managed to make it sound, in the end, like the course of action was his idea. Liam had never needed Marty as much as he did right now.

"Get your executive team and senior managers together and split up the job of reaching out to all your critical contacts—major customers, partners, vendors, and suppliers—to reassure them everything will be fine, and you'll continue to operate an ethical business and honor all contracts. Distance All-American from Honest Abe—you knew nothing of their hiring practices, which you do not condone. Also, I assume there will be an emergency board meeting ASAP, and a statement issued to the media. That should take us through the rest of the day."

A tap on the door was followed by Holly's voice flowing through a crack in the door.

"Mr. Flammer? May I come in?"

"Yes."

Holly stepped in and shut the door, long hair swaying. "Jay's been trying to reach you urgently."

"My phone's off."

"I told him that. He insisted I interrupt and give you this." She handed Liam a pink message slip and backed out of the office.

Liam read the note and crumpled it into a ball.

Marty raised his eyebrows.

"Twelve of our commercial landscaping clients have canceled their contracts, and the financing just got pulled on one of our development projects."

Liam heaved the ball of mashed paper across the room.

***

It wasn't even midnight, but Buwan couldn't rouse a friend to go out on the town with him. Charley was of course indisposed. Sunny was getting settled in their new place—they'd finally agreed to move in with Jess and Xander. Xander was away for a protest in another city. Bu even tried Jess and Terrance—always the least likely to join him—but they also said no. That left him with only the ants under his skin.

He'd put the finishing touches on his latest painting earlier and wanted to celebrate. And possibly tame the ants, if that were possible.

Sighing, he plucked a half-smoked joint from the ashtray on his coffee table and picked up his lighter, but his hands shook so badly he almost singed his eyebrows trying to get the joint going. He threw the roach and lighter down in disgust. Alcohol might help him chill, but he'd already drank all the beer and liquor in the house.

Stability seemed increasingly elusive under his self-medication plan. Maybe he should go back on his meds.

He lay down on the couch and stretched from head to toes. Maybe he could sleep. Maybe.

Fuck it. He was going out.

He jammed his wallet, phone and keys into his white painter's pants. He hit the elevator call button but couldn't wait. He descended the stairs two at a time, bursting out of the building like a swimmer who stayed under the surface two strokes too long.

Dismissing the subway as agonizingly slow, he headed out of the warehouse district on foot toward downtown and the closest bars. A light mist evaporated the second it hit his skin. He walked for blocks. His legs burned. His heart raced. The ants boogied under the skin of his arms. He stopped under a streetlight, half-expecting to see his skin bulging with little ant shapes, but the only raised areas were the same bits of scar tissue that always imbued his dragon tattoo with an undulating, animated presence. For a second, his mind misinterpreted the streetlight glow on the dragon's fanged mouth as moonlight. He stepped out of the streetlight's circle to see his lunar namesake more clearly. He raised his face, closed his eyes, and prayed for the moon to heal him.

Feeling nothing, he walked on, speaking out loud in a sing-song cadence, ignoring the strange looks from the occasional passersby.

"Moon Boy, meet the Bakunawa. Bakunawa, eat the Moon Boy. Moon Boy, meet the Bakunawa. Bakunawa, eat the Moon Boy."

The green and yellow neon sign of the closest bar—a modest one on the outskirts of downtown, near the highway on-ramp—became visible at the end of the next block. He locked his gaze on the colors and let them pull him forward. Maybe a game of chicken when he got to the intersection would satisfy his jones for frenzy.

A childish yelp turned his head as the mist strengthened to a fine-toothed rain shower. A nearly white Labrador retriever puppy peeked out from an alley, holding up a front paw. Bu stepped toward the puppy, who bounced forward, stopped, and retreated back, tail between its legs.

"I won't hurt you, little guy."

A young man with a long beard rushed up, exclaiming, "Skipper, there you are!" He scooped the puppy in his arms. "You scared me half to death." The dog rewarded his person with grateful licks all over his face.

Out of nowhere, sadness coursed through Bu's body. He walked on.

I'll never have a puppy who loves me like that. I'll never have a normal relationship with a woman. Who wants someone like me? Someone who can't control his emotions. Ants under his skin. Limbs afire. No job. Dark skin.

He cursed the finger of depression beckoning to him. One minute up. One minute down. One minute squeezed between the two. The rain thickened. Droplets gathered on his brow. His vision blurred. Reality receded.

The green and yellow neon glare of the bar.

The red hand of the crosswalk.

The changing traffic light.

The rain in his eyes.

The rev of the SUV.

Melding.

He stepped into the street.

Moon Boy, meet the Bakunawa. Bakunawa, eat the Moon Boy.

PART 6:
CROSSING OVER

CHAPTER 28: COMPARATIVELY SPEAKING

Sunny let themself into Charley's apartment using the keys hidden under the loose linoleum on the landing. Charley was awake even though it was three in the morning; all hours were apparently the same to her. She sat on the couch, staring at her laptop, headphones isolating her further from the world. Baggage was perched beside Charley but hopped off and ran to Sunny for a quick rub against their leg. Charley's eyes followed the cat. When they landed on Sunny, a spark followed by a veil passed over them. Charley turned away.

Sunny walked quietly but quickly to the couch. They eased the laptop shut and stood before Charley. Hoping for a look but getting none, they spoke in a quivery voice. "I don't know if you like us or if you hate us. Maybe both. But I'm here to beg you to come out of this,, even if it's just for tonight, because Bu needs you."

Charley blinked twice.

"He was in an accident and he's in the hospital. He's in bad shape. Can you come?"

Charley lifted eyes so mournful Sunny wondered how she stayed upright under their weight.

"I know it's hard to go out right now, but can you do this? I'll help."

Charley stood. Her voice was clear. "Will he be okay?"

Sunny shook their head and held back tears. "They don't know yet. He was hit by a car."

Charley sighed so softly it could have been mistaken for an exhalation. She walked to her bedroom.

Sunny followed, pulling out clothes and helping Charley change into clean pants, shirt, and sweatshirt. The pants were so loose, Sunny wished they'd chosen sweatpants with a drawstring, but they didn't want to take up more time changing. They pulled Charley's hair back into a low ponytail rather than comb it.

As they moved to leave, Charley spoke again. "I need to brush my teeth."

Sunny nodded and watched as Charley spread toothpaste on her toothbrush like a child who'd recently mastered the task and was still enthralled with her achievement.

On the twenty-minute drive, Sunny's thoughts ran willy-nilly—prayers, hopes, and fears, for Charley and for Buwan.

***

Charley thought about what it would feel like to be hit by a car. Or dead. Probably a lot of nothing. So what was the difference between death and her current state? Not too much. But even as she thought this, she knew dead people didn't have these thoughts—they couldn't—therefore she was better off than dead. Comparatively speaking.

***

Sunny and Charley entered the hospital's Intensive Care Unit waiting room, immediately adopting the hush usually associated with libraries and funeral homes. The room was lit dimly, the wee hours cloaked behind vertical blinds.

Jess and Terrance sat beneath the windows, an empty seat between them. Anne Johnson-Bakunawa sat against the far wall, legs crossed, foot bouncing. Two brushed nickel sconces on the mauve wall framed her with narrow cones of light. She held a magazine up as if blocking out her wife Layla, who paced the room back and forth, back and forth. The only other visitors were an old man dozing in his chair and a plump woman holding a pencil poised over a crossword magazine. An employee in a puppy-festooned scrub shirt focused on paperwork at her desk behind a Plexiglas divider.

Layla stopped pacing and regarded the newcomers.

"Hi. I'm Sunny, remember? We met at the Women's March? And Charley?"

Layla nodded. Behind her frameless glasses, purplish half-moons drooped below her eyes. Loose bits of skin marred her lips.

"He's out of surgery and in recovery. We're waiting for the doctor." She resumed pacing.

"Thanks for coming," Anne said over her magazine.

Sunny and Charley joined their friends. Sunny asked in a low voice, "What do we know?"

Jess leaned forward, across the empty chair, in Terrance's direction. Terrance pulled back as Jess spoke quietly. "He was walking on Pearl Street near Congress and got hit by a car. An SUV. Witnesses say he bounced up on the hood and then off. He was brought here by ambulance. His mother found Xander's number in Bu's phone. Texted him. He texted us. That's it."

"Is Xander coming?" Sunny asked.

Jess rolled her eyes as if Xander were her wayward son. "You would hope, but he's out of town for some protest and isn't coming back 'til tomorrow night."

Sunny frowned. "Disappointing."

"Bullshit, you mean," Terrance said. He leaned forward to see around Sunny. "Charley, it's good to see you. How are you doing?"

"I'm okay. Let's worry about Bu."

Terrance gave Charley a thumbs-up. Jess leaned closer. "I'm really glad you came. Anne said Bu was asking for you on his way into surgery."

The swinging doors from the restricted area flew open, admitting the sound of someone whistling. A white-haired man in green scrubs and cap, mask half-untied and dangling at the base of his neck, followed. He went to Anne, who stood. Layla was instantly at his side.

"Mrs. Johnson-Bakunawa. Mrs. Jo—" he stopped rather than repeat himself. "The surgery went as well as it could. There was considerable internal bleeding, a lacerated liver, possibly kidney damage. No rupturing of the spleen—that's good. We tied everything up neatly and now we wait to see if any complications develop."

"Prognosis?" Layla demanded.

"He's young and strong. A full recovery is very possible. But the next twenty-four hours are critical. We'll watch him closely."

"Other injuries?" Layla asked.

"Broken femur—orthopedics will address that soon. A fractured pelvis, cracked ribs." His eyes traveled to the framed watercolor behind Anne's head. "Broken collarbone, multiple lacerations, and extensive bruising." He nodded.

Anne put a hand on the doctor's forearm. "Did you talk to his psychiatrist yet?"

Layla frowned. "Anne, he's been in surgery. That's not his job."

The doctor looked at one mother then the other. "I believe someone is contacting your son's psychiatrist as you requested. Rita," he gestured toward the woman behind the Plexiglas divider, "can give you updates when they're available. She'll also let you know when you can see your son." He nodded and left, resuming his whistling as he pushed back through the swinging doors.

Layla rolled her shoulders up and back. "Really, Anne? Adjusting his meds isn't going to fix his injuries."

Anne sniffed. "Maybe he wasn't taking them. Maybe that's why this happened. It needs to be addressed. What if this was intentional?" She turned to the friends. "Do any of you know if Buwan's been taking his medication?"

Sunny shook their head.

"What was it for?" Jess asked.

"He's bipolar," Charley said. "But we don't know if he was taking them or not. Sorry."

Anne searched all of their eyes as if the truth were hidden somewhere within them. Unsatisfied, she went to speak with Rita. After a several-minute-long consultation, she turned to Layla. "Come on. We can see him now."

***

Bu's parents reported back that he couldn't see any other visitors for a few hours at least, but no one wanted to leave. Sunny rested their head on Terrance's shoulder and napped. While Terrance slept, Jess moved into the empty chair next to him and rested her head on his other shoulder. In his sleep, Terrance's hand slipped onto Jess's thigh.

For the first time in weeks, Charley wasn't lured by sleep's oblivion. When Sunny told her what happened, her body threatened to dump her back into the depths she'd slowly been emerging from. It was only her firm belief that Bu needed her that kept her from sliding down. She felt like she was hanging on by her fingernails, but she owed it to Bu to stay alert and figure out her role in this.

She was still stewing when Xander crept in two hours later.

"I thought you were away at a protest," she whispered.

"I was able to get a bus back." He sat, rubbed his eyes and slept.

***

Anne nudged Charley. "Are you awake? Bu's asking for you."

The window blind had been tilted to allow strips of mid-morning light into the waiting room. Within a few hours, it would be returned to the closed position to block out the day's heat.

Charley followed Anne through the swinging doors, down a bustling hallway, and into a private room.

Bu waited for his mother to leave before speaking to Charley. "Sit. Let me look at you." His wise-ass grin was one of the few recognizable bits of him—that and his thick, short black hair. A large bandage covered half his forehead. His face was a mass of purple, red, and yellow bruises. His dragon arm hung in a sling, looking for all the world like a folded white wing. A long gash, multiple bruises, and an IV peppered the arm with the geometric-patterned tattoos. His splinted leg appeared twice as large as the other leg under the sheet and thin blanket. Humming machines surrounded him like he was a bee in a hive. "You're a sight for sore eyes, Char."

Charley sat in the room's lone, wooden chair.

"How do I look? Tough?"

Charley remained silent.

"No head injuries, so that's good. Having a hard head finally paid off."

Charley pulled the chair by its wooden arms as close to him as possible. "Bu. I'm sorry. I only came to say that. This is my fault."

He squinted. "I was afraid you'd say something stupid like that. The curse isn't real. A curse didn't make me walk into traffic. My brain did." His words slurred a bit.

She didn't react. Just listened to him breathe for a minute.

"I decided I'm going back on my meds 'cause I'd rather be alive than dead, even though dead artists make more money." He laughed, winced, and rested his free hand on his chest. After he began breathing normally again, he moved his hand toward Charley and wiggled his fingers. Slowly, she moved her hand to him. She let his fingers curl around her hand. He closed his eyes. Charley watched his chest rise and fall. She thought he was asleep until his eyes shot open.

He smiled so suddenly, it surprised her and she almost smiled back. The tug of her mouth muscles confused her. He squeezed her hand weakly, so she stretched her lips up in a token smile, for Bu. *I remember this,* whispered her skin cells to her nerves and muscles. *It feels nice,* they whispered back.

"People like us have to decide what kind of life we want to live. It's harder for us to get it, but sometimes we can if we try," Bu said, resting after each sentence. "We definitely can't if we don't try." He paused for breath. "Do you want to live like this? Holed up in your apartment? Feeling responsible for the rest of the world?"

"I don't know. But I keep losing the people I love. And now I'm losing things, too."

"The store."

She nodded.

"If you lose the store, it's not because you're bad or cursed. It's because shit happens. Life happens." His hand jumped. Pain registered on his face. Charley's eyes widened and watered. His face gradually returned to its placid purplish state.

"I should go."

"No. I'm not done. Everybody needs friends. There are two kinds of people in the world. Those who realize it and those who don't. You and I got lucky when we met those guys. Even Jess. Don't throw it away."

Charley stiffened as the sentiment moved through her.

They sat silently for a minute. "That's all I've got for life advice. How are your feet?"

She pulled her hand away and pinned it under her thigh.

"It's okay to talk about it. It's not who you are. It's a symptom of your pain."

Charley shifted and stared at her lap. "I haven't been picking at them as much," she said.

"Why not?"

"Sometimes when I start, Baggage sits in my lap." She felt Bu grinning. She raised her eyes. He looked so victorious she couldn't help but smile back. For real this time. "I couldn't believe it either. Maybe he likes me after all."

Bu laughed as much as his beat-up chest allowed. Charley laughed too, lightly, the sound foreign and echo-like to her ears, medicine to Bu's.

***

After a tasteless breakfast in the hospital cafeteria, feeling no better than before despite Terrance's assurances that food would energize them, the friends lumbered back up to the ICU waiting room. Jess grabbed Charley's arm as the others filed past, stopping her outside the door.

"Can we talk?"

Charley's eyes squeezed shut as if to protect her very soul from the troubles Jess represented. Realizing Jess wouldn't take no for an answer, she simultaneously sighed and opened her eyes.

"Right. You have to know how sorry I am about the bookstore. And for not telling you sooner. I was wrong. But I didn't want to hurt you. Do you believe me when I say I didn't know you when I suggested the company buy it?"

Charley could think of no reason not to believe other than spite, but she only stared at her feet. Jess maneuvered into Charley's line of vision, making her look Jess in the eyes. Charley flinched at something she recognized but hadn't expected to see there: pain. Silent pleading joined the pain. Charley didn't want to cause pain. She nodded.

Jess hugged Charley lightly as if afraid of breaking her. "Thank you. And I'm trying to stop the deal. I found out that All-American's using illegal immigrants and not paying taxes on their wages. I leaked the information to the city's biggest daily and they ran a big exposé on it and we should know soon if that's enough to stop all the company's projects."

Charley's face creased. "What about your job?"

"Friends matter more than jobs." Jess's voice caught on the words. "I'm already looking for a new place to work."

Terrance opened the door of the waiting room, which now harbored only the friends and the old man. "Charley! Jess! Come here, quick!" They followed him in. "Listen to this. Go ahead, Xander."

Xander looked at his phone screen, scrolling as he read. "'The U.S. Internal Revenue Service has opened an investigation into hiring practices at Honest Abe Personnel Management, in particular the possibility the company is hiring undocumented immigrants, paying them cash under the table at rates below minimum wage, and neglecting to report the wages on federal and state tax returns and to pay federal and state taxes on those wages. Because documents suggest Honest Abe's only client is All-American Landscaping Management— AALM—a subsidiary of All-American Development & Construction—

AADC—those companies are also under investigation, as is another subsidiary, All-American Landscaping, Inc. AADC CEO Liam Flammer could not be reached for comment on the investigation or the ICE raids of Honest Abe and AALM last week. AADC's outside legal counsel Marty Murkowski confirmed the companies' bank accounts have been frozen and work on all All-American projects has halted as a result of the investigations.'"

Sunny squealed through closed lips and did a happy dance.

Jess's hand flew to her mouth. "I found the ring."

Terrance hugged Jess and swung her around. "You did it! You saved the bookstore!" He set her down and stepped back, his hands lingering on her arms.

"Couldn't have done it without you, T."

He smiled warmly and nodded.

The old man, roused by the commotion, looked at each of them in turn before closing his eyes again.

Xander went to Charley, who hadn't moved since he announced the good news. "Do you understand the significance of what happened? Flammer won't be acquiring your store after all. Jess saved it."

"Do you think so?" Everyone stopped celebrating to hear Charley's soft voice. "What if Georgina sells it to someone else now?"

"One step at a time, young Charley. We've stopped the imminent sale. While Georgina's ascertaining what comes next, so can we."

Anne poked her head through the swinging doors. "Charley? Sunny? You can all come to see Bu for five minutes." She motioned for them to hurry.

They clustered around Bu's bed, quelling their excitement in keeping with the sedate air in the room.

"Whoa, B, looking a bit rough," Jess said.

Bu smiled weakly. "You should see the other guy. The SUV, I mean. I destroyed it."

Xander leaned close to Bu. "Never you mind what she says. You're still devastatingly handsome in my book."

Bu's eyebrows shot up in mock surprise then quickly fell back, as if the movement pained him. "Why Xander, I never knew you felt that way." He gave an awkward laugh born in his mouth, not in his damaged belly or chest.

"Enough about you. It's not like you've been in a car accident or something."

Bu shrugged minutely.

"Bu, guess what?" Sunny said. "Jess's plan worked. Flammer's being investigated by the IRS and all his projects are on hold. He probably can't buy the bookstore now."

"That's awesome. Way to go, Jess."

"Team effort all the way."

Xander reached into his backpack and began fishing around. "Speaking of team, I have trinkets for everyone. I've been carrying these around, waiting until we were united again."

Charley blushed, knowing it was her fault their reunion took so long.

"I got 4Ocean bracelets for us. For every bracelet, the pelagic crusaders retrieve a pound of trash from the ocean. I matched you up with the animal most like you."

Jess and Sunny exchanged skeptical looks.

"Bring it on," Terrance said.

Xander sorted through a pile of braided strands. He extracted a white one and handed it to Terrance. "You get the polar bear bracelet because like the polar bear, you resemble a teddy bear on the outside but you're strong on the inside and pack a mean bite."

Terrance grinned as Sunny helped him fasten the bracelet. "Hmm, maybe I can dye it black."

"This gray and white manatee bracelet is for Sunny. Manatees are gentle, peaceful plant-eaters."

"Perfect," Sunny and Bu said at the same time. Bu's face pinched, unnoticed by all but Charley in their high spirits.

"Jess gets the black one—the shark. Need I say more?"

Jess snatched the bracelet from his hand. "No. You need not say more."

Xander extracted a purple braided bracelet and put it on Bu's white sheet. "This is mine, the Hawaiian monk seal, which is one of the only two monk seal species still in existence. Charley gets the dolphin, because dolphins are kind, smart, and playful." He handed her a turquoise and gray bracelet. She nodded solemnly.

"And last but oh so far from least, for our Moon Boy, we have the sea otter bracelet—first, because they don't make a Bakunawa sea serpent bracelet, and second because sea otters are good swimmers and highly sensitive creatures." He held a teal-and-black braided bracelet over Bu's bed and considered the left wrist in the sling and the right wrist with its IV. "Hmm, where shall we put it? Will the table suffice for now?" He moved to place the bracelet on the bedside table.

"No, put it on this one." Bu lifted the arm in the sling an inch. "Just try not to pull," he said as Xander fiddled with the bracelet and fastened it. A bead of sweat popped out on Bu's forehead, below the short shock of hair falling across his brow. He closed his eyes. "Thanks, Xan."

Sunny patted Bu's good leg. "We should go. You need to sleep."

"Can we take a picture of our bracelets first?" Charley asked. Bu opened his eyes and nodded at her.

The friends shuffled into position around the bed immediately, as if afraid she might change her mind. She extended her arm over the bed, fingers splayed. The others layered their hands over Charley's, their wrists in their colorful bracelets forming a border around their hands in the center. Xander propped up Bu's arm in the sling.

Terrance pulled his phone out of his back pocket. "I'll take the picture since I've got the longest arms." He reached up and back with his phone and snapped several shots. "Wait—don't move." He checked the photos. "All good. You can relax now."

"The Bakunawa calls," Bu mumbled.

"What?" Jess said.

"I have things I want to say to you guys."

Sunny frowned at his graying face. "Why don't you do it later, Bu? You look beat."

"No. Now." He closed his eyes and slowly re-opened them. "Jessica, go into the sun. Terrance, go with her." He paused, breathing in and out with a subtle rasp.

Confused, Charley looked at Terrance. He narrowed his eyes at Bu. His gaze shifted to Jess and his eyes gradually relaxed. He gave Jess a small smile, which she seemed surprised and then grateful to receive, a sad smile crossing her face.

"Xander," Bu said, "I have a cliché for you to live by: No man is an island."

"Moon Boy, do you speak of social justice or interpersonal relations?"

"Yes." He smirked weakly. "Sunny, it's okay to fight sometimes. Charley, it's okay to ask for help. I love you all. *Now* I gotta sleep." His thick black lashes floated down onto his purplish-bronze cheeks.

Back in the waiting room, Sunny announced they were taking Charley home. "See you back at the apartment," they said to Xander and Jess.

"T, you should come to our place. Don't go all the way back to the 'burbs since we'll probably be coming back here in a few hours."

"Fine idea," Xander said. "You can crash on the couch."

Jess nodded, "Or take my bed. I have to make a quick trip to see my parents. My dad's been asking what's going on at work with the raid and everything. I think I might tell him what I did."

CHAPTER 29: UNINTENDED CONSEQUENCES

Bertie checked the buckle of her granddaughter's booster seat in the kitchen of the carriage house where she, Al, and Dacey lived, tucked back from the Delgados' main house.

"I'll be right back, Dacey. I'm going to get the door."

She opened the front door and flashed her gap-toothed smile at the young, clean-cut man filling the doorway. He smiled back.

"Morning, ma'am. We're looking for Hermenegildo Lopez. Is he here?"

A badge swinging on a lanyard around the man's neck caught Bertie's attention. Terror stole the smile from her round face. She took a step back, one dark hand flying to her bosom.

"Is he okay? Is he hurt?" Her pleading questions tumbled out in heavily accented English. "What happened? Tell me!"

The man nodded. "May we come in?"

Bertie took another step back, allowing the man, and a second one she hadn't seen behind him, into her home.

He no longer smiled. "Where is he?"

"I don't know." Her eyes clouded in confusion. "Has he done something?"

"When's the last time you saw him?"

"More than two years ago." She peered up at the men towering over her, tears pooling in her eyes. "Do you know if he's alive?"

The man stared, his expression unchanging.

"Ma'am, we need you to show us your documents."

Bertie's surroundings dissolved into a dark gray fog.

A motor roared up the carriage house driveway, making the agents turn and look. A riding lawn mower swerved around two dark sedans in the driveway. It lurched to a stop at the cluster of gold daylilies next to the front steps. Al jumped off the mower, his hands black from tinkering with the engine minutes before, his eyes blacker.

"What is the meaning of this?" He pushed past the two men and stood by Bertie's side.

"Sir, we're going to need to see your documents, too."

"Documents?"

"Proof of United States citizenship, a valid visa or other document proving you are authorized to reside here."

"We have lived here thirty years. We have jobs. We go to church. We pay taxes."

"Congratulations. Now show me your papers."

Instead, Al enveloped Bertie in a tight embrace. His bronze arms on her back heaved with his wife's sobs.

Al murmured into Bertie's thick hair. "*No te preocupes, Rigoberta. Michael nos ayudará. Todo saldrá bien.* It will be okay."

***

Valerie leaned into the kitchen sink and inhaled steam from a mug of her favorite coffee. Dressed for work, she sported plum-colored slacks, a crisp white blouse and two-inch heels. She watched a robin hop about the front yard, stopping occasionally to peck at unseen delicacies in the neat lawn.

Michael was concerned with Jess's job situation, but Valerie saw this hiatus as an opportunity to spend some quality time with her only daughter and eldest child. Jess would be by any minute for a late breakfast, maybe more like an early lunch—either way, a rare treat on a weekday. And maybe when Valerie finished her half-day at the dental office, they could meet in the city for dinner or a little shopping.

When a black sedan turned into their driveway, she wondered why a client was visiting Michael here. He'd said he was going into the office late in order to get some work done at home first, but she knew it was more because he was waiting for Jess to arrive. Maybe that's why he scheduled an appointment here.

A second car followed. The vehicles passed the circular driveway in front of the main house and continued toward the carriage house. Valerie's eyes widened. Still staring out the window, she plunked the coffee mug on the counter, precariously close to the edge.

"Michael!" She rushed toward her husband's home office, black hair flying out behind her. "Michael, come here! Hurry!"

***

The couple walked briskly down the driveway toward the carriage house, the crushed stone griping beneath their feet.

Michael muttered. "Don't let them in, Bertie, don't let them in."

Valerie huffed a bit as they walked-ran. "You've told her that, right?"

"Of course. Many times."

"Michael, there's no one outside. She let them in!"

Michael broke into a jog. Valerie jogged, too, but fell slightly behind in her heels.

Two men wearing ICE windbreakers emerged from the sedans. Two other men emerged from the house. One held Bertie's arm and the other held Al's. Bertie's and Al's hands were behind their backs.

Michael reached the house. He raised a hand. "Stop right there! Where are you taking them?"

Valerie landed beside him.

The lead agent perked up. "Who are you?"

"I'm their employer, their landlord, and their attorney. You have no right."

"She let us in, so we have every right. Do you know where Hermenegildo Lopez is?"

Michael closed his eyes briefly, understanding and resignation flooding through him. His face drooped. "No."

Heads turned again as a white BMW crunched down the driveway.

One of the agents mumbled, "More reinforcements at the Alamo?"

Michael watched as his pride and joy emerged from her car, silently begging her to maintain her composure.

***

Jess parked behind one of the sedans and got out. She took in her father's concerned face—a rare look for him, her mother's abnormally pale face, the four agents, Al, and Bertie.

"What the hell is going on?" She stepped toward the closest agent. "Where are you taking them? And why?"

The lead agent studied the growing group of Delgados. "I'm going to need to see all of your papers, too."

A wave of doubt moved through Jess. "Dad, what's going on?" Her voice shook.

Michael stared at the lead agent. "These are immigration officials, Jessica."

The agent tried again. "Show us your papers. Now."

"What papers?" An edge bit through the tremor in Jess's voice.

"Form I-551, form I-766—anything like that will do," the agent said. A self-satisfied half-smile touched his lips. Jess wanted to slap it off.

"We are not required to show you anything," Michael said slowly and firmly. "You have not entered my home, nor do you have a warrant to do so. However, we are all American citizens and we will show you just the same." He turned to Jess. "Show them your driver's license, Jessica."

"What? Really?" Jess's words sounded muffled to her. *Why were they being treated like criminals?* She looked at Bertie. The wild terror on the dear woman's face shocked Jess out of her stupor. "My license?" she asked her father in a firm voice. Michael nodded.

She returned to her car and produced her ID. One of the agents inspected it front and back. "You're lucky we're in a state that requires citizenship to get a license. Otherwise, this would mean squat."

She silently returned the license to her wallet in the car.

"I'll go to the house and get our certificates of naturalization to show you if you will give me a minute." A subtle toss of Michael's head told Jess to accompany him. An agent stepped forward as well, but Michael shook his head, "No, I do not need an escort. You have no right to enter my house. I will be right back. Consider my wife collateral. Apologies for the crass characterization, *mi reina*."

As Michael and Jess walked away, his hand on her arm slowed her. "Don't rush. I need time to think. I'm not an immigration attorney, as you know."

"What's happening? Why can they take Bertie and Al?"

She followed his gaze, staring at his cordovan loafers landing one in front of the other on the crushed stone.

"Because they're undocumented," Michael said.

Jess froze. "What?" she whispered. "No they're not." Her voice rose. "You told me they were legal."

Michael pulled her back into a slow walk. "I have never said that."

"But—but—" For the life of her, Jess couldn't recall her father ever saying it in so many words. "Why didn't you tell me? I should have known!"

Michael shook his head as they followed the driveway around to the front of the main house, out of the agents' view. "It was better that you and Philip didn't know. That way, you couldn't accidentally let it slip, especially as children. And after that—well, I couldn't see the point."

"But why today? Why now? ICE, I mean."

"Probably because of the All-American raids a few days ago. These men came looking for Ozzy. It's typical after a raid to go through employee files and look for people with criminal records. Ozzy's name would've been on the list from that short time he worked for the company. I thought his arrest for possession of illegal substances had been deleted from his record, but they must have learned of it somehow."

Jess froze again. The world spun as if she'd stood up too fast after too many drinks. Her mouth dried up. Her vision tunneled.

Michael grabbed her upper arms. "Jessica. Jessica!" He shook her.

She struggled to focus. "Oh my God, Daddy." She spoke so softly that he had to lean in. "It's my fault." Jess's heart tore as if rent in two by a serrated butcher knife. "It's my fault Bertie and Al are being arrested." A ragged sound escaped her. "Will they be deported?"

Michael wrapped her in his arms and stroked her hair. "Jessie, how could it be your fault?"

"Because I caused the raid. I leaked company information to the newspaper. To get Flammer in trouble."

Michael stopped patting her head. He released her and stepped back. His tan face had acquired a greenish tinge.

"Why did you do that?" His voice was neutral, for which she was grateful. Surely his wrath would come soon though.

"To help a friend. Because of another mistake I made." She gasped for air, half-expecting her lungs to cave in. She squeezed her eyes shut and pounded her fists at the air. "Shit! Shit! Shit! I can't get anything right! Terrance. Charley. Now Bertie and Al! I hurt everyone!" Her face contorted.

"Shhh. Slow down. Start at the beginning."

She let him tow her the remaining few steps into the cool dark house and into his office. She collapsed on the couch, unaware until then of how weak her legs had become. Michael sat beside her.

Jess told him the short version of everything—scouting the bookstore, meeting Charley, the deal going through, Charley's depression, and Jess's decision to go after Flammer.

"Ah, Jessie." He cupped her golden cheek in his palm. "My bold, brave, naïve child. Did you not consider the impact of your actions on the immigrants who work at the landscaping company?"

Her frustration and fury mixed with remorse and fatigue—a volatile cocktail.

"I can't be responsible for everyone! Those workers have to take responsibility for coming here illegally. I was trying to help a friend who was in trouble!"

Michael said nothing.

"Are you mad? You are. But I didn't know! If you'd told me Bertie was illegal, I wouldn't have done this! I would never do anything to hurt her or Al. As it was, I had to protect you!"

His eyes narrowed infinitesimally. "In what way?"

"Liam said he learned how to use illegal labor from you. How do you think I felt when I heard that?"

Michael stared. "And you believed him?"

Jess stuttered a few times. "I didn't want to. I wasn't sure because you never told me about that either. But I made sure your name didn't appear in the article."

He exhaled a small puff of laughter. "Thank you for looking out for your father. But there is a world of difference between what I did and what Liam Flammer does. It's true I hired undocumented immigrants at my landscaping company. Your mother and I didn't end up here on our own, you know. We had help. So I wanted to pay that forward. I hired hard-working people who wanted merely to be paid a fair wage and feed their families. Unlike Liam, I paid these people on the books, and I paid taxes on their wages, which I reported in full. Al and Bertie, by the way—it's the same with them. They file income taxes every year using ITNs since they don't have social security numbers."

As he talked, the fire in Jess's eyes cooled, the outrage gripping her shoulders abated, and an oppressive weariness moved over her.

Michael stood abruptly. "We must get back. I intended to stall them a bit so I could think, but not this long." He moved to the small safe behind his desk and retrieved several documents. "Come."

***

Dacey's shrieks for her grandmother sliced the air. The three-year-old squirmed and struggled in Valerie's tight hold, framed by the carriage house door. Valerie lost her grip on the child's birth certificate, which fluttered to the stoop.

Bertie and Al, one in the back of each car, watched the child forlornly. Bertie leaned through the open window, reciting a mixture of Ixil, Spanish, and English like an incantation or prayer. "No, no. Not again. *Tiioxh qué no me quite otra hijita.*"

Michael's eyebrows lifted. He turned to the lead agent. "They are the guardians of this child, who is a citizen. You cannot detain the parents or guardians of a minor. They must be released and allowed to care for her."

The agent regarded Michael anew. "Who are the parents?"

"Their son Hermenegildo Lopez is the father. The mother— unknown."

"So, he does come here?" Suspicion dripped off the words.

"No. He dropped the girl off on the doorstep nearly three years ago and hasn't been back since. That's why they became her guardians."

"Fine. You can come to the detention center later and make that known. For now, we're taking them."

"I'll follow you," Michael said.

***

Jess and Valerie sat numbly in the carriage house kitchen, Valerie where she could keep an eye on Dacey in front of the living room TV watching *Sesame Street*. Valerie reached for Jess's hand on top of the kitchen table. "Are you okay?"

Jess couldn't bear to admit her culpability a second time in an hour. Instead, she reached for another troublesome thought. "Mom, when Bertie was in the back of the car, why was she praying not to lose another little girl?"

Valerie's eyes teared up. "Because when she and Al and Ozzy crossed the Rio Grande into the U.S., she lost a baby daughter. Itzel."

Jess's hand clutched her heart. "*¡Dios mío!*" Her voice trembled. "You mean, in the river?"

Valerie nodded.

Anger born of despair surged through Jess. "Are there any more secrets you and Daddy are keeping from me?"

Valerie shook her head and wiped a tear.

Jess's heart felt like it was being wrung out to dry. "Why did they come here illegally if it's so dangerous? Why didn't they get in line like everyone else and come in the safe way?"

"Get in line? Oh, Jess, what line? There is no line." Valerie stood and moved to the cabinet, took out two glasses, and filled them with water. "There's no clear path to citizenship for many people. Getting legal status can take years. Millions have tried and are stuck in limbo."

"But can't they apply for asylum?" Jess asked.

Valerie placed the glasses on the table and smiled sadly at her daughter. "Do you think Michael and I haven't looked into all this? Only one or two percent of the requests for political asylum by Guatemalans are granted."

"What if they go back to Guatemala or even Mexico and then come in legally?"

Valerie sighed and sat. "Sometimes, the longer someone's been here illegally, the longer they have to wait after they leave before they can apply for a green card."

Jess frowned. "Talk about disincentive to go through proper channels."

Valerie nodded. "Ironically, IRCA—an immigration law signed by Ronald Reagan soon after we arrived—encouraged more illegal migration. It legalized 2.7 million immigrants at once, making people think they could come here illegally and get amnesty down the road."

Jess wasn't interested in statistics. "Mom, what will happen to Bertie and Al? And Dacey?"

Valerie's shoulders slumped. "Michael will do everything in his power to keep them here."

"But?"

"But we may lose them."

Jess bowed her head. A tear splashed on her lap.

They canceled breakfast. Jess left to be alone with her shame.

CHAPTER 30: TERRANCE'S CROSS

Terrance rapped on the pale blue door of Jess's bedroom, causing Fred to dash over and cock his head as if an enticing secret lurked on the other side of the door. No answer.

When Jess got home from her parents' house, Terrance had been lying on the couch in her apartment. He'd feigned sleep and watched her move about from under nearly closed eyelids. Something about her—a vulnerability—reminded him of when he saw her on the rock in the woods at Bu's summer home.

She'd disappeared into her room and cried for twenty minutes, quiet weeping and occasional sobs seeping through the crack under her door. Terrance had showered, dressing in yesterday's clothes—not his idea of fun—and finally decided he should try to comfort her.

He knocked again. The crying stopped. "Jess?" He tried the doorknob. Locked. "Is it Bu? We're all upset. Let's talk."

"No," a small voice said. "Go away."

"Let me in. We can talk about it."

He waited.

"I want to be alone."

His need to comfort her only intensified. "Don't shut me out, Jess. Please." Fred whined in support.

A faint rustling came through the door. "T." Her voice sounded closer to his face. "You shut me out that night the cops stopped us."

He closed his eyes and murmured to the eggshell door. "I didn't love you then."

He waited. Nothing.

Don't make me say it again, he thought. *It's a surprise to me, too.*

He watched the knob turn slowly. The door creaked open.

Terrance stepped into Jess's room and shut the door. Barred entry, Fred lay down on the other side with a groan.

A pile of shed clothes on the floor marred the otherwise tidy room. Jess—a thin T-shirt clinging to her torso, her legs encased in tight leggings, her feet bare—seemed smaller than her usual formidable self.

He wrapped his arms around her, breathing in her subtle floral smell. "It's going to be okay."

She slid through his arms to the floor and sat back against the door. He slid down and nudged her to the side to make room for his wide frame between her and the bed. His black-clad legs stretched four or five inches beyond her gray-sheathed ones.

A tear dripped from her chin. Her nostrils looked red and tender. Terrance reached for a tissue box on the floor, a pile of used tissues beside it, some smudged with mascara. He handed her a fresh one.

"I didn't think it through enough," she said.

He relaxed a touch. She was talking.

"I shouldn't have given the information to the paper. I shouldn't have done any of this."

Terrance watched her hands twist a tissue into a cylinder. He couldn't make sense of her mood. "You're upset about work? What happened—did they learn you tipped off the press?"

Jess shook her head almost violently. A strand of tear-soaked hair stuck to her cheek. "No. I'm safe," she said with scorn. "But I moved too fast. I didn't have time to think it all through. The consequences."

Terrance removed one of her hands from the tissue and held it. "I know it was a hard decision. But you did it to save Charley. Don't forget that."

Jess scoffed, her disdain confusing Terrance. "I found the ring, but I blew up the wedding party. I may have helped one person, but I lost a family."

"What are you talking about? Is your father mad about what you did?"

She raised her teary eyes to his. Her self-critical tone broke, replaced by raw pain. "I knew the people on the other track, T. The one I sent the trolley down."

Dread crawled in Terrance's gut. "Who are we talking about?"

Jess inhaled and willed her tears to stop. She swiped the tissue across her eyes. "Bertie and Al, and maybe Dacey. They might be deported. ICE arrested them this morning. And it's my fault! Charley was going to lose her apartment and her job. But Bertie is losing everything! Her home for thirty years, her country, her friends, her church. She'll get sent back to Guatemala where they have nothing except crime and corruption and poverty."

Terrance's brow contracted. "They got caught up in the All-American raid somehow?"

Jess nodded.

"Okay. I get it now. Tell me the details later. You need to remember you acted out of kindness. You had no idea this would happen."

He searched for more words that might comfort her but came up empty. He knew it was a futile exercise. Although time would coat her anguish, offering a somewhat protective barrier between the memory and the present, nothing would extinguish it. Ever.

He eased his arm around her. She lowered her head into him.

"Jess, when's the last time you went to church?"

She sniffled. "A few weeks ago. I try to go with my parents every Sunday but sometimes I don't make it out there."

"Would you like to go? With me?"

She nodded, her chin rubbing against his chest. "Yours or mine?" she asked.

"Mine's probably more fun, but whichever one you want."

She exhaled. "I need to go to confession."

He nodded. "Yours it is."

She sat up straight, separating from him. "It's about more than Bertie and Al, you know. What I have to confess."

Terrance extracted his arm and shook it. "Do you want to practice on me?"

She twirled her earring in its lobe, looking in her lap. "If we're going to . . . be friends again, you need to know all of me. This isn't the first terrible thing I've done."

He waited.

"You were right, at Bu's summer house when we were playing Never Have I Ever. I have wished my skin was lighter. I couldn't pass as White when I was a kid—my skin was darker 'cause I practically lived outside. I have gotten racist insults before. For years, I fooled myself into thinking every insult was because of Ozzy. Never me."

Terrance stared at the creases in his knuckles. "Jess, any self-defense mechanism against a racist comment is understandable."

"You don't understand," she said. "I started thinking I was better than him. When he started doing drugs and skipping school, I blamed him. I pulled away but pretended it was him pulling away. I hated him for disappointing me. You know he never even got a driver's—" Jess's mouth hung open.

"What? He never what?"

She closed her eyes. "Oh my God. It all makes sense now. Ozzy never got a driver's license because he couldn't. Because he was illegal. That's probably why he didn't apply for college, even though he was smart enough. Do you know if undocumented immigrants can go to college here?"

"No," Terrance said, "but what about DACA? Wouldn't he be considered a dreamer?"

Jess's brow furrowed. "DACA's not that old. He got his first drug offense way before that. And that's why he ran when he started getting into trouble. He didn't want to put Bertie and Al in danger." Her eyes flew open. "But then I did it. I put them in danger. And now, if he ever does come home, his parents won't even be here." The tears revved up again.

Terrance stood, extended a hand, and pulled Jess up. "The floor's uncomfortable. Can we move to the bed?"

Jess mutely sat on top of her lavender comforter. Terrance put the tissue box on the bedside table. He adjusted the pillow behind her back, went to the other side, took off his shoes, and sat next to her.

"I did something horrible once, too. Something I'll never forgive myself for. You're not alone."

Jess reached for a fresh tissue. "Like what? Not fully analyzing your options before deciding what movie to watch one night?"

He squinted at her. "Was that a joke? Because it wasn't funny."

She smiled. Terrance realized how much he needed that smile.

"Okay. It was a little funny." He settled back against the pillow. "Do you want to know about the terrible thing I did?"

***

Everyone knew Tito was gay by age seven. Before he even knew it probably. But once he was out, he was out. He never hid it. He was one of those guys.

One night the summer before sophomore year, Tito and Terrance were bored. They were leaning on the picnic table in Tito's backyard, swatting mosquitoes. Terrance pulled up the hem of his T-shirt and wiped a spot off his glasses. "Hey, did you hear Kadeem and Duante got fake IDs? They went to a bar last week. I wish we could do that."

Tito perked up. "That's a great idea! Let's do it!" he said.

"What? Get fake IDs?"

"No, go to a bar."

"Are you high, bro? You look like you're twelve."

Tito hung his head.

"That was harsh. Sorry, man. But you do look sixteen and that ain't gonna fly at a bar."

Tito smiled, his pink lips forming a precocious grin—the one that endeared him to teachers when he wasn't trying their patience. "I can just hide in your big-ass shadow." Tito was five-foot-seven, while Terrance was approaching six feet. "Come on. What else we gonna do? Let's try, just to see if we can get in. It'll be fun."

Terrance recognized the hard gleam in Tito's eye—the one that meant he was hanging onto something like a dog on a meaty bone.

Terrance sighed and followed Tito to the bus stop. His bare arms stuck to the plastic bus seat in the humid air. They got off on the far side of town where Tito suggested no one would recognize them. If their parents found them out, they'd be locked in their houses for the rest of high school.

Tito walked purposefully for a few blocks, leading Terrance up and down side streets, many of them with corner bars.

"Slow down, man. You on a mission?"

Tito grinned. "Heard there's a new gay bar in the city. First one. It's supposed to be in this neighborhood somewhere."

Terrance stopped to think, scratching his black hair. He could care less that Tito was gay. He always had Tito's back. He'd stepped into a few gay-bashing confrontations to rescue his friend over the years. He was good with all that. But this was different. He'd be marking himself gay by entering a gay bar. That was asking too much.

The lone streetlight on the block washed over Tito where he stood. "I would go to a straight bar for you." He fluttered his eyelashes.

"Don't do that, man. I hate it when you do that." He sighed and patted his stomach under his shirt, as if confirming he still knew the person inside. "Well, I guess we won't run into anyone we know. Let's go."

Tito jumped a few inches off the sidewalk.

"But you owe me big time!" Terrance said.

"Yes, yes, yes."

They searched for fifteen minutes, going farther and farther from the main drag, but no luck.

"How will you know it's a gay bar?"

Tito smirked. "Trust me. We'll know. Maybe it's that one." He pointed at a small bar in a brick building with a neon sign over the doorway. It sat in the middle of a block, sandwiched by a worn, clapboard-sided building and a narrow alley. "It's called Bennie's."

"So?"

"You know, like 'Bennie and the Jets' by Elton John. I hear there are gay bars all over the country named after Elton songs."

Terrance shrugged indifference.

As soon as they entered the dive bar, they knew they'd made a mistake. The crowd was rough. The customers' Black and Brown skin did nothing to instill comfort in Terrance. Cigarette smoke, cheap whiskey, harsh laughter, and the smack of colliding billiard balls filled the air. Tito in his mustard-colored skinny pants, dark green tank top, and bleached-blonde hair resembled a tropical parrot in a scorched rainforest.

Tito puffed out his chest and clenched his jaw. "Let's have one beer, a quick one, so we don't look like pussies." He ordered two Budweisers from the indifferent bartender who didn't even ask for IDs.

Terrance fought to keep his eyes down, but his reflexes kept dragging his gaze around the small establishment, as if rubbernecking a train wreck that hadn't yet happened. At the other end of the bar, a stocky, dun-colored man with a heavy beard looked at Tito, elbowed his friend, looked at Tito again and laughed. His friend—a bald, dark giant with a wispy mustache that dropped off his chin into two vague points—studied the teens through eyes scrunched into mere slits. He turned his squint on his friend and said something that stopped the stocky man's laugh mid-guffaw. The giant banged his shot glass on the bar and nodded at the bartender for another.

"Let's go, man. Forget about the beer." Terrance turned to leave. To his relief, Tito came with him. Safely outside, Terrance glanced behind him. No one followed them. He exhaled.

As they began to walk away, a door squeaked open in the alley. Terrance and Tito walked faster. A flurry of heavy footsteps landed the stocky bearded guy and the dark giant in front of the boys, making them stop. Two other men emerged from the alley to join the first two. Terrance groaned, not sure if it was out loud or not.

The giant turned out to be only a few inches taller than Terrance but much broader. He stared down at Tito. "My friend says you were looking at me. He thinks you're a faggot."

Terrance tensed, every muscle locking up.

"No, man, I don't know what he's talking about. I didn't even see you in there," Tito said in a casual voice. He always was a solid bluffer.

"You calling me a liar?" the stocky guy slurred, spittle landing on his beard and reflecting in the streetlight.

"We don't want any trouble, okay?" Tito said in a more ingratiating tone. "We're just leaving." He grabbed Terrance's arm and they turned to walk around the men. To Terrance's amazement, they were allowed to pass.

Terrance felt a *whoosh* of air a split second before his friend hit the sidewalk face-first. The giant planted his foot in the middle of Tito's narrow back.

Terrance stood suspended, wondering if he should fight—no, bad idea. Beg? Run?

Tito decided for him. "Go!" he hissed from the ground, blood dripping from his split lip.

Terrance shook his head frantically. The men huddled as if deciding what to do next, the giant's boot still on Tito's back.

"Get help! Go!"

The four men broke their huddle and two of them moved toward Terrance. He bolted as a hand grabbed his shoulder. He broke away and ran to the sound of flesh hitting flesh and a terrifying cracking sound. Terrance sprinted for blocks until he was sure he wasn't being followed. He bent over, insides heaving.

Chattering reached his ears. Two women were walking toward him, a half-block away. He yelled. "Excuse me. Can you help me?"

They flinched but kept walking, heads close together.

He thought he might pass out from frustration. "Where's the closest police station?" he yelled. "What direction?"

One of the women turned and pointed down a cross street. "That way. A few blocks."

He darted toward the intersection and turned the corner, his chest on fire. Down the street, a police cruiser moved away from the curb. For the first time in his sixteen years, Terrance ran toward a cop.

"Wait!" he yelled after it, waving his arms like a madman. "Wait!"

Brake lights flashed on. The cop car backed up and stopped twenty feet from Terrance. He couldn't breathe. He bent over and strained to catch a raspy breath. Ringing bedeviled his ears. Sweat dripped from his nose.

A pair of black-shoe-clad feet appeared before him. Terrance scanned up to see a barrel-chested White cop with a hand on his holster.

"What are you on?" his partner asked, from ten feet back, hand also on his firearm.

Terrance shuddered with three sharp intakes before his lungs cooperated and inhaled shallowly. "Nothing. My friend. He needs help." He stood upright, causing the first cop to hold out his palm, fingers up.

"Stop right there. No closer. Look at me," he commanded while shining a flashlight in Terrance's eyes. "Have you been drinking?"

Terrance shook his head while grasping for another ragged breath.

"Smoking? Shooting up? Which is it?"

The cop lowered the flashlight. Floating black circles hampered Terrance's vision. The black spots began to merge. *Shit, was he going to pass out?* He ducked his head between his knees. The sudden motion sent the cops into action. One grabbed Terrance's wrists and cuffed them behind his back. The other grabbed Terrance's shoulders and pulled him upright. Together, the partners pushed and pulled him toward the cruiser.

"Stop, please! You have to help my friend, Tito. He's getting beat up by four guys, back at Bennie's." Terrance winced as his torso slammed against the cruiser. He lifted his head just in time to avoid his chin being slammed into the metal roof.

"Bennie's. You were at Bennie's," one cop said incredulously while the other frisked Terrance. He chuckled, sending an unnamable emotion straight through Terrance. The cop was laughing! While Tito was being pummeled back there on the pavement. Where Terrance left him.

"Please, please, listen to me. I'm not high. I'm not drunk. My friend Tito is in real trouble. He needs your help. Please."

The first cop grabbed Terrance's arm and spun him around, sizing him up three times before speaking. "Pass our sobriety test and we'll go check on your friend." Terrance saw the partner nodding off to the side.

Inside, Terrance screamed: *For God's sake help me! That's your job!* Outside, he swallowed his terror and anger. A piece of him broke off and disintegrated, lost for good, replaced by something cold and hard and resigned. He spoke calmly. "Okay. What do you want me to do?"

Ten minutes later, Terrance having been deemed not under the influence, the cruiser—Terrance in the back seat—stopped at Bennie's. All three men got out and stared at the empty, blood-soaked sidewalk. As one, they followed a smear of blood into the alley. At the far end, barely visible in the shadows, lay a motionless, prone form.

"Tito, talk to me man." Terrance's foot caught on the concrete as he stepped toward the crumpled pile. A strong hand on his upper arm stilled him.

"Stay here," said the first cop while the other jogged back down the alley to the cruiser. The cop let go of Terrance, walked the rest of the way with gun drawn, scanned the alley, holstered his gun and kneeled before Tito. Peering into the alley, Terrance prayed the face his eyes finally found in the dark was unrecognizable only because of the shadows. Or maybe it wasn't Tito. Maybe he got away.

The cop stood and walked to Terrance, shaking his head. "Come with me. Don't stay here." He led a numb Terrance back to the cruiser and opened the back door. "Do you want to sit?" Terrance shook his head. "How old are you?"

"Sixteen."

"And your friend?"

"Sixteen. But how do I know that's my friend?" he asked, voice high. "Maybe he got away."

The cop's eyes softened. "What was he wearing?"

"Um, these stupid yellowish pants. He's got bleached-blonde hair."

The cop nodded. Terrance's stomach clenched. Dark spots invaded his vision again.

The cop put his hand on Terrance's shoulder and pushed him into a seated position in the back of the cruiser. "Who can we call?"

Who? Terrance wondered. He thought about the faces of Tito's parents if they got the news from a cop. "I don't remember his house number. Call my mother. She'll tell his parents."

The cop nodded, took down the number, and handed it to his partner who stepped away.

"Was he involved in drug-dealing or anything that would make him a target?"

Terrance only stared.

"Come on, son. I need a few more details. Let's start with what the hell happened."

Terrance heard his voice describing the evening, but his ears couldn't make sense of his own words. He had no names for the attackers. He described the first two, but never got a good look at the others.

The partner disappeared into the bar to interrogate staff and customers. An ambulance came. Terrance watched as a gurney squeaked into the alley, returning five minutes later laden with a form strapped in as if it might try to escape. Blood seeped through the white sheet between the bindings. *When did a dead body stop bleeding?* Terrance wondered.

Mary Washington leaped out of her car, eyes wild, arms flailing as she ran. Terrance flinched as she flung herself into him. He slowly let down as she enfolded him, clutching him so tightly he felt short of breath again. His tears soaked her shoulder as he lowered his head and cried like a baby, not caring who saw.

She led him to the car and was planting him in the passenger seat when Tito's father's car pulled up. Terrance struggled to stand but Mary's hand pressed him down.

"Mama, I should talk to them."

Mary studied him, and then the scene, which now included three police cruisers, a number of unmarked cars, and the ambulance. Patrons clustered outside the bar's entrance and chatted quietly as if watching a show. Tito's parents approached the back of the ambulance.

"You stay right here."

A few minutes or fifty later, she returned to the car, got in, and started the engine.

She clutched his hand for a moment, put both hands on the steering wheel and stared straight ahead as she turned for home.

"That's why I tell you to keep your head down." Her voice was flat. Controlled.

The lack of emotion stunned Terrance into silence.

When they got home, Mary helped him undress as if he were five, and bundled him into bed.

She kissed his forehead. "Do you want some hot chocolate? To help you sleep?"

He didn't answer. He had already sunk into a dull state resembling sleep but void of rest, where he would remain for eighteen hours.

✳✳✳

"So you see, Jess. I was wrong to judge you for not telling Charley sooner. We've all done things we're not proud of."

Jess's eyes were dry for the first time in hours. She took his hand and squeezed it. "T, you know it wasn't your fault."

Terrance shrugged wearily. "I gave him the idea to go to a bar. I didn't run fast enough. I couldn't convince the cops to go help until it was too late. And I left him. I left him." He hung his head.

"You know that's not what killed Tito." She waited until he looked at her. "Homophobic assholes killed him. Prejudice killed him. But not you."

The mournful song of a cricket filtered in through the open window. He reached his arm around her. "We're alike, aren't we? Always ruining the lives of the ones we love."

Jess snuggled against him tentatively. "Agreed. But that doesn't make us bad, Terrance. I guess it makes us human."

His phone rang. Sighing, he separated from Jess and answered it.

CHAPTER 31: KEENING

"Is this good?" Sunny motioned to a park bench, tan plastic slats supported by curling black metal arms and legs.

Charley nodded and sank onto the seat. The five-minute walk they'd taken in Founders Park seemed to have sapped the energy she woke with, making Sunny realize how much the hours in the hospital drained Charley's limited reserves and how little a five-hour nap replenished them.

Charley had fallen asleep as soon as she hit the bed that morning. Sunny had looked longingly at the empty half of the bed and placed the faintest of kisses on Charley's forehead before sneaking out of the bedroom like a thief who'd broken and entered. Telling themself it wouldn't be safe to drive home in their fatigued state and that Charley might need support when she woke up, Sunny crashed on the couch, Baggage claiming the nook behind their bent knees.

When they woke, coming to the park was Charley's idea. She'd come into the living room scratching her arms like she had poison ivy or chicken pox but insisting she was well enough to go.

Now she rested, eyes closed to the afternoon sun, chest gently rising and falling.

Sunny reached into their daisy-patterned backpack and pulled out a used paperback. The book soon drifted down to their lap. A few minutes later, their phone rang. They struggled out of semi-sleep and dug the phone from their backpack. No one ever called. Even her mother usually texted. It was Terrance.

"Sunny, come to the hospital now! It's Bu."

Sunny stood. "What happened?"

But Terrance had hung up.

They shook Charley awake.

***

The short walk in the park—the fresh air, the chatter of birds, the sun-dappled greenery—had nourished Charley, only to have the feeding tube yanked away with two small words from Sunny. "It's Bu."

It's not the curse, she said to herself, wanting to believe. *It's not the curse. Bu said so himself.*

They ran into the ICU waiting room and skidded to a stop. Charley swayed like a reed in the wind.

Xander, Terrance, and Jess stood to the side, gray like crumbling tombstones. In the middle of the room, Anne sobbed into Layla's shoulder, sobs that sounded as if they would tear her in two. A younger woman with blonde hair stood with them, arms wrapped around the two mothers. She turned her teary face to the door and Charley recognized a younger version of Anne, she must be Bu's sister, Carrie.

Sunny baby-stepped toward the huddle of women but Terrance stopped them with an arm on theirs.

"I—I just want to—" Sunny faltered.

Terrance steered her away. "We should go." He led them all out of the ICU, to the ground floor and into an inner courtyard with paved walkways slicing squares of grass into triangles. No bench could hold all five, so they settled down to the grass in a circle.

"What—what happened?" Sunny spoke stuffily through tears.

"He's gone," Jess said with disbelief. "Just like that."

"Why?" They all turned at Charley's soft voice.

Xander took her hand and held it in the pocket formed by her legs. "Bu went into hemorrhagic shock from his internal injuries." He stopped talking to swallow.

Terrance picked up the thread. "That's when the damaged blood vessels can't clot so the blood pressure drops, and the organs don't get enough blood and the heart shuts down—" He stopped, as if realizing the gory details didn't help.

"But how?" Sunny wiped the stream of tears on their face to no avail. "They said he would be fine."

Terrance reached his arm around Sunny and pulled them close. "The doctor said there aren't always warning signs for this kind of shock. They thought they caught everything in the surgery. But." He stroked Sunny's arm.

Charley's chest burned like a house fire. She tried to will her protective wall back into place, but her grief was stronger. She visibly shrank into herself as if pressed by the invisible anvil exerting force from above. Xander tightened his grip on her hand. Jess reached her arm around Charley and squeezed.

Sunny's sobs built to a wail, sporadic words interrupting the keening. "It's not . . . Why? . . . He was so . . . Oh, God, no."

The five friends squirmed to their knees and closed the spaces between them. They lifted their arms around each other and—some loudly, some silently—they cried.

***

They broke apart, faces ashen and streaky, countenances grim. No one wanted to leave. No one knew what to do if they stayed.

After mutually deciding to go home and reconvene later, Xander pulled Sunny aside. "I'm worried about Charley retreating again. Can you stay with her? I think you've got the best chance of keeping her with us."

Sunny inhaled with a shudder. They peeked at Charley and agreed with Xander's concern. "I'll do my best."

Xander kissed their cheek. "Thank you. We can't lose another one. Let me know if you need me to come over."

CHAPTER 32: AS RANDOM AS RAIN

Warm mugs of tea in their hands, Charley and Sunny sat at opposite ends of the couch, Charley facing forward, Sunny facing Charley, legs pulled up in a lotus position.

Xander was right. They had to push past the shock and sorrow of Bu and concentrate on keeping Charley with them.

"Charley, can we talk?"

Charley raised her mug, then lowered it without sipping. She turned and mirrored Sunny's position but without the full lotus. Her eyes and face were open. Clear. Sunny thanked God.

"Bu's d—" Sunny stopped to collect themself. "Buwan is not your fault. You know that, right?"

"I don't know anything."

Sunny consulted their tea, the scent of mint barely registering with their nostrils. "Do you believe in God, Char?"

Charley gave a tiny sad shrug. "I want to. But God doesn't seem to fit. With me. With the life I'm living."

Sunny reached down and pulled a book from their backpack. "I want to read you something. It's by Frederick Buechner—he's a minister and an author." They flipped through the pages marked with sticky notes.

Charley adjusted the mug in her hands.

"He says 'events happen under their own steam as random as rain, which means that God is present in them not as their cause but as the one who even in the hardest and most hair-raising of them offers us the possibility of that new life and healing which I believe is what salvation is.'"

Charley turned half-focused eyes on Sunny. "So I'm supposed to feel saved because my parents and my grandparents and Bu are dead?"

Sunny bit their lip. "No. Of course not. But Charley, answer me this: How did your mother die?"

"Plane crash."

"How did your father die?"

"Plane crash."

"How did your grandmother die?"

"Fire."

"How did your grandfather die?"

"Fire."

"What kind of fire?"

Charley squinted at Sunny.

"Did you set it? Was it your fault?"

Charley blinked twice. "The insurance company said they set it themselves in a suicide pact. Because Gram had cancer and Gramps had a heart condition." A touch of passion stole into Charley's voice. "But they would never do that. He told me the night before how excited they were for my graduation."

Sunny inhaled and exhaled for strength. "I'm sorry you had to deal with that on top of everything else."

Charley shrugged in slow motion.

"So back to my point: You didn't cause any of those deaths."

"I know!" Charley's vehemence surprised Sunny. "I'm not stupid enough to think I somehow control airplanes and fires and—and internal bleeding. That's not the problem. Don't you see? The problem is that these things happen to me. People I love leave me. I don't know why. But they do."

Sunny leaned in. "None of them left you. Random acts took them from you. Your parents and grandparents dying seven years apart doesn't mean someone else will be taken from you every seven years.

Bu dying,"—the words scraped at Sunny's throat—"that's just a coincidence, timing-wise."

"No." Charley spoke with reverence, almost as if recollecting a miraculous event. "Twice is a coincidence. Three times is a trend. And seven years before my parents, my dog Chaucer died. Now Bu—that makes four times."

Sunny gestured in frustration, tea slopping onto their pant leg. "What are you going to do? Live your life in fear every seventh year? Don't you hear how ridiculous that sounds? You know I believe in mystical things, but not this curse. Did it ever occur to you that you're putting a lot of importance on your little life, that these catastrophic things happen to punish you somehow? That you're so important that other lives are taken to prove a point to you? That's pretty egotistical, don't you think?"

Charley's mouth drooped open. Her eyes retreated. A gust from the window lifted her bangs off her forehead.

Sunny's face went slack. "I'm sorry. I didn't mean that."

Charley, pale-faced, swallowed. She whispered. "I don't know why I'm still here."

Sunny rested their mug on the floor and moved to the middle of the couch, facing Charley. "You belong here. In this life. Can I read you something else?" Charley nodded. Sunny pulled another Buechner paperback from their bag. They flipped through their place marks. "Here. 'The grace of God means something like: Here is your life. You might never have been, but you *are* because the party wouldn't have been complete without you.' What do you think he means?"

Charley shook her head.

"I think," said Sunny, "that he means God put us all here for a reason, even though we may never know what that reason is, and we all deserve to be here and to be happy. Some people make themselves unworthy through evil deeds. But we all start worthy. And your worth definitely isn't affected by random things out of your control." Sunny scanned the bare apartment. "Is that why you don't have any personal things in here? Books or art or anything? Because you don't think you have a right to be here or to be happy?"

"No," Charley said with a head shake. "It seems safer not to have anything of value here." She closed her eyes. "I'm tired."

Sunny pursed their lips. "There is something of value here. You." They stood. "I'm sorry I made you tired."

They took the half-full mugs into the kitchen, rinsed them, and returned to the couch. They opened the laptop in front of Charley and resumed a program she must have been streaming. *At least that's a good sign*, they thought. *She's moved beyond* Wheel of Fortune. *As long as I haven't set her back with my outburst.*

Sunny settled into the couch, their arm practically touching Charley's.

"Sunny?"

"Hm?"

"There's another reason I think I'm defective."

"What is it?" Sunny asked.

"When I was with Xander, I didn't feel anything. He's so passionate and smart and funny and sexy and I had such a crush on him. But I hardly felt anything when we were together. When I should have felt the most. I'm afraid I don't know how to love anyone."

Sunny hesitated. "Maybe he just wasn't the right person for you."

They stopped talking and watched the show.

"Sunny?"

"Hm?"

"I'm glad you like hanging out with me again. For a while, I didn't think you liked me."

Charley dropped her head onto Sunny's shoulder, her arm twitching. Sunny put their arm around Charley and squeezed her arm in until it quieted. They stroked her hair, letting the sensation of their bodies touching wash over them and praying it would not be the last time.

***

Jess and Terrance collapsed onto her bed on top of the covers, fully clothed.

Jessica's eyes were gritty, her mouth dry, and her muscles heavy. She couldn't sleep. How much time had passed since Bu's accident and Bertie's arrest? Mere minutes or a lifetime?

She studied Terrance. His eyes were shut, but she couldn't tell if he slept. She reached across the foot of space dividing them and wiggled her hand into his.

He opened his eyes and rolled onto his side, facing her. Without his glasses, he seemed less guarded, more open.

She rolled to face him. "I know it's terrible timing, but do you think we should talk? About . . . you know."

He swallowed. "What I said through the door?" he said softly.

She nodded, eyes neutral. "Did you mean, like friends?"

He ran a finger along her cheekbone down her jaw to the cleft in her chin. She shivered. "No."

As that sank in, Jess watched hope and expectation in his eyes turn to doubt and disappointment. She startled.

"Oh! I love you, too," she blurted.

"Don't say it because you think you have to." His voice was dull.

"T." Her eyes traced every angle and curve of his face. "I've never said it to anyone besides my parents."

Terrance's eyes widened. "You're thirty years old and you've never been in love?"

She frowned. "Don't sound so surprised. I'm just really picky. Take that as a compliment."

He didn't answer. Just shifted closer on the bed until she felt the heat emanating from him. Her nerves tingled. Blood swooshed through her. They kissed for a long time like teenagers not sure how to approach second base.

Jess started to unbutton his shirt, but he stopped her with a hand on her hand. "Not yet. I want it to be perfect."

"There's no such thing as perfect," Jess complained, sounding petulant even to her own ears. "No matter how many lists you write, no matter how much you analyze and plan, relationships do not go as planned."

Terrance plumped a pillow against the headboard and sat up against it. Jess shoved her pillow into the headboard and joined him in the upright position. He picked up his glasses from the nightstand, wiped them with the bottom of his shirt, and put them on.

"Jess, I have to ask you something important. What do you want? I'm at an age where I want my next relationship to be my last one. Maybe you're not there yet."

Her eyes flashed. "I may not have been ready to settle down before. Then I met you. But I didn't think we were going to happen. And I don't waste time on things I can't—"

He grinned, making blood rush to her face. "So you're saying you do want me? And have for a while?" He leaned over and kissed her sensuously for three seconds. "Tell me." He kissed her again. "How long?" He moved in for another kiss but stopped and retreated.

Jess narrowed her eyes at him. "Terrance Washington, who knew you were such a tease? Look, if we both want our next relationship to be for real, forever, that's what we'll have."

He shook his head. "I wish it were that simple. But people change. Relationships change."

Jess sighed. "You can't control everything."

"I know. But you have to know what you're getting into, if we do this." He wound his dark brown fingers through her olive ones. "Being part of an interracial couple wouldn't be easy."

"Understood. All kinds of people will judge us."

He cleared his throat. "And some of that judgment might come from family. Can you handle that?"

Jess stared at him. His eyes were intent. Mature beyond their years. She felt unsettled and excited as if meeting him for the first time. "If you can, I can," she said.

He touched her cheek briefly. His voice dropped to a cautious tone. "Jess, do you want kids?"

She nodded.

His shoulders dropped a notch. "Me too. But raising biracial kids wouldn't be easy. And you'd be a White mother of Black kids. We would—"

"Brown," she interrupted, squeezing his hand. "I'd be a Brown mother."

He looked at their intertwined fingers. "Not Black. We'd need to teach them how to act around cops—"

Jess flinched.

"—and to think twice about wearing clothes that draw negative attention, like a hoodie at night. We'd have to make them strong enough to rise above the institutionalized racism they'd confront every day."

Jess's angled eyebrows drew together. "Is it really that bad? A daily thing?"

Terrance perused her from behind drooping eyelids. "Did you know the net worth of the average White family is ten times more than the average Black family's?"

Jess frowned. "That's outrageous. How can that still be happening?"

"Pick your starting point," Terrance said. "Lower-quality homes, worse neighborhoods, less tax revenue for good schools, poorer quality education, higher drop-out rate, more neighborhood crime, jobs that don't pay as well, lower-quality homes. See how the circle goes?"

She nodded. "Depressing, isn't it." She puffed her bangs out of her eyes. "I've always loved Wrighton, but I know now it's a lot more than opportunity. It's racism and sexism and innocent people being hurt too."

Terrance sighed. "No city will ever be my city. We take what we can from it, but don't expect it to give back everything you need." He licked his lips and bit the lower one briefly. "But back to having kids—I don't mean this to sound condescending, Jess, but if we started a family, you'd have to defer to me on things related to being Black. And you'd have to have my back on any decisions around that, even if you didn't agree. Could you do that?"

Jess rested her cheek in her palm and digested his words. "Yes. I learned my lesson. I can put my pride and my need to be in charge aside and assume you know best when it comes to race. As long as you defer to me if the topic is being a Colombian-American accountant." She smiled sweetly.

He answered with the smallest of smiles. "Deal. I know I'm throwing a lot at you. Tell me what you want."

Jess exhaled up at her bangs again, long and slow, smile gone. "First, I think I want to know more about the culture my family left behind. Maybe our kids should learn about their Colombian heritage. Maybe I should." She considered Terrance. "As for us, I just want a healthy, long-term relationship, like my parents have."

"Hm. Do you worry about the relationship growing stale? And the—you know—" He paused.

"The sex?" she asked, her sleepy, heavy eyes opening wide.

Terrance nodded.

"We haven't even slept together yet and you're worried about keeping the spark alive?"

He stared at his hands. "Guilty. I think we've done it in my dreams, by the way. And it was good."

Jess smirked. "I *know* we've done it in my dreams. And it was fantastic. But listen." She took his hand again. "When I run monthly financial statements at work, they look almost the same month to month, sometimes even year to year. The revenue and profits stay within a small percentage range if the business is stable. But behind that, all kinds of small changes are taking place that the numbers don't show."

"And," he asked, "your point is?"

"I'm saying, as long as the general outlook is good, the little daily fluctuations aren't going to hurt the company. Or the marriage. Changes come with the territory. You just roll with it, keeping your eye on the big picture."

"Hmm." He raised an arm and scratched his blonde hair, his bicep moving with the motion. "That's actually a good analogy."

She rose to her knees on the bed, peering down at him. "Don't sound so surprised."

He shifted onto his knees and faced her. "Get used to it, Jess. You surprise me all the time." He reached his arms around her waist and pulled her close. "Now, time to make our dreams come true."

She placed her arms securely around his neck.

***

Later, freshly showered, they lay in bed again, Terrance spooning Jess as she slept.

Had they been wrong to do this right after Bu? No, he decided. Love was love, and Bu saw that before he and Jess even did. But now that he'd eased over the edge of the cliff, he was falling so fast, past the point of no return, that it frightened him.

He loved Jess. And she loved him. This was not how it was supposed to go. She would never know what it's like to be Black in this country. Their children would experience things she'd never fully grasp.

He understood his mother better now. White people brought children into the world full of hope and dreams. Black people brought children into the world with hope shot through with fear.

And Jess—she would suffer in new ways from being with him.

He tightened his arm around her, wishing he could shield her and their unconceived children from the pain that was coming.

***

More dogs than Charley had ever seen in one place frolicked in the park. Not a single one picked a fight or got aggressive with another dog.

Despite the peaceful, playful scene, panic built in her chest, spreading quickly, making her cheeks and fingertips tingle. *Where did her parents go?* She yelled: "Mom? Dad?" She glimpsed a tall man with glowing white hair stepping down a path into thick trees, out of sight. "Gramps?" she called. She chased after him, as fast as her childish legs could go. The aroma of freshly baked chocolate-chip cookies stopped her. *Was Gram nearby?* She peered around, head, eyes, and feet shifting direction erratically. All she saw were trees merging in the dark shadows of a forest. Even the dogs were gone.

She sank to her knees, pebbles biting into the bare skin. *Where did they all go? Why didn't they wait for her?*

A pair of scuffed sneakers appeared before her bent head. She looked up to see Buwan beaming his goofy smile. She reached out her hand, but suddenly he was too far away to touch. She stood on her own. She wanted to go to him, but the weight of loss immobilized her. "Where are they, Bu? I can't find them."

Bu's voice rang loud and clear, even from a distance. "Walk with me and I'll tell you a secret."

Charley reluctantly turned away from the forest. The drag of her steps loosened as she went. Suddenly Bu was beside her. His words reverberated inside her. "Here's the secret, Charley. They're all okay. They're with Chaucer, now. Me, too. Don't worry about us. We're fine. And we love you."

Sharp relief woke Charley.

A warm heaviness pressed on her chest. The pressure began to ease, as if metal bands around her torso were being loosened, one by one. The weight lifted completely away, but the warmth lingered. She closed her eyes and savored the remnants of the dream, the smell of baking cookies lingering in her nostrils.

It felt so real. Were they truly okay? And at peace?

Suddenly panicky, she groped for the familiar feelings: Loss. Pain. Where were they? They couldn't be far, but for now at least, they refused to show their faces. She slowed her breathing. Calm gradually suffused her body.

She threw back the covers and lay there, cool air awakening her body.

Maybe she would try walking two blocks to the bakery today.

***

Instead of the bakery, Charley found herself driving to State Park. Sitting behind the steering wheel felt odd, as if she'd been away from it for years instead of weeks.

Six crows waited when she arrived. They followed her from her car to the picnic table where she sat on top, feet resting on the bench, breaking crackers into crow-sized bites and tossing them on the grass. Her supply exhausted, the crows chattered their way into a nearby tree. Two vaulted off the branch into the pale late summer sky.

Charley closed her eyes and breathed deeply for a few minutes, absorbing the mellow sun and the cool breeze on her eyelids, cheeks, bare arms, and legs. A crow cawed from afar; closer by, birds tweeted and chirped. A rustling noise caused her to open her eyes—a chubby squirrel regarded her innocently. Apparently deciding she was not a threat, the squirrel continued foraging in a pile of leaves, twigs, and moss at the base of a fallen tree trunk. She inhaled the earthy aroma like a balm. Charcoal grill smells wove through the trees from an adjacent picnic area. Childish laughter and good-natured parental admonitions followed. She could almost picture the father chasing his kids around, the kids squealing when caught and tickled.

Charley's throat cramped. Her gut gripped.

She bent over, face on knees, erupting in waves of heaving sobs.

Years of pain.

Abandonment.

Guilt.

Self-loathing.

They gushed up.

Poured out.

And trickled away.

When the spasms slowed, she sat up, stomach muscles aching. "You're okay," she said out loud, then laughed at herself. "But you are, Charley. You're okay."

Spots inside her that had gripped, locked up for years, began to release. Emotions held prisoner began to move, like newly oiled gears clicking into place.

She pulled her lips in between her teeth, released them, and made herself smile to see how it felt. The action triggered a coda of soft sobs and cleansing tears.

She wiped away the final tear with the back of her hand, then pulled her long hair back off her neck, using her thumbs to pry off a few clingy strands. She contemplated the waving trees and the lazy clouds in their peaceful sky.

Suddenly hungry, she walked back to the parking area. Something glinted on the hood of her car—an old-fashioned brass key. She turned it over and over.

She scanned the closest trees until she spotted him. Her smile came unbidden this time. She held the key up high in the crow's direction. "Thank you, Mr. Crow," she cried. "Maybe next time I'll give you a name. Would you like that?" The crow merely cocked his head at her. Charley laughed. "See you soon."

She wrapped the key in her fist and nodded to life before getting in and driving off.

CHAPTER 33: HEART IN THE ROAD

Charley, Xander, Sunny, Jess, and Terrance gathered at the bookstore café, visages resembling warmed wax—eyes sloping down, faces drooping. All wore black, which would have triggered jokes about Terrance's wardrobe choices rubbing off on them had the occasion been a happier one.

"It feels discordant. Being here," Xander said from his usual spot on the leather couch. Jess sat in the middle and Terrance beside her.

From their seat in the yellow armchair, Sunny gestured toward the empty rocking chair. "It won't ever be the same."

"No. It won't," Terrance agreed.

"What transpires from here?" Xander asked. No one requested clarification of his vague question.

"I have something to tell you guys," Charley said softly. "I had a dream two nights ago. Bu was in it." She swallowed hard. "He told me he was okay. And that my parents and grandparents were okay, too. And I—I felt it, you know? That it was true."

She looked at the circle of friends, surprised to see moist eyes all around.

She smiled self-consciously. "When I woke up, I drove to State Park and fed the crows."

Terrance smiled. "That's great, Char."

Charley shrugged like a timid schoolgirl winning a spelling bee. "I didn't jog or anything. But it felt good to be back there."

Sunny sniffled and beamed.

"But this isn't about me. I wanted you to know that I think Bu's okay."

Jess checked the time on her phone and stood. "I hate to spoil this feel-good moment, but—it's time to go."

***

After the funeral and interment, they walked listlessly from the gravesite to their cars, the warm air resting on their skin with subtle weight. They clustered around Terrance's Prius and murmured about nothing while the bulk of the funeral-goers drove away.

Xander kicked at a loose chunk of asphalt at the rim of a pothole in the rutted road. He stared at the resulting shape. "*My heart in the road. Left for all to trample on. What is left for me?*"

Terrance frowned. "That's a bit dark, don't you think?"

"Hmm. It's a dark day, is it not?" Xander pointed out.

"Truth," Terrance replied.

Sunny spoke with spirit. "Let's memorialize Bu with haiku. Right now."

Jess wrinkled her nose. "Too much pressure." She turned to Terrance for moral support, which he declined to offer.

"That's a cool idea," Terrance said. "But I can't do it off the cuff like you guys. Give me five minutes to think of something."

Charley clucked her tongue. "Don't overthink it. Haiku can be beautiful when they're spontaneous. They come quickly; they go quietly."

Xander grinned and put his arm around Charley for a brief hug.

They all closed their eyes to think except Jess, who paced.

Terrance spoke first. "I need to go now before I forget it." He cleared his throat. "*Two kinds of people. That's what you would always say. But only one Bu.*"

Sunny rested a hand on Terrance's arm. "Nice. Okay, here's mine: *Buwan had a light. An aura of love and peace. An artist of life.*"

The others murmured agreement and looked to Jess, now standing on Sunny's other side. "Sorry, I couldn't do it," she said. "But I can say this: Bu, you died too young. You were one of a kind and I'm going to miss you."

Xander laughed. "I think that actually was a haiku, or close to it. But no matter. It's the thought that counts, not the form." He smoothed his beard. "Mine's a tad blue. Sorry. But it feels right to me." He looked to the sky. "*What did you teach us? If we had seen you better, maybe we would know.*" They absorbed his words in silence. "Charley, you ready?"

Charley closed her eyes. "*Bu Bakunawa, the Moon Boy of legend lived; laughed, swam, loved, taught joy.*"

The friends sighed so loudly a nearby bird chattered as if in reprimand, making them laugh softly.

"So, listen," Jess said, "I've been thinking about the bookstore and what C said the other day. What if Georgina decides to sell to someone else now?"

Xander frowned. "An appropriately dreary thought for the day."

"But there's hope," Jess said. "Bu would say the same." They all turned to her. "What if Charley bought the store?"

Charley shook her head. "I have no idea what it costs to buy a bookstore, but I know I don't have that kind of money."

"You don't need to. Some seed money would be good, if you have anything saved. But I could help you apply for a small business loan from one of the city's banks. Some of them give preference to women-owned businesses."

Charley closed her eyes and lifted her face to the sky.

Terrance stood up straight. "We could all help with the business plan. I could be your PR and marketing consultant."

"And I'll be your sales advisor," Sunny said.

Xander bounced on his toes. "I'll function as your green consultant, and we can all serve as your street team in the early days to build buzz."

Jess nodded. "And I'll help with the financial side. But slow down everyone. C, what do you even think of the idea?"

Charley opened her eyes and met Jess's gaze. "Do you guys really think I could do it? Run the store myself?"

"No," Jess said bluntly. "You'd need help. But you'd have us, and the coworkers you're always saying are so great. I could teach you the accounting ropes."

"I know some of it already. I majored in Business in college."

Sunny nodded. "But what about seed money?"

Charley again raised her face, eyes closed. "I have some," she said, lowering her head and opening her eyes. "My grandparents left me a little. I never touched it because it was the only thing I had left of them. But they would like this idea, I think."

"Perfect!" Sunny enthused.

Terrance glanced at the pearly yellow moon emerging in the watery blue sky. "It'll be dark soon. Let's walk Sunny and Charley to their car."

They strolled down the quiet access road bordering the cemetery. The cemetery side of the road was edged by a grass strip and a sidewalk. Light woods lined the street's other side.

"Stop," Xander whispered with force. "Look." He pointed to a spot farther down the road.

A large coyote at the road's edge on the cemetery side ambled into the middle of the road and stopped, looking straight at them. No one moved. Not even the coyote. Its coat was plush and healthy, yellow eyes placid. After a full thirty seconds, the animal thrust its snout skyward, toward the pale moon, before returning its gaze to the group of friends. The coyote yawned with a small squeak and continued leisurely crossing the road, disappearing into the trees.

"Oh my God," Sunny whispered.

Xander spoke with awe. "There's an animal omen for you, Char. Bu's indomitable spirit lives on."

"He's telling us he crossed over," Sunny said.

"Buwan," Charley said.

"Buwan," Jess echoed.

Terrance laughed so loudly it bounced off the trees and back to them. "Buwan! We love you, man!" he shouted, lifting his blonde head and his arms to the moon.

"We love you, Moon Boy!" Charley yelled, dissolving into weak giggles.

Jess laughed but it hiccupped into a sob.

Sunny laughed like music.

Bursting with burbling laughter and weepy smiles, they said good night.

CHAPTER 34: BEYOND MINT

Sunny separated Charley's hair into two sections with a comb and began braiding the left side. Charley, sitting on the floor with her back against her blah couch, had moved past the shock of Sunny's request to play with her hair and the initial grip of her shoulders at the intimate contact with another human being. Now, she relaxed and savored a sensation she hadn't felt since elementary school when her mother braided her hair at least once a week. The brush of Sunny's hands against Charley's neck and the soft tugs against her scalp sent feel-good flutters through her.

"Char, have you decided if you're definitely buying the store?"

"Hmm. Ask me in two days. Jess and I are finishing the business plan tomorrow and on Monday, we meet with the bank."

Sunny fastened the end of the braid with an elastic and began to comb the right side. "That would be so amazing. Can I—" Their hands paused, then resumed combing. "Can I ask you something personal? You don't have to answer if you don't want to."

"Um, okay."

"Your feet. Bu helped me understand why you hurt yourself. But since—are you still doing it? Lately?"

Charley cleared her throat. "You mean since I crawled out of my depression?"

Sunny's hands dropped the comb and separated the right side of Charley's hair into three sections with their fingernails. Charley shivered.

"That, and having the bookstore sale fall through and realizing maybe you can buy it—things are looking up, right?"

Charley waited for a break in the tugging to sip from her mug of mint tea. *It's nothing to be ashamed of,* Bu's voice said in her head. "The answer is no. I mostly haven't made my feet bleed lately."

Sunny's hands rested against Charley's head. "That's such good news."

Charley stared into her mug. "Now, I need to ask you something. Do you think I should see a therapist?" Charley heard Sunny exhale. "I'm sorry to bother you with this or put you on the spot. I don't really have anyone else to ask." Charley's head bowed. "My grandparents sent me to someone a few times after my parents died, but it didn't do much. I don't think I needed it then. But I'm thinking of trying it now. The self-help books in the store only go so far."

Sunny dropped the half-done braid and reached around Charley, their forearms resting on Charley's collarbones for a quick, awkward hug. "I'm honored that you asked me." Their voice sounded thicker than usual. They started the braid over. "I think it's a great idea, and if you're considering it, you're probably ready for it. Lots of people go to a therapist, of course. I know a bunch of people who have benefitted from it and—"

"Sunny," Charley interrupted. "Okay."

"Am I overselling it?"

"Maybe a little."

"I just think it's important to love yourself before you can love anyone else, and therapy can help with that. I don't think you love yourself enough."

Charley exhaled audibly. "I'm trying. Can we talk about something else?"

Sunny leaned back and stretched Charley's hair straight out to braid the bottom section. "Sure." They wrapped an elastic around the completed braid. "First, let me see how you look." They lifted the long braids over Charley's shoulders and moved to view their handiwork from the front. "Perfect. You make an adorable Wednesday Addams."

They lifted a braid and shaped it into a circle on the side of Charley's head. "Or we could pin them up and make you a Scandinavian doll." Sunny laughed. They coiled the braid into a tight bun on the side of Charley's head. "Or there's the ever-popular Princess Leia look."

Charley laughed, endorphins bathing her chest before she batted Sunny's hand away. "You can stop now."

"Okay. By the way, I have something for you." Sunny went to their backpack by the door and pulled out a box. "I brought you a tea sampler, in case you want to try something different. Branch out from your standard mint." They walked to Charley and held the gift out with both hands. "I put it together myself. It's got ginger tea, chamomile, rooibos, raspberry, and a cinnamon-cardamom mix."

Charley regarded the box through narrowed eyes. "Thanks for saying I'm boring."

Sunny's eyes widened and froze. "No! I'm not saying that at all!"

Charley grinned. "Gotcha. Oh my God, the look on your face." She reached up to take the box but Sunny yanked it back.

"I don't think you deserve this after all." They stepped back.

Charley jumped to her feet. "Hey! You can't take it back. That's not fair." She reached for the box but Sunny stepped back again.

Charley feigned disinterest but then lunged toward the box. Sunny ran around the couch holding the box over their head. "Sorry. Changed my mind."

Charley ran at Sunny and chased them around the couch. Two laps of the apartment later, Sunny ducked into the galley kitchen. Charley immediately cornered them. She wrapped her arms around Sunny, pinning their arms to their sides. "Give. Me. The. Tea."

"Okay, okay," Sunny cried. "You win." They wriggled out of Charley's grasp and put the tea on the counter. "Want some?" they asked as if the mad chase hadn't happened.

Charley giggled. Sunny joined in.

Ten minutes later, settled on the couch with a mug of fresh ginger tea in hand, Charley asked Sunny if she wanted to do something—walk in the park maybe.

Sunny stared straight ahead. "I have an idea for something you can do, if you want," they said.

Charley cocked her head. "Okay. What?"

"Do you want to play with my hair now?"

Charley slowly placed her mug on the coffee table. "Um. Are you sure?"

Sunny nodded.

"Okay," Charley whispered.

Sunny moved to the spot on the floor where Charley sat earlier. They leaned back, framed by Charley's jean-clad lower legs.

Charley lifted her hands and hovered.

"Go ahead," Sunny said. "It's okay. While you're at it, you can give me a scalp massage."

Charley lowered her hands, barely brushing the top of Sunny's four-inch-long Afro.

"Are you touching it? I can't feel a thing."

Charley patted Sunny's hair with one palm, then the other. "It's so springy!" She giggled.

Sunny reached up and pulled their cloth headband down over their face and below their chin. "Get in there and dig around," they said in a hushed tone.

Charley pressed her palm down until it rested on Sunny's scalp. Hesitantly, she moved the other hand into Sunny's hair. "It smells good. And it's so soft. Like a fluffy cloud."

"Conditioner," Sunny said. "Lots of it."

Charley played with Sunny's hair for a minute, patting it, tunneling through it with her fingers, straightening strands out to watch them coil back into their preferred shape. She plunged through to massage Sunny's scalp, making small circles with her fingertips, amazed at how their skull felt solid and delicate at the same time.

"That was fun," she announced with a final pat, standing up. "Thanks."

Sunny rubbed a hand back and forth across their eye and stood. "It's getting late. I should go."

Charley plopped back onto the couch. "Or we could order food and watch a movie."

Sunny stopped rubbing her eye. "Indian or Chinese?"

***

"Do you think it's good enough?" Charley asked.

"I do." Jess shut her bamboo portfolio with a snap. "It's a strong business plan."

Charley put her elbows on the wrought-iron, sidewalk café table and dropped her head in her hands, listening to snatches of conversations from the other diners and the pedestrians passing the small restaurant. "This is kind of overwhelming." She looked at Jess who, even in her casual Sunday clothes, looked professional and put-together. Charley sat back, slouching. "I'm pretty nervous about spending this much money. And taking out such a huge loan."

"C, I'm not going to sugarcoat it," Jess said. "You're taking a financial risk. And no one ever said running a small business is easy. I saw a meme once that said it's the only thing more overrated than natural childbirth." She patted her portfolio. "But if the income projections in here are solid, the other numbers work, too."

Charley chewed her lower lip. "Will you stick with me after I buy it? You've done so much already. But I can pay you. I think."

Jess smiled. "I thought you'd never ask. Let's see how much time it takes and then decide if you need to pay me or if you need to hire someone."

Charley held out her hand. "Deal."

Jess grasped Charley's hand and shook. "Deal."

She put the binder in the briefcase at her feet. "We've earned dessert." She waved the waitress over.

Charley fiddled with her nose ring. "So, I've always wondered, what were Xander and Sunny like in college?"

Jess grinned. "The same. I mean, Xander wasn't as confident as he is now. But he always had the passion to change the world."

"And Sunny?"

"Sunny has always been the earth-mother, peace-love-Zen person they are today. To be honest, that rubbed me the wrong way at first. But then I got to know them and—"

"—to know them is to love them?" Charley interrupted.

"I was going to say they won me over, but same thing I guess."

Charley looked at a point beside Jess's ear. "Did you know they were pansexual when you met? Was that weird?"

Jess cracked up.

"Why is that so funny?"

"Because," Jess snickered, "the way I found out was they hit on me."

Charley grimaced. "No way. What happened?"

Jess smoothed back the long side of her asymmetrical hair. "We were in our dorm room, and they offered to give me a back massage, to which I never say no. Their hands kept slipping down my sides, where my bra was, moving toward the front. At first, I thought it was a mistake but they did it again. I point-blank told them not to bother."

Charley stared, the corner of her mouth twitching. "Oh my God, how awkward!"

Jess shrugged. "We laughed about it. They said they were pansexual. I said that's cool but I'm not. And we never talked about it again."

The waitress returned with dessert menus. Jess peered at hers as if it were a year-end profit-and-loss statement.

"Hey, what about the two of them?"

Jess looked up from the menu, raising her eyebrows.

Charley focused on her menu. "Do you think they belong together?"

"Nope," Jess said. "It would have happened by now."

"Do you think Sunny wants to be with a man more, or a woman?"

Charley felt Jess's eyes on her. A blush crawled up her neck onto her face. The words on the menu squiggled like hieroglyphics.

"I don't know," Jess said. "Any more questions, C?"

"Um, yeah," Charley said through the hand at her mouth, "do you think the brownie sundae or the flourless chocolate cake would be better?"

CHAPTER 35: AND THE WALLS COME…

Charley paced around her small apartment, palms sweating. Her therapist's words rang in her ears. "What do you want? What do you want?"

Charley had expected to spend her most recent session re-visiting coping mechanisms: a loosely structured routine that guided instead of stifled, or nightly affirmations about good things that happened that day and good things she had done that day. She would even have settled for discussing painful subjects like her history of self-harm, or how she'd been orphaned twice, or Bu's death. Instead, the therapist focused on basic desires.

Charley did not want to put her basic desire into words. It was bad enough that her mind was playing tricks on her. It wandered away all the time—not completely away into no man's land, like when she was depressed, but into areas where Charley didn't want to go. Whether playing her favorite word game or managing inventory now that she'd returned to work, her mind was frustratingly one-track.

"What do you want?" the therapist had asked. "Don't over-analyze it. Don't question it. Just think about what would make you feel good."

A sharp rap at the door made Charley jump. She let Sunny in. They must have stopped at home after work because they wore a simple, cream-colored macramé minidress instead of their solar company polo shirt and jeans. Their bare shoulders and willowy legs glistened.

"Are you okay? You look pale. Paler than usual that is," Sunny said with a grin.

"Ha ha." Charley scrunched her shoulders up and around twice.

Sunny dropped their backpack to the floor and moved behind Charley. "Shoulders tight?" They placed their hands on Charley's shoulders and explored with their thumbs. "Oh yeah, they are."

Charley wriggled away and went toward the blah blue couch. "What movie should we stream?" she asked as Baggage emerged from the bedroom and claimed one of the couch's arms.

"I'm easy," Sunny said, walking to the couch. "Let me massage your shoulders for a minute."

Charley turned away and pressed her eyes shut for a solid ten seconds. "Okay. Here?"

"Sure. Don't you have almond oil in your bathroom? Lie on the couch and I'll get it." They moved down the hallway, yelling over their shoulder. "Maybe take off your shirt but leave your bra on."

When Sunny returned, Charley lay on the couch, face down on a towel, shirtless and braless. She turned her face to the side. "I didn't want to get oil on my new bra."

"Okay. Cool," Sunny said in a less-than-convincing voice that almost torpedoed Charley's resolve. They knelt beside the couch, applied oil, and began massaging Charley's back.

Charley's body melted and wakened at the same time. Picturing herself half-naked, she nearly shuddered at her vulnerability. But the deep trust she felt with Sunny, and Sunny's nurturing touch, reassured her.

"Are you uncomfortable?" Charley mumbled. "Sitting on the floor?"

"A little."

"You can get on the couch if you want."

Sunny stopped massaging and climbed onto the couch, straddling Charley with bent knees. Charley heard Baggy's paws hit the floor as Sunny ran their hands firmly down her back.

Charley tried to relax and enjoy the massage, but her body inflamed.

"Is this good?" Sunny asked.

"Mmm."

"Any particular place you want me to focus?"

"Sure. A little higher." Charley directed Sunny's hands to right below the shoulder blades, where her bra band usually rested. "That's really tight."

"Really? It doesn't feel too bad." Sunny kneaded with their thumbs.

"Can you go lower?" Sunny's hands traveled lower on Charley's back. "Not that way. Down my sides. It's tight in there for some reason." Charley grimaced into the couch cushion.

Sunny's hands moved toward the sides of Charley's torso. "Here?"

Charley swallowed. "Even lower. Toward the front."

Sunny's hands froze. Ever so gently, their right fingers stroked the outside of Charley's squashed breast. "Do you mean here?" Their voice sounded throaty.

"Mm-hmm."

Charley stopped worrying about what might happen, could happen, should happen. She floated into a delirium of sensory overload, unable to remember ever feeling anything so intensely. Sunny's fingers moved in small circles, igniting sparks everywhere. Charley eased her upper torso off the couch a few inches. Sunny's hand slid underneath and cupped Charley's breast. Charley groaned.

"Stop," she murmured.

Sunny's hand flew out and away. "I'm sorry! I'm so, so sorry."

Charley lifted her head a few inches. "I have to say something." She spoke to the couch cushions. "I am obsessed with you, Sunny. When you're not here, I think about you all the time. I count the hours until you come back." She licked her dry lips. "I am obsessed with all of you." She paused.

"Meaning?" Sunny whispered.

Charley had dived in. She had to keep swimming. "I wrote a haiku about you. *Eyelashes like down. At the corners of your eyes. Delicate feathers.* I couldn't fit it in the haiku, but I really want to kiss that spot." Charley held her breath. "Sunny? Say something, please."

Sunny exhaled. "Can you turn over?"

"Not until you say something about what I said."

Charley felt Sunny breathing through the hands resting on her back.

"Charley, I have loved you for ages, but I never thought you could love me the same way."

A wall in Charley's psyche tumbled down. She shivered and slowly rolled onto her back.

Sunny shifted forward and lowered the side of their face. Charley lifted her head and placed her lips on the thin flesh at the edge of Sunny's eye. Her lips traveled to Sunny's temple. Sunny turned forward. Their lips met.

They kissed and explored for ten minutes, meeting each other in new ways.

Sunny sat back and handed Charley her shirt, which Charley pulled on.

Side by side, Charley snuggled into Sunny, inhaling their unnamable scent, which conjured, oddly, the word "home" in Charley's mind. "I feel like every cell in my body is waking up after a very long sleep," she said.

"Same," Sunny said.

Baggage leaped into Sunny's lap and pushed his head into Charley's hand where it rested on Sunny's leg. Charley stroked his soft fur.

"I've never felt like this. Is this maybe what true love feels like?"

Sunny pushed a lock of Charley's hair behind her ear to see her face better. "Yeah. It is. And I'd say that makes us pretty lucky."

Charley frowned. "I'm lucky. Not so sure about you. I'm unstable. You know that."

"It's okay," Sunny said. "I'm stable enough for both of us."

"I'm pathetic and self-pitying and have no self-esteem," Charley said.

Sunny snickered. "That's a lot of baggage." The cat purred and thrust his head into Sunny's hand. "But don't worry. I have enough self-esteem for both of us." They grinned. "And the therapist will help. Keep up with that. God, keep up with that for sure."

"Ha ha." Charley shifted and ran her finger along the row of tiny gold hoops outlining Sunny's ear.

Sunny's face grew serious. "This is really and truly what you want? Us?"

Charley's eyes glistened. "Sunny, I've never felt as sure about anything in my life as I feel about you right now."

EPILOGUE

A few months later

Charley hung up with the contractor she'd hired to convert the second floor of the building from an apartment into retail space for ten thousand more titles. The bank had approved a loan for the renovation and start-up operations. Charley planned to allocate a small section of the new space for an Activist Corner with pamphlets and books related to various causes and to host monthly Act Up nights for local nonprofits to talk about their missions and volunteer needs.

If Sunny agreed, Charley planned to convert the third floor from storage space into an apartment for her and Sunny and Baggy—one filled with light, plants, photos, and built-in bookcases. Her father's books would occupy a prime spot on one shelf.

She hadn't asked Sunny yet. She'd only recently begun waking up dread-free, no portents or animal omens—real or imaginary—hanging over her head. Her feet had healed. She was coping. She wanted to savor her new self a bit longer before starting the next chapter.

She turned off the computer and locked her office door.

Wandering a crooked path through the store, eavesdropping on customer conversations, she passed the section where she and Jess were building a resource bank for immigrants looking for legal advice, government program information, or simply news from home in the form of international newspapers and magazines. Jess now worked at the real estate development and construction company founded by

Charley's grandfather. She didn't like to talk about Bertie and Al; their case would be tied up in court for years. At least they had been released on bond and deportation wasn't a given. Still, any mention of the situation brought Jess to tears. She seemed to find some solace volunteering at an immigrant services agency in an effort to spare others the pain she'd heaped on herself and her family.

Terrance had publicized the bookstore's change in ownership and its new programs, which included a monthly scavenger hunt, a PJ Story Hour for kids, and Xander's favorite—Book-A-Birthday, in which people who brought in a friend within a week of the friend's birthday and bought them a book got twenty percent off their purchase.

Charley made a point of waving goodbye to the bustling café staff as she passed. She smiled at the new bins Xander had set up for recycling paper, plastic, and glass. Eventually, they would collect food scraps for compost. Xander promised energy-efficient and cost-saving lighting and heating would be next.

Stepping out the front door, she texted Sunny she was ready.

***

They were the first to arrive at the Johnson-Bakunawa's summer home. The door was locked, so they went around the house and sat in the Adirondack chairs at the cold firepit to wait. A bracing breeze off the water hinted at colder weather on the horizon. Charley zipped her hoodie and clipped her windblown hair back.

Xander bounded around the corner of the house ten minutes later, Fred at his heels.

"Sorry to be unpunctual. But Anne texted and they're running late too."

Fred rushed to greet Sunny and Charley with sloppy kisses, but quickly shifted focus to the Frisbee in Xander's hands.

"Quick game while we wait?"

They spread out into a triangle on the sand. Sunny lobbed the Frisbee in a deflated arc that Fred immediately intercepted. Disc in mouth, he lowered his front legs to the ground, butt in the air, challenging Sunny to chase him.

"Where are Jess and Terrance?" Sunny asked as they stepped toward Fred, who quickly twisted his torso away and ran in a small circle. "We have so much catching up to do."

Xander cornered Fred and wrestled the Frisbee from him. "Jess doesn't love us anymore. She didn't text once during their extended weekend away."

Charley was about to chide Xander for being needy when she heard "Hey," from behind them. Jess and Terrance walked into the backyard, swinging a cooler between them.

Terrance's hair was black, not blonde. His shirt was white, not black.

"Whoa, it's like I'm seeing you in negative," Xander said.

Sunny rested their fingertips on their skull. "Mind twist, I can't handle it." They made an explosion noise and spread their fingers in the air.

Jess grinned as they dropped the cooler beside the chairs. Her face and arms glowed with a deep tan acquired on their four-day tropical getaway. Charley hadn't seen Jess so happy since before Bu's death and Bertie's arrest, although the somber shadow her features acquired during those ordeals lingered, as Charley guessed it would for a long time.

"Doesn't he look handsome?" Jess asked.

"Why the change?" Charley said.

Terrance looked at Jess. "I've paid homage long enough."

Jess grabbed his hand and held it between them. "Tell them the other reason. The one they'll understand."

Terrance scratched his head with his free hand. "I thought a more traditional look would be good, because I'm running for city council."

Sunny clapped once. "Perfect! What a good idea!"

Xander plopped into a chair as Fred deposited the slimy Frisbee at his feet. "We'll be the street team for your campaign, of course. But don't you have to reside in the city to run?" Fred lay down with a dog-sized sigh.

Terrance sat. "Mm-hmm. That's another bit of interesting news."

Jess also sat. "We're moving in together," she said. "We're buying a condo in the city."

Xander jutted his lower lip out. "You're moving out, Jess? I can't believe you're abandoning us." Sunny punched his arm and he grinned. "Just kidding. Sensational news. Congratulations."

Charley's brows knit together. "Will 'living in sin' hurt your chances of getting elected?"

Jess and Terrance grinned at each other and kissed.

"There's one more part of our announcement." Jess rested her left hand against her cheek, the uncharacteristic gesture making Charley cock her head. Sunlight sparkled through the new ring she wore. "We're engaged."

"Oh my God!" Sunny jumped up and practically fell on Jess in their haste to hug her. Charley followed.

"A fantastic and fitting miscegenation, albeit potentially risky given your short courtship," Xander announced, rising to get in on the hugs.

"X, it feels like we've known each other forever. What could we possibly go through that we haven't already?"

Terrance chuckled. "Rest easy, Xan, we've thoroughly evaluated the risk. We think a year of living together will be enough time to make sure we're ready for marriage."

After they settled back in their seats, still bubbling, Xander said Anne told him where the house key was hidden, if they wanted to move inside.

Jess turned her face toward the sun. "I'm good here."

Sunny fiddled with the long end of their headband. "So, are you guys thinking about kids?" they asked.

Jess and Terrance traded a glance. "Yep, someday," Terrance said.

"That is so awesome." Sunny's voice caught.

Charley cleared her throat. "Sunny and I joke that if we could have kids together, they'd come out with sepia-colored skin."

Sunny laughed lightly. "Or like a Creamsicle—orange on the outside, white on the inside."

A smile touched the corner of Xander's mouth. "I can envision you two as parents. Definitely." He nodded. "I sense your wheels turning, Sunny, but there's no need for sympathy because I'm not in love like the rest of you." He swiped on his phone several times. "I've got a new boyfriend, named C.J. We've been dating for a month. I hadn't apprised because—well, I just wanted to see how it went first."

"Wise," Terrance said. "No need to introduce someone to this gang until you're feeling stable about it."

Jess shook her head slowly. "No, X. This isn't going to work."

Xander stared at her, speechless for once.

"What am I going to do with a name like C.J.? That's too many initials, but I can't call him C because we've already got Charley."

Xander turned to Terrance. "What monikers will she bestow upon your kids? A, B, and C? Or go crazy and call them X, Y, and Z?"

Jess laughed. The others joined in.

Xander held out his phone, showing off a photo. Sunny peered at the screen. "Ooh, cute. Where did you meet him?"

Xander squirmed his mouth to the side, holding back a smile. "In jail. After the riot." The smile burst free as they all cracked up.

"What does he do for work?" Jess asked.

"Financial services."

Jess's eyebrows flicked up and down. "Wasn't expecting that. He must make decent money."

"So mercenary of you," Xander said.

Jess sighed. "Why do I always have to be the only practical one here?"

"Is he an activist on the side?" Sunny asked.

"Hmm. Sort of. The riot was his first protest, so he's a little gun-shy now. But he donates to some good causes." No one responded. "What? Is it so implausible that I would date someone other than a hard-core activist? There's value in work-life balance, you know." He scanned their blank faces. "Does this lower your estimation of me?"

Sunny patted his arm. "No, it raises it."

Fred barked and bolted around the house as car doors slammed in the driveway. He returned a minute later, escorting Bu's moms into their own backyard. Anne carried a large parcel wrapped in brown paper. Layla stopped to kick off her shoes.

After polite greetings all around, Anne asked if they wanted to move inside. Layla looked up at the window of the sitting room that had served as Bu's studio. "I'd rather stay out here, if it's not too cool for you, Anne."

Xander and Terrance dragged two more chairs over for the mothers.

Sunny spoke first. "We're so sorry we didn't help Bu more. We didn't know what he needed."

Anne shook her head. "On the contrary, you grounded him. He was happier since he started hanging out with all of you than he'd been in a long time."

Layla perched on the edge of her seat. "The past few months have been hard, so we hope you won't mind if we do this quickly," she said, nodding at the parcel set by Anne's chair. "One of the paintings in Buwan's loft had your names on the back. We don't know when he planned to give it to—" Her voice drifted off and her gaze wandered across the water.

Anne patted the brown wrapping paper. "This is for you. That's really all we have to say." She stood and wiped her hands on her slacks. "Stay as long as you like. The house is open now. We won't be back until tomorrow. Just lock up if you leave."

The mothers walked off, side by side but untouching.

The five friends remained silent until the car engine faded in the distance.

"I guess we should open it," Jess said.

Sunny nudged Charley. "You do it."

Charley took the package to her seat, gently pried open the thick brown paper and set it on the ground. She propped an unframed canvas on the arms of her chair and stood back.

A finely detailed, vivid purple dragon with iridescent scales formed a border around the painting, bleeding off the edge in spots. The torso draped down the left side of the canvas, a gold-trimmed, red wing nestling at its side. The tail traced the bottom of the canvas before tapering and climbing up the right side, the fins at its end positioned as if about to cradle or swat at the moon painted there. Above the moon, the beast's open, fanged mouth hovered.

"Look," Sunny whispered. "From a certain angle, the shadows in the moon look like a boy's face."

The curled dragon encircled a storm of colors that began as clearly defined sections of throbbing red, smooth gold, spring green, pale turquoise, and electric blue at the dragon's inner border. Those sections blended with their neighbors as they moved toward the center in psychedelic swirls and curlicues, creating new hues out of the two original ones. Those colors then merged with their neighbors to form even more new colors. The colors seemed to move, flowing into each other and toward the center like flames or water. In the center, all the colors—which seemed infinite in number at that point—converged and disappeared into a marble-sized orb of pearly white.

Sunny swallowed audibly. "It's stunning."

The others murmured in agreement.

Charley knelt before the painting. "It's all dots." She turned to face her friends. "Everything inside the dragon's circle is painted in tiny dots, like the grains of sand in a monk's mandala."

Terrance approached for a closer look. "That's amazing."

They took turns inspecting the painting up close, then moving backwards until the dots blended before their eyes.

Sunny played with their lower lip. "And those blocks of color closest to the dragon—those are us. They match the shirts Bu gave us at the reggae festival."

"Wasn't Bu's color purple?" Terrance asked. "I don't see purple."

Sunny released their lip. "Because he's the dragon. And the moon boy."

Charley took Sunny's hand. "Where should we keep it?"

"We could put it in our new condo when we move in," Jess suggested.

Xander shook his head. "We need a location where we can all appreciate it. The bookstore café?"

Charley shook her head. "I don't want it getting splashed with coffee or smelling like pastry." She scratched her nose. "Bu loved you all equally. We should rotate it."

"One month per person," Terrance suggested.

Jess picked up the canvas, looked at the back, and smirked. "Want to hear how he put our names on the back?" She read the small lettering brushed in one corner. "It's a haiku. *Charley, Sunny, Bu. Terrance, Jessica, Xander. Six meld into one.*" She replaced the canvas in its chair, her smirk fading as she sniffed.

Sunny's arm shot into the air, making Charley jump. "Charley, look!" they exclaimed. "A hawk!"

A large russet-colored bird with a pale underbelly banked and turned overhead, low enough for Charley to make out the hooked beak and individual primary feathers at its wingtips.

"There are two of them." Xander pointed. "See the companion over there?"

"Hm. A pair," Jess said, standing for a better look.

Charley stood and craned her neck back as far as it would go, watching a third hawk join the first two. "No—a family." She turned to follow the movements as another hawk joined the group. Then another. Then another.

"Oh shit, it's becoming like the movie *The Birds*," Jess deadpanned, a hand shading her eyes from the sun.

"Shh." Terrance stood behind Jess and wrapped his arms around her. Their heads tilted back in tandem to watch the show.

The growing flock glided in a lazy, noiseless circle, a pair of hawks occasionally breaking out of the pattern to swoop away and back, as if playing tag. More hawks continued to come.

"Wow," Xander said. "I can't even count them all now. There are forty at minimum. It's called a kettle by the way. What we're witnessing."

Sunny reached for Charley's hand again. "I've never seen anything like it. This is incredibly perfect," they said.

"I love how they soar, not even flapping their wings. It's so peaceful," Charley whispered. "Effortless."

"Is it me or are they getting smaller?" Jess asked.

"They're ascending," Xander said. "Riding a thermal. See how long they go without flapping? They're letting the wind carry them up."

They watched the kettle rise until the hawks reduced to mere dots, and then disappeared altogether.

THE END

ACKNOWLEDGMENTS

Many talented sensitivity readers gave generously of their time and expertise to educate me and keep me honest. Immense thanks to: Annabel Harz (who went above and beyond) and Ofelia Brooks, for editing with sensitivity, experience and insight; Susan Mills, who patiently educated me on all things immigration—any inaccuracies in that area are wholly on me; Vanessa Charles, who graciously allowed me to use her pain in order to teach; Robert Irwin at the University of California, Davis, Humanizing Deportation Project; Debbie Drew, who opened a window into her life that validated and improved the story; and mental health professionals Lucinda Nightingale and Richard Schwindt (Richard is also an excellent fiction writer!).

Many alpha and beta readers helped improve the story and shape it into its final form. I thank them all: Susan Roney O'Brien, who is generosity personified—any success I may achieve is directly traceable back to her support; M.T. Maliha, whose camaraderie has sustained me through many a dark spell; Tina O'Hailey, a kindred spirit in ways I don't even fully understand yet; Gabby Boucher, one of my guiding lights, whose sharp editing skills extend from high-level thematic and structural down to line editing; Cindy Stevenson, my mom, my original editor, and my first inspiration for a female writer; Joan Bulman, whose enthusiasm for the characters boosted my spirits during times of doubt; Amy Atwood, who has made me one of her altruistic endeavors, for which I am eternally grateful; Suzanna Roberts, who always manages to squeeze me in between the horses and chickens and to sell a few books at her farmstand; Helen Fremont, for her candor and jogging/laundry insights; Terry Farish, Heleen Kist, Eileen O'Finlan, Bonnar Spring and Ruth F. Stevens; and Liam Lassiter for Wednesday Addams and other astute improvements.

A massive thanks to Natalie Simone, whose impact far outweighs the time she spent correcting and educating me. Her generosity of spirit in discussing sometimes difficult and all too personal subjects with me, yet another time, is appreciated more than I can ever say.

Thanks to Craig Stevens for the Spanish translations; Russell White for his legal expertise; Michael Herrmann at Gibson's Bookstore in Concord, NH, for explaining life at an independent bookstore; Heidi Burkhardt for her paramedic skills; Katsy Garcia for informing the portrayal of a Filipino-American artist; and The Rev. Jane Willan for her input into Rev. Marcus Culpepper—one of my favorite characters who, alas, didn't make the final cut. Thank you to the Monadnock Writers' Group for giving Queenie—another cut character—new life in its *Smoky Quartz* journal.

My writers' group cohorts carved into various drafts with glee and frankness: Rox Burkey, Joseph Carrabis, Joe Della Rosa and Tina O'Hailey; Kathleen Fagan, Jody Graydon, Kristen O'Neill and Jen Stocks (thanks to Bianca Marais for bringing us together); and Devon Evans, Owen Johnson, Andrea MacRitchie and Charlie Oroszko.

Thanks to 4Ocean for allowing me use of their name, and to Frederick Buechner Literary Assets LLC for allowing the inclusion of Mr. Buechner's wisdom.

Most of all, thanks to my daughters and my husband Craig, for being my biggest fans, as I am theirs.

READING GROUP DISCUSSION QUESTIONS

This discussion guide contains spoilers.

1. Which of the friends did you relate to most? Why? Did you dislike any of them?

2. The novel includes emotional scenes related to mental health, racism and immigration. Did any of those scenes change your perspective on these issues?

3. Do you think Charley's beliefs in animal omens and her seven-year curse are well-founded or irrational? What purpose do they serve her, if any? Does her belief in superstitions change by the end of the story?

4. Buwan hides his Bi-polar 1 from his friends, other than Charley. Do you think he should have been more open? Might that have made a difference in his life?

5. Jess and Terrance form an unlikely pair, yet they connect in numerous ways. Why do you think they are attracted to each other? Do you think their relationship will last?

6. Xander is traumatized by his treatment at the community meeting to discuss plans for the nature preserve. Why was he so upset? Do the feelings evoked by that scene call to mind any other scenes in the novel?

7. Xander's violent behavior at the protest-turned-riot horrifies him after the fact. Why did he vandalize the police cruiser? Is his reaction understandable, or simply unacceptable in our society?

8. What Charley perceives as back-to-back betrayals—Xander's personality change at the riot, and the pending sale of the bookstore orchestrated by Jess—send her spiraling into a deep depression. Were you surprised at this development? Why or why not?

9. Jess's decisions—in particular not telling Charley about the bookstore sale, and leaking the immigration story to the newspaper—hurt people she cares about. Do you agree with her choices or not? Do you think she learns anything from these experiences?

10. How would you handle the trolley dilemma described in Chapter 26? Does your view change if you know the one person but not the five?

11. The characters have differing views on immigration. Did Bertie's story change your personal views at all? (To read Bertie's full story, access Bonus Materials on the author's website at AuthorSMStevens.com)

12. Do the racism episodes ring true to you? Have you experienced or witnessed similar behavior? How did reading those scenes make you feel?

13. What do you think of Terrance's commitment to only marrying within his race?

14. Which of the characters' views on activism change during the novel? Did your own view change at all?

15. Do you think Bu's accident was truly an accident or was it intentional?

16. Were you surprised by Charley's attraction to Sunny? Why or why not?

17. The novel incorporates racism, immigration, mental health, women's rights, gender identity, sexual orientation, and even environmental justice. Is this a realistic portrait of life in America today?

ABOUT THE AUTHOR

S.M. Stevens began writing fiction during back-to-back health crises: a shattered pelvis and ovarian cancer. She writes contemporary novels and short stories designed to make readers laugh, cry and think. In addition to her focus on adult fiction, she has published novels for Young Adult and Middle Grade readers. She lives in New Hampshire.

www.AuthorSMStevens.com.

NOTE FROM S.M. STEVENS

Word-of-mouth is crucial for any author to succeed. If you enjoyed *Beautiful and Terrible Things*, please leave a review online—anywhere you are able— even if it's just a sentence or two. It would make all the difference and would be very much appreciated.

Thanks!
S.M. Stevens

We hope you enjoyed reading this title from:

www.blackrosewriting.com

Subscribe to our mailing list – *The Rosevine* – and receive **FREE** books, daily deals, and stay current with news about upcoming releases and our hottest authors.
Scan the QR code below to sign up.

Already a subscriber? Please accept a sincere thank you for being a fan of Black Rose Writing authors.

View other Black Rose Writing titles at
www.blackrosewriting.com/books and use promo code
PRINT to receive a **20% discount** when purchasing.